EVENING COMES

A NOVEL

STUART FABE

Evening Comes

Copyright 2016 by Stuart A. Fabe

All Rights Reserved

For information about this title or to order other books and/or electronic media, contact the publisher:

Stuart A. Fabe
Greencastle, Indiana
stuartfabe@gmail.com

ISBN: 978-0-692-65481-1

Printed in the United States

Author's Note

Evening Comes is a work of fiction and is written solely for entertainment. Any resemblance to specific people or places is purely coincidental.

Dedication

For Marla . . . Always.

Chapter 1

CLAY ARNOLD STEPPED into his photographic darkroom and was immediately enveloped in the warm glow of its amber safe-light. He'd lost count of the number of times over the years he had returned to this inner sanctum. Certainly scores upon scores, and here he was again surrounded by that soft, embracing light.

The familiar odors from the chemicals in his trays filled his nostrils. The Dektol developer, the stop bath, the rapid fixer and hypo-neutralizer . . . all noxious chemicals to humans and yet all necessary elixirs for conjuring his photographic art. Here in this room, in the basement of the nineteenth-century brewery that he called home, he was free to create whatever images he wanted. He was free to be himself.

From his Bose stereo the smooth sounds of Weed Rawlins's mellifluous voice and the beseeching tremolo of his blues harmonica filled the darkroom and further separated him from the world outside. Weed and Clay had been close friends since childhood,

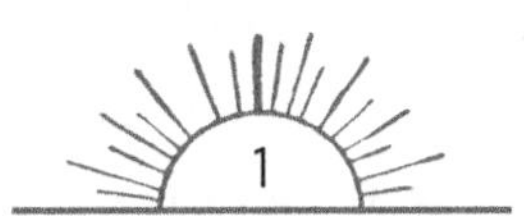

and hearing Weed's music helped bring a feeling of insulation from a sometimes harsh world that had recently shattered Clay Arnold's life.

Here, fifteen feet below the old brewhouse, Clay's senses of sight, smell, and sound were all supercharged as he worked in his darkroom. Here he was alone like a monk illuminating a manuscript in a monastic cell. It was in this place that he sometimes found an elusive peace.

In truth, Clay welcomed spending his precious-little free time creating artistic black-and-white prints. He'd grown up admiring the work of so many magnificent predecessors in photography; the legends like Edward Weston, Edward Steichen and Alfred Stieglitz, Yousuf Karsh, Edward Curtis, Dorothea Lang, Gordon Parks, and, of course, Ansel Adams. Photographic icons, all.

Although Clay had earned a reputation as a world-renowned photographer in his own right and had no shortage of professional labs eager to digitally print his work, the basics of black-and-white printmaking that he learned at a young age still called to him like an irresistible mistress. Over the years Clay had perfected many of the photographic tools available through Photoshop, but when it came to his private time, he chose the solitude of his wet darkroom. Now, at age thirty-two, he was a master at his craft.

He took his time reviewing the contact sheet of images and selected a very special subject he was eager to print. His eyes fell on the portraits of a beautiful, smiling young woman whom he had come to admire and adore. Clay let out an audible gasp when he saw the series of diminutive portraits he'd shot two months prior in the park along the White River. Immediately he selected one image in particular and found himself just staring at it. He was seized by its attraction like iron to a lodestone.

Jennifer Skyler was the love of his life pure and simple. They had met a year ago at the opening of his photography exhibition featuring his recent images of people living on the street. The art media had gushed such adjectives as *evocative, seminal,* and *searing.* It wasn't Clay's intention to have his work reviewed or labeled by anyone, least of all by critics.

This series of photographs was his reaction to walking the streets of several American inner cities seeing the faces and places of those folks just trying to get by, trying to eke out whatever existence they could. Their faces were mostly marked by stress and forlornness. Their eyes tried to show bravery, to show some hope, but there was an overriding sense of sadness, all except for the children.

At one point during the exhibition, Clay had torn himself away from a small throng of admirers and found himself staring at a large framed print of a young black boy sitting in the shadowed doorway of a deserted brick building. The boy was a bit of an enigma to Clay because, while the other children were running and playing in the street, this youngster sat by himself in a tenement doorway. The mood that the scene created left a lasting impression on the photographer. It tugged at him. It was an intersection of art and humanity, and the image he took became one of Clay's all-time favorites.

Before long Clay sensed another presence standing next to him staring at the same picture of the boy. He turned to see who had invaded his private reunion with this image and saw a woman whose serene beauty literally took his breath away. It was Jennifer Skyler.

Without any introduction Jennifer asked Clay, "What do you think he was thinking when you took his picture?"

Clay just looked at her. He peered deeply into her dark eyes and visually absorbed her exotic features. He slowly closed his eyes for a moment to retrieve his equilibrium and then replied.

"Well, he was probably thinking *who's this white guy taking my picture which I'll never get to see anyway; so why should I do what he wants?* Perhaps, he was thinking something like that."

Those were the first words that Clay Arnold and Jennifer Skyler spoke to each other, but they would not be the last.

Clay returned his attention to Jennifer's portrait on the contact sheet and then retrieved the corresponding negative from his file folder. He inserted the negative into the carrier in his old Omega D5 enlarger and carefully focused the image that appeared on his easel. He paused to study various areas of the negative's image and made notes regarding his exposure time and where he needed to dodge and burn to maximize the greatest tonal quality.

From his years of printmaking, Clay knew that color images could often stand on their own by virtue of their bright hues, but he had learned that fine black-and-white prints always required the manipulation of the light during the printing process. At these times he often felt like a magician painting with light.

After Clay rechecked his focus, he selected a pristine sheet of 11" × 14" Agfa Brovira Speed photo paper and secured it in his easel below. Now he turned the enlarger on again and began exposing the photo paper. His old Gralab timer started moving, and the low hum of its motor actually blended nicely with the sound of Weed Rawlins's harmonica.

He artfully waved his burning and dodging tools like an orchestra conductor adding light to certain areas of the portrait, holding light back from others. He worked quickly since the overall exposure time was set for twenty-eight seconds. He burned some extra light onto the chin and cheek areas to deepen their tonal qualities, and he dodged light from the eyes and hair to keep those areas from getting too dark.

When Clay was in his darkroom, he was no longer a photographer. Now he was a printmaker, and he wanted this print of Jennifer to be something extraordinary, something enduring.

In the weeks and months that followed their first brief conversation at the exhibition, Jennifer and Clay found themselves increasingly intrigued about each other, and soon they were spending more and more time together. Clay was initially captivated by Jennifer's exotic features: her long, raven-black hair; her deep, dark, shining eyes; her pretty mouth and engaging smile; her trim, athletic figure; the easy and confident way that she moved. All of these features created a woman who was just remarkable in her loveliness. And the more Clay got to know Jennifer, the more he was struck by how bright and witty she was, and how fiercely committed she was to her medical career and to helping women and families lead better, healthier lives.

Dr. Jennifer Skyler was an OB-GYN by training, having gone to medical school at Johns Hopkins University and then returned home to her Hoosier roots in Indianapolis, where she did her obstetrics and gynecology residency at Indiana University Hospital. She was a star in her field, and the combination of her skill, reputation, and personality made Dr. Skyler heavily sought after by premier medical centers all across the country.

More than anything, Dr. Skyler found true fulfillment in helping women become more knowledgeable about their bodies and gain understanding of family planning. Growing up in urban Indianapolis, she saw many single girls and married women of all economic backgrounds make questionable decisions about their health and sexuality.

Her goal was to provide the best medical care she could for her patients, and to make certain that women and their husbands and partners understood the full array of family planning options available to them. So it came as no surprise to her family, friends, and colleagues when she became the medical director of the Planned Parenthood Center in the Broad Ripple community in northern Indy.

Beyond work, both Jennifer and Clay were swept up by the joy and passion of their maturing relationship, and they made efforts to be together despite their insanely busy careers. Jennifer's work at the Planned Parenthood Center required a tremendous amount of medical oversight and management. Providing outstanding medical care and counsel for every woman who came through their doors was paramount, and Jennifer set high standards for herself and the Center's staff.

Then there were the storm clouds that certain frightening elements of the community rained on the Center because of its policies for providing contraception and legal abortions. Planned Parenthood faced a torrential assault from various religious groups, and there was always some politician, looking to showcase his piety and devotion to God's word, advocating that the federal government cease its funding for Planned Parenthood.

And, of course, there was often some nut job out there who'd gone off his daily meds or wanted to grab some attention by hurling obscenities at the Center's staff when they entered or left the building.

At first, the negative attacks on the Center's mission were merely annoying to Jennifer, but she sensed a growing trend toward violence; so even with their increased security systems, Jennifer was more than just a little concerned.

Despite her dedication to her career, Jennifer was finally ready for a committed relationship, and she believed that handsome, poised, world-famous photographer Clay Arnold could be just the right guy.

For a very long time both of them had thrown themselves into doing whatever it took to achieve their professional goals. Now with their careers very well established, Clay and Jennifer felt it was finally time to nurture a romance. And, as with their careers, they were very good at it. They were in love, and with each day that passed, their devotion to each other grew.

As for Clay Arnold's passion for his career, he had been totally intrigued with photography ever since his parents gave him a 35mm Canon FTb camera on his fourteenth birthday. He was fascinated with all the dials and settings, and with terms like *f-stops* and *depth-of-field.* He was further infatuated when at

Christmas his parents gave him a 24mm wide-angle lens and 200mm telephoto lens to go along with the 50mm lens that had come with the camera. Clay was hooked on taking good pictures, and he took his camera everywhere with him.

In turn, his parents were thrilled to see young Clay read everything he could get his hands on about photography and all the different equipment and techniques that were available. He hounded his mother to take him to the public library so he could haul home stacks of fine art photography books to see how the really good photographers made great photographs.

Clay became mesmerized by the incredible range of subject matter that these photographers covered: sports, portraiture, fashion, fine art, industrial design and advertising, journalism and nature photography. Before long, he had an excellent working knowledge of the settings on his camera and could very competently compose an image and produce an accurate exposure.

Clay spent many a day wandering the paths along the White River close to his home. He used his wide-angle lens when he wanted to capture a broad picture or to increase the depth-of-field of his focus. He was thrilled at how close to his subject he could get with his telephoto lens. Birds and squirrels, or the occasional couple necking, came into close view for his playful voyeurism into their worlds.

During his teenage years Clay's curiosity about photography grew. In addition to constantly reading about the history of early photography, he became enthralled by the incredible variety of cameras manufactured in the years after Louis-Jacques-Mande Daguerre had introduced photography in 1837. Clay was intrigued by the size and beauty of the early wooden view cameras with their large brass lenses. To him the nineteenth-century cameras were like works of sculpture.

Clay's parents were encouraged by his serious approach to his hobby and were good sports about helping him buy equipment, but they were taken aback when, at age sixteen, he asked to build a fully equipped darkroom in the basement.

With his darkroom in place, he soon realized that there was a vast difference between being a good photographer and being a good printmaker. His goal was to become excellent at both disciplines.

In the years that followed high school, Clay rapidly matured as an individual, and he had an uncanny talent for succeeding in whatever photography assignment he was given, whether as a college student at Yale University or during his graduate studies at the Art Institute of Chicago.

Tragically, Clay's parents were both killed in an Alpine automobile accident while touring northern Italy. Clay was away at graduate school at the time, and their sudden deaths rocked him in a way that caused him to escape even deeper into his education and career. He had no siblings and no close relatives; so in some ways he felt like an orphan. His close childhood friends, Weed Rawlins and his sister Tori, were the closest people he could call family. He treasured them.

The only other good news was that Clay's parents left him their sizable, seven-figure estate, and so he was free to travel the world and virtually choose his work assignments. He preferred to work with clients whose photographic interests mirrored his, and financially he was able to do so.

Professionally, Clay made a name for himself quickly. His travels to Africa, India, China, Eastern Europe, and the Amazon earned him no fewer than four *National Geographic* covers while he was still in his twenties. His real love, though, was for capturing the essence of people's souls through his portrait work.

He blended his portfolios with pictures of various international leaders and with actors and rock stars who asked him to shoot their likenesses. Clay's approach was unique, however, because his photo books and exhibitions also included the likenesses of everyday people living on the street. His subjects were an interesting combination of princes and paupers.

"People are people," he liked to say. "A person's character flows from within, not from the trappings of wealth and power that they wear."

By the time Clay turned thirty, he was among the most famous photographers on the planet. Clay's life, however, was not a storybook dream. Yes, he was very comfortable financially, and he had achieved great professional success, but he had also lost his parents, and another tragedy shook him to his very core. He looked again at the portrait of Jennifer that he was in the midst of printing, and his knees buckled.

Six weeks previously he had received an unexpected phone call from another long-time friend, Trent Reynolds. Trent was a detective with the Indiana State Police, and he had managed to track Clay down during a photo shoot for a winery in Napa Valley.

"There's been a bombing, Clay, and you need to come home immediately," Trent had advised.

Clay stared at the portrait of Jennifer he was working on. Weed Rawlins's voice softly echoed throughout the darkroom. It was a song about lost love.

After receiving Detective Reynolds's phone call, Clay chartered a private flight back to Indianapolis from California, and Trent met him at the airport. They drove back to Clay's home, and Trent filled him in with what he knew.

"We don't have a lot of details yet, Clay," Trent had sympathetically spoken at the time.

Clay recalled Trent's every word that night. Each one was seared into his consciousness.

"What we do know," Trent continued, "is that the Planned Parenthood Center was bombed around 8:30 last night by an unknown assailant, and four people were killed, including Jennifer, a nurse, and two clients."

"I am so sorry, Clay. I know she was a very fine woman, and I can't find the words to express how badly I feel for you right now. About all we really know is that the assailant spray-painted 'baby killers' on the outside of the Center; then he bombed it with what looks like a homemade device. The lab is working on it now, but from the damage it wreaked, it must've been pretty big. I know this is very little consolation, but I don't think she felt much, Clay."

Clay just stared straight ahead and said nothing. He was overwhelmed and in shock.

Trent Reynolds went on, "The security cameras were destroyed in the explosion and subsequent fire, but we're looking at a camera from the convenience store down the street to see if it recorded anything significant. It was fairly dark outside at the time of the bombing, and there were no eyewitnesses. We've been leaning on our informants, but unless the camera from the convenience store shows something or a witness comes forward, it looks like the bomber got away. I'm really sorry, Clay."

Clay silently stared straight ahead as Trent shared this heartbreaking information. Now, six weeks later in his darkroom, Clay fixated on Jennifer's portrait as it came to life in the tray of developer. Weed's mellow voice sang to him from his stereo, and Clay just continued to stare at the picture of the only woman he had ever really loved. The portrait in the tray of developer continued to get darker with each second that passed, and after about two minutes of staring, it faded to black.

"Don't go!" Clay groaned, but the love of his life, and now her image, were gone.

Chapter 2

MAURICE "WEED" RAWLINS stepped out on to the front porch of the old wooden frame house that he and his sister Tori called home. The evening sun was beginning to set, and it radiated a panorama of golden light onto his unshaven face.

He was dressed in faded jeans, an old Chicago Cubs T-shirt, and no shoes. In one hand he carried a short glass with a few cubes and a bottle of Early Times. In the other hand he cradled his harmonica. It was one of those rare late-September days that had warmed into the midseventies earlier that afternoon but would cool to the upper thirties by dawn.

Weed was going to enjoy the warm weather as long as he could. With each passing day he was more aware that before long another midwestern winter would settle in for a dreary four months. By early December he could count on Indy's frigid temperatures to bite into his life, and he wasn't thrilled by that prospect.

Sure, Weed was growing weary of Indiana's winters, but he was also a dedicated Hoosier, and he knew he had a lot to be very

grateful for, living where he did. He was also smart enough to schedule several weeks of his winter music gigs in warmer cities, and he had no shortage of friends and female admirers wherever he performed.

He was also lucky enough to have a great friend like Clay who owned a secluded contemporary lodge just outside of Tucson. Clay made it clear to Weed and Tori that they were welcome to use it as often as they wanted. To Clay, it was their home, too, and they all reveled in their frequent winter retreats there.

They'd all had some terrific times at the Arizona lodge, especially when Jennifer was still alive. Jennifer and Clay, Tori, Weed and their close friend Mace, plus Lex and Satchmo. They had all created a warm and loving family.

But those days with Jennifer were gone, and the memory of them got trampled on by the reality of her tragic death. Weed shivered in the warm light just thinking about it, and about how much trouble Clay was having in recovering from her loss. Weed was determined to be a good friend. Tori, too. They all were.

Weed looked around his surroundings and smiled at his good fortune. He loved living in the large, multibuilding complex that was originally built by the Block Bros. Brewing Company around 1855.

Weed took a soft sip of his Early Times and let the smooth whisky roll down his throat. He closed his eyes and felt a different kind of warmth touch him from within. He leaned against one of the porch posts and coaxed some improvisation from his harmonica. The sound was melancholy and yet upbeat in tempo. Weed Rawlins loved his blues harp and whisky. He felt like they put him in a soulful place where he was meant to be.

He heard a snuffing sound and looked over to see Satchmo, their enormous Maine Coon cat, walking along the handrail to greet Weed with his whiskered muzzle.

"C'mon over here, you big ol' beast," Weed cooed at Satchmo. "I swear you get bigger every time I see you. You haven't been eating sheep again, have you?" he joked.

Truth was: Tori and Weed adored this gorgeous feline. His magnificent silver-gray fur was damn near regal, and he strutted with a confidence that added to his majesty. On the molecular level, Satchmo was one very cool cat. He reveled in his independence, and he controlled the pest population around the old brewery like a sentry on guard.

He just showed up one day about two years before and took to Clay and Mace, and then he eventually started sleeping at Tori and Weed's house. Satchmo became their collective mascot, and even he and Lex, Mace's black Lab, figured out a way to make their relationship work.

In return, Satchmo also enjoyed the company of these humans who seemed to want him to be very comfortable. So, being a very smart kitty, he graced them with his presence and returned their affection with rubs and mews and the almost daily gifts of rodents and birds.

From inside the house Weed heard the sweet sound of Tori's voice singing along with an old recording of Ella Fitzgerald crooning a tune from the Cole Porter songbook. Tori's voice was so pure that it was hard to tell the difference between hers and Ella's.

"Well brother Weed, good evening to you," Tori said as she joined Weed on the front porch. She heard Satchmo's familiar purr and greeted him with a few scratches under his chin.

"And good evening to you, too, Mr. Satchmo," Tori said brightly. "I trust you've had a productive day keeping our home free of rodents and safe for democracy."

Satchmo purred even louder, then bounded away to resume his appointed rounds of the property.

Tori was Weed's younger sister by about eighteen months, and they were about as close as two siblings could be. They actually grew up three doors away from Clay's family on Elysian Lane near the White River north of Broad Ripple. Their families were good friends during their youth, and they remained very close nearly three decades later. Like Clay, Tori and Weed had lost their parents, a shared grief that forged an unbreakable bond. They were family now.

Like her brother Weed, Tori was trim and very good-looking, with honey-colored hair and an easygoing personality. Like her brother, too, she had chosen music as her favorite artistic medium. She could sing like an angel and play the keyboard with incredible virtuosity. She loved all genres of music, but she definitely favored the soulful sounds of blues and jazz. Tori and Weed played beautiful music together and often performed before large, enthusiastic audiences at Stella's Diner.

Aside from gender, of course, the only difference between the two siblings was that Tori had been blind since birth.

Standing on the porch with him, Tori said to her brother, "Tell me what you see, Weed."

"Aw heck, Tori, you know every inch of this entire complex as well as, if not better than, any of us except maybe Satchmo!"

"I know, Weed, but I just want to hear you describe it for me again, and tell me the history of the place again, too," she prompted. "Your words make pictures for me. Please."

The waning, evening sun cast the last remnants of its life-giving warmth on their faces, and Weed eyed the details of where he and Tori, Clay, Mace, Satchmo, and Lex lived.

"Okay," he began, "From where we're standing I see the front of our farmhouse, which used to be Henry and George Block's home when they arrived here from Bavaria. As the story goes, the Block brothers emigrated to Indianapolis, where they were sponsored by some relatives who had already come over from Germany."

"Within a couple of years," Weed continued, "Henry and George came north to the Broad Ripple area and purchased some twenty-five acres along the White River for their new brewery. The Block brothers liked this site for two main reasons: One, it reminded them of the Rhine River valley back in Germany, and secondly, the waterway provided another means of transporting their beer to other communities. Aside from that nasty bit of history called Prohibition, the Block Brothers Brewing Co. remained in existence for 100 years."

"Go on!" encouraged Tori. "I wonder how different the place was back then . . . the voices and the sounds and the smells. Imagine the stories these buildings could tell, and all of the people who have come and gone."

"From our porch," Weed continued, "I see our cobblestone courtyard that measures maybe forty by sixty feet and is bordered by our frame farmhouse and the other buildings that the Block brothers built over time. All of the buildings have lush English ivy growing on them that gives the complex a rich, verdant, nineteenth-century air about it."

Weed went on, "Clay was very smart in purchasing the complex and the acreage when he did, and he's done a great job in maintaining much of the historical integrity of the brewery complex while making great homes that we all enjoy."

Tori nodded agreement.

"Straight ahead," Weed went on, "is the power plant that was originally constructed to provide energy for all of the buildings in the brewery complex. That's where Mace lives, along with his black Labrador, Lex."

"Originally, it was just an old brick power plant, but Clay and Mace put a lot of back-breaking work and money into making it a very comfortable home for Mace when Clay bought the property about ten years ago."

"I love being in Mace's home," Tori beamed. "It's always comfortable and cozy, and hearing Mace's stories creates a lot of wonderful pictures for me."

"The power plant is still probably capable of providing energy for the entire complex," Weed continued, "but over the years, Mace and Clay determined that it was more efficient and economical to upgrade the utilities for each individual."

"Next to Mace's place, of course, is the old stone brew house where Clay lives. It's a multilevel stone and brick structure with Clay's spacious living quarters on the second and third floor. It also has a large basement where Clay's darkroom is located and a sub-basement that the old brewery used for storing their barrels of beer.

"The sub-basement is thirty feet underground and maintains a steady temperature of fifty-five degrees. Clay told me the other day that he wanted to speak with me about a special construction project for the sub-basement. He didn't elaborate, but he told me he needed my special expertise. I'm very curious to hear his plans."

"The first floor of the brew house," Weed went on, "has a separate entrance which leads to a gorgeous photography gallery that is free and open to the public. Our friend Clay spared no expense in creating a brightly lit gallery where he could exhibit his favorite photographs and a space to showcase his museum-quality collection of antique cameras and early precinema devices."

"As you know, Tori, guests come to Clay's museum every day that it's open, and it's become a bit of a mecca for students of photography and communications. I understand that his collection of Daguerreotype and wet-plate view cameras is among the finest anywhere in the world. Mace has volunteered to meet and greet folks that visit the museum and distribute literature. He's gotten really good at it, and it all works well."

"The second floor is Clay's main living space with his study, kitchen, and great room. His roof garden, which is situated off his third-floor bedroom, has a wonderful view of the White River. But, you already know all of this, Tori."

"I know, Weed, but thanks for telling me what you see. It really helps to have your eyes into the visual world," she sighed.

The sun continued to drop lower in the western sky, and Weed and Tori caught its fleeting warmth on their faces. Weed took another sip of his Early Times and proceeded to play a soulful tune on his harmonica. Tori joined in humming her own harmony as she had done since they were both young children.

Before too long Satchmo reappeared with a mouse that he laid at Tori's feet like a sacrificial offering. He rubbed against both of them and then went bounding off to greet Mace Davis and Lex who had heard their music and were walking across the courtyard to join them on the porch.

"Evening, Mace," Tori called to him. "I was wondering if you were home."

"Yes, I've been home most of the day, Miss Tori, just catching up on some household stuff and making sure we've got enough seasoned firewood for the winter. I've been seeing a lot of those big, black wooly worms in the woodpile, which is not a good sign, and the Farmer's Almanac predicts that we're in for a long, bitter winter."

Weed shivered at the very thought of that prognostication and took another sip from his Early Times. He blew a brief, shrill note on his harmonica as if to ward off the specter of Old Man Winter. Tori and Mace laughed because they knew how much Weed hated being cold.

Mace Davis rounded out the constellation of unique characters living in the old brewery complex. By all accounts, Mace, whose real name was supposedly Macedon Reginald Davis, was a fine and upstanding gentleman of African heritage.

He never knew his father, and his poor mother had virtually no education. She gave birth to Mace at age fourteen and suffered a fatal heart attack at age twenty-two attempting to give birth to another baby who died. Mace was alone and on the streets of Freeport on Grand Bahama Island at age eight, and he got by however he could. He doesn't talk much about his childhood.

Mace told Weed once that the priest and nuns at St. Francis took him off the street and educated him in their school for three years. Every once in a while he recites some Latin prayer and smiles at the memory.

At around age twelve Mace jumped on a ship he thought was going to Kingston, Jamaica, and he landed in New Orleans. He scrounged around New Orleans for about two weeks, nearly starving, until he met up with some older boys who said they were going to work in a lumber mill in a faraway place called Indiana. Mace figured he'd just tag along. Nearly sixty years later, Mace is still rooted to this property.

Turns out Mace was hired by the Jeffries Woodworking Mill to do general shop clean-up and any other tedious jobs that needed to be done. He didn't care, though. He made a little money, which he saved, and Mr. Jeffries let him sleep in the old workshop. Mrs. Jeffries was very kind and always remembered to give him something to eat each morning and at night.

Over the years Mace closely watched, listened to, and learned from the great woodworkers at the mill. He became a master cabinetmaker, and thanks in large measure to his skill, the Jeffries Woodworking Mill became highly sought after for fine cabinetry and architectural millwork. The mill thrived and its reputation grew . . . for the next fifty years.

Then, after being in business for over five decades, the Jeffries Woodworking Mill closed its doors on its long and glorious run; similar to what its predecessor, the Block Bros. Brewing Co., had done fifty years earlier.

Mr. Jeffries's decision to sell the property to Clay Arnold came with one deal-breaking stipulation: "that if Mace Davis so desires, he should be given free lodging in the brewery/mill complex for as long as he wishes."

Clay and Mace subsequently spent a weekend together in the old brewery complex becoming familiar with the property and each other. At the end of the weekend, they jointly decided that Mace's living on the property not only made sense from a property-management point of view, but it was also unequivocally the right thing to do. In their ten years there, neither man had ever regretted their decision for a second.

Mace joined Tori and Weed on the porch of the old farmhouse and took a seat in an old wicker rocker. Lex and Satchmo nuzzled each other for a brief second, and then Satchmo found more interest in a moth that had glided into his territory. Weed handed Mace a short glass with three fingers of whiskey, and they toasted each other's good health.

"Tori, have you talked with Clay today?" Mace asked. "He left me a note saying there was something he wanted me to help him with."

"No, I haven't, Mace," she replied, "but from the faint odor coming from the vent pipe near Clay's place, I'd say he's been down in his darkroom most of the afternoon printing some photographs."

The three of them faced the setting sun, and they grew quiet in its fleeting warmth.

After a few moments Tori said, "I'm very concerned about Clay. He's just not been the same man ever since Jennifer died."

"You mean was *murdered*, don't you?" came Weed's frank reply. "Sorry, Tori, and I agree with you. Clay is a lot quieter than usual, and he's staying withdrawn. It's not something that any of us should take personally. I just think he needs more time to process his heartbreaking loss of Jennifer. I can also sense that he is very angry, first of all because Jennifer was so important to him, and also because the cops have no plausible leads."

Mace listened intently to what Tori and Weed were saying about Clay and how he was dealing with Jennifer's death.

"You know, we can't walk in Clay's shoes," Mace said somberly. "He knows we're all here for him. He's taken a heck of an emotional beating, and I agree with Weed that he's coping with a lot of grief and anger at the same time. When he's ready, he'll come to us . . . and we'll be here for him."

Tori asked Weed to pour her a short tumbler of bourbon with a little ice. She softly started humming an improvised melody with her warm voice, and after a few moments Weed brought the most soulful sounds out of his harmonica.

Mace took special notice of what was unfolding around him. The sun was setting with an expansive array of reds and purples. It wasn't too chilly yet. They were on the porch of the brewery complex's old wooden farmhouse. Whisky was warming their insides, and the Rawlins's spirited music was warming his heart. He was with friends.

Mace had lived on this property for nearly six decades. The Block Bros. Brewing Co. had closed before he arrived at age twelve, but the Jeffries Mill had been his life. He had a lot of memories, most very good, and at this moment, he couldn't remember ever feeling more content than he did right now.

After a few minutes Clay emerged from the darkness of the courtyard and into the light of the reverie occurring on Tori and Weed's front porch.

"There you are," Weed said in greeting. "We were wondering if you'd ever come up for air and spend some time with your charming and adorable neighbors!"

Clay smiled at him and settled into another of the porch chairs next to Tori and Mace. Weed handed him a libation, and Satchmo jumped up on his lap and started rubbing his muzzle against Clay's chin.

"Well, I had some images I wanted to print in the darkroom, and I guess time just got away from me."

It was nearly dark now, and the last orange remnants of the setting sun reminded Clay of the darkroom's amber safelight, which in turn reminded him of the sadness of printing Jennifer's portrait. He grew quiet again but felt some satisfaction in merely listening to the voices and banter of his good friends. In truth, Tori's assessment of Clay was accurate. He wasn't the same man as he had been before Jennifer's murder.

"Well, it's getting a bit late for me," Clay said after finishing his drink. "I've got some major photo assignments that will take me away for a couple of weeks, and I probably should turn in. Mace, are you available around ten in the morning to take a trip to downtown Indy with me? I have some unfinished business I feel a need to complete, and I could use your help, if you're free."

"Sure enough, Clay," Mace replied. "Anything you need me to do in advance?"

"No, I think just having access to your counsel will be more than adequate," Clay said cryptically.

"And Weed, if you're free sometime tomorrow afternoon, I have that project in the sub-basement I'd still like to discuss with you. You, too, Mace, if you're available. I'll be leaving day after tomorrow and hope you're willing to get a head start on the project while I'm gone."

"We'll be here, Clay. Tori and I will be practicing some new music sets we want to try at Stella's Diner this weekend. Just give me a holler when you're ready, okay?"

With that, Clay rose from his seat, said his goodnights, and slipped back into the darkness of the courtyard. Satchmo bounded after him. Tori, Mace, and Weed remained on the porch for another hour or so trying to regain the euphoria they'd felt earlier, but all three were suffering for their friend. They wondered how they might help.

Chapter 3

CLAY CLIMBED THE TWO FLIGHTS of stairs to the roof garden outside his bedroom in the old brewery building. He could've taken the private elevator he had installed when he built the museum, but he needed the exercise to exorcise the grief and anger that still plagued him over Jennifer. Plus, Satchmo had already bounded up the stairs in front of him, leading a noble charge, so it only made sense to fall in line behind.

Clay turned on his Bose music system and poured himself a generous snifter of Graham's Port. The stereo was tuned to his local public broadcasting station playing Igor Stravinsky's *Rite of Spring*. Clay took a sip of the port, closed his eyes, and listened to the dramatic primal sounds filling his head . . . tribal drum beats and savage beasts trumpeting. Organic and raw.

Clay wondered what Tori's reaction would be to the intensity of Stravinsky's *Rite*. He wondered whether a sightless person heard

and processed the sounds of music, especially very dramatic music, the same way a sighted person did.

Clay knew this work very well because on more than one occasion his father had him, as a teenager, listen to its highly charged passion of Stravinsky's opus. At first Clay found it disturbing and a little frightening in places, but once he listened closely, he began to feel a certain kinship with the visceral emotions the music created.

The *Rite of Spring* concluded, leaving Clay feeling breathless. The PBS station turned its programming to the national news and immediately went to a breaking story about another mass shooting. This time at a school near Louisville, Kentucky. Eight children dead, aged six to ten. Four more kids seriously injured and rushed to hospitals. One teacher killed and two others gravely wounded. Shooter still on the loose. Lots of trauma and confusion. Details were sketchy.

The combination of the powerful music, the port, his emotional experience printing Jennifer's picture in the darkroom, the news of yet another mass shooting at an elementary school—all of these things had a seismic, transformative effect on Clay. His blood boiled with outrage on numerous levels. He'd fucking had it. "Enough, goddamnit, enough!"

Clay regained most of his composure, and he turned off the stereo. Right now he just couldn't listen to one more account of mass shootings, or killings of unarmed black kids, or harassment of gays or women wearing yoga pants.

Then there were the attacks on Planned Parenthood centers by religiously-inspired zealots and certifiable whack-jobs, all in the name of the Lord and saving babies.

Clay was fed up with the ignorance of self-righteous politicians and right-wing pundits who declared blind idolatry to guns and the NRA. He was angry and ashamed that a huge number of Americans, including many congressmen and media personalities, didn't want to have systems in place to prevent crazies from getting assault rifles and handguns.

He stood at the handrail looking at the starry sky. He faced east and immediately recognized an old friend, the heroic constellation Orion. The Hunter.

Clay felt an immediate uplifting to his spirits. Orion had always been his favorite constellation, and it had been gone from view for much of the last six months. Now it was beginning to return, low in the eastern sky, and soon it would be the major constellation in winter's southern sky.

Clay didn't put a lot of stock in the concept that things happened for a reason. He just never found any evidence to support that philosophy. Regardless, he was curious to note that, within a couple of minutes, he had both heard the old primal rhythms of the Rite of Spring and seen Orion, the Hunter.

He didn't honestly regard these as prophetic signs, but the occurrences caused him to stop and think seriously about what he really wanted to do. And, what he wanted to do more than anything was to tilt the playing field in favor of the victims. To avenge them. To even the score.

Satchmo materialized like a fluffy ghost from the roof garden's autumn foliage. He walked over to Clay and sat by him on the handrail. The two of them remained still, each listening to the night sounds along the White River.

Clay thought back almost twenty years ago to when he had his first camera and would hike along the White River near his parents' home, taking pictures of whatever caught his eye. And now, here he was along the same river again, with a lot of water having flowed by here since his youth.

Satchmo reached up and touched his forehead to Clay's and snuffled. Clay smiled, flattered by Satchmo's expresion of affection. This cat definitely showed a lot of character. Subtle but fascinating.

He made a mental note to shoot a series of portraits of animals and their personalities. Nothing hokey, though. Images with their eyes serving as windows to their souls.

"Well, Mr. Satchmo, I appreciate your friendship, too! You are a mensch, and I'm proud to have you as my confidant."

Then Clay turned serious again. "I suppose you realize I've got to make careful preparations for my upcoming evening shoots."

Satchmo gave a hearty meow, then brushed against Clay's side and trotted back to the cover of the autumn foliage.

Clay returned his gaze to the starry sky and quietly bid Jennifer a good night.

"Soon," he whispered to himself. "Very soon, the evening comes."

Chapter 4

CLAY MET UP WITH MACE a little before 10:00 AM in the courtyard area between Mace's home in the power plant and Clay's
brewery building. There was a slight chill in the late September
air, but the skies were mostly clear, with a comfortable breeze
coming out of the southwest.

"G'morning Clay," Mace cheerfully greeted. "Hope you had
a good night's rest. Tori, Weed, and I stayed up for a little while
after you left. Wished you'd hung out with us. Tori and Weed
sang, and, of course, we drank and smoked a little. It was a really
mellow evening. Next time, okay?"

Clay nodded his agreement and deflected Mace's comment
by asking his trusted friend, "Have you had breakfast yet, Mace?"

Mace held back a small smile, recognizing that Clay preferred
to dodge the subject of sociability for now.

"Sure did, around 6:00 AM. You know me, Clay, after all of
these years of getting up early for work, my internal clock won't let

me lay around past six-thirty. Now having said that, I'm definitely up for another breakfast if you are."

"Give me five more minutes, Mace, and I'll drive us down to Stella's Diner. It's been a while since I've seen our spirited friend, Mrs. Vance, and I've missed her maternal way of offering unsolicited advice."

"Yeah," Mace replied. "Stella does have a very unique way about her, that's for sure. It's probably what's allowed her to be such a successful businesswoman."

Clay stepped back inside his entrance to the brewery building, then descended in the elevator to his darkroom located in the brewery's basement. He turned on the white light, instead of his safelight, and went to the desk situated immediately inside his darkroom. He found the file he was looking for and removed a five-by-seven-inch photograph. He placed the photo in a brown envelope and slipped it inside his jacket pocket.

"I'm ready, Mace," Clay called out as he returned to the courtyard and opened the driver's door to his silver Toyota Tacoma.

A moment later Mace let Lex outside and shut the door to the power plant. Lex barked a few times to announce his presence and then scampered off behind the farmhouse where he found Tori working on raised beds in the garden.

Mace climbed inside the truck, and the two men drove out of the brewery complex heading for Stella's Diner on the edge of Broad Ripple.

Stella's Diner was a well known and highly regarded establishment. Stella's started out in its early days as a simple roadside diner and earned a reputation among the locals as a place to come for good, wholesome, home-style cooking that was affordable. Under Stella Vance's smart management and savvy investing, it grew to become a popular regional club, attracting musicians and visitors from throughout the midwest and beyond.

The original diner building served as the main entrance to a much larger facility. You could still get a classic Stella's Diner breakfast there in the morning, but after high noon the original building became the lounge for the trendy night club that emerged behind it. It was quite a juggling act, but Stella made it all work.

And Stella herself was an institution. She was an astute promoter who showcased great musical talent, pretty waitresses, fine home cooking, and premium liquor. None of the success would've been possible without Stella's vision, and she was very picky about who worked for her. Stella set high standards. No trash.

Now in her very late thirties (no one knew her exact age for sure), she had three boys, ages ten to fifteen. She had been raising them by herself for the last four years ever since her late husband, Norbert, got run over by a cement truck. The driver, failing to see him, backed over him at the cement plant where he worked. He was mashed into an unrecognizable slurry of organic material and gray-colored goop.

Stella carried on, though, and the women working at the club actually enjoyed helping to look after the boys. The boys were thrilled to get a close-up view of the club's operations. It was a mesmerizing experience for them. They also delighted in having the opportunity to see some very pretty women in alluring garments. They were boys, after all.

Stella stood about five feet and five inches, with a tanned complexion, heavy make-up, and black-rimmed glasses. She had long auburn hair, a brassy color that came out of a bottle. While the unique tint looked a little trashy, it fit her personality perfectly and became her signature feature. Well, that and the leopard, tiger, or zebra print tights that she wore, along with a hot-pink, form-fitting top. Stella was quite a spectacle!

True, Stella might've looked like she came out of a trailer park, but there was nothing unseemly or illegal about her establishment. Stella's Diner was a multimillion-dollar business, and Stella was smart enough to create the glitz and even smarter not to throw its success away by getting in the gutter.

The waitresses were very well trained in dealing with patrons who had too much to drink and got a little too friendly. Stella's security personnel were trained to be polite, but they were highly effective in maintaining decorum, if necessary. Stella made certain to keep a respectful working relationship with the local police. She knew it made no sense to have them as enemies, and it was reassuring to know that the cops were around if she needed them.

Everyone respected Stella, and everyone came to her diner for fun.

Weed and Tori Rawlins were regular performers at Stella's Diner, which meant that Clay and Mace often showed up to enjoy watching Weed and Tori electrify their audiences. Their range of music could get you up and dancing like you were on fire or crying in your beer with sadness. They could spin your head with their spectral voices and sounds and then have you begging for more.

The brother-sister duo were regional music sensations. Professionally, Weed traveled more frequently than Tori, not because of her blindness, but because he really enjoyed performing on the road, and Tori was perfectly happy performing closer to home.

Like Clay, Weed had never been married. He wasn't against marriage, but right now Weed was a single guy who enjoyed being single. He loved making a good living playing his music. He was a happy dude.

He also loved his sister and was totally devoted to her. Even when he was gone, he made sure that Tori had back-up help if she needed it. Weed didn't hover, but he kept a protective, brotherly eye out for her.

"Well, I'll be," said Stella when Clay and Mace entered the diner. "If it's not my two favorite fellers over age fifteen. Mace, it's about time you dragged that handsome photographer down here. Where in the world have you been off to now, Clay?"

"Stella, it was actually his idea," Mace said. "Clay told me he wanted to have a good, home-cooked breakfast and hopefully catch a glimpse of that gorgeous, hot chick who owns the place," Mace fibbed.

Stella just beamed at the compliment, and Clay shot Mace a look that said, "Don't you dare say another word!"

Stella led the men to a booth and told them that she needed to cover the cash register for a little while.

"I'll be back in a few minutes," she said. "But Abby will be happy to take care of you. She's new here and is waiting tables in between journalism jobs. She's working hard so you gents be sweet to her and don't tease her too much, okay?"

"Yes, mother Vance," came Mace's compliant reply.

Abby approached their table, introduced herself, offered two menus, and asked if they wanted coffee. In his usual outgoing manner, Mace introduced himself and Clay as two guys who come here frequently. He said "yes" to the coffee.

Clay didn't even bother to look up. He just said, "Coffee, two scrambled eggs, sausage links, hash browns, wheat toast."

Abby fumbled with her pad and pencil to get the order down before she forgot.

"Uh, okay," she managed to reply. "And you, sir," she said to Mace, "do you want to order now or wait until I bring your coffee?"

"I'll just have the same as him, but coffee now would be good," Mace said in a soothing tone.

Abby left for the kitchen, and a little silence settled over the table. Abby returned a few moments later with a fresh pot of coffee and filled their cups. Clay remained quiet while she was at the table, but Mace politely thanked her. Clay finally made eye contact with Mace.

Without preamble, Clay said, "I really need your advice on something that's been gnawing at me quite a bit. It's a little weird, and that's why I want your reaction to it, and maybe your help."

Clay and Mace had known each other for over ten years by then and had grown to respect and rely on each other, despite their differences in age, race, and upbringing. Clay respected Mace as a wise, older man who he could count on, and he regarded him as a close friend.

Mace had known a lot of men over the years, some very fine and some hellishly cruel. Within thirty minutes of meeting Clay, Mace knew he was a straight-shooter, and he was never disappointed. If Clay needed him, he'd be there.

"So, what shall we discuss?" came Mace's question to Clay as they sipped their coffee.

Clay began, "I can't remember if I ever told you about the first time I met Jennifer."

"At the opening of your exhibition a little over a year ago, right?" Mace asked. "I was there, but I didn't meet Jennifer that night."

"She came up alongside of me as I was staring at an image that I shot of this black kid sitting in a shadowed doorway," Clay recalled.

"I remember saying to her that the boy probably thought he'd never see the picture that I was taking of him." Clay pulled the picture out of his jacket pocket and laid it on the table for Mace to see.

After a few awkward seconds, Mace said, "So we came all the way down to Stella's so you could tell me that?!"

"No, Mace, I want you to help me find him," Clay said solemnly.

Abby returned and brought them their breakfast platters and refilled their coffee cups.

"Now let me get this straight," Mace began again. "You want to drive into the inner city in Indianapolis and look for some street kid that you saw very briefly a year ago and give him this picture."

"Yeah, that's pretty much it," Clay admitted. "I know it sounds bizarre, Mace, but I feel like this is something I need to do or my head's going to explode with anger, grief, and frustration."

"I understand that, Clay, but you don't even know if the kid is still alive, or in reform school, or moved away or is living with his sweet Aunt Tootie. He could be anywhere . . . and you don't even know his name." Mace shook his head.

They ate their breakfasts quietly, and Mace's thoughts returned to his own youth, living alone on the streets of Freeport in the Bahamas. Long ago, he had learned to forget much of the suffering he endured as a youngster on his own: the constant fear; the distrust, the old used clothes, the lack of affection; and the hunger . . . always the hunger.

It wasn't until he was rescued by the good souls at St. Francis that he even had an inkling that his life could be better. Throughout his life Mace never felt a spiritual closeness with God, but he never forgot the way that the good people at St. Francis reached out to him and literally saved him.

Abby returned to offer more coffee and clear their dishes away. For the first time since they'd arrived, Clay noticed her. She caught him looking at her, and he looked away feeling embarrassed and a little ashamed for noticing a woman other than Jennifer.

Abby West's appearance caught Clay by surprise. She was very pretty with hair the color of corn silk and sky-blue eyes that glowed like pale sapphires above rose-colored cheeks. She had a warm smile, but she maintained a very professional demeanor.

"Anything else I can get for you gentlemen?" she asked.

Mace and Clay looked at each other, and Mace said, "I think we're both good. Just need to pay. Thanks."

Abby left the bill on the table and turned to face Clay.

"You're Clay Arnold, the photographer, aren't you?" she said.

Clay was stunned by her recognition of him. Of course, he and his work had earned international fame, but to Clay it was his photography that he wanted recognized far more than him. He was always surprised if someone identified him personally.

"Uh, yeah, that's me," Clay managed. "Do you mind my asking how you knew?"

"Oh, I'm a huge fan of fine-art photography, especially street photography, and I've followed your career over the last couple of years. And, because I'm pretty smart, too." With that Abby smiled at both men, spun around, and walked away.

Mace and Clay enjoyed Abby's clever departure. She had surprised them both.

"That young lady appears to have some spirit, and pretty, too!" Mace said.

"Yeah, spirit," Clay replied.

They met up with Stella who was still manning the cash register. She looked a little harried, and Clay asked what was up.

"Oh, pains-in-the-ass is what they are," she said bluntly. "A couple of weeks ago we put in a major shower facility at the rear of the property so campers and truckers could rent vehicle space for the night and be able to get a hot shower.

"Anyway, long story short. It's been very popular, but lately we've had this loud, black pickup truck coming around harassing our guests. A lot of hollering, cussing, accusing my employees of being whores and faggots. It came to blows once. The cops got here fast, but those cowardly jerks got away first. They've been here three times now. Same black pickup, sporting a Confederate battle flag as its front license plate.

"Actually, Clay, your friend Detective Reynolds from the Indiana State Police arrived first last night and is handling the state's investigation. He said he would have a man on duty in the parking lot in an unmarked car for the next few days in case the bad guys come back."

"I'm really sorry you and your guests have to deal with that kind of ignorance," Clay said. "Trent Reynolds will get the situation under control, I'm sure."

But inside Clay could feel his blood beginning to boil again at the thought of self-deluded hoodlums victimizing innocent people.

"I'm going away on assignment in Charleston, South Carolina, for a few days, but I'd like to hear more about this when I return, if that's okay with you, Stella."

Stella looked into Clay's steady, penetrating eyes and nodded affirmatively at him. "We'll talk," she said.

Mace and Clay sat in the Tacoma in the parking lot and talked about how they should go about finding the boy. They didn't talk much about what they would say to him if they found him, and Clay was relieved to have Mace's experience to fall back on.

"Let's start at the beginning," Mace said. "Let's go back to where you shot the picture and see who's around. Then we'll take it from there, okay?"

Clay had traveled to Indianapolis's inner city many times in his life, mainly to shoot pictures that were compelling to him, not necessarily to his clients. He didn't know the area in southern Indy like the back of his hand, but he had a decent knowledge of the key landmarks. When they arrived at their destination, Clay saw the old building and pulled his truck to the curb. Mace and Clay got out.

Chapter 5

I T WAS ABOUT NOON, and the sunlight cascaded down the sides of the buildings onto the pavement below. With the sun overhead, Clay missed seeing long dramatic shadows cast on the buildings. He knew that he would have to be here in the early mornings or late afternoons to see them. They added an artistic dimension that he often incorporated in his images.

He recognized the building he was looking for because he had admired and photographed it on other occasions. In an earlier time it had been a stately, old brick Victorian, probably a wealthy merchant's home. Now it still projected a noble street presence, but it needed some serious help.

533 Rose Street had been sandblasted fifteen or more years ago during a revitalization program by the city. But that was a long time ago now, and no one had shown much interest, especially the owner. The wood trim around the front door had begun to rot. The old box gutters were in bad shape and leaked in places

they weren't meant to. A second story window was cracked, and the chimney hung at a precarious angle.

Regardless, Clay viewed this edifice as an aged grand dame. He pulled the photograph out of his pocket and walked over to the spot where he likely stood when he took the boy's picture. There was no boy, and there were no shadows, but he knew he was at the right place.

Further down the block there were several kids playing ball in the street.

Mace said, "C'mon Clay, let's head on down there and have us a little conversation. Somebody should know something about our little Mr. X. It all depends on how much they choose to talk to us."

"Would you mind taking the lead, Mace? I don't mean to lay all of this on you, but I think they'll react better to an older black man more than some white guy they probably don't trust."

Mace knew he was right, but he said, "Trust me, my being black doesn't necessarily mean squat to these kids either. They'll want to know what's in it for them, and will they get in any trouble."

Clay and Mace ambled down the block about a hundred yards and stopped on the sidewalk to watch them finish their inning. Clay took in the scene. He smiled because it reminded him of a painting by Roberto Fabiano, rather than a photograph.

The scene was composed of Victorian-era rowhouses, old leaning telephone poles, and street urchins running and playing. Clay marveled when he thought about the number of ballgames that must've been played on this street over the decades. Play was timeless.

The inning came to an end, and a boy around thirteen saw Clay's camera hanging around his neck and said, "Hey mister, you wanna take a picture?" Then he puffed his chest out largely and pretended to be a superhero.

The other kids laughed, and Mace and Clay took this as their cue to talk with them.

Mace fibbed, "I used to play on these same streets around here when I was a kid; a long time ago. I remember when Timmy Snodgrass knocked a home run right through old man Clodfelter's parlor window right over there."

"My friend and I are looking for someone; nothing about the cops or anything like that, but my friend asked me if I'd come back to the old neighborhood and give him a hand."

Several of the kids went back to tossing a baseball, but a small cluster of three stayed and listened to Mace.

"What did this boy do?" the youngest of the boys asked.

Mace looked at Clay, and Clay responded by simply telling the truth.

"I'm a professional photographer. People pay me to take pictures. Sometimes I take pictures to make a statement, and sometimes I take pictures just for myself. A couple of years ago I took a picture of a kid sitting in the doorway of that building down there, and it turned out to be one of my very favorites. I want to thank the boy and give him the picture I took."

The kids just stared at Clay. "Really!?" one asked. "Why would you want to do that?"

Mace tried to conceal a smile, but Clay caught his feeble attempt.

Now Mace said, "I know it sounds a little funny, but it's important, and we were hoping you might know him. We might be able to make it worth your while."

Clay gave the kids the photo. No one showed an immediate reaction. The oldest boy was named Marcus. He looked at the two younger kids and told them go back to the game. They went running back to join the others, arguing over whose turn it was to bat.

Mace looked at the boy and said, "Son, can you help us out here? I grew up on these same streets, and I know it's best not to say anything, but the boy in the picture is not in any trouble. We just want to talk with him."

"Is there a reward if I know something?" the boy asked.

"Yes," Clay said, "if you can help us locate him."

"How much?"

"How's twenty dollars?"

The boy started to walk away. "Man, twenty dollars doesn't buy shit."

Clay said, "I'll give you a hundred dollars if you help us find him. Fifty now and the other fifty when we find him."

The boy stopped and walked back. Clay discreetly handed him fifty dollars so the other kids wouldn't see.

Clay showed Marcus the photograph again.

"Yeah, I know him," he said. "That's Rennie. Rennie Cotton. He used to live around here a few years ago. He's staying a couple streets over now. I think he's living on his own. Been that way with him for a while."

Mace asked, "Would you be willing to ride over with us to where you think he stays?"

Marcus grew suspicious about getting in the truck with two strangers, but the allure of the additional fifty dollars was hard to resist.

"All right, but no funny stuff, you hear me?!"

"We hear you," Mace said. "Don't we, Clay?"

"Yessir, we sure do," was all that Clay could think to say.

Marcus yelled over to the other kids telling them he'd be back tomorrow. Then the three of them climbed into the Tacoma. They drove about six blocks past some new streets that had been built in recent years. The city elders had ultimately decided that it was cheaper to tear down the old brick Victorians and construct townhouses. They looked nice, but Clay knew there was no way they'd hold up as well as his "aged grand dame."

Marcus pointed to an old shack at the end of Hill Street. "I think he stays there," he said. "Lives alone."

Clay looked at the shack and muttered, "Jesus."

Mace was also taken aback by how ramshackle the place looked. He tried not to think about his own younger days trying to survive on the street. Those were not pleasant memories, and seeing this shack brought back a heartache that he thought he had left behind.

Marcus said, "Can I have the other fifty now? I showed y'all where Rennie lives."

Clay said, "Sure." He handed him the rest of the money and offered him a ride home, but Marcus said he lived the next street over. He bolted out of the back seat of the truck and took off running for home.

"Well," Mace said, "I guess we're about to find out if we got snookered by a thirteen-year-old con man, or if this Rennie Cotton is who we're looking for."

"Mace, listen, I really appreciate your coming along with me on this. You probably think I've lost my mind. Maybe I have. All I know is that I've really struggled emotionally ever since Jennifer was killed. And the cops still haven't come up with any tangible leads. I've just had this weird feeling that maybe finding this kid and helping him out will allow me to feel human again, instead of angry all of the damn time."

"Anger is an insidious thing," Mace said. "It causes a lot of damage. I know. I felt anger for a lot of years, still do. It probably kept me from getting married all these years. We all have to find our own ways to deal with it, or it will consume us."

Clay just shook his head. "Well, I'm starting to feel consumed."

"C'mon," Mace said. "Let's see if anyone is home."

They got out of the truck and dodged the broken glass on the sidewalk. Mace took the lead, and they walked up to the shack's door and knocked. There was no sound from inside. Mace knocked louder this time. There was a scuffling sound, and the door slowly opened a crack to reveal two youthful eyes peering up at them.

Chapter 6

"WHAT DO YOU WANT?" came the adolescent voice from within. "I ain't buying nothing; so get the fuck out of here." He slammed the door in their faces.

"A real charming young man, wouldn't you say, Clay?" Mace offered sarcastically.

"Yeah, real charming," Clay repeated. "Knock again, Mace."

This time the door opened a crack and the short barrel of a pistol pointed through the opening.

"I said I ain't buying nothing," Rennie declared in a more menacing voice. "Now get out of here before I start shooting your asses."

"Now son, put the gun down," Mace said calmly. "My friend and I aren't here to mess with you. We have something we want to show you."

"Well, unless you brought me money or food, I ain't interested. Now get on out of here." He cocked the revolver.

Clay said, "Okay, okay, just take it easy." He pulled the photograph from his pocket and put it up to the crack in the doorway for the boy to see. "I just wanted to give you this."

The boy took the picture and closed the door so he could look at it more closely.

A few seconds later the door reopened and Rennie said, "Where'd you get that picture, mister?"

"I took it about two or three years ago over on Rose Street," Clay replied.

Clay could see the wheels turning in Rennie's mind and a flash of recollection appear on his face.

"You're that photographer man who used to come around here and shoot pictures of us poor people so you could make money off of us. Yeah, I remember you. What do you want?"

"Well, do you mind if we step inside and talk with you?" Mace asked. "I don't like transacting business from the sidewalk."

"Business, what kind of business? And, hell no, you can't come inside."

Rennie had lowered the gun, but he stayed very alert in case these old dudes tried to pull something funny.

Clay pulled a twenty dollar bill out of his pocket and flashed it at the kid with the gun.

"Just want to talk with you, is all," Clay said. Mace nodded his agreement.

Rennie reached through the opening in the door, grabbed the twenty-dollar bill, and slammed the door shut. Mace and Clay just stood there a moment wondering what would happen next, and then the door opened slowly again. No shots were fired. When they peered inside, they saw the boy sitting on an old wooden chair with the pistol in his lap.

Mace and Clay entered the dimly lit shack and were stunned by the barrenness of its interior. There was one chair, currently occupied by Rennie Cotton, a small wooden table with a candle and matches, a mattress on the floor, and a large can that apparently served as Rennie's toilet. No electricity, no running water. The place was a pitiful hovel.

Mace looked around the one-room shack and saw a scene of poverty the likes of which he hadn't witnessed in a very long time. He felt a heartache that made him literally touch the wall to steady himself.

Likewise, Clay eyed the interior of the shack and was surprised that anyone lived like this in America in this day and age. He was equally shocked that this adolescent boy had eluded Human Services and school authorities for as long as he had. Rennie Cotton had slipped through the cracks of society and was going through life alone.

"So, talk!" Rennie said.

"I understand your name is Rennie Cotton. Is that correct?" Clay asked.

"How'd you know that?" a wary Rennie asked.

"Word on the street," Mace answered. "Look, my friend here just wanted to give you that picture he took of you, okay?"

Rennie said nothing. He just stared at the two men.

Mace continued, "How old are you, son?"

"Old enough, and I ain't your son," Rennie spewed.

"You live here all by yourself? You got any kin?" Mace asked quietly.

"Naw, no kin. What's it to you anyway?"

"Just asking, is all," said Mace. "You got a job? Fella's got to be able to buy food, right?"

Clay and Mace could see that their conversation with Mr. Cotton wasn't going to get all warm and fuzzy, but Clay wasn't prepared to just say goodbye. He and Mace shared a pained look at the plight of this kid's life.

Clay blurted out, "I'm looking for a reliable worker at the place where Mr. Davis here and I live. It's good work and the pay's good, if you're interested in something steady."

Clay just let the words hang in the air.

"I don't need your damn charity, mister," was Rennie's frosty response.

"It's not charity, Rennie," Mace said. "We're offering you an opportunity to work hard and get paid well, too, but if we walk out that door, the offer goes away. We need someone we can rely on. Your choice."

Rennie just stared at the two men. After a few more awkward moments, Mace turned to leave the shack.

"What kind of work?" Rennie asked.

"Mostly odd jobs around our place at the old brewery/mill complex north of Broad Ripple," Clay said. "Hauling firewood, sweeping out buildings, pretty much whatever we need you to do. Eight dollars an hour and lunch. Mace will pick you up in the morning and bring you back here in the evening."

Rennie looked at the two men suspiciously.

"Why are you doing this? Why are you being nice to me?"

"For now, let's just say it's your lucky day," Mace said. "But young man, let me tell you this, you steal from us, you give us a bunch of lip, and your lucky day will disappear fast. We're not playing any games with you, Rennie, and if you're as smart as I think you are, you'll put your pride aside and come to work for us."

He stopped talking and watched Rennie struggle with what he should do.

"What time?" Rennie asked. "What time you gonna pick me up?"

Clay and Mace gave each other a private smile, and Mace said, "eight o'clock AM sharp. Do you need a watch?"

"Naw, I get up early," Rennie said. "This is straight-up business; no funny stuff, right?"

"Straight-up business, Rennie," Clay said. "You work eight o'clock AM to five o'clock PM. Eight dollars an hour, plus lunch. That's seventy-two dollars a day, cash."

"Alright, I think I can help you out," Rennie said. Clay stuck his hand out, and Rennie reluctantly shook it to seal the deal.

"Good," said Mace. "I'll see you tomorrow morning at eight o'clock sharp."

Clay and Mace left the shack and walked back to the truck.

"Thanks, Mace. I have no idea how this will work out with Rennie, but I really appreciate your agreeing to give it a try."

Mace agreeably nodded his head, but his mind had drifted back to his hard youth on the streets of Freeport, and to the way the priests and sisters at St. Francis had pulled him from the brink.

"Yeah," he replied to Clay. "We can make this work."

Chapter 7

CLEMENT HACKER WAS AN unhappy man, which unfortunately meant he was also a very unpleasant man.

His late wife, Ella Marie, fell to cancer a few years back, and Clement never recovered from the shock of her death. He was consumed by the anger he felt. He directed most of that rage toward hospitals, doctors, and health insurance companies, but hell, before long he included the whole freakin' government, too! In his mind Clement Hacker went from feeling like a victim to believing he was an anointed warrior. He was on a deeply personal mission.

Clement wasn't alone in his vitriol toward a lot of people. His twin sons, Newt and Twit, were the spitting image of their father when it came to being generally pissed-off, obnoxious louts.

The three of them lived together at their secluded cabin in southern Indiana. The twins were in their midtwenties and had no interest in leaving home. They really had nowhere else to go, anyway, but Clement made sure they knew he expected them to

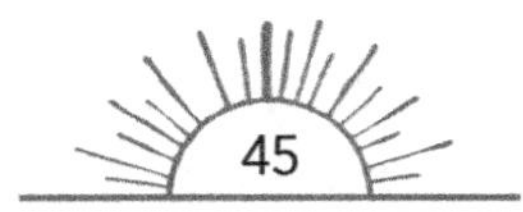

stay home and do his bidding. Clement was the alpha male, and Newt and Twit accepted that fact.

The three men had worked together at the Wallace Concrete Co. for a few years, but one of the three was always angry with some other co-worker, and Mr. Wallace had finally had enough of the ugly talk and aggressive behavior coming from the Hacker men. He told them to go find happiness and professional fulfillment elsewhere.

"Get the hell out and don't come back!" were Mr. Wallace's parting words.

Fortunately, Clement and the boys were good at auto and truck repair, welding, hauling, and other tasks that were often needed in the country. Their skill level was fairly basic and definitely not very high-tech. Regardless, the father and his two sons were able to make ends meet.

"You got that exhaust system fixed yet for the black Dodge pickup?" Clement bellowed in Newt's direction.

"Getting close, Pa. Just finishing up, and we gotta see how she sounds when I start her up."

"I can't believe you and your brother fucked it up in the first place."

"Now, Pa!" Newt started. "We told you we was hell-bent-for-leather getting away after messing with those folks at Stella's Diner. We did as you told us and cruised around behind Stella's and gave folks shit. I think waving our Confederate battle flag was a real nice touch. Sure seemed to get a bunch of jiggaboos all riled up."

"Last time we went, though, there was a police car waiting for us. Fortunately for us, we spotted each other at about the same time. We took off over the curb, through some shrubbery, and down a short flight of concrete steps, but we got away safely. Unfortunately, the tailpipe and muffler got a bit scrunched."

"Yeah, well," Clement said, "serves those whores and sinners right at that Stella's Diner. That trip was a good warm-up for you and Twit for what I have planned in the future. And make dang sure that muffler is quiet. We don't need to draw any more attention to ourselves than we already have."

"And, by the way," Clement continued, "where is that seedy-looking brother of yours, anyway?"

"He's down at the feed and grain store. Don't you remember you sent him for the fresh supply of fertilizer?" Newt prompted.

"Oh yeah, but remember," Clement cautioned, "we've got to be real quiet about that. If anyone knew what we're doing with that fertilizer and the other chemicals, we'd have a swarm of government people snooping around where we don't want them. Remember that!"

"I remember, Pa, and Twit knows to be careful, too. Most of the time."

"All right, then," Clement said. "I'll be here in the pole barn mixing up a batch of stuff. You finish up with that truck. When your brother gets back, you boys come see me so I can show you again how we mix the ingredients."

"Then I've got another assignment for you. We're gonna teach those corporate crooks and sinners not to mess around with the Lord's laws, and us! Transgressors is what they all are . . . blasphemous transgressors! You boys just remember we're on the side of righteousness."

"Yessir, Pa. Me and Twit, we'll do whatever you say."

A few minutes later a heavy rumbling sound scattered the birds roosting on nearby trees. Twenty seconds after that, a battered and dusty unmarked pickup pulled into view. The direction of the sun and the dust swirling around the car made the scene almost spectral. The truck was dark gray in color and had no identifying badges or chrome. In the diffused light, the truck looked like a large, menacing ghost.

Twit Hacker pulled the truck into the yard and parked it next to the entrance to the pole barn. He saw Newt coming toward him and got out.

"Did you get it all?" Newt asked his brother. "Pa's inside the pole barn ready to give us another lesson in the finer qualities of ANFO."

"Yeah, I got it all," Twit said. "And I remembered what Pa said about keeping my mouth shut and my mind on business. No joking around, no storytelling at the feed store. Just get my order filled and politely leave."

Newt asked, "Did anyone at the feed store comment on how much fertilizer we've been buying lately?"

"Not really," Twit said. "The clerk at the counter just said he was glad to see that our business is so busy. Nothing more than that."

"Good. C'mon, let's go see Pa."

They entered the large, metal building that measured some thirty by fifty feet. On the floor there were two old transmissions and a large Ford diesel engine leaning against what appeared to be the shell of an old snowmobile. There were motor-oil cans and five-gallon gas cans lined against an entire wall. Machine parts littered the old shelving units, and hand tools were scattered helter-skelter around the shop.

The only power tools they had were an old Craftsman radial-arm saw, a huge air compressor, a welder, and various power saws, nailers, and drills. At the rear of the pole barn was a large, wooden workbench with an old, fluorescent light fixture hanging from chains overhead.

Clement sat at the workbench focusing on a manual and a small booklet containing old, hand-written notes. He looked up from his reading when he heard his boys approaching.

"You get everything I ordered from the feed store, Twit?" Clement asked without any preamble.

"Yessir, Pa, I did just like you said. I was just telling Newt that I got everything you wanted and didn't say nothing to nobody. Just picked up the order and left. Didn't talk to anyone, except the guy behind the counter."

Clement looked hard at his two boys for a few seconds to see if they were telling him everything. He didn't want to risk failing in his mission and possibly going to prison if his boys couldn't follow orders.

"All right, then," said Clement. "You boys best go pull that truck inside the barn so you can unload. And remember: treat that stuff real tenderlike, or we'll all be seeing Kingdom Come sooner than we want."

"Yeah, boy!" Newt said. "I remember when we delivered righteous revenge on that Planned Parenthood place in Broad Ripple. Ooh, that abortion clinic was there one second and mostly gone the next. ANFO baby."

Clement shot Newt a serious look. "I told you it's best that we don't talk about that bombing. We should practice our ignorance on that, just in case we're ever questioned about it. Do you understand what I am saying to you boys? We've got to stick together on this."

"Yessir, Pa," both boys said simultaneously.

"Now then, you boys grab those stools and bring them over to the workbench." He waited for them to get settled.

"ANFO is your basic fertilizer bomb," Clement began. "And it's an excellent way to get people's attention!"

He referred to his little notebook, "That's ninety-four percent porous prilled ammonium nitrate which is your fertilizer, and six percent number two fuel oil. Says here the ammonium nitrate (AN) works kinda like an oxidizing agent and helps to soak up the fuel oil (FO). Pack it in a confined container, detonate, and kaboom!"

"Hell, all I know," Twit chimed in, "is it'll blow the shit out of some pretty big buildings."

He and Newt fell out laughing until their Pa brought them back down.

"You boys listen good now, and I've warned you about getting too gabby about what we're doing. I'm planning on you two taking another trip soon, and you'd be very wise to give our friend, ANFO, here a lot more respect."

"You gonna let us use the ANFO this time, Pa?" Twit wheedled. "We promise we'll be real careful and follow your instructions to the letter. Won't we, Newt?"

"Maybe soon," Clement offered, "but not this time. Besides, I've got something else in mind, and don't you bug me about it. I'll let you know when I'm ready."

Clement began reading again from the little notebook. He wanted to make sure Newt and Twit grasped the destructive capability of the ANFO and would not be too casual with it. For him, ANFO spelled armageddon.

Chapter 8

THE RIDE BACK TO THE BREWERY complex from southern Indy was quiet. Neither Mace nor Clay felt a need to say much. They both had come to the same conclusion about bringing Rennie to work at their place. Each thought it was the right thing to do, but for different reasons.

For Mace, the emotional pang that he felt when he saw Rennie living in squalor was undeniable. Even now at age seventy, he always felt the painful memory of his own destitute youth just under the surface. Now, to see an adolescent boy existing in a similar way was all too vivid a reminder of the pain Mace had tried to forget.

Mace didn't have a rescue fantasy for Rennie, but he was starting to believe that maybe the priests and nuns at St. Francis had pulled him up from the depths of despair for a reason. Maybe, Mace thought, it was time to pay back and pay forward by helping Rennie Cotton.

For Clay, his motivation for wanting to help Rennie existed on several levels. The most immediate motivation for Clay was that it connected him to Jennifer. Clay was still struggling to deal with the rawness and suddenness of her murder. Any positive thoughts he had of their happy times together got instantly swept away when he flashed on her death.

The portrait of the boy, and now the boy himself, allowed Clay to feel connected to the woman he loved. Intellectually, he knew this thinking was folly, but he was powerless to break free from the gravity of his heartache.

There was another reason, though, that motivated Clay to want to help Rennie.

Clay sensed that he was a changed man in the aftermath of the Planned Parenthood Center bombing. He had always been an observant man. After all, it was how he made his living through photography. Now his visual senses were no longer merely observing, though. They were on high alert. He felt like he was on speed, keenly aware, ready to react. He knew it was just a matter of time before the magma within blew the lid off the mountain.

At times, Clay also felt like he was losing control of himself, and it was not a feeling he enjoyed. He attempted to manage it as best he could, but he believed he was starting to lose his grip on the finer aspects of his humanity. He wanted to punish certain people, and he wanted to take his time to exact his unique mode of retribution.

And while the majority of Clay's anger stemmed from Jennifer's murder, there was so much crazy shit going on out there in the world today that listening to the news for only a brief time confirmed that a lot of people just weren't behaving like caring citizens.

Pick a political or socioeconomic topic, any topic, and the polarization that Clay witnessed, and the out-and-out pure igno-rance when it came to matters such as gun violence and science and women's health, was more than he could stomach. And the media and office seekers stirred up a ton of disenfranchised, scared, and angry folks. Everyone was pissed anymore, including Clay.

So, on the one hand, Clay was aflame with blood lust, and on the other he was grasping at the most improbable of straws to keep himself from emotionally going totally over the edge. Helping Rennie Cotton could well be Clay Arnold's last chance before he just didn't give a damn about much of anything anymore.

Clay thought it was probably nuts investing his time and interest in Rennie, but he also knew that it was the right thing to do. He and Mace could make this work, if Rennie would meet them halfway. Clay also knew that Tori and Weed would graciously welcome their new helper.

Thirty minutes after leaving Rennie in Southern Indy, Clay and Mace turned into the brewery complex. Detective Trent Reynolds was waiting in the courtyard when they arrived. He was talking with Tori and Weed.

"Afternoon, gentlemen!" came Trent's friendly greeting to Clay and Mace.

Mace and Clay got out of the Tacoma and walked over to the three of them.

"Well, to what do we owe the honor of a visit from the State's Finest?" Clay asked Trent.

Clay and Trent had known each other ever since elementary school. Weed and Tori, too, for that matter. They'd even played varsity football together in high school. Trent and Clay were never best friends, but they both liked and respected the other, and they shared some mutual friends which brought them into contact with each other more frequently than otherwise.

"Well, I wish I could say I was just in the neighborhood and wanted to catch up on old times," Trent said, "but I've got a little information about the Planned Parenthood bombing that I thought you should know."

Clay closed his eyes and hung his head. He waited for Trent to go on.

"You remember that I told you there was a convenience store down the block from the Planned Parenthood Center and that their security camera might've recorded the bombers?"

"Yeah, I remember. I'm surprised it's taken this long to find anything out," Clay said evenly.

"Me, too," Trent agreed. "Apparently, the store's camera is a real piece of shit, and from what our tech guys say, it's amazing they were able to retrieve anything from that distance in the dark. We got some images, though."

Clay stood stone still. He wanted to hear what Trent had to say next, but he was very anxious, too. His emotional wounds were still very raw.

Clay believed that the police were working as hard as possible to clear this case, and the continuous presence of the media in the wake of the Center's bombing kept everyone on their toes. But, at this point, Clay's confidence in the police investigation had begun to cool, and his blood began to simmer.

"The video showed a dark pickup truck barreling away from the scene of the Center bombing. It didn't have a rear license plate, but the camera caught the image of a Confederate flag on the front plate."

"Did you get a make of the truck?" Mace asked.

"No make, Mace, but we had Wilbur Hoyt from the county garage take a look at the video, and he swears the truck is an older model Dodge Ram. We've got the Bureau of Motor Vehicles checking their records, but honestly I doubt this truck is the same color it started out being."

"Funny thing, though," Trent continued. "It was a dark, unmarked pickup truck that was used to terrorize Stella's Diner, and a dark pickup truck was sighted at that horrible elementary school attack near Louisville."

Trent's words hung out there for everyone to consider.

"There's something else, too, Clay," Trent said. "The lab finished their examination, and it appears that the terrorists used a very large ANFO fertilizer bomb to blow up the Planned Parenthood Center."

"Since each bomb is homemade, they each have their own chemical signature, almost like a fingerprint. Now we're investigating who's buying a lot of ammonium nitrate and who's nutty enough to blow up buildings with people in them."

"I know there are a lot of dark trucks out there and a lot of farmers who buy large quantities of fertilizer, but these are the first real breaks we've gotten in this investigation. We've got the FBI helping us out to identify suspects based on the video and the bomb composition, but it may take some time. I know it's not what you want to hear, Clay, but at least we're making some progress."

Clay just nodded and said thanks to Trent for letting them know.

After Trent departed, Clay and Mace talked with Tori and Weed in the courtyard for a bit. They related the news that Rennie Cotton was coming to work for them. Tori and Weed were familiar with the photograph that Clay had shot of Rennie, and they were eager to see the young guy in person.

"I could sure use some help in the vegetable garden," Tori urged. "I've already been harvesting tomatoes, squash, and beans, but there's a lot more that'll need to be picked or we're going to lose some great veggies."

Mace said, "I had better begin a project list for young Mr. Cotton to tackle. Let me know what you all want, and then we'll try to prioritize. And remember, the kid isn't even a teenager yet, so let's not try to kill him on the first day."

They chatted for just a few more minutes, and then Clay said he had some things he needed to take care of in his office.

"Weed, do you have about an hour of time you can give me in the camera museum in about thirty minutes?"

"Sure, Clay," Weed replied. "I'll meet you there. Is this about the project you mentioned a couple of days ago?"

"Yeah, it is. I could use your engineering background and your creative thinking. Mace, if you've got time, I think it would be important for you to join us, too."

"Sounds mysterious," Mace said. "I like mysterious. See you in a little bit."

Chapter 9

CLAY ENTERED THE ENTRANCE to his home and took the elevator to the second floor. He went to his study and checked his computer for recent e-mails and his phone for any messages. There was a cheery voice message from his agent, Lily Deupree, confirming his itinerary for upcoming photography assignments.

"Good morning, Clay," came Lily's pleasant voice on the answering machine. "I just wanted to confirm your upcoming assignment in Charleston, South Carolina. Your airline and car rental reservations have been made, and I've got you staying at the Ventana Inn again as you requested."

Clay sent Lily a quick e-mail saying thanks and confirming he'd be flying out of Indianapolis the next afternoon for Charleston. Then he began checking his photo equipment to make sure he had everything he needed.

While many photographers carried tons of equipment for photo shoots, Clay preferred to travel light. He always liked concentrating on his subjects rather than ruminating over a bunch of camera

bodies, lenses, and filters. It was an approach that worked well for him, and he had a lot less equipment to haul along.

He charged up the extra batteries for his Canon camera and then proceeded downstairs to the first-floor camera museum to meet Weed and Mace.

It was late in the afternoon now, and the Vintage Camera Museum was closed for the day. Clay arrived first and turned on the museum's specialized lighting. It had been a while since he had taken the time to be alone with his collection, and being here again with these iconic pieces of camera history was like being surrounded by old friends.

It was not a huge collection, numbering perhaps no more than one hundred antique cameras and early precinema devices, but anyone who was familiar with such collections knew that Clay Arnold's museum was among the five best in the world.

Clay entered the main gallery and approached an ornate cabinet that displayed an array of very early Kodak cameras that he had acquired. He admired this group, which included an Original Kodak camera, two Satchel-Style Folding Kodaks, and a No.1 Cone Pocket camera. What made these cameras even more significant was their condition. They were pristine. They had virtually never been used.

He smiled at the old memory of reading as much as he could about cameras like these when he first started collecting. He often wondered if he could ever put together a meaningful camera collection that showcased the evolution of photography.

As he got into his midtwenties and his career began taking off, Clay found himself in a financial position where he could indulge himself a little. So, when an extremely fine piece became available, he paid the price. Each camera in this case had a pleasant memory attached to it, and Clay smiled his appreciation at them.

But this was just the tip of the iceberg. To the right of the cabinet stood a stately oak pedestal. On top of that pedestal sat one of the rarest cameras imaginable. It was one of three known original Daguerreotype cameras made by Alphonse Giroux in 1837 for his famous brother-in-law, Louis-Jacques-Mande Daguerre, the inventor of photography. It was among the world's first successful cameras, and with Louis Daguerre working his chemistry, it changed the world.

Clay was shaken from his reverie with his collection when he heard Weed and Mace enter the museum's main gallery. He made a mental note to return soon so as not to neglect these wonderful pieces of history.

Mace came to the museum regularly to help with tour groups and to keep an eye on things, so he knew the antique camera collection well.

"Clay, I replaced the spotlight shining on the Edison Kinetoscope," Mace said. "It just wouldn't be right if visitors couldn't view Edison's early projector because of a burnt out light bulb, also invented by Edison."

"Thanks, Mace. I really appreciate everything you're doing to keep it open and fresh for the public. It was not my intention to saddle you with all you do here, but I'm awfully glad that you enjoy it."

"It's not a problem, Clay," Mace said. "It's all good, and the kids and other visitors are generally interested and respectful. I had to laugh the other day when I heard a young girl ask her father what film was. Everything and everyone comes and goes, I guess."

As for Weed, he had certainly also been here often over the years, but not so much recently. When he entered the museum and saw what was on display, he was reminded of what an impressive collection Clay had acquired, and of how terrific he thought it was that he was sharing it with the public.

"I love this place!" Weed exclaimed as he made a sweeping motion with his arms.

Clay and Mace couldn't help but smile at Weed's enthusiasm, but Clay soon brought the three of them back to the reason for their meeting.

"Okay, I know you're both busy guys, so I'll get right to the point. Frankly, I am really fed up with the hateful attitudes and the violence that is being perpetrated on innocent people all across the country. Damn well fed up!"

"Every time I turn on the news or go online there's a fresh story about a new school or theater shooting, or a Planned Parenthood Center bombing, or a church shooting, or a congresswoman being shot, or wacko libertarians taking over federal property. I am beyond being pissed off."

He continued. "Every day, we get another vocal right-wing prick who thinks we should have more guns everywhere to stop the bad guys. Yeah, like that's going to work when no one can tell a good guy from a bad guy," he said sarcastically.

"And it's not just what happened to Jennifer, although that's still at the top of my list. The conservative politicians and wing-nuts can't even agree that background checks for gun buyers are sensible. I feel like 'we the people' are being held hostage by our own leaders. No more, goddamnit!"

He went on, "And, I see the hollow eyes and shocked expressions on the faces of family members and friends of the victims. Their lives are forever changed. We owe it to them to even the score."

Clay looked directly into Mace and Weed's eyes. "I want to do something about it, and I'm no longer interested in waiting for law enforcement or our feeble politicians to deliver justice.

"Believe me, fellas, when I tell you that I'm not trying to pressure you into anything. Whatever you decide is okay with me, seriously. No harm, no foul. But I'm not going to give this up."

Mace and Weed stood silently waiting for their friend to finish speaking, and then Weed said, "Clay, we know that Jennifer's murder was an unspeakable act; one that would seriously affect anyone in your situation, but I hope you've really thought through how you plan to deal with your grief."

"I have," Clay responded. "I've thought about it a lot, and if you're willing, I'll need your help. Let me show you a little of what I have in mind; then I'd like you both to please think about it and let me know your decisions."

Mace stood silently listening to Clay. He had learned a long time ago that it was often best to remain quiet and wait until all parties had had a chance to fully voice their thoughts before offering his.

"Why don't you fill us in, Clay," came Mace's level words.

Clay led his two friends to another display case in the museum. It contained an unusual grouping of very uniquely designed cameras.

"In the early days of photography, inventors were inserting cameras into all manner of commonplace objects. Today, historians refer to them collectively as 'detective cameras' because they were devices hidden into everyday things like rings and canes and books, even clothing."

"Truth was," Clay continued, "there were no telephoto lenses back then, so if a photographer wanted to get a candid shot without the subject knowing it, the photographer often used a cleverly hidden camera to snap a picture. Seeing my collection of these has given me an idea!"

"So," Weed said, "why do you need us?" But he had a feeling he already knew the answer to that question.

"Well, Weed, with your engineering background, I thought you might like to try your hand at weaponizing some new, improved, detective-style cameras for me."

"Are you serious?" Weed replied.

"Deadly serious," came Clay's direct reply.

"Okay," Weed said, "let me get this straight. You want me to make you some weapons out of your old cameras?"

"Yeah, sorta. Maybe using some of my spare parts to fabricate something new. Items based on their original clandestine designs though," Clay stated.

Clay just let his words hang out there for Weed and Mace to consider.

Weed looked closely at the unusual cameras in the display case. He whistled a little tune to himself as he considered Clay's proposition.

"And if I agreed to do this, Clay, just where do you propose that I could design, machine, and test these little beauties?" Weed asked.

"I'm glad you asked that. Come with me," Clay said, and he led Mace and Weed from the museum gallery and returned to the elevator.

The three men descended from the first floor to the basement level where Clay's darkroom was located. The darkroom was located approximately fifteen feet below the complex's courtyard. Clay faced the elevator's control panel and pressed his password into a separate key pad that he had added when the elevator was installed.

"Both of you should memorize my new password," Clay instructed. "Evening. As in evening comes."

Mace and Weed looked at each soberly. They realized that their friend Clay was not fooling around.

The elevator now descended another fifteen feet and came to a stop at the entrance to the rarely visited sub-basement in Clay's brewery building. They were now thirty feet below the brewhouse and courtyard.

Weed let out a low whistle again as he scoped out the old brewery's large barrel room.

"Wow!" Weed exclaimed. "I think you showed me this room once several years ago, but I must admit that I had forgotten about it."

Mace said, "The three of us are the only ones who know about this room. It was built by the Block brothers when they constructed their brewery in 1855. This far underground the temperature maintains a pretty steady fifty-five degrees, and the Block brothers found that to be an ideal temperature for storing their barrels of beer prior to shipment."

The three men walked into the barrel room, and they marveled at how dry and comfortable the twenty-by-forty-foot space was.

When Clay purchased the brewery complex, he had the elevator installed and also made upgrades to the barrel room's ventilation system. He added WiFi for his laptop and a landline telephone. The barrel room even contained a small refrigerator and a little bathroom. Clay had spared no expense in modernizing the space.

It had been a long time since even Mace had descended into the barrel room. There had been no real reason to do so.

"The Block brothers were ingenious men," Mace said. "Come to think of it, I don't think we even used this room during the heyday of the Jeffries Woodworking Company. We had plenty of space above ground."

Clay walked around the room admiring the old stone and concrete walls and the medieval-looking arched ceiling.

"Should we show him, Mace?" Clay asked.

"Show me what?" Weed wondered out loud.

Mace nodded affirmatively to Clay, and Clay walked over to a large wooden wall panel that had five bronze hooks for a coat rack.

"This," Clay said to Weed, and he pulled down on the bronze hook on the left side.

An audible click was heard, and the wooden wall panel pulled an inch away from the wall. Then Clay inserted his fingers in the opening, flipped a small latch, and pulled the panel fully open. It revealed a tunnel leading into darkness.

"Get out of town!" Weed whooped. "Holy shit, is that really a secret passageway?"

"Well, let's just call it an alternate entrance," Clay mused. Mace grinned.

"Unbelievable, Clay. So where does it lead?" Weed asked.

"You can credit those ingenious Block brothers again," Clay began. "When they built the brewery and power plant in 1855, they also built the farmhouse where you and Tori live. As you know, that was the Block brothers' home, and they wanted a secure underground passage that would connect their house to the brewery building. Immigrant labor was cheap, and so they built the passageway."

Then Clay continued, "When prohibition came, they upgraded the passage and used it as a way to sneak guests from their house to the barrel room for their alcoholic beverages."

"So, where does the tunnel lead to at the farmhouse?" Weed wanted to know. "Tori and I have lived here a long time now, and I've never see the other entrance at the farmhouse."

"Are you sure about that?" Clay asked.

"Uh, yeah, pretty sure," came Weed's confident reply.

"Well, you know that old potting shed immediately behind your house?" Clay prompted.

"Yeah, Tori uses it for her gardening," Weed said.

"Next time you're in there, take a real close look at the floor. There's a trap door that has a workbench over it. The bench keeps the door very well hidden. If you were to move the bench and open the trap door, you'd see a stout, metal ladder that descends to a landing about fifteen feet below. Then another ladder leads you down to the sub-basement level. The underground passageway goes beneath the courtyard to where we're standing now. Pretty ingenious, eh?!"

"You're shittin' me, right?!" came Weed's snarky reply. "All this time and you never told us about it!"

"Honestly, Weed, I had pretty much forgotten about it, and I never knew how safe the tunnel was, so I didn't want to encourage its use. Anyway, when I started thinking about using the barrel room, I remembered it had some secrets."

Clay closed the wooden wall panel and pushed the bronze coat hook in an upward motion to reseal the opening to the passageway. It now looked as innocuous as before.

"So, what I'm thinking," Clay said, "is that the two of you build a laboratory of sorts for Weed to create the weaponry. I was thinking that Mace could construct the workbenches that you'll need, and that you, Weed, could outfit your shop with whatever equipment you need to machine and test the devices."

Weed and Mace looked at each other soberly. This was a huge undertaking; not just the fabrication work, but the emotional investment as well. They knew that if they proceeded in helping Clay, they could be complicit in murder.

"If we agree to help you with this," Mace said, "when would you want to begin?"

"As soon as possible," Clay said. "I'll be away in Charleston for maybe a week, but I'm hoping you guys can get started and have something to show me when I return."

"Wait, wait!" Weed interrupted. "This is some major, serious shit, Clay!"

"Look man," Weed continued. "I don't care for those crazy right-wing motherfuckers any more than you do, but are you sure this is something you really want to do?"

"You know, Weed, I could go into a long dissertation about why I need to do this, but I'll spare you my rationalizations. It's time to even things up, and the law and the lawmakers aren't getting it done."

"So, what?" Weed asked. "You want to go around whacking bad people instead of letting the cops do it?"

"It doesn't sound quite as heroic when you put it that way," Clay replied. "But, yeah, I think that pretty much sums it up."

"And Mace, you go along with this, too?" Weed asked.

"Weed, I've spent nearly seven decades trying to do what I thought was the right thing. In my younger days, it was because I didn't want to draw any attention to myself. After a while, I just got busy working hard at the Jeffries Woodworking mill. It wasn't like I turned a deaf ear to the evil that some men do, but I was intent on looking after myself. I wanted to feel secure, and I felt I had no choice."

Mace continued, "With age comes some perspective, and anymore I don't have enormous faith in our leaders' abilities to protect and defend us. In fact, I find many of those duly elected officials and corporate leaders to be the root of the problem. And Holy Mother of God, we're out of control with gun violence. True leadership is handcuffed by the paranoia of the ultra conservatives. It's nuts. So yes, I go along with Clay 100 percent."

Mace went on, "We each have to make our own decisions, Weed, and neither of us will pressure you into going along with us. While Clay is in Charleston, I'd appreciate your helping me get the workshop set up, and then you can decide what you want to do, okay?"

"Yeah, Mace, I'll help you outfit the shop," Weed replied. "But I would like to think about being an accomplice to vigilantism and murder. That's a huge burden.

"And Clay, you know our friendship is unbreakable; so even if I choose not to work with you and Mace, my lips will be shut as to what you're doing. That's a promise."

"That's all I can ask for, Weed," came Clay's frank reply.

The three of them spent a few more minutes in the sub-basement talking about what Mace needed to get a workshop set up.

Weed's head was spinning. He didn't like the way people were getting victimized with mass shootings and attacks on women's rights and well-founded principles of science. It was like the world had lost its ethical and rational compass, even in the name of God.

Weed needed more time to process how Clay's mission would affect all of their lives. He was a musician and a loving brother to Tori and a friend to Mace and Clay. He yearned for it to stay that way, but he also knew that something had to give. He knew that sometimes you just can't sit on the sidelines when crimes are being committed and people are being led down a path to perdition by our own leaders.

The three men rode the elevator up to the first level and chatted for a few more minutes in the courtyard.

"I'll be picking Rennie up in the morning, Clay. Anything in particular you need him to do?" Mace asked.

"I haven't given it a lot of thought, because I need to prepare for my South Carolina photo shoot. Whatever you have him do is fine with me; plus it would be great if he could help Tori in the garden. You can always call or text me if you have questions. I've got ample cash in my office so you can pay Rennie, and in case you need to purchase any special supplies."

"And, Weed, try not to worry too much about my plans. I haven't lost my sense of humanity yet, and I sure don't plan on getting caught or implicating any of us."

Weed nodded his understanding, but he still wanted to think about the new path he was being drawn toward.

Chapter 10

THE NEXT MORNING DEBUTED with a pastel-fingered dawn. Venus welcomed the rising sun from high above in the southern sky. A waxing, gibbous moon was low in the west. A new day had broken. The three brightest bodies in the sky would be visible together for only a brief time, then pass on to their next stops along their celestial journeys.

As usual, Mace climbed out of bed around six o'clock and began his routine of daily morning chores. He prepared his breakfast, made his bed, emptied the ashes from the bottom of the wood furnace, and burned the trash in the complex's incinerator.

He still had a few minutes before he needed to leave to pick up Rennie, so he thought he'd see if Tori was up and about. He knew she was usually an early riser, and he wanted to talk with her about Rennie.

"Well, there you are, Mace," came Tori's hearty welcome. "Please tell me it's a gorgeous day, because the sun on my face feels delicious!"

"It is indeed a glorious day, Tori, made even more so by your radiance," he said melodramatically.

They both laughed and Tori offered Mace a cup of coffee.

"Thanks, Tori, I just had a cup, and I need to go meet young Mr. Cotton in thirty minutes. I wanted to ask you, though: Would you be willing to work with me and Rennie on different things when you have free time?"

"Truth be known," Mace stammered, "I've never been around young kids much, and I'm not exactly sure if I'm going to be good working with Rennie. I mean, I want it to work out for all of us, and I just don't want to screw anything up. Does that make any sense, Tori?"

"Of course it does, Mace. I'm obviously not a parent, but from what I understand, there aren't any engraved roadmaps for being a good parent or guide. Just being yourself is the only way to be. Kids are smart, and they see through bullshit. This kid's been around the block so much there's not much that he hasn't seen. Am I right, Mace? So, just be cordial and instructive, and remember he has suffered even more than he's going to let on.

"Mace, I'll be here when you and Rennie get back. I'll see if I can convince Lex and Satchmo to join in a little welcoming committee. Then, we'll see what work needs to be done."

"Thanks, Tori. You're really helping to put my mind at ease. This kid brings up a lot of powerful memories, and I'm a little apprehensive about what else I'll recall. You've been a big help, though. Thanks."

Mace walked across the courtyard toward the power plant and climbed into his 1955 GMC Series 100 pickup truck. It had belonged to the Jeffries Woodworking mill and had seen years of use, but under Mace's continuous care, the truck remained a reliable vehicle.

When the Jeffries Woodworking mill closed, the owners thought it was only fitting and proper to give the truck to Mace since he was the truck's principal caregiver. He'd been driving and maintaining it ever since.

Rush-hour traffic in Indy this time of morning was always congested. Mace had to seriously concentrate on his driving, which was probably a blessing keeping his mind off of yesterday's intense conversation with Clay and Weed.

Mace knew he was 95 percent comfortable going along with Clay's plans to take it to the bad guys, but he'd been a law abiding citizen for many years, and he knew that going along with Clay would change all of that. He wasn't feeling as conflicted as Weed, but this was a very big step.

Mace pulled the truck onto Hill Street just as his watch chimed eight o'clock. The street was quiet as he pulled up to Rennie's shack. He hoped that Rennie would come bounding out of his door, enthusiastic about starting his new job, but Rennie was nowhere to be seen.

Mace waited in the warm truck for a few minutes but soon realized that Rennie wasn't coming out.

Mace got out of the pickup, walked up to Rennie's door, and knocked. There was no sound from inside. He knocked again. Again, nothing from within. Mace pushed the door open and saw Rennie's motionless body lying on his mattress.

Mace rushed over and knelt down beside the unmoving boy. He saw that Rennie's face was bruised and swollen. He had been badly beaten.

"Rennie, it's Mace Davis. Are you okay?"

He lightly touched the boy's shoulder, and Rennie stirred a little.

"Oh my," Mace said. "What have they done to you?"

Mace went back out to his truck to retrieve his bottle of water. He placed a few drops of water on Rennie's parched lips and was rewarded by seeing the boy's mouth open a little to receive the wetness.

"Rennie, it's Mace Davis," he said again. "Can you hear me all right?"

Rennie groaned and said, "Yeah, I hear you. Go away!"

"Son, you are a mess. Can you see if you can sit up?" Mace prompted.

Rennie tried to move, but he was in a lot of discomfort.

"Ooh, it's my ribs," he moaned. "They stole my money and kicked me in my ribs and left me in the gutter. After they left, I crawled back home."

Mace offered Rennie more water, but he could see that the boy was struggling even to drink.

"C'mon," Mace said. "You can't stay here in the condition you're in."

Mace carefully kneeled over the boy and gingerly picked him up from the mattress. Rennie was in no position to resist Mace's help as the big man carried him to the truck. Once inside, Mace fastened the boy's seatbelt and headed back toward the highway.

Rennie nodded off as Mace drove north. The hum of the truck's internal rhythm was like a narcotic to the young guy.

Mace periodically looked over at Rennie as he drove. He didn't appear to have the kinds of injuries that required a doctor's immediate attention, so he made the decision to go home instead of the emergency room. Mace knew, though, that people who have any head injuries should be monitored closely for several hours.

He was eager to get back to the brewery complex because he wanted Tori's help in assessing the extent of Rennie's injuries. He paid close attention to the road, and his trusty pickup maintained a steady pace.

Mace exhaled audibly. The day that had begun with a glorious, pastel-fingered dawn was developing into a hazy unknown.

Twenty minutes later Mace pulled into the courtyard in front of Weed and Tori's farmhouse. Rennie had slept during most of the drive here, but he became more alert when the truck stopped and the hum of the engine went silent.

"We've got us a hurt boy here," Mace called to Tori as she and Lex came out to the front porch to meet them.

Mace went around to the passenger's side and gently lifted Rennie from the car seat. Rennie winced a little, and again he didn't resist Mace's help.

"He got whupped pretty bad," Mace said to Tori.

"They stole my money," Rennie moaned.

"Here, Mace, let's put him in the guest room," Tori directed.

They got Rennie settled on the bed, and Lex came bounding in to see what all of the excitement was about. His tail was wagging only a little as he approached this new smelling human, and his big nose started a full-body scan of the reclining figure.

Rennie opened his eyes wide in astonishment when he saw the size of this big, furry creature giving him the once-over.

"It's a black wolf!" Rennie cried out loudly, and he tried to get away, but the combination of his exhaustion and Lex's encroaching friendliness made it impossible for Rennie to escape.

Then Lex put his big wet nose up to Rennie's face and made a grand slurp with his tongue.

"He's trying to eat me!" Rennie wailed, and he started flailing around on the bed to get away.

Lex, of course, thought Rennie was playing now, so he stretched his front paws onto the bed to get even closer.

"Okay, Lex, that's enough for now," Tori said. "We promise you can eat him later if you're good."

Lex took a final sniff, sneezed, and went to sit by Tori's side. Mace stood quietly in the doorway appreciating the scene. Tori sat on the edge of the guest bed and introduced herself to the bruised and battered kid occupying her guest room.

"Hello. My name's Tori, and I understand from Mace that you are Mister Rennie Cotton, is that correct?" Tori led.

"Yeah," Rennie said feebly. "I don't know about the mister part, but yeah—that's me."

"Rennie, I'm not a doctor, but I know a lot of things about human anatomy, and given the beating you've had, I want to make sure you have no broken bones. Is it okay if I check you out?"

"Uh, yeah, I suppose," he said flatly. "I don't want you putting no needles in me, though."

"No needles, Rennie," came Tori's soothing reply.

Rennie lay on his back, and Tori began a careful examination starting at the top of Rennie's head and slowly feeling tissue and bone all the way down to his toes. There was nothing lurid about the examination, and by the time Tori had examined from Rennie's head to his chest, Rennie had already drifted asleep under Tori's healing touch.

"Mace, I think he's okay physically. Beaten for sure, and equally exhausted, hungry, and dehydrated. He needs some bed rest, and fortunately I've got the time to look after him."

Tori went on, "He's definitely going to need some new clothes, because I'm burning the rags he's got on. He'll need underwear, socks, shirts, pants, a belt, a toothbrush and comb and stuff. Might as well add a coat, gloves, and hat to the list, too. Oh, and his shoes are total trash. I'll give you my best estimate on sizes. Keep your receipts, and we'll figure out reimbursement later, okay?

"Probably find everything you need at Walmart," Tori suggested. "Heck, while you're there, pick up whatever else you think we might need. I just made up a batch of Mama Tori's hearty vegetable soup and a loaf of bread. Why don't the three of us have some lunch when you get back. Sound okay to you?"

"You got a deal," Mace agreed. "I'll do the best I can with the clothes and sundries. Looks like we'll have a houseguest for a while. Thank you for being so willing to help him. I hope Weed shares your enthusiasm."

"Weed will be fine. Rennie will be a new audience for him to perform for," she laughed.

Tori dictated some clothes and shoe sizes for Mace, and he went back to the pickup and took off for the store.

Tori turned back toward Rennie to listen to his breathing.

"You're blind, aren't you?" came Rennie's surprised and direct question.

"Yes, I'm blind," came Tori's matter-of-fact reply.

"Like, you can't see nothing?" he inquired.

"Blind as a bat," she replied. "But I'm a lot cuter!"

"Dang!"

"So, Rennie, since I can't see nothing, what say you get those clothes off and climb into a nice warm bath? I don't even want to know when the last time was you had a bath."

"Been a while," he offered.

Surprisingly, Rennie slowly moved, and it was clear his ribs were very sore. He dragged his legs over the side of the bed and cautiously stood up. He managed okay, barely.

"You sure you're blind?" he insecurely asked again.

"Since birth, sir, so you don't need to worry about me seeing Mr. Happy."

Rennie slowly took off his shirt, which aside from being filthy, was too large for him and was missing two buttons. His belt was leather with an old metal buckle. His pants were dark, stained chinos that looked like they'd been originally much longer and then cut to a shorter length by its current owner. Rennie took off his pants and socks. He had no underwear, and his shoes were worthless. All he wore now, in his nakedness, was the soot and grime of living on the street for eleven years.

"I got to pee," he said.

"Come with me," Tori said. "I'll run some bath water for you, too."

After Tori heard the toilet flush, she knocked lightly on the bathroom door and re-entered.

"Rennie, here's the soap, some shampoo, and a wash cloth. May I suggest, though, that after you get in the water, you just lie there and soak for several minutes? It'll help soothe your sore muscles. Just don't fall back to sleep. Here's a towel and my spare robe when you're done."

Rennie walked over and put his foot in the water. Immediately he felt the attraction of its warmth. He balanced himself and put his other foot in the water, then ever so gingerly he sat down, stretched out his legs, and laid back until his body was submerged. He let out a breath as if all of his cares just drifted away. He told Tori he was okay, and she said she'd be back in a few minutes to check on him.

Rennie closed his eyes and let the balmy water cover his ears. The sounds from beyond became fuzzy, discordant. All of his senses were centered on relaxing in this tub of soothing water. Rennie opened his eyes and looked around the bathroom. It was in an old house, but it had a very cozy, friendly look about it.

Here, in this strange place with these new people, he felt oddly secure. However, after years of wary living on his own, that feeling of security and temporary kindness from strangers scared him almost as much as the boys who had beaten him. Trust was an emotion Rennie hadn't had much success with.

For now he just wanted to enjoy the moment. Rennie slipped his ears below the surface of the water and listened to the resonant sounds of his own breathing. The bath water engulfed him, and he let it soothe his aching body.

Chapter 11

Newt and Twit Hacker rode in Twit's dark-gray pickup along I-65 north heading toward Indianapolis. The autumn sun seemed to be struggling against the low-hanging cloud cover, but it eventually peeked through by the time they passed the exit for the outlet malls.

"I figure we've got another hour or so of driving before we get to the first location that Pa wants us to check out," said Newt.

Clement Hacker had chosen a Sunday to send his boys on their little reconnaissance mission. He figured there'd be a lot fewer people around who might remember their pickup truck.

"Now remember what I'm telling you boys about keeping your mouths shut," Clement had warned his twin sons again as they left their secluded home in Southern Indiana.

"There's a lot at stake here, and I need you boys to be our eyes and ears in planning our next attack," Clement continued. "That

includes not getting spotted or pulled over for some stupid traffic violation. You hear?!"

"We hear you, Pa," came Twit's dutiful reply. "We ain't going to do nothing to draw attention to ourselves. Don't you worry. Right, Newt?"

The twins maintained the 70 mph speed limit and cruised through the rolling farmland. The dark truck blended in with the overcast day and the large number of other pickup trucks common in these parts.

"Here, Newt. You want another beer?" Twit asked as he passed a can of Bud Light to his brother. "I thought having a six-pack along would make the ride less boring. Fucking breakfast of champions, baby!"

"Good thing Pa doesn't know," said Newt. He'd have a shit fit if he knew we were doing anything that strayed from his specific instructions."

"Well, Pa ain't here, is he?" Twit said. "And besides we're old enough to do what we want. We'll get his recon mission done, but no reason why we can't have a little buzz going while we're doing it."

The pickup chewed up the miles along I-65, and before too long they merged on to I-465 South near Indy. A few miles later they headed for I-70 and the Illinois Street exit. It was shortly before ten o'clock in downtown Indy. The streets were mostly quiet with the exception of a few young families who were hustling to their church services.

Newt pointed at a very large office tower and told Twit to pull the truck over to the curb.

"There it is," said Newt. "The headquarters for the Hoosier Homestead Insurance Company."

Hoosier Homestead was a venerable old insurance company that had started business about eighty years ago, mostly selling homeowners' and renters' insurance. Like many insurance companies, they had branched out to other promising markets and several years earlier had started selling health-care insurance. They made a ton of dough doing it, mainly because their mantra when it came to paying claims was *deny, deny, deny.*

From their curbside vantage point they saw that the office tower was an extremely well built, twelve-story structure that had an underground parking garage. Newt pulled out his cell phone and began taking pictures of Hoosier Homestead's corporate headquarters. He used the zoom lens function for close-up views of the entrance to the underground garage.

"Okay, Twit, I think I got what we need. But let's drive around the block again to scope it out from different angles. My guess is that Pa's going to want to use the garage as his point of attack, though."

Twit cruised around the block another time, and then they agreed to head north to their next destination.

Conner Prairie Hospital, north of Broad Ripple, had long been recognized as an excellent primary-care facility. It was a regional hospital specializing in basic medical/surgical cases, but through the recruitment of specific medical practices, the hospital had built a solid reputation for excellence in cardiac care and treating difficult cancers.

When Clement Hacker's wife Ella Marie was diagnosed with Glioblastoma Multiforme, a particularly deadly form of brain cancer, Clement had decided to go with Conner Prairie Hospital over the medical centers in Louisville even though they were closer.

It was a decision he regretted. Even though he knew Ella Marie's type of cancer was a one-way trip to oblivion, Clement was beyond consolation with his wife's death. He became bitter that she died while under the care of Conner Prairie's so-called renowned physicians and staff. He wanted someone to pay. Hell, he wanted a lot of people to pay.

"Fucking bastards, all of them," Clement had repeatedly told his boys. "Goddamn doctors, with all their smart talk and driving around in their fancy Mercedes. They killed my Ella Marie with that radiation and chemotherapy poison. They all think they're so smart. Well, they ain't!"

"And that fucking Hoosier Homestead Insurance Company," Clement would often rant. "Deny, Deny, Deny! Every time we submitted a claim for Ella Marie's care, the insurance company claimed bullshit about a pre-existing condition or having used up her lifetime medical benefits."

Newt and Twit pulled the pickup truck into the hospital's large parking lot near the entrance to the outpatient clinic and turned off the engine.

"It's a big place," Twit remarked. "Let's take some more pictures for Pa."

It was a big place, indeed. There was the original hospital building constructed several decades ago, plus the renovations and additions from ensuing years.

The hospital complex now included a medical office building, a seven-floor patient tower, major imaging facilities, an emergency room, and an impressive outpatient clinic and same-day surgery center.

The outpatient center was where Clement had brought Ella Marie for her treatments. It was an ornate, glass-and-steel structure with a grand atrium that had been named after some wealthy benefactor.

"Ooooeee!" Twit exhaled. "Pa sure picked us a big place to bring down!"

"Yeah," Newt agreed. "We're going to have to pick just the right spot to do the most damage," he surmised out loud.

After taking the pictures, Newt and Twit decided it was best not to dawdle in the hospital lot. They didn't want to have to answer any questions from a security guard.

And since it was after noon, they agreed it was time to find a place for lunch. Twit began driving south, and soon he spotted a sports bar microbrewery near the Conner Prairie Interpretive Center.

"Let's hang here for a while," Twit said. "Maybe take in the Colts game. They can serve beer on Sunday because they brew it here."

"I don't know, Twit. Pa usually likes us to come straight home after a mission. Maybe we ought to call him."

"Oh, fuck that, Newt, we're grown men," Twit lectured his twin brother. "We don't need Pa's okay on everything. Besides, I think it would be fun to stay on the road for a couple of days. Might as well take us a little vacation. We'll call Pa later. How's that sound, brother?!"

Newt shook his head in surprise. "You sure are talking big when Pa's not around."

"Yeah well, he ain't around, is he?" Twit managed to say.

The two men entered the sports bar and requested a booth with a good view of the wall-mounted TV. They got settled in their seats, and their server took their order for a pitcher of beer. The Colts game was scheduled to begin in about ten minutes, and leading news stories were being aired. The events in Ferguson led.

"Well, look at all that race crap going on over in Missouri," Twit reported. "I know how I'd deal with them coons if they ever pulled that crap in Indiana."

"Keep your voice down, Twit," Newt admonished. "Pa warned us about talking too much, and you need to hush up!"

"Aw, Newt, quit being such a dang pussy. Ain't nobody gonna hear me."

"All the same, shut the fuck up!"

The brothers were accustomed to arguing with each other. They'd done it for as long as they could remember. It always blew over, until the next time.

Their server brought them another pitcher and took their lunch orders. They both ordered pork tenderloin sandwiches, bowls of chili, and fries.

Another news story came on. This time about the evangelical college president who was exhorting his student body to arm themselves.

"Now we're talking! Heck, I'd think about trying to go to college if I could carry some protection with me, and I don't mean rubbers."

Newt looked at his brother and just shook his head in disbelief. The server brought their lunches and a third pitcher of beer.

The news stories continued for another few minutes, and the more beer that Twit drank, the more color commentary he was providing on the news stories.

At one point a family of four looked in their direction because Twit was getting a little too boisterous. Twit flipped them the bird, but he quickly calmed down when Newt grabbed him by the front of his shirt and told him, "Enough goddamnit! Remember what Pa said!"

Newt was fed up with his idiot brother. He quickly scarfed down the rest of his lunch and waited for his knucklehead brother to finish his. He then put on his coat, took the bill the server had left on the table, and marched off to pay it.

Twit stumbled to catch up with his less inebriated brother and managed to make it out to the truck without messing himself or falling down.

"No, Twit, I'm driving!" Newt commanded. "Now get in the truck and we'll decide where we go next."

Twit emitted a loud, odoriferous belch and said, "Wee, look at me. I'm on vacation!"

"Okay Twit, now settle down," Newt said. "I got me an idea. Now listen up! I'm thinking we get ourselves a motel room close by, and grab us a nap and sober up a little bit. Then, tonight we head back on over to Stella's Diner and see what kind of mischief we can get into there."

"In fact, I'll give Pa a call when we get in the room and tell him about my plan. I think he'll appreciate our taking the initiative. After all, they're all a bunch of whores and sinners, right?"

Twit was three sheets to the wind at this point, but the idea of more mayhem tickled him.

"Yessir, brother Newt. Take a nap and then go fuck with people. I like the way you think!"

Chapter 12

CLAY'S FLIGHT TO CHARLESTON, South Carolina, was uneventful. After retrieving his personal bag and camera gear he headed for the car rental booth and pulled away from the airport in a silver Lexus SUV.

While Clay considered himself to be a dedicated midwesterner, he always enjoyed being in the South, especially as winter approached. As he drove along the highway, his acute visual sense was tuned into the exotic local flora. The ubiquitous palmetto trees, Spanish moss, and kudzu were constant reminders that he was in a ecosystem very different from Indiana's leafless trees and harvested fields.

He entered Charleston and was flooded by mixed feelings. How could such a lovely city, one that was very unique in American architecture and Southern progressive thinking, also be a place of such horrific racial divide?

As Clay approached the iconic Emanuel African Methodist Church, he felt great sadness and shame for the senseless murder

of nine congregants, including the pastor, by some stupid-ass, twenty-one-year-old kid looking to ignite a race war.

Clay shook his head at the brazen ignorance of it all. He also sadly knew that there were many other people who supported this boy's murderous act.

"Will we ever learn?" he wondered out loud. His blood boiled because he doubted that we humans as a species ever would.

A couple of minutes later Clay pulled up to the curb outside of the Ventana Inn and was greeted by a black gentleman in a doorman's uniform.

"Good day, Mr. Arnold," came Robert's friendly drawl. "Welcome back to Charleston and the Ventana Inn, sir!"

"Good day to you, too, Robert. It's been a while since I was last here, and I'm flattered that you remember my name. I trust you've been taking good care of yourself."

"Of course I remember you. How could I ever forget that photo series that you did of our old homes south of Broad Street? I've lived here my whole life, and I don't think I ever saw those streets and homes in the same light."

Robert took Clay's car keys and handed them to a younger man to park his car. Clay entered the Ventana Inn and was warmly greeted by an attractive young woman at the registration desk.

"Ah, Mr. Arnold, we are so happy to have you as a guest again. When your agent, Lily Deupree, called to make your reservation, she asked that we put you in our Palm Room just like before. Is that okay?"

"That's perfect," Clay replied. "And your name is?"

"I'm Grace," came her smiling reply. "You're a bit of a legend around here because of your photography. Please let me know if there's anything we can do to make your visit memorable."

"Thanks, Grace. It's a pleasure to meet you. I'm probably a little early for check-in, so if you need more time to get the room ready, I'll be happy to go to the Veranda Room for lunch."

"That'll be helpful. I know that Lawsie is preparing to clean your room next. Maybe need another thirty minutes or so, okay? I'll be happy to safely stow your bags until then. I can let you know when it's ready."

"Thanks, Grace. Take whatever time you need. I suppose people around here are pretty excited about the South of Broad Street Art Festival."

"Oh, yes," Grace replied. "Although, ever since the church shooting, I think it's taking some time for all of us to regain our confidence as a community. I think many folks hope that the Festival will brighten our spirits again."

Clay nodded his understanding, and for the first time since his arrival, he took notice at how lovely and poised Grace was. He privately chided himself for even noticing, and he felt disloyal to Jennifer's memory.

"Heartbreaking," was the only word he could think to voice. "I'll check back with you after lunch, then."

Clay entered the Veranda Room, which was situated just off the main lobby, and was led by the hostess to a table with a window view. The room was warm in its decor, with pecan paneling on the walls, which also sported tastefully framed paintings of sailing ships and hunting scenes.

Clay had dined there several times on previous visits, and he welcomed the charming elements of its Southern heritage. He knew all too well, though, that beneath the charm of Charleston's stately appearance was an undercurrent of racial division and hatred. He came to the city's Festival with the photographic goal of capturing both Charlestons.

From his window view Clay watched the bustling of local folks as they went about their daily routines. He watched Robert amicably greet hotel guests and residents as they passed the hotel's entrance. He was a perfect front man for the Ventana Inn.

As Clay was finishing his lunch, he heard a raucous commotion coming from the hotel's barroom. Two businessmen were apparently arguing about the Charleston church massacre.

A middle-aged man wearing a seersucker suit was berating the other man about the biased news stories that the national media outlets were reporting. He was well into his cups, and the alcohol had taken control.

"Goddamn darkies!" he ranted. "Those sons of bitches got what was coming to them in that church," he slurred.

The other businessman wasn't having any of this guy's vitriol and suggested that he needed to go sleep off his lunch and maybe get some counseling for anger management.

"Fuck that counseling shit, I just want these people to understand their station in life, is all."

Clay could feel his blood beginning to boil again, and it was everything he could do to not confront the seersuckered shithead.

The other businessman loudly told his lunch partner to go fuck himself and stormed out of the bar. He passed where Clay was sitting and exited the Ventana Inn in a huff. Clay saw that "Master Bigot" was still sitting at the bar, nursing his cocktail and muttering to himself.

Fortunately, Clay's anger was soothed a few moments later when Grace came from the front desk to tell him his room was ready and that his bags had been placed inside.

"Thank you, Grace," came Clay's acknowledgement, and seeing her friendly smile helped reduce the temperature of his boiling anger to a low simmer.

"So, are you on assignment in Charleston the whole time you're here," Grace inquired, "or are you going to be able to spend some time getting to know our beautiful city better?"

"I've been to Charleston several times over the years," Clay said, "and I've gotten to know the battery area fairly well, but I'm sure I don't know it as well as the locals. I thought I'd go out later this afternoon with my camera to get reacquainted and see how setup is going for the Festival's artists. Aside from that, do you have any suggestions?"

"Oh well, yeah, lots of suggestions," Grace offered, "but it would probably be easier to show you than tell you."

Immediately Grace became embarrassed by her comment because she didn't want to come across as being too presumptuous and forward.

"Sorry," she interjected quickly. "I hope that didn't come across as too pushy. I was just trying to be helpful."

Clay smiled at her embarrassment and chose not to tease her about it.

"No, you're fine, Grace," Clay replied. "You're just doing your job and being friendly. But since you mentioned it, I could use a knowledgeable guide to show me places I might have missed along the way. I'm game if you are."

"Well, I'm going to have to plan us a little adventure," Grace said warmly. "Maybe go to some places that I haven't seen in a while, too. I get off work at five o'clock. If we leave shortly thereafter, will you still have enough good daylight left to take pictures?"

"I think the light will be fine," Clay answered. "This will give me some time to organize my camera gear, send a few e-mails and maybe catch forty winks. Why don't we meet in the lobby at five then. Okay?"

Just as they were turning to leave, a long, loud string of profanity erupted from the barroom.

"Goddamn darkies! And those greasy Mexicans and Cubans. This country belongs to the whites, and I'll shoot any sumbitch that says otherwise."

Grace immediately returned to her desk to call Mr. Delacroix, the Inn's manager.

Clay stood in the doorway between the Veranda Room and the lobby, and soon the big-mouthed drunk came lumbering from the bar toward the lobby.

The drunk businessman bashed hard into Clay's shoulder as he tried to pass him.

"Hey, watch it, asshole," the drunk slobbered at Clay. "Watch where you're going next time."

Clay stood his ground, and the drunk finally managed to make bloodshot eye contact with him.

"Who the fuck are you?" he slurred at Clay.

The drunk was probably six-foot-two in height and tilted the scale at about two-hundred-and-forty pounds. A big man. Clay was approximately five-foot-ten and weighed about one sixty. No contest, but Clay really had to control himself not to hit the bastard in the face as hard as he could. His blood was on fire.

"Let's just say," Clay said in very distinct words, "that you would be wise never to come back here again."

The drunk was then confronted by the manager, Mr. Delacroix, who had come immediately at Grace's request.

"Sir, we don't tolerate that kind of language or behavior here at the Ventana Inn. May I suggest that you find a more plebeian establishment to quench your thirst in the future."

"Fuck you, you little prick. I'll go where I please and say what I please."

And with that the drunk stumbled out the front door, gave Robert the doorman the finger, and lumbered away.

With the drama over, Clay turned to Grace and said, "See you at five o'clock."

Chapter 13

ORI LIGHTLY RAPPED on the bathroom door and listened for
Rennie's response.

"How are you doing in there?" she inquired.

"I'm all right," came Rennie's soft reply.

Tori opened the door a crack and asked if he needed any help.

"Naw, I'm okay, just putting on the robe you loaned me. I'll
be out in a little bit."

Tori heard the toilet flush again, and a minute later Rennie
slowly came out of the bathroom. He looked reasonably human.

"Where are my clothes?" he asked. "You can't expect a man
to go around wearing a girl's bathrobe."

"Well, you can say goodbye to those clothes," Tori stated.
"They're not even worth washing. Mace has gone to the store to
buy some new things for you. He should be back pretty soon, and
then we can have some soup and bread that I've prepared."

"Those boys stole my money. I can't go buying new clothes,"
he lamented.

"Let's not worry about that now," Tori soothed. "How are you feeling?"

"I hurt pretty much all over, but especially my ribs where those boys kicked me. Hurts even more since they stole my money. It was all I had." Rennie said sadly.

"Come sit here in the kitchen with me. I'll make you some herbal tea, and we can get to know each other a little until Mace gets back from the store. Then we'll have some lunch, okay?"

Lex came bounding into the kitchen and right up to Rennie. Lex did another full-body sniffer scan and then sat next to him, leaning his flank against Rennie's leg.

"Lex seems to like you, Rennie, and that's rare for Lex," Tori said.

"I thought he was a big old black wolf at first," Rennie admitted. "I thought he was gonna take a chomp out of my leg."

"Well, he's certainly capable of doing it. I'll never forget the time he chased off the Jehovah's Witness people," Tori laughed.

Just then Satchmo came strutting into the kitchen. Rennie took one look at the enormous Maine coon cat, and his eyes widened in surprise.

"Wow, that's the biggest dang cat I've ever seen," Rennie said. "Is he mean?"

Satchmo walked up to Lex and began rubbing against him and purring loudly. He kept a safe distance away from the boy, though.

"He's very friendly once he gets to know you. For now just ignore him when he comes around. Satchmo hates to be ignored. Before too long, he'll come to you. He likes to be coy.

"As I think of it," Tori continued, "it seems you two have something in common."

"Yeah, like what?" Rennie asked. "He's a cat!"

"Well, to begin with," Tori answered, "you both lived alone on the street for much of your lives, and you know how to take care of yourselves."

"I don't know," Rennie said quietly. "Those boys beat me up and got my money. I sure don't call that taking care of myself."

Lex laid his head in Rennie's lap and looked up at him, his tail wagging.

Rennie looked down at the huge creature leaning against him and said, "You ain't going to eat me, are you?"

But by now, Rennie was beginning to realize he was in safe company.

Satchmo rubbed against Lex again and then trotted off toward the front door. A moment later Tori heard Mace's truck pull into the courtyard in front of her old farmhouse. She left Rennie in the kitchen and went to the porch to offer assistance to Mace, who was loaded with bags of clothes and groceries.

"I think I got a little carried away," Mace admitted.

"Well, this is certainly not like you, Mace Davis: spending money like this," Tori said.

"I know," Mace agreed. "A lot of memories have been bubbling to the surface."

Tori reached out and Mace placed several bags in her hands. With Lex trying to sniff everything they carried, and Satchmo underfoot, they somehow managed to get to the kitchen.

"Oh, hello again, Rennie. It's good to see you up and around. How are you feeling, young fella?"

"Better. A little tired maybe," Rennie admitted. "What you got in all of those bags?" he asked.

"Oh, I don't know," Mace feigned. "Maybe some clothes and stuff for some young man who just got the daylights walloped out of him."

"Really?" came Rennie's surprised reaction.

"Tori, give me a hand here, will you please?" Mace asked.

The bags were on the kitchen table, and Tori handed each one over to Rennie for him to open. At first, Rennie was very hesitant to take anything out of the bags.

Mace realized the boy's reluctance and said, "Unless, of course, you want to go through life wearing a woman's flowery bathrobe!"

Rennie didn't need to be teased about the bathrobe twice, so he slowly began removing articles of clothing item by item from the bags. First came the socks and underwear, which were received with a muted thanks. Then, came a toilet kit containing a brush, a comb, a toothbrush, and toothpaste, followed by his new leather belt, shirts, and pants. A new winter coat was next in the flow of garments, along with a blue knit cap and leather gloves. A small mountain of clothes grew on the kitchen table.

Finally—the ultimate of all ultimates—came the shoes!

Mace had sprung for a high-end pair of Nike athletic shoes, and Rennie's eyes grew even wider than when he first saw Satchmo. He was stunned.

"I can't pay for any of this," he said somberly. "This is way too much!"

"Rennie, I know everything that has happened to you today— from your getting beaten to your coming here, and now all of the clothes and everything—I know all of it has been a total surprise, but I'd like to share something with you that I rarely ever talk about. Tori already knows about my early years."

"I'm listening," Rennie said respectfully.

Mace closed his eyes and began to speak again. He told Rennie about being an orphan on the streets of Freeport, and how the clergy at St. Francis had taken him in and educated him, and how he—at about the same age Rennie is now—had come north from New Orleans to Indiana to find work.

Rennie listened attentively, and Mace continued to tell his life's story. He told about coming to work at the Jeffries Woodworking Co. and how he has lived here on these grounds for nearly sixty years.

"And of the many things I learned along the way, the one thing that your situation reminds me of the most is that there are good, kind people out there in the world, and when they offer you a helping hand, take it. It can save your life. It saved mine."

Mace let his words hang in the air, and he saw that Rennie was considering his words very intently.

Recognizing that Rennie wasn't yet ready to comment on Mace's advice, Tori strategically changed subjects and uttered the immortal words, "Who's hungry?!"

The serious mood changed instantly, and Mace and Rennie began collecting the bags of clothes.

Tori said, "Mace, why don't you and Rennie put the clothes in the guest room for now? After lunch we can remove their tags and put them away."

Rennie was very sore, but he wanted to help, so he gingerly got up with a couple of shopping bags and followed Mace into the guest room. While there, he slipped out of Tori's spare bathrobe and put on some of his new clothing, minus the tags that Mace snipped off. Everything fit remarkably well, and Rennie was excited beyond belief about his new athletic shoes.

"It ain't easy for me to say 'thank you' 'cause I've never really had much to say 'thank you' for, but I want you to know I am grateful for everything that you and Tori are doing for me. Just want you to know, is all."

"You're very welcome, Rennie," came Mace's warm reply. "Why don't we go get some lunch? You must be starved. I sure am. C'mon."

Tori had set the table from memory. It was one of the kitchen duties that she learned at a very young age. Their mother made sure that both Tori and Weed had equal household responsibilities, and their father welcomed Tori's companionship and extra pair of hands when working in his shop or in the yard.

Tori's parents did the best they could in raising a sightless child. They were not wealthy, but they were well enough off to make sure she got a very good education and was exposed to many diverse cultural and athletic events.

They also invested heavily in music lessons for Tori's magnificent voice. No parents could have felt prouder than when they heard Tori and Weed sing together at the Palladium and the audience went wild. What they got in return for their guidance as loving parents were two devoted siblings who could rely on each other long after they were gone.

As for Weed, he was often astounded by how well Tori functioned in her sightless world. Given her obvious limitations, she did remarkably well. Tori chose not to dwell too much on the seriousness of being blind; she had made peace with this fact of life a long time ago.

In fact, another major element that Tori and Weed's parents insisted upon in their children's upbringing was a sense of humor.

"Without humor, all is lost," their father would often say. "Not everything is a joke, but not everything is deadly serious, either."

So, humor of all forms, especially laughing at oneself, became a staple in their childhood home. All was not lost.

Mace helped Tori ladle the soup into bowls and set them at each person's place. The aroma was magnificent, and the steam from the soup wafted above the table. Tori sliced the multigrain loaf she had baked earlier and brought out an assortment of fresh fruit and veggies.

"Dig in!" she announced, and she and Mace picked up their soup spoons and began to enjoy their bountiful lunch.

Rennie was a little slow in starting his lunch. Mace looked over and saw that there was a tear in his eye.

"You okay, Rennie?" he asked.

"I'm okay," he said softly. "I was just wondering if this is what Thanksgiving is like."

Tori managed to hide a sudden catch in her throat. She knew she had missed out on many things in life being blind, but she had always been surrounded by a loving family, including Weed, Clay, and Mace. For a child not to know the warmth of Thanksgiving was a heartbreaking revelation to her. Mace, too.

"I guess this is very much what Thanksgiving is like," Tori said. "Except we don't have any turkey, of course. Now, let's dig in before our soup gets cold."

"Agreed!" said Mace.

Despite his physical discomfort, Rennie did, in fact, dig in. His ribs were still very sore, and his face was puffy from the pummeling he took, but the soothing bath and Tori's healing touch had his recovery off to a good start.

Before long, Tori's astute ears picked up the sound of a familiar vehicle pulling into the courtyard.

"We've got company," she said.

A few moments later, everyone heard the soulful blues notes coming from a harmonica. Weed had arrived home. He kept playing his tune as he came through the front door and strode back to the kitchen.

"Good afternoon, everyone!" Weed sang out. "Tori, it sure smells good in here! Do you have more soup? And who is this young fellow sitting where I usually do?"

"This young fellow is Rennie Cotton," Mace stated. "He's the young man that we talked about with Clay. He's going to be helping us out around the brewery complex."

"You're Weed, aren't you? Weed Rawlins, the musician?" Rennie asked.

Weed stopped blowing to cool the soup on his spoon and smiled at Rennie.

"Now, how do you know who I am?" Weed inquired.

"Because everyone in the hood knows who Weed Rawlins is!" Rennie declared. "Your music tells it like it is, and—well, the older boys like to joke about your name, Weed. They say you must smoke a lot of herb."

Tori laughed out loud. "If our parents knew that the nickname they gave my sweet, adorable brother would be confused with marijuana, they'd have a cow. Fact is, he grew so fast as a child that our parents said he grew like a weed, and the name stuck."

"Actually, both theories could be true, and I'm not saying anything else without the benefit of legal counsel," Weed joked.

"Now, Weed, cool it!" Tori said, and Weed got the message to change the subject.

"Maybe later on, after I finish my chores, would you play a little more harp for us?" Rennie asked.

"I'm sure Weed would be delighted to have you as a captive audience later, but right now, sir, you need to lay down and rest some more," Tori stated. "Weed and I will clean the dishes, and there will be plenty for you to do tomorrow. Fair enough?" Tori asked.

"Fair enough," Rennie replied. "And thank you for helping me. I told Mace I'm not used to people being nice to me. So . . ."

Weed took a more serious tone. He looked the boy in the eye and said, "Rennie, you're welcome to stay here while you heal. Where you choose to go after that is your business. Nobody's going to force you into anything. You don't need to make a decision now. Right now everyone wants you just feeling strong again."

"There's only a couple of rules you need to follow while you're here," Weed continued. "No stealing from us and no lying. We all work hard and look after the property and each other. All of us stick together around here. Isn't that right, Mace?"

"Right as rain, my friend. We stick together!"

"I hear what you're all saying," Rennie said. "I'm used to being on my own, though. May take a little getting used to. Don't mean no disrespect. I'll work hard though, I promise. I need to make me some money. I'll follow the rules, too, Weed."

They finished their conversation on solid terms. Tori walked to the guest room with Rennie and helped him put some of his new belongings away before he laid down to rest.

Weed said to Mace, "I've got a couple of hours before Tori and I need to leave for our performance tonight at Stella's Diner. You want to take a look at the detective-style cameras Clay was talking about in the museum and then drop down to the sub-basement?"

"Sure," Mace said. "Are you feeling more comfortable about participating in Clay's plan?"

"Closer," Weed replied. "And every time I read or hear another news report about some senseless attack, I get even closer. Believe me, I understand why Clay is so pissed!"

Mace and Weed went to the guest-room doorway and thanked Tori for the great lunch. Weed reminded Tori that they had a gig that night at Stella's Diner, and Mace said he'd be happy to look after their new house guest.

"Tori, do you play music, too?" Rennie asked with high interest.

This time Weed spoke for his sister and said, "You ain't heard no sweeter sound than when my sister starts singing the blues!"

Rennie was impressed.

"Let's plan on leaving for Stella's around six," Weed suggested to Tori.

"I've been practicing, and I'm ready with our new tunes," Tori beamed.

"Okay, then. Mace and I need to check on some things in the brewery building that Clay asked us to handle," Weed concluded. "I'll be back in time to clean up, and then we'll go light up the Diner!"

Chapter 14

AFTER THE UNPLEASANT episode in the Veranda Room restaurant, Clay went to his room to organize his gear and send an e-mail to his agent Lily to confirm details for his upcoming photo shoots.

In addition to his current assignment at the South of Broad Street Art Fair in Charleston, he asked Lily to work out the details for upcoming assignments in Santa Fe, San Diego, and a couple of other projects that still needed to be confirmed.

Clay then phoned Mace to see how things were going at home. Mace and Weed were in the camera museum when Clay called, and Mace filled him in about Rennie's beating and subsequent temporary residence with Tori and Weed.

"Wow, it's amazing Rennie has lasted as long as he has on the street. I'm sorry I'm not there to be more helpful, especially since it was my idea to have him work for us in the first place," Clay lamented.

"Don't worry about it, Clay," he heard both Weed and Mace say almost in unison. "Tori has been terrific helping him," Mace added. "And we're all fine with his being here. We made sure he understood about no stealing or lying. He seems okay with it."

"I'm not sure where he'll want to go after he heals," Weed began, "but we can cross that bridge when we come to it. For now, we'll just let nature take its course."

"He needs money now, though," Mace stated. "So I'm pretty sure we can count on his working with us around the brewery complex for a little while, anyway. Whether or not he chooses to go back to his shack on Hill Street at night remains to be seen."

"Now, about these antique, detective-style cameras in your collection," Weed continued. "What do you have in mind?"

"Basically, I want to see if you can develop devices that will allow me to get up close and personal with my subjects, but I'll need you to tell me what you think is doable in terms of reliable weaponry, especially on short notice. You've got carte blanche with your ideas, my friend. Please just keep in mind I need at least one device very soon that you are sure will work," Clay stated.

"I've been giving it some thought," Weed said. "Mace and I are standing in front of your collection if you want to discuss specific cameras."

"Great," Clay said. "I've been giving this some serious thought, too. I really do not want to use my prized cameras as weapons. They are just too special to me, but like most collectors, I also have acquired a supply of very rare but incomplete cameras that I use for spare parts. If my memory serves me correctly, I think you should be able to cobble together some new devices from them."

"Cool!" Weed cooed. "This could be a very intriguing enterprise. And, my professors at MIT never thought that a musician like me would ever use what they taught me! I'm already getting closer to liking Clay's plan, Mace."

"Mace, if you guys are willing to get started while I'm gone, have at it," Clay encouraged. "I think you know I have a supply of spare camera parts and special tools in the storage closet next to my darkroom. Why don't you cart what you think would be useful down to the sub-basement so Weed can get started? When I get back in a few days, I'll look around to see if there is anything else in the way of parts we should use."

Clay continued, "Now, then—in the display case look for the following cameras: The Stirn's Vest Camera, my Ben Akiba Cane camera, my Photo-Cravate, the Steineck ABC Watch camera, and the KGB Ring camera. Oh, and one of my favorites, the Demon Detective camera. I'll be happy to text you these names when we hang up."

"We'll see what we can find in the storage closet, Clay," Mace said. "We'll carefully transport the vintage cameras down to the sub-basement for Weed to refer to. It appears we are moving forward. I'll set up the workbenches and lighting this afternoon yet."

Clay hung up the phone and texted the camera names and then laid back and closed his eyes.

Clay had hoped to catch a brief nap, but his mind was racing. He realized that he had influenced Mace and Weed in evening the score—not that they weren't capable of making up their own minds. They were their own men. Now, they were like kindling wood, and Clay was the spark.

He pictured Jennifer's face and felt disappointed with himself because his mind's eye was losing some of her details. Clay pulled out his cell phone and looked at pictures of her he'd saved. The images took on almost dream-like qualities.

"Did I really know you, Jennifer Skyler? Were we lovers? Had we planned to marry?"

Clay knew the answers to all these questions, but he struggled to find solace in their memory.

Clay set the alarm on his watch for four-thirty and closed his eyes again. This time he drifted off to sleep and soon began to dream.

Images flashed in his mind. Black-and-white images. Color images. Pictures from different projects and exhibitions. A silent cacophony of scenes and portraits. Soon the flood of pictures began to ebb, and Clay dreamed of a hooded executioner cloaked in a long black robe. The man was featureless except for his dark eyes which held a steely stare. It was Death. Like smoke, Death drifted over to within a yard of Clay and stared into his being.

"You wish to be like me, Clay Arnold?" came a voice that had no caring.

"Not like you. Like me," came Clay's dreamed reply.

"Oh, so you think you are different from me?" the specter asked. "Death is death, yes, whether it comes from your hand or the stuff of nightmares like me. Once you have dipped your finger in blood, the stain never goes away."

"I don't care about stains. I want revenge and justice," Clay said coldly.

"Be careful what you wish for," Death advised. "Or as I warned Dante at the gates of hell centuries ago: Abandon all hope, ye who enter here."

Clay stirred in his sleep and found himself awake, looking across the darkened room. The fan from the air conditioner made the curtains move, and for a brief moment Clay thought that the figure of Death was there with him. He shuddered, but the ethereal visage of Death had vanished just as surreptitiously as it had arrived.

Clay looked at his watch. 4:27 PM. He turned off the alarm and went to the bathroom to freshen up. He looked in the mirror and thought about his dream. "Be careful what you wish for," he repeated to himself.

At five o'clock sharp Clay emerged from his Palm Room and walked the short distance to the lobby to meet Grace for her guided tour of the Battery area. He had his camera with him and was eager to see areas of the Charleston peninsula he had never seen before.

Grace came promptly to the lobby and told Clay she needed five more minutes to make sure the receptionist taking over her duties knew about some last-minute changes.

Clay walked out to the street and spoke with Robert the doorman.

"Good evening, Mr. Arnold," came Robert's positive greeting. "I see you've got your camera with you. Anything in particular you'll be taking pictures of?"

"Not sure yet," came Clay's honest reply. "Grace has offered to show me around the Battery, and I thought it would be fun to see how the artists are doing in setting up their canopies for the South of Broad Street Art Festival."

"Well, you've got yourself an excellent guide, and she's pretty, too," he said with a wink.

Clay let the latter part of Robert's comment go past without a response.

"Robert, do you mind if I ask you a question about the episode that occurred earlier?"

"You mean the drunk who stumbled out of the Inn?" Robert asked.

"Yes," Clay responded. "Who was that guy, anyway?"

"Oh, that was Jefferson Talbot. He doesn't come around very often, but when he does, there's always some turmoil. Rumor is he's the behind-the-scenes leader of the local KKK. Apparently, he has other lackeys doing his public speaking for him, but he's the real guy calling the shots."

"How nice," Clay said icily. "It seems he's not only a big-mouth but a coward, too. I told him he'd be wise never to return here again."

"Good luck with that warning, Mr. Arnold. I'm afraid Jefferson Talbot feels like he's got enough support and money that he can do and say whatever he chooses."

Just then Grace came gliding out of the front door, slightly out of breath.

"Sorry for the delay," she offered. "We have a new employee working the desk, and I needed to make sure she was ready for her shift. It looks like you two were having a serious discussion. Did I interrupt anything?"

"No, no," came Robert's quick reply. "Mr. Arnold and I were just discussing some of our city's more colorful personalities."

"I see," Grace said. "We certainly have our share!"

"Well, Grace, I'm ready for our walking adventure if you are," Clay suggested. "We'll catch you later, then, Robert."

The sun had begun to dip lower in the western sky, and the evening light cast a golden glow on the waterfront. Grace and Clay walked a few blocks east and came to the Water Front Park along the Cooper River and Charleston harbor.

Clay's eyes scanned his surroundings, and he took a few pictures of sailboats cruising near Fort Sumter.

"Let's walk down East Bay Street to White Point Gardens," Grace suggested. "We'll see the artists setting up for the art show, and then we can take some of the lesser traveled lanes."

The October temperature was still a balmy seventy-five degrees, and Clay thought how much chillier it must be back home in Indiana. The two of them walked past artists who were busily putting their artwork on display. They saw all manner of colorful art glass, wood turnings, paintings, jewelry, and, of course, photography.

Clay was impressed with the diversity of talent, and he reflected on how very fortunate he was to have achieved great renown and financial success with his photography. A rare achievement, indeed.

After about forty-five minutes of touring the art show set-up, Grace said, "Let's walk over to look at the stunning architecture of Number Two Meeting Street, and then I have some other places to show you."

Number Two Meeting Street was an iconic home with gorgeously sculpted architecture. Clay shot several images of it and felt no different than the multitude of other tourists who had fallen under its artistic charm.

"C'mon," Grace urged, "before we lose the afternoon light."

She led him along streets named Legare and Tradd, Gibbes, Lamboll, and Murray. Clay was familiar with some of the streets and houses, but many were new visual delights for him. He took his time viewing various scenes and made notes about where he would like to return when the sunlight was in a different position in the sky.

Grace was an ideal guide, and Clay found himself enjoying her company. After about two hours Clay suggested that they return to the Inn because he knew it had been a long day for Grace, and because he wanted to rest up again for a full day of shooting the next day at the art show.

They arrived back at the Ventana Inn shortly before seven-thirty, and Clay thanked Grace for the great tour. Robert was still on-duty at the Inn's front door.

"That was fun," Grace said to Clay. "If you want to continue our tour again just let me know."

Clay thanked her again and said he'd enjoy that very much. They parted company after a brief hug, and Clay watched her glide away.

Chapter 15

"YOUR FRIEND'S HERE again," Robert quietly informed Clay.
"Oh," came Clay's solitary reply.

"He's pretty loud," Robert went on. "I informed the new woman on the desk that if he gets out of hand not to hesitate to call Mr. Delacroix. Mr. Talbot has been warned before, and I doubt Mr. Delacroix will be very pleased that he's returned."

"Hmm," came Clay's noncommittal reply. "I think maybe I'll have a drink and just turn in now, Robert. It's been a long day."

Robert watched Clay enter the Inn and was surprised that Clay had dismissed any further conversation about Jefferson Talbot.

Clay went to his room and pulled his camera bag on to the bed. He rummaged through his equipment until he found what he was looking for. He slipped two items into his pocket, left his room, and went to the Veranda Room bar.

Jefferson Talbot was sitting on the same bar stool he had claimed earlier in the day. It was about eight o'clock now, and several hotel guests and other tourists had come for dinner. The

large-screen TV was turned to a national news channel, and Mr. Talbot was loudly expressing his personal commentary on each story.

At first the guests tried to ignore the man's boorish remarks, but now Mr. Talbot began directly challenging some of them on their political beliefs. The bartender tried to have Mr. Talbot tone his language down, but his polite efforts failed. Mr. Talbot continued his ugly, harassing comments.

"Fucking coons, Mexicans, and Chinese are taking over the country, and that big-eared monkey in the White House is letting them get away with it."

"Okay pal, that's it!" the bartender said with clear exasperation. "I'm calling the manager, and if you can't behave yourself, I'll have to call the police, too. It's your choice."

Clay stood by the entrance to the bar and smiled a little, but there was absolutely no humor in his expression.

"How dare you speak to me that way!" Jefferson Talbot snarled at the bartender.

"Okay, that's it, mister. Get out or I'm calling the cops," the bartender declared, and to provide added emphasis he pulled a mean-looking club into view.

"I'm leaving, you low-life prick!" Talbot slurred, and without paying his tab he slid off the bar stool and staggered toward the doorway where Clay stood.

For the second time that day, the drunk bashed into Clay's shoulder as he attempted to navigate his way out of the bar.

"Hey, watch it, asshole!" came the same words the drunken bigot had directed at Clay earlier in the day.

Clay let him pass without comment and watched as Talbot made his way toward the lobby and then exited the front door. Robert moved out of the way to give the drunk easy access to the public sidewalk. Talbot managed to compose himself and began walking south on Church Street.

Clay watched him leave the Ventana Inn. Fifteen seconds later he walked out the front door, nodded a brief greeting to Robert, who was assisting other guests at curbside, and began following Jefferson Talbot.

Clay couldn't help noticing that it was a gorgeous evening in Charleston. The sun had recently set, but the western horizon was still aglow with pink and mauve streaks. Soon the colors would turn to a flat gray color and then be swallowed by the darkness of night. Evening comes.

Jefferson Talbot seemed oblivious to the world around him. His gaze was firmly fixed on the walkway in front of him, and his gait was slow but steady. He was unaware of Clay's presence some thirty feet behind him.

Before long Talbot came to the intersection of Church and Tradd streets and stopped for a moment to catch his breath. Clay slowed his pace so he wouldn't overtake his target before he was ready. Up ahead he saw the old cemetery that he had explored on previous occasions and decided to quicken his pace. He passed Jefferson Talbot without commenting to him, but Talbot was characteristically rude.

"Hey, watch it, asshole," came his favorite choice of words as Clay passed him on the sidewalk.

Clay walked ahead of Talbot and reached the entrance to the cemetery. He turned and faced Talbot's oncoming stride. His hands were in his pockets.

Talbot looked up from the sidewalk and saw Clay blocking his path.

"Hey, faggot, get out of the way," he spewed at Clay.

Clay stood there staring at him and waited for the drunk's next insults.

"Fitting that we're at a cemetery, don't you think, Mr. Talbot?" came Clay's rhetorical question to him.

"What are you talking about, asshole?" came Talbot's terse response.

"A cemetery . . . you know, where we put dead people," Clay replied.

An expression of confusion dominated Talbot's face, and then a moment of recognition took over his features.

"Oh, yeah—you're that guy at the bar," he said. "Well, if you're after my money, forget it. I'm not giving you shit, so get the fuck out of my way."

"Gee, now how did I know you were going to say something profound like that?" Clay said. He continued to stand his ground, blocking the sidewalk.

"I don't have time for your bullshit, mister, and besides, I have to take a wicked piss, so beat it."

Clay stared at Talbot and saw that his prey was clearly a larger man. He knew that even drunk Jefferson Talbot could deliver a stunning punch, so he planned his next move carefully.

"I said move it, asshole, or I'll kick the crap out of you and piss in your mouth," came Talbot's colorful threat.

Clay feigned an apology to his drunk adversary and stepped to the side of the walkway.

"That's better," came Talbot's assuaged reply.

Clay quickly scanned his surroundings and saw that there were no other pedestrians or drivers. As Talbot began to pass him, Clay took his hand out of his pocket and with viper-like speed leaped forward and tightly wrapped his camera's cable-release cord around Talbot's pudgy, sweaty neck. It was like a garrote.

Talbot immediately began to struggle, flailing his arms around to try to loosen Clay's grip and strike back.

Clay held on with all of his might and hoped that his cable-release didn't snap. The more Talbot struggled, the tighter Clay pulled the cable until Talbot's eyes began to bug out and his complexion turned the color of the evening sunset.

"Over here," Clay said to the taller man, and he began to drag Jefferson Talbot into the solitude of the old cemetery.

Talbot had no recourse but to follow. Clay dragged him about twenty feet to an area in the verdant graveyard and forced him to sit down on an old, wrought-iron bench that faced a mausoleum featuring the sculpture of a heroic angel.

Talbot reached his hand to his throat and tried to claw the cable release away from his neck. His bulging eyes looked at Clay, and Talbot knew from the intensity of Clay's expression that his tenure of life was about to end.

Clay spied a section of rusty iron fence lying on the ground and snapped off a twelve-inch metal spike. Talbot's eyes widened even further when he saw the menacing spike, and he tried a final time to squirm away.

Clay forced Talbot to make eye contact with him.

"So, you think you're entitled to treat people like dirt, don't you, Mr. Talbot? You think you are better than everyone else, yes? You think that the white race needs to take up arms against people who aren't like you, yes?"

Jefferson Talbot frantically began to shake his head no, but the temperature in Clay's blood had reached the boiling point, and there was no going back. He took the rusty spike and placed the tip of it to the soft tissue under Talbot's chin. With one deft and violent motion, Clay forced the spike upward through Talbot's mouth until the tip exited his head through his left eye socket. A momentary expression of shock dominated Jefferson Talbot's face. Then, he was dead.

But Clay wasn't quite finished. He leaned the slumping bigot against the back of the iron bench and reached into his pocket for the second item he'd brought from his camera bag. It was an old pocket knife that he kept for various uses. Clay pulled out the shorter of the two blades and leaned close to Jefferson Talbot's deformed face. He carved KKK into the dead bigot's forehead and stared at Talbot's disfigurement.

"Evening comes," Clay whispered to himself.

By now it was dark. With his handkerchief Clay wiped the blood from the knife blade and any tissue from Talbot's neck off the cable release. He then carefully wiped his fingerprints off the iron spike and looked for any telltale signs of evidence that the police might discover. Finding none, he looked around to see if there were any witnesses. Again, there were none.

Clay calmly pocketed his tools and took a final look at Jefferson Talbot's lifeless body. He exited the cemetery and didn't look back. It was the first time Clay had ever killed anyone, and he was flooded with a range of emotions. No, he didn't for one minute regret what had just occurred. He believed that Jefferson Talbot's life justified his murder.

But the thought of taking another human life, however despicable, was something he would have to work on reconciling. For now, though, Clay felt the boil in his blood begin to simmer, and he thought wistfully of Jennifer. He knew she would never approve of his behavior, but . . . well, things were different now.

Clay maintained a steady stride along Meeting Street and was relieved to see few folks out for an evening stroll. Several blocks from the cemetery Clay noticed an obscure sewer, and he crammed his bloodied handkerchief down its dark maw. Clay heard the bells toll from the Emanuel African Methodist Episcopal Church. He respectfully waited for them to end and then resumed his solitary walk back to the Ventana Inn.

Chapter 16

STELLA'S DINER WAS ALIVE with excitement. The parking lot was filled to capacity, and there was a twenty-minute wait for folks wanting a table. Stella took up her position as hostess decked out in her tight, leopard-print yoga pants and fluffy, hot pink top. She looked like a hooker from the Taj Mahal, but it was all part of the partying persona she wished to portray.

Tori and Weed arrived with ample time to speak with their friend Stella and to get set up for their performance. Any time Tori and Weed performed, Stella could count on packing the Diner with guests, but tonight was especially busy.

"We've got some new tunes we want to debut tonight," Tori said to Stella.

"Darlin', anything you and your handsome brother want to play is fine with me," Stella said. "All I have to do is advertise that the Rawlinses are performing, and we got people hanging from the rafters. So, have at it!"

Tori and Weed could see that Stella had her hands full greeting guests, so they said they'd talk later and went backstage to make last-minute preparations for their performance. Tori called Mace's cell phone to see how things were going with Rennie.

"Mainly, I'm just letting him sleep," Mace said. "I've checked on him a couple of times, and he appears to be sleeping comfortably. I don't think you need to worry about anything," Mace offered. "Just have fun and leave your audience begging for more," he laughed. "We're fine here."

People kept pouring through the Diner's doors, and Abby West joined Stella as a greeter and to help escort guests to their tables when their names were called.

"Wow, we are really rocking tonight," Abby said to Stella. "I've never seen it so busy!"

"They're here to hear Tori and Weed. Do me a favor and keep an eye on things for a minute, will you? I see that Detective Reynolds just came in, and I need to talk with him about security. I'll be back in a few minutes," Stella declared.

A few moments later the Diner's house lights went low, and a blue spotlight highlighted Tori sitting on a stool at center stage. She held a microphone and looked heavenward. She absolutely glowed. The crowd immediately broke into applause.

The room fell back into silence, and Tori began singing a soulful song a cappella. At first it sounded like an old Negro spiritual, but soon Tori was adding blues and jazz elements into the melody. Her voice sounded like something only an angel could produce. The audience was enraptured by her mellifluous voice, and even the serving staff stopped in mid-stride to enjoy her special talent.

After several bars the stunning wail of a blues harmonica was heard offstage, and then Weed made his grand entrance and joined Tori center stage. The crowd went totally nuts.

For the next forty-five minutes Tori and Weed captivated their audience with a combination of classic and new Rawlins's songs. Typically, Tori sang and Weed played harp, but at times Tori played her keyboard and Weed sang heart-warming tunes about love—lost and regained.

It was one of those mesmerizing performances that made all in the audience leave their cares and differences behind and share a warm, common bond made possible by the universal language of music.

"Thank you, folks!" Tori began. "It's always a pleasure to perform at Stella's, and Weed and I are grateful for y'all coming out tonight. We're going to take a short break, and then we'll come back to share a few very new tunes we've have been working on just for you."

The audience broke into a very appreciative applause, and Weed and Tori waved as they left the stage. With a break in the music, Stella joined Trent Reynolds at his table near the front door.

"Seems like everyone is pretty well-behaved tonight," Trent said to Stella.

"So far, so good," Stella agreed. "But Tori and Weed usually attract a fairly tame audience.

"Do you have any more information on the jerks in the pickup that have been harassing my customers?" Stella inquired.

"I wish I had more to offer in the way of information, Stella, but they've pretty much vanished for the last couple of days. Since we haven't had any trouble recently, I've had to reassign the officer that I had here, but I thought I'd keep an eye out tonight from the parking lot."

"I appreciate that, Trent," Stella replied. "I hate tying up your time like this since I'm sure you're very busy. Let me get you some dinner before you head out to the lot. I'll send Abby over to get your order. On the house."

Trent had already put in a solid twelve-hour shift and wasn't going to argue with Stella about a free dinner. A few minutes later Stella relieved Abby at the hostess station, and she came over to take Trent's order.

"Good evening, Detective Reynolds. I'm Abby. Do you know what you want, or do you need to see a menu?" she asked.

"No, Abby, I think I'll have the special tonight, medium-well, please."

Abby went off to the kitchen to deliver his order and then back to the hostess station to see if Stella needed more help.

Again the house lights were turned low, and Weed and Tori returned to the stage to continue their performance.

Without preamble, Tori began singing one of her favorite songs, "God Bless the Child". The song had always been special to her because, as a sightless person, she knew how important it was to be independent despite having a serious physical handicap.

Now this song had even more significance because Rennie was also a child who had needed to stand up to the vagaries of the world. She thought of Rennie when she sang the soulful tune. Weed accompanied her beautifully on harmonica, and together the audience was spellbound by the transformative power of their talents. You could hear a pin drop.

Abby returned to Trent's table with his order of apple-bacon pork loin and stayed there to listen as Tori and Weed concluded their song.

Trent said to Abby, "I've known those two ever since we were little kids, and somehow I always knew that they would be successful at whatever they chose to do. Do you know that Weed has an engineering degree from MIT? He doesn't talk about it much, only because he's so turned on by music. He's a multi-talented guy."

"No, I wasn't aware of his degree," Abby said. "But he sure can play the blues. It's funny how life can take you in different directions, I guess."

Trent looked at Abby, smiled and said, "Oh, so you're a philosopher, too."

"No, just someone who has to decide about a major career change coming up. I'm actually a journalist by profession," Abby stated. "But my liberal leanings didn't exactly match up philosophically with my newspaper editor's or the governor's for that matter. So I got fired. Stella has been kind enough to give me work until I can figure out my next career move."

Just then a commotion occurred by the front door, and Trent turned to see a valet rush through the entrance looking for Stella, but he went directly to Trent when he saw a man in a police uniform.

"They're back," he said breathlessly. "Those guys in that pickup truck with the Confederate flag. They're out there taunting people, especially our black and Hispanic guests. It's ugly."

Trent told the valet and Abby to find Stella and make certain the Diner's security staff was alerted. He suggested that they do it discreetly so as not to alarm the guests. They took off, and Trent turned and went outside to the parking lot.

Sure enough, a dark pickup truck with a Confederate flag for the front license plate was cruising up and down the parking lot. A defiant young man stood in the bed of the truck waving a large Confederate flag and spewing profanity and racial slurs at persons of color.

Trent immediately radioed the situation to his dispatcher and called for backup.

"Come on, you dark-skinned, faggot motherfuckers. Let's play tag, with my truck!" the driver snarled.

The driver steered the pickup on to the sidewalk and began knocking pedestrians out of the way like bowling pins. Trent managed to catch up to the truck and leaped onto the driver's running board. The jerk in the truck bed attempted to stab Trent with the flag's pole, but Trent deftly deflected it and yanked it out of the man's hands.

The pickup driver saw what happened in his side view mirror and pulled a handgun from his jacket. Bam! The gun discharged in Trent's direction, but fortunately the driver's aim was off.

The Diner's security personnel came pouring out to help, but at the sound of the gunshot they all ducked for cover. The man in the truck bed reached for his own gun, and Trent saw that he was in an untenable position with two armed bad guys.

Despite that, he knew that innocent people had already been injured and that many more would be if he couldn't contain the violence that was erupting. He reached for his own holstered firearm, which was a challenge given the erratic motion of the truck. He was too late. Another shot rang out, and Trent felt the hot, searing pain of a .38-caliber bullet shear through his right shoulder. He immediately fell off the moving truck and lay face down on the pavement.

"Newt, let's get the fuck out of here!" Twit hollered. "I just shot us a cop. We gotta git!"

"Copy that, brother!" and Newt stomped on the accelerator and made a beeline for an adjacent service road.

Now, pretty much everyone at Stella's Diner was aware that there was a major problem outside. People began heading for the rear exits, and the security guards were trying to maintain order.

Abby had witnessed the terrifying shot that knocked Trent from the truck. He was lying about twenty yards away, and she went running to render assistance. Stella had also seen Trent get gunned down and went rushing after Abby to help.

"Oh, no!" Abby cried out when she got to Trent. His shoulder was bleeding profusely, and he appeared to be in shock.

Stella arrived by her side two seconds later, saw the gravity of the situation, and pulled out her cell phone and dialed 911.

"This is Stella Vance, owner of the Diner. We have just been attacked by two white men in a dark pickup truck, and we have an officer down. We need immediate medical assistance."

"Yes ma'am," the operator said. "Help is on the way. Officer Reynolds already radioed for backup, but I'll make sure we dispatch ambulances from the area hospitals."

A moment later a security guard came up to them with a first-aid kit. Abby grabbed whatever gauze and bandages she could find and began carefully applying direct pressure. It would have to do until the emergency personnel arrived.

Stella and Abby gingerly moved Trent onto his back to take the pressure off of his bleeding shoulder. For a brief moment he opened his eyes and looked at Abby.

"Did they get away?" he asked.

"Yes," Abby said. "Now just lie still, okay? You've been shot, and help is on the way."

Tori and Weed were outside now with everyone else, and Weed told Tori that their long-time friend was lying on the pavement. They rushed over to offer assistance, too, and the driver of an EMT transport vehicle saw Stella waving her arms and veered in her direction.

Five minutes later the EMTs had reduced the flow of blood and loaded Trent into the ambulance.

"Where will you take him?" Abby asked.

"Conner Prairie Hospital," came the reply. "Your first aid likely saved his life, miss. I think he should survive, but his shoulder is going to need some major surgery."

Stella, Abby, Tori, and Weed silently watched as the ambulance pulled away with its siren blaring.

"Whew, what a night," Weed finally said. "God, please let him be okay."

They all went inside the Diner, which at this point was virtually empty of any guests and staff. Stella went behind the bar and started pouring drinks for anyone who wanted one.

They all sat at the bar having a stiff drink, and then Tori and Weed helped Stella and Abby close up the Diner for the night. Each of them was stunned by the evening's events and still couldn't believe what had happened. Stella prayed that everyone would heal fine. She also prayed that she didn't get sued.

"The police tell me no one was killed by those jerks," Stella reported. "But five people required serious medical attention and were transported to area hospitals. That's in addition to our friend Trent. If it hadn't been for his bravery, I shudder to think how many fatalities would've occurred."

Weed called Mace to let him know what had transpired and to say that they would be home in a little while.

"What a tragedy, Mace," Weed declared. "I just can't believe anyone would behave like that. It's barbaric! I'll call Clay first thing in the morning to let him know what happened. He's gonna be mad as hell."

"One thing's for sure, Mace," Weed continued. "I am damn well ready to move forward with Clay's plans in the sub-basement. Let's get together early in the morning, okay? Because I am royally pissed off!"

"Don't worry, my friend," Mace assured. "We'll take care of business. The three of us!"

Chapter 17

"Wow, Pa, you should've been there!" Twit gushed on the phone to his father. "We went through the parking lot at Stella's Diner like rhubarb through a rat. People were flying off the sidewalk, and then we shot us a cop."

"Goddamnit to hell," came Clement Hacker's reply. "I wanted you boys to do a little recon mission, not go shooting some dang cop. Now, we'll really have a shitstorm to worry about. I want you boys to come straight home and try not to shoot anyone else before you get back."

"I swear," Clement muttered to himself. "Both of them are dumber than a bucket of worms."

But the brothers did not come straight home. They agreed that there would be cops everywhere, so they decided the best thing to do was to hunker down somewhere for the night.

"Pa's gonna be hopping mad we didn't come straight home," Newt said.

"Yeah, well, like I said earlier, Pa's not here," came Twit's lame reply. "We'll get home when we do. I know a place we can go to hide and get us some shut-eye after all of that excitement. Hell, I'm getting a boner just thinking about it."

Twit managed to find the trailer park he was looking for a few miles from Stella's Diner, and Newt drove the pickup to the rear of the park.

It was quiet as a graveyard, and they selected a hiding place among several dilapidated vehicles.

No one saw them pull in. Newt killed the truck's engine, and they scrunched down in their seats and pulled their hats low for additional concealment. They had managed to elude the law.

The next morning broke with a calmness that belied the violence that had occurred just a few hours earlier at Stella's Diner. Twit and Newt spent the night in the truck and woke up to the comical commotion of a territorial male cardinal pecking at his reflection in the driver's side window.

"Hey, Twit, wake up. It's time to hit the road," Newt advised.

"I gotta take me a piss first," his grizzled-looking twin announced.

"Me, too. Then let's hit the road. We better stick to the backroads. I got a feeling the cops will have the interstate pretty well patrolled. We really should dump this truck and steal something else, but we're only about three hours from home, and I just as soon keep my truck and make a run for it."

"From here," Twit suggested, "I think we ought to take the road that runs along the White River. Probably lots of places to hide if we need to."

They did their business and climbed back in the truck. Newt was at the wheel again. He pointed the truck south and exited the trailer park.

"I guess this means no coffee or breakfast this morning," Twit whined.

"Yeah, well," Newt said sarcastically, "why don't we just try to stay out of jail. Chew on that."

Rennie woke up early. He didn't have a watch, so he wasn't exactly sure what time it was. The dawn light was barely peeking through the guest bedroom window of the farmhouse, but it provided enough light that he could see his surroundings.

He moved slowly under the blanket to test his comfort level, and although his ribs were still very tender, he felt better after his warm bath, Tori's meal, and a good night's sleep in a real bed. He slid the covers off and stood up by the side of the bed. He was plenty sore, but he could walk okay.

He had to pee, and he opened the bedroom door and listened to see if Weed or Tori was stirring. Satchmo came sauntering up to him and followed him into the bathroom, purring loudly.

"Quiet, now," Rennie said to the huge cat. "Don't go making any noise or nothing."

Satchmo purred even louder. Rennie peed and went to the sink to wash his hands which he rarely ever did.

He looked at himself in the mirror and frowned at what he saw. He knew he was surviving okay living in his shack on Hill Street, but he knew he was paying a price, too. The beating he'd taken was just one episode among many traumas that he'd had to endure. Yeah, he could make it on his own, but the cost was high.

He opened the bathroom door, and Satchmo took off down the hall. Rennie followed him and heard Tori humming a melody from the kitchen. He went back to his room, quickly dressed in his some of his new clothes, and returned to the kitchen.

"Is that our young house guest coming down the hall," Tori called out. "Or is it just another big old cat?"

"It's me," Rennie said sheepishly.

"And how do you feel this morning?" Tori inquired. "I bet you're still plenty sore."

"Yeah," Rennie admitted, "but I think I'm okay, thanks to you and Mace and Weed. Can I help you with anything right now?"

"I have the skillet warming up. Why don't you get the bacon out of the fridge and put about nine slices in to fry," Tori suggested. "Then, if you want to crack some eggs and put them in this bowl, we'll add them to the skillet when the bacon is finished."

Just then Weed came rolling into the kitchen with Lex at his side.

"Sure smells good," he remarked. "And I see you have yourself an excellent helper here."

"G'morning Weed,"Rennie said. "How'd you guys do last night at the club?"

"Well, we had us an exciting evening, wouldn't you say, Tori?"

"Uh huh, you could say that, Weed," she said, but Rennie noticed that her words and her reaction didn't exactly match up. They decided to change the subject.

"So, how are you feeling this morning?" Weed asked Rennie. "Your face isn't quite as puffy, and you seem to be moving better."

"I'm okay," he said stoically. "I can work, if that's what you're wondering."

Just then Mace rapped on the door frame and joined the group in the kitchen.

"Hmm, bacon and eggs!" Mace said enthusiastically. "Now I'm sorry I already had my breakfast."

"Well, have a seat anyway, Mace," Tori suggested. "We've got plenty of coffee and some extra bacon and toast. Please help yourself."

Rennie noticed how well the three of them got along together. Actually the five of them if you included Lex and Satchmo. It was a caring family; something he had never really known before. He ached for it.

"I spoke with Clay a few minutes ago," Weed told Mace. "His reaction about Stella's was pretty much what we expected it would be," he said cryptically because Rennie was there. "He said he'd be home in a few days after he finishes up in Charleston. He's eager for us to move forward with the project we discussed."

"Good," came Mace's reply. "I'm ready to start when you're finished with breakfast."

"Can I help, too?" came Rennie's request.

"Why don't we give you another day to heal," Weed suggested. "What Mace and I will be doing is fairly physical work," he fibbed, "and I know Tori has some things she'd like for you to help with. Trust me, there will be plenty of things Mace and I will need your help with, but let's give you another day to recuperate, okay?"

"Okay," Rennie said. "I may be little, but I'm strong."

"Don't worry, Rennie," Tori consoled. "I really need your help in the garden and then if you're feeling up for it later this afternoon, I thought we might take a hike along the White River to help loosen up those sore muscles of yours. How's that sound?"

"Sounds fine, Tori. I ain't never worked in a garden before."

"Good, it's settled then," Mace said. "Weed and I will probably grab some lunch at my place so we can stay focused on our project. We'll touch base with you guys later in the day, and I've got my cell phone with me if you need us."

Weed tossed a piece of toast to Lex who caught it on the fly. They all finished breakfast, and Rennie helped Tori clear the table and wash the dishes. They both had a growing feeling of trust but not quite a bond.

It was a good start to what would prove to be a long and arduous day.

Chapter 18

CLAY WOKE UP AT SIX-THIRTY when he heard the same church bells peal as the evening before. He lay in bed a few minutes to regain his equilibrium. He knew he had a full day of shooting at the art fair, but he also wanted to reflect back on murdering Jefferson Talbot.

Clay promised himself he wouldn't dwell on the prick's murder very long, but like sex, his first time would always be memorable. He thought the KKK engraving made quite a declarative statement.

Clay shaved and showered quickly and dashed off to the restaurant for a quick breakfast and to review his notes for the day's assignment. The art show's organizer didn't want Clay to simply shoot pretty scenes of the art fair. She could've paid anyone to do that. She wanted to make a cultural statement with this show and she was counting on Clay's photography to help catapult her production company to a new level among art fair promoters.

Clay chose a table that had a good view of the television in the bar. He was pleased that there had been no report made

of a murder in the cemetery, but he knew that would change soon.

Clay's breakfast came, and he read through his notes well enough to have a strategy for his shots. Walking through the art fair with Grace yesterday while the artists were setting up had been helpful, and he was looking forward to the challenge of making this photo shoot very unique.

Clay's phone rang as he was finishing his coffee. It was Weed. Clay listened intently as Weed explained what had transpired at Stella's the night before. Clay closed his eyes as Weed shared the sad news that Trent had been shot, and he made a mental note to ask his agent Lily to please send flowers to the hospital.

"How are you and Tori doing?" Clay asked.

"Well enough. It's not something I want to go through again," Weed lamented. "Several good people got hurt by those same two jerks who've been driving around Stella's in that pickup truck waving the Confederate battle flag."

"Lovely!" came Clay's sarcastic reply. "How's Rennie doing by the way? I almost forgot to ask."

"He's doing better," Weed answered. "I think it's the resilience of youth. That, and we've got him hanging with Tori and Lex today so he can heal more. It also frees Mace and me to work in the sub-basement. Honestly, Clay? After last night's attack at Stella's, I am anxious to get some of our weaponry created by the time you come back. The weapons will be pretty straightforward devices. I want to keep it simple."

"Okay, I'm sorry, Weed, but I can't talk too much longer right now. Will you please thank Mace for me again and keep me informed about things, especially anything you hear about Trent? I'll call you back later today."

They hung up, and Clay sat at his table staring straight ahead thinking about the attack on Stella's Diner. If anything, Weed's report reinforced Clay's desire to even the score.

"Well, you look pretty focused this fine morning," came Grace's direct but cheerful greeting.

"Oh yeah, good morning, Grace. I get fairly fixated when I'm preparing a photo project. I take it you're already working your shift."

"Yeah, I began at seven, and I'm off at five; then I have a meeting of the women's writing group I belong to," Grace stated.

"I really appreciated your taking the time yesterday to stop by the art fair with me, and then to show me some of your favorite sites in the Battery."

"Happy to do it, Clay. If you still want my friendly guiding services, just let me know. I don't think I have time to go all the way out to Indigo Plantation like we discussed, but there's still a lot to see and do in historic Charleston.

"I think so, too," Clay answered. "Let's see if we can make our schedules work."

"Well, I'm off tomorrow, so if you're free to explore in the afternoon, just text me or stop by the registration desk." Grace offered.

"That could work very well. It would give me time tomorrow morning to meet with the show's organizer and review what I shoot today. I'll know more when I get there this morning. I'll look for you when I return toward the end of your shift this evening. Right now, though, I am going to be late if I don't scoot down to White Point Gardens. We'll connect later, okay?"

They parted company, and Clay drove the Lexus, which Robert had retrieved for him, down to the gardens. Along the way, he thought about his conversation with Weed. He was damn glad to have both Weed and Mace in his corner.

The South of Broad Art Fair promised to be a delightful show. The weather forecast called for a stunning Charleston day, and the setting along Charleston's Battery was admired by both artists and visitors alike.

Clay went to the show's office and met with Natalie Barrows, the show's organizer. It was the first time they had met in person, and Natalie, who was usually quite loquacious, became utterly speechless when she laid eyes on the handsome, world-renowned Clay Arnold.

"Oh, my, Mr. Arnold, it is such a pleasure to meet you," Natalie finally gushed.

"Please call me, Clay," he replied. "May I please call you Natalie?" he asked with an air of casual sophistication.

"Why, yes, of course, Clay," which she replied excitedly.

Natalie Barrows was a petite, plump woman around forty-five with bright red hair. She had developed a very successful art show production company, but, alas: her success came at the cost of her having very few meaningful, intimate relationships. Being in close proximity to Clay was very arousing to her.

They spent the next fifteen minutes discussing the photo project and the various promotional uses Natalie had in mind for Clay's images. They agreed that Clay would stop back around noon so they could take a look at some of what he'd shot.

As Clay left the Art Fair office, Natalie stared vacantly at his rear end, fanning herself with a show program as he walked away.

"Oh my," she breathed.

Clay spent the next couple of hours doing what Clay Arnold did best which was capturing the spark behind people's eyes and creating a mood with his subjects and settings.

Candid portraits of children were always easy because of their uninhibited nature. Clay was very pleased with several that he'd taken. He knew that Natalie wanted to portray the family-oriented atmosphere at her art shows.

Clay was patient and able to capture fun or fascinating images of all sorts of people; old, young, racially diverse, male, female, and a few he guessed to be transgender. Each scene held a creative opportunity, and Clay used his artistic mastery to take many compelling images.

He stopped by each artist's booth and was again reminded of the sheer number of very talented people out there. At one booth a glass artist was showing her work to a potential customer. No one but Clay noticed how the light from the glass was shining on the customer, and he took a picture that showed a glorious rainbow of colors on the customer's face.

It was just one of those wonderful artistic surprises, but Clay had a unique talent for finding them.

Clay visited many booths that morning and found something worth photographing at nearly each. He stopped at another photographer's booth and saw some very exciting black-and-white infrared images. The two photographers enjoyed comparing stories about shooting on the road.

Clay spent the next three hours touring each booth and waiting for those golden moments to snap the shutter. His patience and good eye for detail were rewarded.

Around noon Clay felt like he had quite a large file of images to review with Natalie. She had arranged for lunch to be served for them in her private office, and she looked like she had freshened up quite a bit.

"Come have a seat, Clay," Natalie invited as she patted the chair right next to hers.

They downloaded the images from Clay's camera onto Natalie's laptop so she could select the ones she liked most.

Even at just a cursory glance, Natalie could tell that Clay had taken many terrific images. She was mightily impressed, and seeing this collection of great photographs taken just that morning reminded her why she was paying him so much for his talent.

"If you want me to continue taking pictures, Natalie, I'll be happy to do so," Clay said. "I think we have some pretty good stuff as it is, but it's your call."

"Yes, yes, quite so," she said. "I agree. No need to send you out in the heat again. You are . . . I mean, these pictures are amazing."

"Why don't we do this," Clay suggested. "Why don't you take the rest of the day and tonight to review the images, and I can come by around nine tomorrow morning for us to do some further editing. Then I think we can handle much of the rest by e-mail and phone."

What Natalie really wanted to do was invite him for dinner at her hotel and let nature take its course. Instead, her bravery got stuck in her throat, and she could only say that it sounded like a good plan.

Clay bid her adieu, and she sighed as she watched his firm rear end move further and further away.

Chapter 19

W ITH BREAKFAST OVER, Mace and Weed went to Clay's brewery building and got started on their work for Clay. They rummaged through Clay's collection of spare antique camera parts in the storage closet and took them down to the sub-basement.

Mace was almost finished with the workbenches, and he and Weed laid out the available camera parts and the tools that Weed would need to craft his new weapons.

"I think we have a good enough collection of spare parts to easily convert the Stirn's Concealed Vest camera and the Ben Akiba Cane Handle camera into something that Clay can use secretly and effectively," Weed declared. "I want to have at least one very effective weapon for him when he returns from Charleston."

Mace nodded affirmatively and asked Weed what he had in mind.

"Originally," Weed began, "the Stirn's Concealed Vest camera was a flat, bronze, six-inch disk that hung around the photographer's

neck with a cord. It took six pictures on round glass plates. It was concealed beneath a vest and the camera's lens poked through a buttonhole on the vest. It looked like just another button. Another cord ran down the photographer's sleeve, which the user pulled to take a candid picture of his subject."

"My goal," Weed continued, "is to replace the interior glass photo plates with a small group of explosive projectiles that Clay can shoot through the vest with each tug of his cord. I think we can use .22-caliber bullets, which at close range would be more than adequate to seriously injure or kill a bad guy.

"We'll start with those and then see what else we can salvage for the other devices. I'll have to go to the hardware store to pick up a few items, and I'll need some timing devices and detonators, wiring, and circuits. Gotta pick up a little gun powder and some .22 rimfire cartridges, too. It shouldn't be hard to do what I'm thinking with the vest camera."

Mace again nodded his understanding and then placed a sturdy, black wooden cane on the workbench. It was made of ebony and looked like a gentleman's walking stick with an elaborately engraved steel handle.

"Ah!" Weed praised. "The Ben Akiba Cane Handle camera. Let me take a moment to read Clay's notes about it."

"Okay, says here this camera was made by a German guy named Emil Kronke in 1903. A hinged plate in the front of the handle swings downward to reveal the camera lens. For our purposes the lens will be replaced with a short gun barrel, and the handle will be converted into a pistol of sorts. It'll be mounted on the ebony cane which serves as a monopod. A very elegant, simple, stable design."

"You can really do this, Weed?" Mace asked.

"Yeah, I can do it," Weed replied. "You pretty much know me as a blues musician which is fine with me, but when I was at

MIT, I guess I showed a certain aptitude for blowing shit up with small devices. The Pentagon wanted me to work with them, and a fellow who said he was with the Bureau of Mines came to see me unannounced once. Intense guy. I don't think he was really with the Bureau of Mines."

"I never knew," Mace said.

"They all made it pretty clear," Weed admitted, "that I was never to speak of their offers of employment. I took their 'request' seriously. Clay knows, and, of course, Tori, too. So yeah, Mace, I can really do this."

"In any event, let's keep working. I figure it'll take us the rest of the morning to get everything set up," Weed said. "Why don't I run to the stores to get the supplies, and it would be great if you could erect some targets at the end of the room. I better get a bunch of ear plugs, too."

The two men talked over some construction details for a few more minutes, and then Weed took off to procure his materials.

In the silence of the sub-basement, Mace reflected on what he and Clay and Weed would be doing with the antique camera weapons. Knowing the character of his partners as he did, he was comfortable as an accessory to . . . a reckoning.

Tori led Rennie out the rear door of the farmhouse to the garden area beyond. The morning sun was above the trees in the southwest and cast its warm countenance on the young boy and his blind garden guide. Satchmo materialized out of nowhere and followed along with them.

Both Mace and Weed had helped build her garden. Instead of simply tilling one large garden plot, Mace had constructed raised beds for her. Each bed had a wooden framework around it, with pathways in between, which made it much easier for Tori to locate and work on them.

"Here we have our squash," Tori remarked. "Over there we have our watermelons and cantaloupes. Then beyond them we have our tomatoes and beans. Garlic and potatoes are over there next to the beans. And we also have various kinds of peppers and cucumbers. It's really late in the growing season, so everything needs to be picked."

"Wow," Rennie said, "I ain't never seen a garden like this with all those wooden borders around them. How do you keep track of everything?"

"Well, for one thing, since I can't see, I've developed a pretty darn good memory of where things are. Besides that, I have touched every last inch of this garden, either planting or tending to it, so I know my garden pretty well.

"Then there are some plants that I can just smell. Like Marigolds. Anyway, it works for us, and we've already harvested a lot this year. Real soon the frost will kill off everything but the heartiest of plants, and that's why I need your help in harvesting things now."

Lex came bounding into view and joined Satchmo for a morning jaunt between the raised beds. Tori had planted catnip next to the bed she reserved for herbs. Satchmo was literally rolling on the herb as if it held mystical powers. Rennie laughed at the huge feline's unabashed delight.

Tori led Rennie to each raised bed and spent the first hour giving him a lesson on what each plant was and how to care for it. She then had Rennie harvesting green beans and peppers off the vines and gently picking the tomatoes she would freeze for use later that winter.

After working for about two hours, they took a break inside the old shed that sat next to the garden. Tori kept her tools on an old workbench, and there was an old hydrant inside that was connected to the original well that the Block brothers had installed in the mid-1850s. It provided all the water Tori needed for the garden.

"How're you feeling, Rennie?" Tori asked. "Gardening doesn't look like hard work, but there's a lot of bending and stooping, and it can get to you after a while."

"I'm doing okay," Rennie replied. "My ribs are still sore, but I'm better than I was when Mace came and got me at home."

Home. The very mention of the word sounded wrong to Rennie, especially when he compared where he'd been living on Hill Street with the friendly confines of the brewery complex.

From the weight of the baskets that Rennie had filled, it was clear he had done a very good job with his first harvest.

"Wow, we got us a lot of vegetables!" Rennie said proudly.

"And, it's all really good for you, too," Tori added. "Not like that deep-fried stuff you buy at those fast-food places. Why don't we head inside and wash the vegetables, and then we'll make us some lunch. I'm starved, and I bet you are, too."

"Oh, yeah, I can eat," Rennie proclaimed.

They put their garden tools back in the shed and walked back inside the house to clean up and prepare lunch.

"Do you mind if I ask you a question?" Tori asked Rennie.

Rennie shrugged and said, "I guess so."

"Don't you ever get lonely living alone on the street?"

Even though Rennie liked Tori and was starting to feel like he could trust her, he was reluctant to answer her question at first. His loneliness was something that he chose not to talk about with others because it pointed to his vulnerability. He learned a long time ago not to show that side of himself to others. People could take advantage of you.

"Yeah, well, a little, I guess," was all he felt comfortable admitting.

"Uh huh," Tori said softly.

She decided to let Rennie take all the time he needed to talk about himself. Besides, she didn't always like to answer personal questions, either, especially about her blindness, even though most folks were just trying to be sensitive.

After they had their lunch and cleaned up the kitchen, Tori said, "I'm tuckered. Why don't we each take a brief nap in our rooms, and when we get up we can take a little hike on the trail along the White River? Lex needs some more exercise, and I think it would be good for both of us, too."

"That's sounds good to me," Rennie agreed. "I wouldn't mind resting up for a little bit. Thanks again for lunch, Tori, and for letting me work with you. I enjoyed being in the garden, and I'm looking forward to seeing the river. Never really seen a river up close before."

Tori went down the hall to her room with Satchmo in fast pursuit, and Rennie headed for the guest room with Lex at his side. It had been a healing morning for each of them, both physically and emotionally, but neither of them could foretell what lay ahead later in the afternoon.

Chapter 20

"GOLL DANG THOSE two boys," Clement muttered to himself. "I distinctly told them to come straight home, and it's morning now, and there'll still not here."

He tried calling them on his cell phone and only got the recording of some dumb-ass female saying that the person he was trying to reach was currently unavailable, and to leave a message.

"I'll leave a goddam message, all right!" Clement bellowed. "You two little pissants better get your scrawny asses back here ASAP, or they'll be hell to pay."

Meanwhile Newt and Twit Hacker were in their pickup truck heading south when Twit's phone rang.

"It's Pa," Twit said. "I really don't feel like hearing his shit right now."

"So, don't answer it," Newt advised. "He's going to be pissed at us no matter what, so we might as well put off his lecture until we get home."

Newt followed Twit's earlier suggestion that they steer clear of the interstate and take the back roads along the White River until they got further south of Indianapolis.

"I'm really getting hungry," Twit remarked, and Newt heard his own stomach starting to grumble, too.

"Maybe we can find us a fast-food joint soon. I really need me some coffee," Newt said.

The October sun rose higher in the sky, revealing a glorious day made even brighter by the autumn colors. Newt drove until he found a place for breakfast and pulled up to the drive-thru window.

"Now, mind your manners here," Newt advised. "We don't need anyone remembering us if we can help it."

After their quick stop to load up on breakfast, Newt found the entrance to the county road that ran along the White River, and he maintained the speed limit as he drove through the Streamside Country Club. The only people he saw were a few golfers in their carts. There were virtually no other drivers and no cops in sight.

"Now looky there at those faggy boys playing that sissy game," Twit guffawed. "Hey, Newt, there ain't nobody around; why don't we go mess with those boys when they get around that bend behind the trees . . . just a little fun before we get home and Pa lights into us."

"All right," Newt relented. "But I don't want us killing no one. Deal?"

"Deal," Twit agreed. "But you know I get to defend myself, too, right?"

Newt slowly drove the pickup off the road and on to the fairway. The two golfers looked up and saw the truck, which they thought was a maintenance vehicle for the country club. Newt edged to within fifty yards of the golfers and came to a stop next to a sand trap.

Twit grabbed a ball bat from behind his seat and got out of the truck's cab. He jumped up into the rear bed and erected the Confederate flag so it unfurled boldly. He surveyed the situation, looking at his prey as well as scanning for any witnesses.

"Now, take it slow and easy, Newt, and when you get within twenty yards of these pussies, gun it! I'm gonna whomp 'em with this baseball bat when you pass 'em. You know, like we used to do with the mailboxes."

"Oh, shit," was Newt's resigned reply, as he slowly began to move the truck forward.

The two golfers had just completed the eighth hole and were in their cart heading for number nine. The weather couldn't have been better, and the two men considered themselves lucky to have blown off work to play golf.

"Batter Up!" Twit hollered, and Newt began to increase the speed of the truck. Newt looked in his rearview mirror and saw his dipshit twin taking practice swings. The rebel battle flag waved fiercely.

At this point the golfer in the passenger seat saw that a grimy looking pickup was heading straight toward them.

"Uh, Walter, I think you'd better step on it," Norm encouraged. "These guys don't look like maintenance men to me."

Walter took a quick look over his shoulder and tried his best to execute an evasive maneuver. A menacing-looking pickup truck chasing a golf cart down the middle of the fairway made for a comical scene, but nobody involved was feeling any amusement.

"Gun it, brother!" came Twit's battle cry, and the truck lurched forward with fearsome speed.

Twit was damn near drooling with anticipation as Newt closed the gap between the two vehicles.

Crunch! came the sound of the ball bat on fiberglass as Twit smashed it into the cart's left-rear section.

"Dang it, Newt, get me closer next time. That sissy boy swerved away at the last second."

Newt used his brakes to create a spinning turn, and within seconds he was on the trail of the golf cart again.

The two golfers were absolutely terrified by the maniacs in the truck. Norm reached into his golf bag and retrieved his pitching wedge.

Walter saw what he had done and could only reply, "Seriously?!"

But it was too late to switch clubs. Newt had the golf cart directly in front of him, and he gunned the engine again. It emitted a guttural sound like an enraged banshee.

Thwack! came the sickening sound of the bat meeting the back of Walter's head. His eyes immediately stared blankly, and he slumped in the driver's seat.

"Yee-Yee!" Twit whooped. "I got him good, Newt!"

Norm took one look at his friend Walter's bloodied head and heaved his breakfast all over himself. The cart continued to move steadily forward under the weight of poor Walter's heavy foot and rapidly approached the large water hazard near the ninth hole.

Norm heard the pickup truck regain its traction and speed toward him for the coup de grâce. He did the only thing he could think of and stomped his foot on top of Walter's, and the cart shot forward and launched itself into the pond just as Twit was preparing to play home run derby again.

"Dang it!" Twit cried out. "Those sissy boys got away."

"Good," Newt said. "Now let's get the fuck out of here while we still can!"

The truck disappeared as quickly as it had arrived. Norm sat in shock in the passenger's seat as the cart began to submerge in the pond. He looked over at Walter's lifeless body and then at the pitching wedge still in his hands. He heard a bubbling sound and felt the water begin to soak his legs. He wondered if it had been such a good idea to blow off work after all.

Newt and Twit beat a fast exit from the country club and continued heading south on the county road running beside the White River.

Newt looked in the rearview mirror again and saw his moronic twin brother shouldering the baseball bat and grinning like he had just signed a Major League contract.

Chapter 21

TORI AND RENNIE GOT UP from their naps at about the same time. She had heard Weed's vehicle return from his trip to wherever he'd gone and figured she would see him and Mace around dinner time. She didn't know what project he and Mace were working on for Clay, but they appeared very intent on doing a lot of work today.

"Are you about ready for our little adventure along the White River?" Tori asked Rennie.

"Yes ma'am," Rennie replied.

Lex saw Tori reach for her red-tipped cane and a leash and began prancing with anticipation.

The old brewery/mill complex was located adjacent to the White River. The Block brothers had chosen this site because the river reminded them of the Rhine river in Germany, and also because the river provided an excellent means for transporting their barreled spirits.

It was a beautiful autumn afternoon, and the sunlight played a silent symphony of color.

"Listen!" Tori said to Rennie as they approached the bank of the river. "Close your eyers and listen to the sound of the wind through the trees and the flowing water."

Rennie did as Tori asked and then watched as she became enraptured by the sounds of her sightless world.

Tori breathed a deep, cleansing breath and bent down to undo Lex's leash. The happy labrador took off running and barking at nothing in particular. He just wanted the world to know he was on the job as guide and protector.

The path Tori chose was well-worn by hikers and had very few roots and rocks. Over the years Tori had come to know this path very well and was able to anticipate several natural obstructions. Despite this, she rarely ventured out here alone. She always had her cane, and Lex was never far away.

The river was stunning this time of year. The water rolled by displaying white-and-silver eruptions wherever it found an area of rocks and gravel. But it was the reflection of the vibrant colors from the leaves that gave it an almost mystical feel. Much of the river's course was within fifty yards of the road, and the foot path ran evenly between the two. Lex could be heard splashing about in the shallows.

"Mind if I go over and see the river?" Rennie asked. "I can't swim, so I'm not gonna get too close."

"Sure thing," Tori encouraged. "Lex loves the water, and he's actually a very good swimmer."

Tori sat on a large rock on the path near the road. She listened as Lex and Rennie played together by the river's edge.

"Throw a stick in the water and tell him to fetch," Tori called out. "There's a reason why Lex is called a retriever."

Rennie did as she suggested and laughed with delight when he saw the big dog dive into the water after the floating stick.

Tori smiled at the thought of this ghetto kid enjoying the great outdoors for the first time with a loyal and obedient dog. They spent the next several minutes swept up by the joy of being by the river, and Rennie and Lex slowly went on ahead of Tori's position as they innocently played.

There were still no other hikers along this section of the alluring stream, and the traffic from the nearby road was virtually nil. Tori decided to remain seated and quietly listened to the world around her.

The only sounds she heard were the winds in the trees, the rushing river, the rhythm of her own breathing, and a dog and boy bonding over a stick and flowing water. She felt at peace.

After a while Tori thought she heard a low rumbling noise that she dismissed as some vehicle way off in the distance, but eventually the noise grew steadily louder.

Newt and Twit cruised along in the pickup, with Twit feeling especially ebullient after trashing the golfers. They had no idea that they had actually killed the driver of the golf cart, but they really wouldn't have cared, either.

Twit's cell phone rang, and he saw that Pa was calling them again. This time he answered it and prepared himself for his father's verbal assault.

"Howdy Pa," Twit said cheerfully. "How're you doing today?"

"How the hell do you think I'm doing, you freakin' sack of frog turds!" came Clement's strident reply. "I told you and your worthless brother to come right home. Where the hell are you?"

"Oh, Pa," Twit said evenly. "We're still north of Indy. We thought we'd try our hand at a little golf," he lied.

"Golf?! What in the sweet lord's name are you doing playing golf?"

"Well, we sorta invented a new game. It was a combination of golf and baseball," he giggled.

Clement had no idea what his son was talking about and really didn't care about their recreation.

"Now, I told you two to get home, and I mean it! I want to hear about your recon mission of the insurance building and the hospital. We've got plans to make, and I need your asses back here now. Understand?!"

"Yes, Pa, whatever you say. We should be home in about two hours."

They ended the call, and Newt looked over at his twin brother. He just shook his head in disbelief at the way he fibbed to their daddy.

The twins continued on south along the county road until they reached a turn off for the White River Road.

"I'm turning here," Newt said. We'll have more places to hide, if need be, and I recall that there are some pretty isolated places just up ahead."

"Sounds good to me, brother. Let's just blend in and enjoy the view," Twit agreed.

It was mid-afternoon now, and the river road made a steady transition from its course through gentle rolling farmland to occasional locust and walnut groves to a denser forest with a canopy of autumn splendor overhead.

Even Newt and Twit were affected by the change of scenery. With no one behind him, Newt reduced his speed to enjoy the scenery.

"Hey, hold up, Newt!" Twit declared. "Who's that up ahead on that path?"

"Slow down, Newt, I wanna take a look."

"Sure enough, Newt, it's a girl, and she's sitting there all by herself. Pull up over there so I can get a better look."

Newt did as his brother requested and was rewarded with Twit's gleeful declaration, "Ooo, she's a pretty one!"

Tori had certainly heard the truck coming from a half-mile away but didn't give it much thought. Now that the harsh-sounding truck was close by with its engine turned off, she became alert.

"Well, hi there, little lady," came Twit's most charming greeting. "What're you doing out here all by yourself? Pretty thing like you."

"I'm enjoying the day, and I'm not here by myself. Is there something I can help you with?"

"Well," Newt interjected, "we'll just be on our way. C'mon brother."

"Now, not so fast, Newt. Seems like the pretty lady just asked if there was anything she could do to help. Isn't that right, pretty lady?"

Tori's senses were now on high alert, and she held her cane at her side in a defensive posture. Another move by either of these guys and she would start screaming bloody murder.

"Her cane's got a red tip, Twit," Newt pointed out. "She's blind."

"Oh, you're blind!" Twit parroted. "And you're out here all by yourself, looks like. Looks like party time to me, brother."

"You get out of here now," Tori seethed with fire, and then she began screaming at the top of her lungs.

"Quick, grab her, Newt. Don't let her get away."

Newt lunged forward, and Tori went into the warrior pose she had learned in martial arts class and made a fierce, sweeping motion with her cane. The cane caught Newt along the left side of his face, and he went down to his knees emitting a keening cry.

Tori continued to scream and used her acute hearing skills to determine the location of her attackers.

Newt was recovering slowly from the surprise blow, and Twit went on the attack.

Tori faced his direction, and screamed, "Lex! Lex!"

She heard him bark in the distance. He was coming. Rennie, too.

Twit made a fast, low move and dodged the sweep of her cane. He moved quickly again and made a vicious low kick at Tori's shin. He connected and she went down very hard, hitting her head.

Now there were arms and legs flying everywhere as Newt and Twit tried to subdue her, and Tori was hellbent on preventing that.

She screamed at the top of her lungs, "Lex!!!"

Tori barely heard Rennie's voice calling her name because it was drowned out by the snarling sound of an attacking dog.

Lex tore into Twit, who had been trying to rip off Tori's jacket. Lex's assault was ferocious in its violence and bloodcurdling in its sound.

"Get it off," Twit bellowed, but Lex tore at his hands and forearms. "Get it off!"

Tori continued to kick and claw for her life, and she and Lex were hanging in there for everything it was worth.

Newt regained his composure and pulled his pistol from his holster. He was trying to get a straight shot at the beast, when from out of nowhere, this kid came charging in with a stout tree limb and whacked Newt hard between his shoulder blades.

Newt lurched forward from Rennie's blow, and the gun went off, striking Lex in the hind leg. The poor dog let out a sad yelp and fell away. Tori intuited what had happened to Lex, and she renewed her rage like a protective mother.

Newt ran over and grabbed Twit by the back of his shirt and pulled him off of Tori.

"Twit, goddamnit, we gotta get out of here! People could've heard the gunshot, and the cops are looking for us, anyway. We gotta go! Now!"

Twit reluctantly got up, and they both ran for the truck.

"Yeah, you better run!" Rennie yelled after them.

The truck roared to life and produced a rooster-tail of dirt and gravel as it sped away, heading south on White River Road.

Rennie ran over to Tori and saw that she was having some trouble moving. Lex was bleeding from his leg and seemed to be in a state of shock.

"Oh, Tori, are you okay?" was all that Rennie could muster to say. He was scared.

"My head hurts, and I don't feel too well, Rennie. Help Lex. And, here: take my cell phone and call Mace and Weed. Tell them we're on the path by the rock I like to sit on. They'll know where."

She took the phone first and felt the braille buttons for speed-dialing Weed. Then she handed the phone to Rennie to talk.

"Help Lex," she managed to say and then passed out.

Weed answered the phone on the second ring and was surprised to hear Rennie's frantic voice.

"Weed, it's Rennie. You gotta come quick. We're down by the river and we got attacked by some rednecks. Tori's hurt bad. She said her head hurts and she passed out. Lex got shot in the leg. He's bleeding bad. Tori said to tell you we're on the path by the sittin' rock."

Mace had been standing next to Weed and heard Rennie's plea. Within seconds he was out the door of the sub-basement running for his first aid kit and his old truck. Weed was just a few steps behind him trying to get Rennie to calm down.

"Do what you can for Lex, but stay on the phone, Rennie. We're on our way," Weed said.

Mace's old truck flew out of the courtyard, and the men made a beeline for the river road. Given their knowledge of the trail along the river, Weed and Mace knew exactly where they were heading and wasted no time in getting there in under five minutes.

"Oh, no!" Weed said as he saw Tori and Lex lying on the ground with Rennie standing guard in case the rednecks returned.

Mace immediately went to tend to Lex's injuries, and Weed kneeled in the dirt next to Tori and cradled her head.

"Mace, please call 911 and have them meet us at our place," Weed said.

"She's not responsive right now, but her breathing seems to be okay."

Mace placed the call, and then he brought the truck closer to the path. He and Weed carefully lifted Tori into the bed of the truck along with Lex. Weed rode in the truck bed with them, and Rennie rode in the cab with Mace.

"Tell me what happened, Rennie," Mace directed.

"Me and Lex were playing along the river, and Tori was sitting on the rock. We were playing fetch with a stick and had moved down the river a little ways. All of a sudden we heard Tori screaming for Lex. We came running, and there were these two trashy looking white men in a dark pickup truck with a flag that had weird bars and stars on it. They attacked Tori. She tried to defend herself with her cane."

"Lex tore into one of them, and the other man shot him in the leg. I tried to break it up with that big stick, and they took off after they shot Lex. Then Tori dialed your number and gave me the phone. That's pretty much what happened."

"Do you think you'd recognize these jerks or their truck again?" Mace asked Rennie.

"Yeah, I think so. The men both looked alike, and like I said, the truck had that old redneck flag. Are Tori and Lex gonna be okay?"

"I sure hope so," Mace lamented. "It looks like Lex has lost a lot of blood, and Tori probably has a concussion. They both need medical attention."

Two minutes after they arrived back at the brewery complex, the EMTs arrived and carefully examined Tori and Lex. They tended to Lex's injury as best they could and managed to stop his bleeding.

"We've done what we can for the dog, but he's gonna need to see a vet," the lead EMT said. "But first we have to get the young lady to the hospital. We think she's suffered a concussion, but otherwise her vital signs appear to be stable."

Weed jumped into the rear of the emergency transport vehicle to ride with Tori to Conner Prairie Hospital's ER. It was the same place that Trent was taken when he was shot at Stella's Diner.

Mace and Rennie called ahead to the vet's office to let them know they were on their way. All things considered, it could have been far worse.

"You helped saved their lives, Rennie," Mace said to the young boy. "Thank you."

"I was scared and mad, is all," Rennie replied softly. "I didn't want them hurting my friends."

Mace looked over at Rennie and gave his shoulder a reassuring squeeze.

"You did good, young man," Mace said. "You did really good."

Chapter 22

CLAY WOKE UP AROUND seven o'clock and took his time cleaning up and organizing his camera gear. He walked through the lobby and waved a friendly greeting to Grace, who was currently busy at the front desk helping guests check out.

He enjoyed a leisurely breakfast in the Veranda restaurant and reviewed the images he'd saved on his camera. The television in the adjacent bar room was turned to a local news station, and his ears immediately perked up when the news anchor reported a breaking story about the apparent murder of a man named Jefferson Talbot who was found dead in an old cemetery in the city's historic district.

The newsman reported that the cause of death was being withheld pending the coroner's exam, but that the deceased had the initials KKK carved into his forehead. Clay knew it was only a matter of time before the story broke nationally.

Clay glanced at the chair at the bar that Jefferson Talbot had occupied two days before and smiled a mirthless smile to himself.

"That's one bigot who won't be terrorizing anyone anymore," he murmured to himself.

Clay finished his breakfast and stopped by the front desk to talk with Grace.

"I've got to head down to White Point Gardens in a few minutes to review the images I shot at the art fair yesterday with the show's organizer. When I'm finished I'll come back to the Inn, and we can see when you're free to continue our exploring," Clay offered.

"Looking forward to it very much," Grace replied enthusiastically.

Robert had retrieved Clay's car for him and was standing next to it when Clay emerged from the Inn.

"I understand our friend Jefferson Talbot met an untimely death recently," Robert remarked to Clay.

"Yeah," Clay said. "I just saw that on the morning news. Pity, huh?"

Robert and Clay held each other's steady gaze for a second, and then Clay left before another word was spoken.

It was another gorgeous day in Charleston, and Clay enjoyed his brief drive down East Bay Street. He looked out across Charleston's harbor and saw Fort Sumter in the distance.

He reflected on the Fort's historic significance as the site of the first military action of the Civil War. He wondered how far America had truly come as a freedom-loving nation when the vitriol toward persons of color remained so prevalent more than 150 years later. He was very pleased that a person like Jefferson Talbot would never utter another hateful word.

Clay arrived promptly at nine o'clock for his scheduled meeting with Natalie Barrows. Anticipating the opportunity to be with Clay again, she made sure that she would not be interrupted with art-show details.

Her assistant was a young woman named Heather McGinnis, and Natalie had the poor woman in a tizzy with a gazillion spur-of-the-moment tasks. Natalie was clearly excited, and whenever she got excited about something or someone, she tended to bark orders about trivial stuff. Heather was bearing the brunt of Natalie's excitement this morning.

"Good morning, Clay," she sang out when Clay entered her office. "It's such a lovely morning. Why, it almost feels like love is in the air, don't you think?"

"Yes, it is a very lovely morning, and you seem very cheerful," Clay said politely. "I take it you feel the art show is going very well."

"Yes, the show is proceeding quite well. We've had good crowds and the artists are reporting brisk sales. Plus, I have the world-famous Clay Arnold doing his photographic magic for me. Here, come have a seat by me, and we'll discuss your images in more detail."

Natalie patted the seat of the nearby chair, and Clay took it and moved it a few inches away, ostensibly for more elbow room.

"I take it you've had an opportunity to study the images I shot of the art fair yesterday?" Clay asked professionally.

"Yes, indeed I have, Clay, and as I mentioned yesterday when we took a cursory glance, I see some things that are very exciting to me."

Clay wasn't sure, but he thought he saw Natalie wink at him as she moved shoulder-to-shoulder with him.

Clay maintained his position, and he began pointing to several images that he thought were special given the parameters of the assignment.

Natalie cooed her concurrence. She shifted in her chair and brought her ample bosom to rest on top of Clay's forearm. He literally had to hold back a smile at the thought that Natalie Barrows was actually putting the moves on him at nine-fifteen in the morning.

"You know, Clay," she said steamily, "I'm free for dinner this evening, and I would be delighted to treat you, provided you're available, of course."

"Well, uh, I might be," he began.

But then he was saved by his phone's ringtone, and he rose to answer it. It was Weed.

"Natalie, would you please excuse me a moment? I need to take this call from home."

He didn't wait for her reply but stepped outside her office for more privacy, and to forestall the romantic launch sequence that Natalie had attempted to initiate.

"Hey, Weed, what's going on?" Clay asked innocently. "Everything okay?"

"No," came Weed's one-word answer.

Clay stood stone still and waited for his friend to go on.

"Yesterday afternoon Tori and Rennie and Lex were attacked on the trail by the White River."

"How bad?" Clay asked softly.

"Could've been worse, but bad enough," Weed stated. "I'm at Conner Prairie Hospital now. The EMTs brought us to the ER here, and she was admitted for observation. At the very least, Tori has a concussion. Two 'rednecks', as Rennie called them, attacked her on the trail. Rennie and Lex had gone upstream a little ways to play, and these two assholes showed up and tried to take her."

Clay closed his eyes and hung his head as he heard Weed continue to speak.

"Lex got shot in the leg, and Mace and Rennie rushed him to the vet, but I haven't had a chance to connect with them yet today. I'll call them when I get off the phone with you.

"Oh, man," Clay managed to say. "I'm about finished here in Charleston, and I'll make arrangements to get the first flight I can back to Indy. I'll call you and let you know when I'm scheduled to arrive."

"I'm really sorry, Weed," Clay continued. "I am so sorry Tori got hurt, and Lex, too. How's Rennie doing with all of this?"

"Rennie seems okay," Weed reported, "but it was very upsetting to him, too. He told me he saw Tori swing her cane at one of the attackers, and apparently she smacked a bad guy in the head really well. Rennie told me he clubbed that same guy with a big branch, and I think that turned the tide in the fight. Unfortunately, Tori got thrown to the ground hard and hit her head, and Lex got shot during the attack."

Clay's blood began to simmer with rage. "I'll get home as soon as I can, Weed. Will you please keep me informed, and if you get a moment will you also go and see Trent? I can't imagine he's been discharged yet, given the seriousness of his gunshot wound."

"Will do, Clay, but I need to get off the phone now," Weed said. "The nurse said the doctor wants to speak with me."

They hung up, and Clay stood very still processing everything Weed had told him about the attack. He placed a quick call to his agent Lily and asked her to book a flight back to Indy for him. Then he turned to go back to Natalie's office.

"So, as I was saying," Natalie started, "I would be happy to treat you to dinner and other earthly delights."

"Natalie, I am very sorry, but the phone call I just took was not good news. Some very close friends of mine were brutally attacked, and I really need to return home. I'm afraid we're going to have to take a rain check on dinner. I think we can handle anything else you need by phone or e-mail. I'll call you in a day or so to follow-up."

"Why, yes, of course," Natalie replied. "I hope your friends will be okay."

Clay gave her shoulder a friendly squeeze and thanked her for being so understanding. She watched as he turned to leave and lamented that she wouldn't get to squeeze him in return.

"Well," she muttered to herself, "a phone call or e-mail may take care of business, but not everything else I had in mind."

Natalie's assistant Heather saw Clay leave hurriedly and noticed the disappointed look on Natalie's face. She had a sinking feeling it wasn't going to be an easy day for her.

Clay arrived back at the Ventana Inn several minutes later and asked Robert to please keep his car at curbside. He received a text from Lily who informed him he was booked on a 1:00 PM flight back to Indy.

Grace saw Clay enter the Inn and commented, "Wow, that was quick work at the art fair."

"I received a very disturbing phone call from home about some close friends who were attacked yesterday afternoon. I'm very sorry, Grace, but I need to return to Indianapolis to be with them. Obviously, that means we won't be able to get together later today. I was really looking forward to it, and I hope you won't think me terribly rude for leaving."

Clay could see the look of disappointment on her face.

"No, of course not," she said supportively. "I'll prepare your bill for you while you're getting your belongings."

Clay rushed to his room and returned to the front desk five minutes later.

"I'm very sorry, Grace. This wasn't how I wanted my trip here to end. Maybe we can get together again on a return visit to Charleston," Clay added. She leaned forward and kissed him on the cheek and nodded yes.

Chapter 23

Four hours later Clay pulled his Tacoma into the courtyard at home. Both Mace and Rennie came outside to meet him.

"Hey, Mace. What's the good word?" Clay asked hopefully.

"Hello to you, too, my friend. The good word is that Tori's going to recover. It'll take a little time, but the doctor plans to release her in a couple of days to recuperate at home. Physically, they don't expect any long-term damage from the head injury. Emotionally, it may take a little time longer.

"Weed called me last night from the hospital, and he's concerned, not to mention very angry. His concern is that the attack may shake her confidence. We all know Tori is a very capable person, but being attacked and having to fight blind would be very unsettling to say the least. So we need to be sensitive to that."

"She's a tough lady," Rennie added. "I was still a little ways away when she got attacked, but I saw her whomp that redneck up the side of his head with her cane. She kicked his ass!"

Clay and Mace couldn't help but smile at Rennie's frankness.

"I want to get cleaned up a little and put some things away," Clay said, "and then I want to go to the hospital to see Tori and Trent. You guys wanna come?"

"Yeah!" Mace said. "Rennie, would you be okay staying here with Lex and Satchmo for a couple of hours?"

"Oh damn! I forgot to ask about Lex. How is he?" Clay cried out.

"He's missing a leg now," Rennie stated bluntly.

"What?!" Clay shouted.

"They shot him, but, boy—you should've seen how Lex tore into that man who was trying to hurt Tori. I thought he was going to eat him! Then he got shot."

"The bullet did a lot of damage to his hind quarter," Mace said, "too much for the vet to repair. So, he had to take the leg. Lex is alive and on the mend here at my place, but he's hurt bad."

"I want to see him before we go, Mace," Clay said. "Gimme fifteen minutes, and I'll stop in, okay?"

Clay headed for his home in the old brewhouse, and Mace and Rennie went inside Mace's power plant to check on Lex.

Lex was lying on his left side on a woven oval carpet in front of Mace's wood-burning stove. His right hip area had a large bandage, and he was asleep. Satchmo was curled up sleeping next to Lex as they had often done before.

"Rennie, I've been so concerned about Tori and Lex that I've neglected to ask how you're feeling."

"I'm okay. My ribs are still sore, but I'm okay."

"So," Mace began, "you're comfortable taking care of Lex and the wood stove while I'm gone? If Lex needs to go outside, will you be careful and patient with him?"

"Yeah, yeah," Rennie said. "I can do it, Mace. We'll be cool. Go on with Clay and see Tori and that policeman. We'll be fine here."

Mace looked closely at Rennie to see if he was being completely honest about feeling comfortable taking care of things. Mace saw sincerity in the young man's eyes.

"I want to ask you something else, too," Mace said. "When I get back from the hospital, do you want me to run you back to your place on Hill Street?"

So much had happened to Rennie in the last two days that he hadn't really even thought about Hill Street.

"Oh, that. No, I'd really like to stay here with all of you. You know, help y'all out. If that's okay with you, Mace."

"I think the way you helped save Tori and Lex's lives might've removed any question about you staying with us, my young friend. I guess we're a little unusual here. Except for Weed and Tori, none of us are blood relatives, but we have a very special bond. We don't take that bond lightly, and you need to know that."

Rennie nodded his head affirmatively. "I'm good with that," he added. "You can count on me, Mace."

A few moments later a knock was heard on the front door to the power plant and Clay came in. He kneeled down next to Lex and gently stroked his flank. He placed the back of his hand up to Lex's nose so the drowsy dog could smell his scent. He lightly stroked the top of his head and whispered soothing words to his wounded friend.

Satchmo yawned and purred when Clay scratched gently behind his ears, then promptly fell back to sleep.

"Rennie says he's got everything covered for us while we're at the hospital; so I'm ready when you are, Clay."

"Thanks, Rennie. Thanks for taking care of our buddy here. We'll catch up when we get back," Clay said gratefully.

Mace made sure that Rennie knew what he had available for food, and then he and Clay climbed into his truck for the drive to the hospital.

"It's been a helluva couple of days," Mace said. "I'm glad you're back."

Clay looked over at his old friend and shook his head in disbelief and anger.

"First Jennifer, then Trent, and now Tori, Lex, and Rennie," Clay said solemnly. "Did you and Weed have a chance to work on things in the sub-basement while I was gone?"

"We made some good progress, and Weed has come up with some very clever designs with the parts from your old cameras. And now that Tori and Lex have been hurt, I imagine he's going to really want to get you outfitted with some killer stuff."

They drove silently the rest of the way to Conner Prairie Hospital, but their silence was deafening. Each man knew what the other was thinking. The evening was about to come.

Chapter 24

CLAY AND MACE ARRIVED at the hospital around 6:30 PM and went straight to the information desk to get room numbers for Tori and Trent. They were directed to the fifth floor in the patient tower, room 514. The door to Tori's room was closed as they approached, and Mace knocked lightly on it.

Weed opened it a moment later, and his eyes lit up when he saw his two close friends standing in the light of the doorway.

"Oh, Clay! Man, am I glad to see you!" Weed said with an air of relief. "Mace, how's Lex doing, and Rennie?"

Weed looked exhausted. He was physically and emotionally spent. He hadn't left Tori's side since picking her up from the trail, except when the hospital staff took her for some scans.

"How's she doing, Weed?" Clay asked. "What do the doctors say?"

"She's seems to be doing better. They gave her a mild sedative, and she slept pretty well through the night. The nurses came in

a couple of times to check on her, and they seemed satisfied with how she was doing."

"The doctors say she suffered a concussion, and—barring any setbacks—they'll probably dismiss her tomorrow."

"Weed," came Tori's plaintive voice. "Who else is here, Weed?"

Tori had regained consciousness and was trying to get her bearings.

"It's me and Mace, Tori. You know, the two best-looking guys in the world," Clay said brightly.

A small smile formed on Tori's lips, and Clay leaned forward and kissed her lightly on the forehead. Mace followed suit, and Tori tried to bring her arms up into a big hug around both men.

"I called the nurse," Weed joked, "to get these two vagrants tossed out, but it didn't work, so I guess we're stuck with them."

"Thanks for coming, guys," Tori said with a tear in her eye. "You know I never want to be a bother."

"Nothing could keep any of us away, Tori. You know that," Mace said softly.

"How's Lex? Where's Rennie? Are they okay?"

The more alert Tori became, the more details she remembered about the attack.

Weed and Clay looked to Mace to answer her questions.

"Lex was shot in the leg, and the vet couldn't save it. Lex should recover with some loving care, but we are now the proud caregivers of a three-legged labrador."

"I'm so sorry," she sobbed. "He was so brave! When I was attacked, I kept calling his name, and he came out of the brush with a fury that I never felt possible coming from him. Then I heard the gunshot and his yelp. I don't think I would be alive today if it weren't for Lex and Rennie."

The three men looked at each other and voiced their understanding.

"So, would you guys do me a favor?" Tori asked of Clay and Mace. "When you leave, would you kindly take Weed with you, so he can get rested and cleaned up?"

"Now, Tori," Weed began to say, but Tori had regained some of her strength and silenced him with the wave of her raised hand.

"Weed, you've been great. You're the best brother a woman could have, but it's time for you to look after yourself now. I'll still be here in the morning; so skedaddle. The nurses will know to call you if anything happens, which it won't, so let a beautiful woman get some rest, okay?"

Weed abided by his sister's wishes, and after a few more minutes of talking about her condition and reassuring themselves that it was all right to go, they left Tori in room 514 and went to find their good friend Trent.

Detective Trent Reynolds lay in his hospital bed staring at the television set with the sound muted. When the EMTs brought him to the ER after the attack at Stella's, he was rushed into surgery.

After the surgical team worked to repair his decimated shoulder, he spent the next two days in the intensive care unit under heavy sedation. Just today he had been brought to a medical/surgical nursing unit where he was receiving close attention.

Trent surveyed his surroundings and was dismayed to see heavy bandages on his upper torso and tubes sticking into his body. He saw the IV drip and lifted the bed sheets and saw a catheter. He cringed briefly.

His shoulder felt very stiff, but given the intravenous pain medication he was receiving, he didn't feel much discomfort. In fact, he didn't feel much of anything, except sadness for the other people who had been hurt and disappointment that he hadn't been able to subdue the attackers at Stella's.

The gun shot to his shoulder at close range had been very destructive, and the doctors were surprised that he even survived the trauma.

Despite the surgical team's best efforts, the lead surgeon had told him earlier in the day not to expect a full recovery.

Trent knew his career was going to change dramatically, and he wondered whether he would ever be the same man again. He closed his eyes and tried not to think about it.

There was a soft knock on the door, and Trent expected it would be his nurse checking on him. He chose to keep his eyes closed and hoped his pain meds would carry him away to another place.

In the quiet of his room, he heard his visitor set something on his night table, and through bleary eyes he recognized a small bouquet of flowers.

He heard his visitor preparing to leave, and he asked, "Who is it?"

"Trent, are you awake?" the soft voice answered. "It's me, Abby West, from Stella's. I can come back another time if you're not up for a visit."

Trent shifted his position in bed and opened his eyes more to bring himself back to full wakefulness.

"Oh, Abby! Of course, I remember now. You tried to help me when I got shot. How did you know I was here?" Trent asked innocently.

"The EMTs told me they were bringing you here, and I wanted to see how you're getting along. I thought these flowers might brighten your spirits a bit."

"That is very kind of you, Abby. I've never had anyone bring me flowers before." He managed a smile and said, "Maybe I should get shot more often."

"You were awfully brave jumping on that truck like you did. I am very sorry you got hurt so bad. Stella and I both know you saved a lot of lives. For what's it's worth, we made sure that point was well noted in our report for the police. She plans to come and see you very soon."

"I appreciate that, Abby. Stella's a mighty fine woman. You, too."

Abby had just asked Trent when he thought he might be discharged when another knock came on his door. This time Clay's face peeked through a crack in the door, followed by Mace and Weed, who gently pushed their way into the room to see the patient.

"Oh, Jesus, somebody please call Security," Trent said when he saw his three old friends standing at the foot of his bed.

"Didn't they teach you nothing at the state police academy?" Weed chimed in. "You're the guy who's supposed to do the shooting; not get yourself damn near killed."

As numb as he was feeling, Trent was very happy that these guys had come to see him. He didn't have a lot of close people in his life, and this was a special moment for him.

"Abby, I believe you may know these three juvenile delinquents who stand before us," Trent stated amicably.

She smiled and nodded affirmatively. "It's good to see you all again."

A brief, awkward silence ensued, and Abby said to Trent, "Listen, why don't you visit with your friends, and we can catch up when you get out, okay?"

Trent looked directly into Abby's eyes and thanked her very much for coming to see him. "I'd like that, Abby. Thanks again for the flowers."

Abby said goodbye to Weed, Mace, and Clay and slipped out of the room as quietly as she had entered.

After the door closed, Trent squared his sights on his friends and said, "Don't give me any shit, guys. She was just being nice. Nothing more."

"Did we say anything?" Mace said with feigned innocence.

Clay changed the subject. "How're you feeling, Trent?"

"They've got me so doped up, I'm not sure what I'm feeling yet. It's probably gonna hurt like a motherfucker for a while, I suspect."

Trent's three visitors selected chairs and gathered around his bed. Over the next fifteen minutes they talked about the attack at Stella's. Trent gave a blow-by-blow account, including good descriptions of the truck and the two attackers.

"I think they're brothers, maybe twins, because they looked a lot alike. The truck was a black, unmarked pickup. The one guy tried to push me off the truck with a Confederate flag, and then the prick shot me."

Clay and Mace quietly listened to his account, and then Weed picked up the conversation.

"There's been another attack, Trent. This time Tori was nearly raped on the trail along the White River. She got roughed up and ended up with a concussion. She's here at Conner Prairie Hospital. Two floors below you."

Trent closed his eyes and shook his head.

"No, not Tori. Is she all right?"

"Yeah, I think so," Weed said. "It may take a little time to regain her confidence, but she's a strong woman, and we'll all help look after her until she's back to being Tori again."

"There's something else I've been thinking about, Clay," Trent said tentatively. "I'm not so sure that the assholes who attacked the Diner and Tori aren't the same guys who bombed the Planned Parenthood Center and killed Jennifer."

Clay stared at Trent stonily. "What makes you think that?" Clay asked evenly.

"Just a hunch, my friend—nothing I have hard evidence for, but the description of the dark truck and the Confederate flag sounds very close to what the videotape at the convenience store recorded."

"Any way you look at it," Trent continued, "we need to stop these neanderthals. They enjoy hurting people too much."

Clay was very tempted to begin telling Trent what he planned to do to bad guys with Weed and Mace's help, but he respected that Trent had taken a solemn oath as a law enforcement officer. He didn't think it was appropriate, or even advisable, to be totally frank with him.

The men commiserated for about another ten minutes, and then a nurse entered the room to check on Trent.

"Visitors' hours are almost over for the day, gentlemen. Detective Reynolds needs his rest."

The men took that as their cue to leave and told Trent they'd check back with him very soon.

"I appreciate you guys coming to see me," Trent said. "It means a lot."

The ride back to the brewery complex was subdued. Mace drove the old truck. Weed was emotionally exhausted, and Clay simmered with anger.

They agreed to meet early in the morning in the sub-basement. They had urgent work to do.

Chapter 25

CLEMENT HACKER MUTTERED to himself as he worked alone in his pole barn.

"Oh, Ella Marie, I swear to you those goddamn doctors and insurance crooks are gonna pay for your dying. Sons of bitches, all of them!"

In his more rational moments, Clement knew that his late wife would not approve of the violence that he and the boys were committing in the name of justice and the Lord, but he was beyond consolation. Besides, to Clement there had been plenty of other reasons in life to be pissed off enough to harm people he didn't care for.

"And those fuck nuts in Washington. Throw them in with the whole lot of the other greedy bloodsuckers. They talk about all this trickle-down economic horse shit, and about the only thing trickling down on the little guy is horse shit."

Clement knew he had to be smart about his crusade against the establishment. He knew the law was already hot on their tails,

and those twin sons of his had just complicated his plans one-hundred-fold by shooting the cop and whatever else they'd done.

Some thirty minutes later Clement heard a familiar rumble as Newt and Twit finally arrived back home in their dark pickup.

"Oooeee, Pa!" Twit squealed. "We had us a highly successful reconnaissance trip, didn't we, Newt?"

"Uh, sure did, Pa," Newt said evenly.

"You boys know I wanted you home yesterday, don't ya? You boys know the cops are after you, don't ya? You know we got to finish making plans to get those people who killed your ma, don't ya?"

"Well, sure, Pa," Twit started, but Clement shut him down with a stare that could melt steel.

"Now, get over here," Clement snapped, "and tell me everything, and I mean everything, about the recon mission to the insurance company and the hospital, and anything else you boys have been up to."

"Yessir, Pa," Newt said in submission. "Well, we went to both places like you said and took some pictures for you to see. The Hoosier Homestead Insurance Company's office building is a real solid-looking, twelve-story structure. You can see here that it's got a large parking garage underneath the building."

"Conner Prairie Hospital is huge," Newt continued, "so we took pictures from different angles: the main entrance, the ER entrance, the outpatient entrance, and the patient tower. Big complex with lots of places to do damage."

Clement closely studied each picture and took his time figuring out where and how he wanted to deliver the fertilizer bombs.

"You boys done good. I think you got me pretty much what I need to make some decisions. And, in case you're wondering, I do, indeed, intend for us to blow both places to kingdom come."

In truth, the boys had always figured it would be one building or the other, but Twit in particular saw the beauty in his pa's thinking.

"Lordy, lordy!" Twit chirped "We're gonna have us a hootenanny!"

"All right, then," Clement said officiously. "Tell me what the hell else you boys got into while you were up north. And what's this crap about playing golf?"

Newt and Twit just stared blankly at each other, neither one wanting to be the first to speak.

"Well, Pa," Twit began, "it was like this. Me and Newt were driving along this county road trying to be real smart and stay away from the cops, and we came across a golf course. We saw two sissy-looking boys playing golf, and well, Pa, you could just tell by looking at their clothes and all that they were sissy boys."

"So, I says to Newt that if you were with us you'd want to teach those faggot sinners a thing or two, so we did."

"You did what?" Clement asked seriously.

"Well, Newt was driving, see, and I got in the bed of the truck with my baseball bat and played a little home run derby in the Lord's name. It took me two swings, but I split that boy's head like a melon. They were riding in this golf cart thing, and dang if it didn't end up sinking in a pond with that other sinner in it."

Clement Hacker closed his eyes and thanked the Lord that Ella Marie was no longer around to hear what her lovely sons had done.

"You realize, of course, we really got to lay low for a while now," Clement scolded. "The owners of the golf course where those sissy boys play is gonna be hopping mad about you killing someone on their property. And believe me, the cops are gonna be looking under every rock for you."

"Well, yeah, but nobody saw us, and Newt and I were just doing what we thought you'd want us to do," Twit fibbed.

"What else?" Clement demanded. "What else did you boys do when you were up that way?"

"Well," Twit began again, "we sorta roughed up this young woman we saw on a trail between the road and the White River. Had to shoot her dog."

"You what?" Clement bellowed.

"She was blind, too, Pa. My genius brother tried to rape a blind woman," Newt said.

"Well, Mr. Fancy Perfect, thanks for throwing me under the bus with Pa," Twit whined.

"You attacked a blind woman?" Clement said with incredulity in his voice.

"Would've gotten her too, Pa, if that little nigger boy hadn't whomped Newt with a log. Newt's gun went off and shot the dog. We figured we better get away before the cops showed up. So we did."

"Holy mother of God!" Clement wailed.

"Now listen up, you two," Clement went on. "We all need to lay low for a while and let things cool down. I want you staying close to home for a couple of weeks. It'll take us that long anyway to make up enough ANFO for both buildings. You hear what I'm saying?"

"Yes, Pa," came the twins' submissive response. "We were just doing what we thought you'd want."

"Well, quit thinking, dammit! Let me do the thinking, and I'll let you two know when it's time for your part of the mission. Are we clear on that?!"

"Yes, Pa," Newt and Twit said in practiced unison; but somehow Clement wasn't exactly sure he could trust their word.

Chapter 26

CLAY AWOKE EARLY the next morning and lay in bed thinking about all of the pain that he and his friends had endured at the hands of some very ignorant and nasty people.

He was relieved that Tori was going to be okay and that Trent was at least alive. In his mind, however, their survival was the positive tip of an emotional iceberg that belied the anger he felt just below the surface.

From out of nowhere Satchmo materialized on his bed like a ghost.

"There you are, my friend. I could sure take some lessons about stealth and hunting from you, couldn't I, big fella?"

Satchmo purred loudly and rubbed his cheek against Clay's chin. The two of them watched the sun break over the eastern horizon and bring clarity to Clay's world.

"Well, c'mon now. We've got things we got to do," he said to himself as much as to Satchmo.

Clay put coffee on to brew and then went off to the bathroom to clean up. He also answered an e-mail that his agent Lily had sent to him regarding photography assignments he had coming up in various cities.

Fifteen minutes later he let Satchmo outside to continue his appointed rounds of the brewery complex, and then he took the elevator down to the sub-basement.

Clay was not surprised to see Mace already there sweeping up detritus from Weed's machinations on the weaponry and putting targets up at the far end of the room.

"G'morning, Mace. You're up early as usual. How's Lex doing this morning?"

"I think he's doing a little better every day," Mace said. "Rennie and I carried him outside so he could do his business, and Rennie agreed to keep a close eye on him while you and Weed and I work down here."

"So, what do you think, Mace? Is Rennie going to hook up permanently with our merry band of miscreants?"

"Well, I'm not exactly sure what a miscreant is, but, yeah: I think we have a new, loyal member of the tribe. I think he's feeling a special bond with Tori and Lex given what they went through together."

A few moments later they heard the quiet hum of the elevator descending, and Weed exited with a cup of strong coffee in his hand and a weak smile on his face.

"Morning, gents," he said as he approached Mace and Clay. "I trust you fellas got a decent night's rest."

"I called the nurse's station a few minutes ago to check on Tori," Weed reported. "Apparently she slept well through the night, and the doctor just left her room. They're thinking seriously about discharging her later this afternoon, so I'm hoping we can get a lot of work accomplished down here before I need to go get her."

"Wow, you guys made some fast progress down here while I was in Charleston," Clay said enthusiastically. "Did you get an opportunity to finish any pieces for me?"

Weed and Mace smiled and pulled the cloth cover off of the workbench to show Clay what they'd created.

"The man's a genius!" Mace said about Weed. "He basically took pieces of some of your leftover antique cameras and made what we think will be very effective weapons for you. We were preparing to test-fire two in particular this morning."

"Ah, yes!" Weed exclaimed with caffeinated enthusiasm. "Allow me to introduce the new, improved, and highly lethal Stirn's Concealed Vest camera."

Weed opened a wooden box and placed the five-inch round metal disk on the countertop.

Clay beamed his satisfaction at what he saw. As a collector, he had always loved this camera because it was meant to be concealed to capture candid pictures. Seeing what Weed had created from a few spare parts was impressive.

"Can we give it a try?" Clay asked like a kid with a new toy.

"Step over here," Weed directed.

He opened the camera's body and showed Clay how to load the four cartridges into the camera body plus one in the chamber.

"The lens is your gun barrel. Here, put this vest on," Weed instructed.

The Stirn's camera had a cord attached to its sides, and Weed slipped the cord over Clay's head so the camera rested comfortably on his chest.

"Now button up the vest and put the camera's gun barrel out of the closest button hole."

Clay did as he was told.

"Now, then. Instead of using a separate cord to discharge the weapon, I've synched a wireless signal on the side here to the detonator in your camera. All you need to do is depress this button and the gun will fire."

Mace looked on with growing anticipation as Clay followed Weed's directions.

"Okay, Clay, move over in front of the wall target and stand about five feet away," Weed said.

Again, Clay did as he was told.

"Now, remember this is a first trial for this weapon, and I'm not sure what kind of a kick you're going to feel. I actually chose a very light .22 load for this test, mainly because it's resting so close to your heart."

Clay faced the target, which was made of paper about four feet tall featuring the black outline of a human head and torso.

"Hey, Mace, nice artwork," Clay joked. "Where'd you get it?"

"Sotheby's." Mace deadpanned.

"Now aim your chest at the center of the target and press the button. We ought to hear a nice bang."

Nice bang hardly described the explosive sound that came out of that light load Weed had placed in the bullet. In their haste to see what this little baby could do, all three of them had forgotten to wear ear plugs. The sound that erupted off of the sub-basement's stone and brick walls was cacophonous.

All three reached their hands up to cover their ears from the reverberation.

"Holy shit!" Weed chuckled. "And, look at the target!"

The hole in the target wasn't huge, but it was big enough to cause a recipient to be severely compromised, or worse.

"Great shot, Clay!" Mace hollered because all three of them were still getting their full hearing back.

They all approached the target to see better.

"How do you feel, Clay?" Weed asked. "Was the kick from the discharge too strong?"

"Not really, Weed. In fact I think we can use standard issue .22 shells."

"I can do that," Weed said confidently. "Now, then: you still have four bullets left. Three are in the body of the camera, and when you just shot the camera, it mechanically moved the next shell into the chamber. It's basically a semi-automatic weapon."

"And you did this in, like, two or three days?" Clay marveled.

"See, and you thought I was just a charming and talented blues man," Weed kidded.

"I can see this being a very effective weapon, especially if the bad guy is someone who I want to see up close and personal," Clay intoned.

"Why don't you put the Stirn's Vest Camera aside for now and come over and see what we have for the truly discriminating gentleman avenger?"

Weed held up his replicated version of the 1903 Ben Akiba Cane Handle camera.

"I must compliment you as a collector, Clay. Your foresight in acquiring the major parts of these rare cameras is allowing me to construct some very intriguing devices."

While Weed was now, and would forever be, a blues musician, he had to admit he was finding this project a sweet way to use his engineering talents to help even things. The attack on Tori had sealed the deal.

"Wow, let me see that!" Clay said excitedly.

Weed's creation was indeed impressive. He had located an old, sturdy, ebony cane that Tori sometimes used in their performances and had securely fitted his new handle to it.

"I realize I don't need to tell you the unique features of this rare beauty, but I replaced the lens at the front of the handle with the barrel of the gun. Just flip the small metal plate down to reveal the barrel, and push this little button to take the safety off. Now, you're ready to fire. Very easy."

"Did you use the same .22 cartridges as in the Stirn's Vest Camera?" Clay inquired.

"Yes," Mace said. "I think it's probably best for us to standardize the caliber we use in all of our weapons. That way you can purchase bullets anywhere they sell shooting supplies. I doubt you want to carry special ammo with you and have to explain it each time to airport security."

Clay stood in front of another target Mace had placed on the wall. This time they all put earplugs in to dampen the explosive sound.

"You have five shots," Weed confirmed, "like the Vest camera. Four in the handle's grip and one in the chamber. You can either use the cane as a monopod for stability or hold the camera's handle out in front of you at arm's length."

"Let's try both positions," Clay said eagerly.

Bang! The cane-handle weapon fired beautifully. He fired it four more times from various positions, and a light haze of blue smoke hung in the sub-basement's air. The target was shredded in the abdomen area.

"I think we have a winner!" Mace announced. "Very cool, Weed!"

Clay stared at the tattered target and then at his two friends.

"Whew!" Clay exhaled. "That is killer, pardon the pun!"

"Okay," Weed said, "once I make a very minor adjustment to the weapons to accommodate the standard shells, you'll be ready to take the vest and cane cameras with you. I imagine that as someone with your reputation, Clay, as a photographer and collector, you shouldn't have any difficulty transporting these antique cameras anywhere."

"Were you able to come up with any other ideas from the spare antique camera parts?" Clay asked hopefully.

"Show him, Weed!" Mace encouraged.

"All right. We have two other devices that I think I can modify soon. You had an extra KGB ring camera that I plan to alter so it opens to hold a nasty dose of cyanide or some other poison that can be slipped into your target's drink."

Weed continued, "We have your antique Steineck ABC wristwatch camera that I believe can be fitted with a powerful taser charge. It won't be lethal, but it should totally incapacitate anyone on the receiving end. Then the rest is up to you."

"Incredible, Weed!" Clay replied. "Remind me never to piss you guys off!"

Just then Weed's phone rang. It was the hospital informing him that Tori would be discharged later that afternoon and that he should plan to pick her up around four o'clock.

"Good news. I can bring Tori back home this evening," Weed informed. "If she feels up for company, it could be great to have all of us around the table together. Oh, and I imagine you guys agree that we should keep our sub-basement projects to ourselves."

Mace and Clay did indeed agree. No sense bringing Tori and Rennie into it.

In fact, Clay thought it was best not to tell Mace and Weed about his first execution of Jefferson Talbot in Charleston. There was nothing to be gained by making them accessories after the fact. Certainly nothing to be gained by boasting about it. He felt no delight in his murder. No, Clay chose to keep this secret to himself.

A few minutes later Clay's phone vibrated, and he saw that he had a text from his agent Lily.

"Looks like I'm leaving tomorrow afternoon for a photo shoot in Santa Fe and then going on to San Diego and Chicago."

"Busy man," Mace remarked.

"Yeah, busy time," Clay admitted, "but I'm sure we'll keep in touch via phone and e-mails."

"So, if you guys don't mind my leaving you to your devices, I really need to get some things organized and packed before I leave tomorrow. I also hope to stop by and see Stella if there's time.

We didn't get a chance to finish a conversation we were having at the Diner.

"Most of all," Clay continued, "I'm really looking forward to our all being together this evening with Tori and Rennie. I'm so relieved she's going to be okay, and I haven't had much of an opportunity to get to know Rennie. It already feels like ages ago, Mace, that we first talked with him on Hill Street."

The three men said their goodbyes, and then each got down to work.

Chapter 27

CLAY TOOK THE ELEVATOR UP to his living quarters and looked around at his home. It was a large open space with contemporary Danish furniture and richly hued, handwoven carpets over polished hardwood floors.

Some of his favorite photographs were artfully hung on the walls, and his favorite early American Daguerreotype camera, originally owned by Mathew Brady, stood nobly on its studio stand in the corner. Artifacts of different varieties and from different parts of the world occupied niches on pedestals and shelves. It was a living museum.

Years ago Clay had replaced the brewery's original small windows with large walls of glass that welcomed light. He used vertical blinds to control the amount of light, like an iris in a camera, but right now he wanted to bask fully exposed to the source of life, the sun.

Clay closed his eyes and felt the warmth of the autumn sunlight bathe him in its baptismal stream.

"Give me strength," he whispered. "Keep my friends safe."

Clay sat at his computer and saw that Lily had forwarded his flight numbers and lodging details. The project in Santa Fe was going to be a promotional photo shoot of several art galleries along Canyon Road. He had been there a few times before and always found unique objects of interest.

Clay chuckled to himself when he saw a mushy e-mail from Natalie Barrows in Charleston saying how much she had enjoyed working with him, and that she would just have to come up with another reason to hire him again.

The next e-mail he read was brief, but it got his attention in a way that surprised him.

"Hope your trip home was safe and that your friends are doing well. I enjoyed our time together very much. Warmly, Grace."

Nice, Clay thought. Very nice.

He looked over to the low coffee table and stared at a portrait of Jennifer. Her death seemed so long ago now, but he wasn't emotionally ready to let go of her and be intimate with another woman. Besides, he had work to do and a mission to fulfill. He believed Grace was a very special lady, someone whom he might be willing to get to know better, but timing was important.

Satchmo snuffled a greeting to Clay as he entered the room. The big cat had an almost preternatural sense about Clay's temperament, seeming to want to be there for him when he was in need.

"There you are again, my spectral friend," Clay said to Satchmo. "Have you come to brighten my spirits?"

Satchmo rubbed his long body against Clay's calf and let out a loud meow as if to answer affirmatively.

Clay and Satchmo spent the next hour together as Clay answered a few more e-mails and began packing his camera gear and clothing for his upcoming trip to Santa Fe. Clay carefully reviewed the scope of work that he was being paid to do in Santa Fe, and he felt he had a solid plan for the various locations on Canyon Road he needed to photograph.

"Well, that's about it for now, Satchmo," Clay summed up. "I still have time to run down to Stella's Diner before coming back for our family dinner with Tori."

With that summation, Satchmo turned and scampered out the door.

Clay's drive to the Diner was relatively uneventful despite the rush hour. His radio was tuned to a national news channel, and he listened as a litany of stories featuring unpleasant human behavior were dissected by pundits for a hungry audience.

"A list has been published by a major consulting firm of the elected officials in America who benefited the most financially from supporting Wall Street banks . . ."

"There was an attack on a mosque in central Indiana with slurs against the prophet Mohammed smeared with pig's blood on the front doors . . ."

"A congressman from Alabama decried efforts by his liberal colleagues to fund a comprehensive study of the science of climate change . . ."

"An attack occurred on a library in Southern Missouri for having books about evolution in its circulation . . ."

"Antigay protestors showed up at a gay pride rally in Pittsburgh hurling insults against 'lurid fornicators' . . ."

"Right-wing journalists joined together calling for more investment in the drilling for fossil fuels and the dismantlement of the EPA . . ."

"The president of an evangelical college called for students to arm themselves."

"And in breaking news, Jefferson Talbot, a central figure in South Carolina's white supremacy movement, was found murdered with the initials KKK carved into his forehead."

That last report certainly got Clay's attention, but there was no further mention of suspects or witnesses; so he settled back into his seat for the duration of the news reports. He shook his head in total disbelief that American culture had slid so far backward into the clutching hands of mean-spirited demagogues.

"Evening comes," Clay whispered to himself. "Evening comes . . ."

Ten minutes later Clay pulled his Tacoma into the lot at Stella's Diner. He sat in the truck for another minute until his anger had subsided to a less volatile level. Then he went looking for his friend Stella.

"Hey, handsome!" came Stella's warm greeting as Clay entered the lounge area. "What mischief and mayhem have you been up to since last week? You haven't been breaking any girls' hearts, have you?"

"Hey, yourself," came Clay's friendly reply. "Oh, you know, Stella, just trying to make an honest living with my camera," he said with a smile.

"We never did get to finish our last conversation about those jerks in the pickup that were harassing your place," Clay added.

"Yeah, well, I suppose Weed and Tori filled you in about what happened the last time they paid us a visit," Stella said unhappily. "And Abby told me she saw you at the hospital in Trent's room. So, I imagine you've gotten his account of what happened, too. I swear, Clay, I never saw anyone act as bravely as that Detective Reynolds friend of yours did. He saved a lot of lives that night."

"Yeah, and damn near paid the ultimate price for his bravery, too," Clay said somberly.

Stella asked one of her staff to cover the front desk for a while, and she and Clay moved over to a private table out of earshot from any guests.

Clay and Stella had always enjoyed a friendly relationship, but they had never really shared their personal points of view regarding politics or social issues. It wasn't that they didn't trust each other. They were both smart, savvy people who knew that their thoughts were often best kept to themselves.

"I hear a lot of talk in here, Clay, often from folks who have had way too much to drink for their own good," Stella offered. "The other night good old Dutch Ferris was spouting off how he was here the night those jerks attacked the Diner, and that he thought he recognized them."

"Did he tell the police?" Clay asked.

"No, he's a bit of a wacko libertarian who thinks it would be an infringement of the attackers' rights to free expression, so he chose not to say anything."

"Oh, gee, there's a patriotic American for you!" Clay said derisively.

"Well, I haven't seen him since then, but I believe with a few more drinks and some flash of cleavage the next time he comes in, I might be able to get some more information out of him. You interested in what I find out?"

"Very!" Clay said. "I imagine Trent would be very interested as well."

Just then Abby West saw Clay and Stella conversing at their corner table, and she came up to say hello.

"Am I interrupting?" she asked politely.

"No, not at all," Stella said. "I was just telling Clay about Dutch Ferris's big mouth, and what he said about knowing our visitors in the pickup truck."

"Hi, Clay," Abby said, "Dutch was letting his alcohol do his talking for him. Pretty pathetic bragging about knowing the criminals who caused a tragedy. It would be great if we could get him to say more."

"I have faith in both of you," Clay said.

"By the way, Clay, have you been back to see Trent since I saw you at the hospital yesterday? He seemed really down when I saw him, but then you guys helped left his spirits."

"No, I haven't," Clay replied. "Tori's being discharged today, and Weed is driving up to the hospital soon to bring her back home. If time allows, I'm sure he'll stop in to see Trent again, and I'll definitely give him a call."

"On a happier note," Clay continued, "provided she's feeling up for it, we're all having dinner tonight to celebrate Tori's homecoming. I'm leaving tomorrow for Santa Fe for a project so it's really great we'll all have this time together."

"That's wonderful," Abby said. "Clay, there's something else I wanted to speak with you about. I've been doing some thinking about an article I'd like to write, and I'd like your opinion."

She went on, "You know I got fired from my last job at the newspaper because my editor and I had some major differences of opinion about many of our cultural issues today—gun violence being one of them, abortion another, and the list goes on."

"I recall," Clay said sympathetically.

"Well," Abby continued, "I was thinking about writing a piece about gun violence from law enforcement's point of view. Do you think that Trent might be willing to be interviewed on the subject?"

"One way to find out, Abby. Just ask him. He might feel a little conflicted given his usual reluctance to say anything that might reflect badly on his profession, and I presume he would want to clear it with his supervisors."

"On the other hand," Clay went on, "getting shot by redneck pricks who shouldn't be permitted to own firearms might change his attitude a bit. You should ask him, though. He might surprise you."

Abby thanked him and said she needed to get back to work. After she left, Stella commented on what a fine woman she was and expressed the hope that she could find another news job where her talents were truly appreciated.

"Let's do this, Clay: give me your phone number and e-mail address, and I'll keep my ears open for anything else I hear. I have always had this sense that you and I are coming from the same place about exacting justice."

They let those cryptic words hang in the air, but each nodded quiet agreement.

"I gotta go, Stella, but let's keep in touch, okay? I want to nail these bastards every bit as much as you do, especially since Trent told me he thought they might be the same men who blew up the Planned Parenthood Center."

They let those words hang in the air as well, and then Clay departed.

Chapter 28

RENNIE AND LEX WERE curled up together on the woven rug in front of Mace's wood stove. Rennie gently stroked Lex's flank, and the black Labrador occasionally exhaled a moan of trust and contentment.

In truth, it was the first time that Rennie had ever had to care for another creature other than himself, and he found a growing feeling of camaraderie in the relationship.

"There you go, Lexie," Rennie said softly. "That's a good dog, yes. You and I are partners, aren't we?" he cooed. "We've both been whomped on by mean people, and look, here we are. Maybe we're a little tore up, but we scared off the bad guys, didn't we, big fella?"

Lex moaned contentedly again and licked Rennie's hand as Rennie stroked his nose and muzzle.

The two of them spooned for several more minutes and basked in the glow and warmth of the wood stove. Lex exhaled a different-sounding moan this time, and his ears went to full attention as he

heard a familiar sound. A few seconds after that, Rennie heard the crunch of gravel in the courtyard as Weed pulled his truck in front of his and Tori's farmhouse.

"C'mon Lex, let's go see Tori and Weed," Rennie encouraged.

Lex struggled at first to get this three legs under himself but was determined to be a part of the homecoming greeting for Tori. Rennie opened the door to Mace's power plant, and Lex and he managed to stand on Mace's front porch as Tori and Weed exited the truck some twenty yards away.

"C'mon, boy," Rennie urged the injured dog again, and he helped Lex slowly descend the three wooden porch steps to the courtyard.

"Hey, Tori!" Rennie yelled out when he saw her by the car. Weed was offering her his arm, and Rennie came running over to her.

"Hey, Tori, welcome home, man! It's good to see you," he said.

Tori opened her arms, stepped toward Rennie's voice and pulled him to herself.

"Thank you so much, Rennie. You saved my life," she said with a breaking voice. "I'll never forget that."

"Well, it was Lex and me. Lex got to you way before I did. He's a hero!"

At the mention of his name, Lex let out a plaintive bark as if to say, "Hey, what about me?"

"Oh, Lexie!" Tori immediately called back and began walking in his direction.

Lex began his three-legged walk toward her, and Rennie caught up with both of them as Tori sat down on the ground to be with her hurting friend. Lex literally fell into her lap and began licking her chin.

"Oh, Lexie," Tori said softly. "You are the best friend anyone could ever have. Thank you. Thank you, my friend." She cradled him.

Weed bent down to see Lex, too, and told Tori what he saw. Tori gently ran her hand over the lab's bandaged leg, and he whimpered just a little.

"We're going to get you all healed, aren't we, Rennie?" Tori declared.

"We sure are. Lex is gonna be the best three-legged dog ever!" Rennie said triumphantly.

Just then, Mace emerged from Clay's brew house where he had been working in the sub-basement.

"Tori!" he called out briskly as he approached them.

"Hey, Mace, come give a beat-up blind girl a hug!" she sang out.

And for the next few minutes they all reconnected. Bonds were being reinforced. Now all they needed to do was get Tori settled, make sure that Lex was okay, and wait for Satchmo and Clay to complete their family's constellation.

Weed asked, "Tori, do you think you might be up for a nice family dinner and a little entertainment, or would you prefer to rest?"

"No way!" Tori replied. "I'm tired of being a victim and a patient. Yeah, time to rejoin the human race so—sure!"

"Okay," Weed said. "We'll have it at the farmhouse just because it's most familiar to Tori, but under one condition: Tori, you have to agree to let all of us take care of everything tonight; and you get to be the queen."

"But!" she began.

"But," Weed said, "why don't you select our music for tonight? And maybe Rennie will help you set up the table. Mace, how about you and I handle the cooking and cleanup?"

"Sounds like a plan," Mace agreed. "I'll bring some food, too. C'mon, Lex, let's get you over by the stove again."

"Rennie, you want to come in with Tori and me?" Weed suggested.

"Sure!" he said eagerly. "Just let me know what I can do to help!"

Tori took Rennie and Weed's hands and said, "It's good to be home."

As Clay drove his Tacoma out of the Diner's parking lot, he knew that he'd likely be crushed by the onslaught of rush-hour traffic. Regardless, he wanted to visit Trent in the hospital again before he returned home to celebrate Tori's homecoming.

His conversation with Stella had galvanized his anger over the men who had victimized innocent people, including the love of his life, Jennifer. Clay also had the feeling that Trent might be willing to keep him informed of any new information about the attackers.

Clay purposely kept the radio off so his blood pressure wouldn't spike over the constant string of negative news reports, and he arrived at Conner Prairie Hospital without too much traffic delay.

"Come on in," he heard Trent say upon his knock at the door.

"How's the patient today?" Clay asked as he entered the darkened room.

"Frustrated!" came Trent's frank reply. "I want to get the hell out of here and go back to work. I feel like each day I'm in this bed, the bad guys who tore up the Diner and the Planned Parenthood Center are getting farther and farther away."

"Have the doctors told you when they might be ready to release you?" Clay inquired.

"Probably tomorrow, but they may want me to go to a rehab facility for a couple of weeks since I have no one at home to look after me. I am not too keen on doing that, but we'll see how I feel without the pain meds."

"My boss wants me to take a desk job for a while, and the thought of not being in the thick of things on the street bothers me. I know my career is likely to change, but I've got to feel like I have more value to the department than sitting my ass behind a desk. Yeah, I'm frustrated. But enough about my woeful crap," Trent concluded. "How's Tori doing?"

"Weed picked her up at the hospital a little while ago, and he called me to say she seemed much better and that they were on their way home."

"Good!" Trent said positively. "She's lucky to have you and Weed and Mace to lean on."

"Yeah, we're all lucky to have each other," Clay sighed. "For that matter, if you find that you need a place to crash for a while instead of your home, you're more than welcome to bunk at my place. I'm going out of town for a while on various assignments, and Mace and Rennie and Tori and Weed could be very good company for you."

"You're very kind to offer," Trent said. "May I think about that and let you know tomorrow once I know for sure what the doctors decide?"

"Of course," Clay said. "Whatever you feel comfortable with is fine with us, okay?"

The two friends spent the next few minutes talking about the attacks by the men in the dark pickup truck. Clay pressed Trent for more information about the attackers, but Trent had been out of the loop since being shot. That was the major reason he wanted to get out of the hospital and back on the job.

"What I said to you yesterday, Clay, about the attackers at the Diner possibly being the same perps who blew up the Planned Parenthood Center is mostly speculation on my part, but over the years I've come to trust my gut in such things."

"I just left Stella's prior to coming to see you, and she said that a guy named Dutch Ferris was bragging recently that he knew who the bad guys are. You might want to have a friendly little conversation with him, because if I do it myself you might not have much of a potential witness left if he chooses not to cooperate with me."

Trent sat up very attentively in his bed, and Clay was pleased to see him getting more animated at the thought of catching the bad guys.

"I'll do it," Trent said. "Thanks for the tip, and thanks also for the offer to bunk at your place."

Just then a knock was heard at Trent's door, and Abby's smiling face came into view.

"Well, twice in one day!" Clay said as Abby entered the room and stood next to him at the foot of Trent's hospital bed.

"You haven't told him about our conversation at the diner?" Abby asked Clay.

"No, I haven't," Clay said honestly. "That's your business."

"What are you two talking about?" Trent asked in confusion.

"It's a literary project I think I could use your help with," Abby suggested.

Clay looked at his watch and said, "I think it's time for me to leave you two to discuss it, and I need to scoot back to the brewery complex to be with everyone before I leave for Santa Fe tomorrow."

Clay wrote down his cell phone number and e-mail address again in case Trent needed it.

"Let's keep in touch, my friend," Clay said seriously. "Abby can fill you in more on what she knows about Dutch Ferris. My guess is that guy could steer us in the right direction."

Trent nodded his head affirmatively and thanked Clay for being a good friend. A few moments later Clay was gone, and Abby and Trent were left alone with their futures as unilluminated as the room itself.

Chapter 29

CLAY ARRIVED BACK AT HIS brew house some thirty minutes later. He'd chosen not to listen to the radio on the way home. With his frank conversation with Trent still ringing in his ears, he had enough to contemplate without getting worked up over yet another unpleasant media report.

He exited the Tacoma and was greeted by the spectral appearance of Satchmo.

"I swear you just come out of nowhere, you big old cat. I'd put a little bell on you if I didn't think it would really piss you off," he kidded.

Satchmo leaned the full weight of his flank on Clay's lower leg and meowed a friendly salutation.

Clay bent down to pick him up, which was rare since Satchmo tipped the scale at about sixteen pounds.

"C'mere, you beast!" Clay groaned as he lofted the big feline. "Are you going to be okay if I leave you for a few weeks? Huh? Are

you going to keep a close eye on everything around here while I'm gone? Huh? I sure hope so. I'm counting on you keeping us safe, okay? Good boy!"

Satchmo snuffled and purred and rubbed his forehead and his muzzle against Clay's chin and cheek. Clay marveled at this cat's personality.

"Thanks, buddy!" Clay said as he put Satchmo back down. "Looks like everyone's at Weed and Tori's. Shall we head on over and join them?"

With Thanksgiving just around the corner, the sun was very close to setting as Clay and Satchmo approached the farmhouse. The house looked darkly lit on the outside, but it literally glowed from the warm lighting within. From ten feet away, Clay could hear Weed singing a soulful tune.

Clay stood still for a few moments with his Maine Coon partner at his side and took it all in. He knew he had chosen to take a very violent path to even the score with many deserving candidates. He knew he might somehow pay an emotional price for his actions, but hell, he figured he had already been paying a huge price since Jennifer's murder.

Clay surveyed his brewery complex: His brew house, Mace's power plant, Tori and Weed's farmhouse. This was his home and his family. He knew he was comfortable with what he had chosen to do, but he originally didn't intend on putting Mace and Weed at odds with the law.

He also knew that these were two very wise and independent men. They didn't need Clay's permission to participate in vengeance. They felt similarly to Clay, and they were committed to standing by their friend. Their mantra was: *We stick together!*

"Well, good Lord, look what the cat dragged in!" Weed exclaimed robustly as Satchmo and Clay came through the kitchen door.

"Howdy, Weed! How are you, Tori?" Clay replied, and he went over to give her a warm hug.

"I think I'm fine," Tori said. "I don't enjoy hanging around hospitals too long. You don't do anything physically except lie there, and a little of that goes a long way with me. So, yeah, I'm fine and feeling strong, too. Thanks for your concern, though, Clay."

"Well, I'm glad you're feeling better, because if I'm not mistaken I hear Mace and Lex getting ready to come through the door, and then it'll probably get a little cacophonous for a while."

"Cool!" Tori chimed. "Let the cacophony begin!"

And so it did . . .

Rennie came out of the bathroom after freshening up for dinner and was immediately joined by Lex, who seemed to be ambulating fairly well. Granted, his gait was a little unusual, but he was getting around.

"Well, looky there! That Tori Rawlins sure is pretty now that she's home from that Conner Prairie spa!" Maced euphemistically called the hospital. "Great to have you back, darlin'," Mace said sincerely.

"Thanks, Mace! Now, then, about this dinner tonight! Who's in charge?"

"I am," both Mace and Weed announced in unison.

Everyone started laughing, and then they all harmoniously got down to preparing what was possibly going to be their only Thanksgiving dinner together this year, given Clay's travel schedule.

Rennie and Tori set a beautiful table, and Tori selected a CD of Weed's greatest hits. The brother and sister duo sang along with each song, and the others basked in the glow of an evening for which each had many reasons to be thankful.

Tori had her arm around Rennie, and Lex lay comfortably at their feet. Satchmo knew a love fest when he saw one and strode over and plopped down by Lex's belly.

After a while, Tori told Rennie that she wanted to go outside to feel and smell the night air. She led a comical parade of Rennie, Lex, and Satchmo in single file out the front door to the porch.

Mace, Weed, and Clay made eye contact and cryptically talked about meeting early in the morning to finish the clandestine project. In truth, the first two weapons were ready for him to take. Clay was ready, too.

"I'll bring you up to speed tomorrow morning about my conversations with Stella, Abby, and Trent," Clay said quietly. "For now, just know that we have allies."

Chapter 30

For the umpteenth time Clement Hacker looked at the pictures of the two targeted buildings that Newt and Twit had taken on Newt's cell phone. The enormous structures would be challenging to blow up.

The headquarters for the Hoosier Homestead Insurance Co. looked like it was built to withstand a nuclear blast. Clement tried to estimate how much concrete and steel went into constructing the massive twelve-story structure, but he just stared at the pictures and absently shook his head in near awe.

"Everyone and everything comes and goes, ain't that right, Ella Marie?" Clement intoned to himself. "You were taken from me, and now it's time for the doctors and insurance people to learn what it means to come and go."

Clement looked around the interior of his pole barn to assess his inventory of ANFO for the fertilizer bombs. He then looked ruefully back at the pictures of the two buildings he hoped to level.

"One thing's for certain, Ella Marie," he said out loud. "We're gonna need some bigger bombs!"

A few moments later Newt and Twit came trotting into the barn. They had been confined to their property for only a couple of days since returning from their recon mission, but they were already antsy to leave the property and create more mischief.

"We're bored, Pa," came Twit's sullen comment. "Can't Newt and I go run some errand for you? Maybe go to the feed store or something?"

"Bored, huh? Well, maybe you juvenile delinquents should've thought of that before you started attacking faggy golfers and a blind girl! I told you we need to lie low and not draw any more attention to ourselves until we're ready. Come to think of it, though, why don't you boys head on down to the feed store and pick up some more ammonium nitrate and fuel oil."

"Sure thing, Pa!" Twit sang out gleefully. "Just tell us how much you want, and Newt and I will get all you want."

The three men spent the next few minutes discussing the best ways to do the most damage to the insurance company's building and the hospital.

"Looks to me," Clement said, "like the best thing we can do is drive a pickup truck full of ANFO into Hoosier Homestead's underground garage and leave it next to the elevator. That way when the bomb goes off it'll explode upward through the elevator shaft and tear out the building in all directions."

"Oooee!" Twit squealed. "What about the hospital? Where do you think we ought to blow that up?"

"That's a different story," Clement said, "because the hospital has so many different entrances. Probably need to drive the truck right into the main entrance and kiss the lobby, the doctors' lounge, and the administrative offices adios!"

"Yee-yee!" Twit giggled nonsensically. "When do you think you want to do this, Pa?"

"Well, like I said, we need to get some more supplies for the fertilizer bombs, and then I think a joint strike by you boys on Thanksgiving day ought to make a real loud holiday statement. How's that sound?!"

"How're we gonna set the bombs off?" Newt asked.

"With cell phones," Clement replied. "I've been doing me some reading, and it looks like we can hook the phones up to the ANFO, and with another phone we can dial a number and—kaboom! You boys just need to make sure you get far enough away from the building before making the call. My plan is that we blow both buildings at the same time for maximum impact."

"Well, how're Twit and I gonna get away if we blow our trucks up in the process?"

"Now, don't you fret about that," Clement stated. "I'll be up there, too, and I'll have to figure out those little details some more.

"Now, then: why don't you boys head on back to the feed store and pick up our supplies, and then I want you to come straight back home. I don't want you talking to nobody, and I sure as hell don't want you getting into a skirmish with anyone."

"Yes, Pa," came their pitiful replies. "Can we at least go over to Jeffersonville for the gun show? It's real easy to buy whatever we want there."

"No, goddamnit! The feed store and then home. That's it!"

"Yessir, Pa . . . eyes open, mouths shut, and then straight back home. We understand, don't we Twit?"

Meanwhile, back at the brewery complex Weed rose early to check on Tori and Rennie, who had decided to sleep in a little after the previous night's excitement. He prepared coffee, made a light breakfast, and then headed over to the sub-basement of the brew house to meet Mace and Clay.

"G'morning, gents," Weed said to his friendly co-conspirators as he entered the underground room. "It's a glorious day! Are you ready to kick some redneck asses?" he asked rhetorically.

Mace and Clay nodded affirmatively, and then Clay proceeded to tell them about Stella and Abby's suspicion that Dutch Ferris knew the men who'd attacked the Planned Parenthood Center, Stella's Diner, and Tori, Rennie, and Lex.

"I told Trent about Dutch Ferris," Clay stated. "I think he's going to make interrogating him his top priority when he's discharged from the hospital. He said he was going to call his office after I left and have them run a background check on the man."

"No doubt," came Mace's even reply. "I sure wouldn't want to be Mr. Ferris if he isn't forthcoming with information for Trent about the attackers. In fact, that's a conversation I wouldn't mind witnessing," Mace continued.

The three men worked side by side for a couple of hours putting the finishing touches to the KGB Ring camera, which had a secret reservoir that Clay planned to fill with poison. Fitting the Steineck ABC Wristwatch camera with a taser-like device was a little tricky, but Weed managed to finally get it figured out.

"So, at this point," Weed concluded, "we have converted four of your antique cameras into devices capable of disabling or killing your subjects. Do you think these should meet your needs?"

"Absolutely," Clay replied. "It might be easier just to shoot the fucking bastards, but using these weapons is really more my style. I'm going to have to leave you now to get ready to head for the airport. We'll keep in touch, but let's be very cool about what we say in our communications. The last thing I want is for us to get caught."

"Hallelujah to that, brother!" Weed said.

"Amen!" Mace added.

And then Clay left to prepare for his photo project in Santa Fe, and to contemplate his new career as an avenging assassin.

It was finally time to even the score for the innocent victims—past, present, and future.

Chapter 31

TRENT REYNOLDS HAD HAD enough convalescence. "I can't clear these cases lying around a damn hospital bed," he lamented to himself.

The doctor had already removed his catheter, but he still had an IV inserted in his arm. He examined it carefully, reached down and pulled the needle out. Free at last!

A few minutes later he was dressed in the same pants he'd been wearing when he got shot. Fortunately, the hospital's housekeeping staff had had them laundered while he was in the ICU. His shirt was in tatters from the gunshot, so he wore a surgical scrub shirt for a top.

Trent quietly called his ISP associate Rebecca Willett, fibbed to her that he was being discharged, and asked her to come immediately to the hospital and give him a ride home.

Trent watched the nursing station from his darkened room, and when the coast was clear, he slipped out of his room and stealthily walked to a nearby stairway. So far, so good!

He descended to the first floor, exited the stairway and walked to a position near the main hospital entrance, where he waited for Rebecca to arrive. No one paid him any attention.

"Well, you look better than you did when I visited you in the intensive care unit, but not by much," Rebecca cheerfully greeted her supervisor.

"Thanks, I think," came Trent's reply as he painfully strapped his seatbelt into place.

"Where to?" she asked.

"My home, so I can get a change of clothes and then to the office," Trent replied, "and if the hospital calls looking for me, you haven't seen me, understood?!"

Rebecca had been Trent's associate at Indiana State Police headquarters for nearly six years, and she'd learned a long time ago to trust her boss's judgement.

"Oh, did we leave the hospital against medical advice?" she asked like a scolding parent.

Trent dodged the question.

"I need you to find out what you can about a man named Dutch Ferris," Trent stated. "Dutch probably isn't his real first name, so you're going to need to do some digging. Actually, we should pay a visit to Stella's Diner and see if they can give us a make, model, and possibly a license number for his car."

Rebecca understood the drill. During their tenure together, she had helped find several dangerous people for Trent with even less information.

"I'm on it, boss," Rebecca replied officiously.

"Great. Now let's get the hell out of here. Hospitals make me nervous."

Clay's direct flight from Indianapolis to Santa Fe was uneventful. Even going through airport security went off without a hitch. Clay always carried his camera gear on board the aircraft with him, not trusting the baggage handlers to treat his fragile equipment with the same care that he did.

Clay packed Weed's newly fabricated weapons along with the rest of his photography gear, and security gave them only a cursory look seeing them nestled along with other camera bodies and lenses.

Although Clay was a dedicated midwesterner, he certainly understood the fascination with the southwestern United States. Not only a landscape different with its mesas and scrub brush, but even the light itself seemed to be clearer and more intense. He flashed briefly on the artist Georgia O'Keeffe and understood why she'd moved out west so many years ago. It was the light, he thought. And to a photographer, it was all about light.

On the drive to the Monastery Lodge where he would be staying, Clay telephoned Maggie Bodine to let her know that he had arrived, and to confirm their dinner meeting later that evening at the Lodge. He had worked with Maggie before and found her to be a very accomplished professional.

In truth, they knew each other very well personally, too. Way before meeting Jennifer Skyler, Maggie was a woman that Clay had worked with on some promotional projects. He found her more than a little intriguing. Work schedules and miles between them kept them from developing much of a relationship, but there was a definite physical attraction on both parts. As self-confident as Clay was, he felt a little nervous at seeing Maggie again.

Margaret "Maggie" Bodine was a success story in her own right. She had started her own design and advertising firm some fifteen years earlier, cultivating it into a highly successful company that promoted many of the new art galleries blossoming in old Santa Fe and along Canyon Road.

She was thrilled to have Clay Arnold's exceptional eye and reputation for the visuals of a holiday promotion that would attract many well-heeled clients to the city.

Her real curiosity, however, was just seeing Clay again. She knew that they'd had a special connection a few years back, and now she felt almost embarrassed at her undeniable excitement.

Clay drove through the center of old Santa Fe, marveling at the combination of native culture with sophisticated modernism. If he weren't so happy living in Indiana, he could easily see himself living out here.

A few miles north of the city, Clay pulled into the grounds of the Monastery Lodge and admired the loveliness of the setting. There were low, sand-colored adobe structures scattered over several acres. Each one sported a ceramic tile roof, and when Clay squinted a little and used his imagination a lot, the scene looked like it might've been from over a hundred years ago.

He saw that there was quite a bit of activity going on, with guests participating in various activities and the housekeeping staff quietly servicing the facilities.

Clay entered the impressive main lodge and was immediately greeted at the registration desk by a lovely, tanned, teenage girl with almond eyes and raven hair. Her name badge read *Carmelita*.

"Buenos dias," she said sweetly. May I help you, sir?"

"Yes, my name is Clay Arnold. I believe you're holding a room for me."

"Of course, Mr. Arnold . . ."

And a few minutes later Clay was checked in and on his way to his room across the parking lot from the main lodge. It hadn't been an especially long day, but Clay felt a little weary from traveling and decided to rest up a bit before joining Maggie for dinner at eight in the Monastery's dining room. He laid down, set his alarm, closed his eyes, and soon drifted off to sleep.

Chapter 32

REBECCA AND TRENT ARRIVED at his place several minutes
later, and while Trent applied a fresh dressing to his shoulder
and changed clothes, Rebecca began her search of police databases
for information about Dutch Ferris.

At first she came up with blanks, and then she noticed that
Dutch Ferris was a gun aficionado who enjoyed making purchases
at regional gun shows.

"He's got no criminal record—just some minor traffic viola-
tions," Rebecca informed Trent when he came downstairs.

"And buying and owning guns sure isn't a crime," Trent
replied. "But if he can point us in the right direction to find these
jerks, it'll be the first solid lead we've had for a while. Let's head
over to Stella's Diner to see what we can find out."

On the drive over, Trent gave Stella a quick call to let her know
they were coming and to ask for any information on where Dutch
Ferris lived or worked.

As usual, Stella's Diner was a hopping place. Trent hadn't been back since the attack, and he paused at one point in the parking lot to examine a large, dried blood-stain on the pavement. It was where he had fallen, and he knew it was his blood.

Stella came rushing out to greet Trent and Rebecca.

"Trent, I'm so sorry I didn't get a chance to see you in the hospital," Stella said sincerely. "I've just been slammed with work and trying to do right by the people who got injured during the attack. So far, no one's sued me, and the insurance company seems to be cooperating."

"Not a problem, Stella," Trent assuaged her. "I doubt I would've been very good company, anyway."

"What are you doing out?" came Abby's admonishing voice from the Diner's front door. "I seriously doubt that the doctors released you so soon."

"Busted!" came Rebecca's muffled comment to Trent.

"I got antsy," Trent replied defensively. "Besides, these bad guys are still on the loose, and I figure a lot of people are counting on us catching them. And, I'm one of them!"

"How can we help?" Stella asked.

Rebecca explained that they wanted to check the Diner's office for any identification on file for Dutch Ferris, and to ask if the valet parkers might have any information regarding his vehicle.

"Let's go see," Stella said to Rebecca, and the two of them went back to her office.

Once they'd left, Abby said to Trent, "You really should still be in the hospital, you know. How are you feeling?"

"I've felt better," Trent said with a weak smile. "I really appreciated your visiting me in the hospital."

"Just doing my civic duty for a wounded first-responder," she offered, but they both knew her visits were more personal than that.

"Do you think that once you've recuperated a bit more," Abby said, "you might be willing to be the subject of an interview about gun violence?"

"Maybe," Trent suggested, "but it's something I'd have to think about. Perhaps we might be able to discuss it over dinner sometime soon."

That suggestion of dinner together totally surprised Abby, and she tried to maintain a professional demeanor when she replied that it sounded like a very good idea.

A few minutes later Stella and Rebecca rejoined them, and Stella said, "That was a very smart idea having me check our records, Trent. Apparently we had a picture of Dutch Ferris's driver's license on file. We often do that to verify that a patron is of legal drinking age."

"We've got a photo of the subject," Rebecca said, "and an address and his plate number."

"Good going, you two!" came Trent's excited reply. "C'mon, Rebecca. Let's go see if we can convince Mr. Ferris that his cooperation with law enforcement is a good idea," he said euphemistically.

Trent thanked Stella for her help and told Abby he would be in touch very soon.

***

Dutch Ferris sat in front of his television set in his boxer shorts and an old Indianapolis Colts T-shirt. He had a tall glass of bourbon in one hand and a bowl of Moose Tracks ice cream in the other. Life was good!

The news channel that Dutch was watching featured a story about a college president in Southern California who was urging the student body at his school to take up arms.

"Hells bells!" he belched. "Now that's what I call my kind of college president. It's about time someone took a stand against those liberal pricks who don't understand that our founding fathers wanted us citizens to embrace hand guns and assault rifles in the name of freedom. Yessir!"

Dutch poured a little of his bourbon into his bowl of ice cream and sloshed it around. "Everything goes better with bourbon," he slurred.

Dutch was about to nod off from his exciting dessert when he heard a car pull into his driveway.

"Now what?" he muttered to himself as he peered through his venetian blind at the dark sedan outside. He reached for an old, tattered bathrobe as he heard footsteps approaching his front door and then a sharp rap of purposeful knuckles.

"Yeah, what do you want?" Dutch hollered through the closed doors at his uninvited guests.

"State Police, Mr. Ferris. Open up, we need to talk with you," Rebecca declared.

"About what?" came the reply from within.

"Just open the door, Mr. Ferris," came Trent's perturbed voice. "If we have to get a warrant and haul your ass to the station to ask you a few simple questions, I doubt that you'll be very happy with our accommodations. Now, open up!"

"Hold on, dang it. Fella can't even eat his dessert in peace anymore," Dutch declared as he unlocked and opened his door.

Rebecca and Trent both had their police credentials out when Dutch Ferris's unshaven, unkempt face peered out at them.

"Mind if we step inside, Mr. Ferris?" Rebecca inquired.

"All right, c'mon in, but I ain't done nothing wrong," he said sourly.

Trent and Rebecca slid inside his door and looked around. Trent kept Dutch company while Rebecca did a quick scan of the first floor to see if anyone else was in the house.

"What's this about?" Dutch asked with a twinge of anxiety in his voice.

"We understand you were at Stella's Diner the night of the attack," Trent said.

"Yeah, so what? A lot of people were there that night," Dutch retorted.

"True, but you were the only one claiming to know the attackers," Trent said forcefully.

"So what?" Dutch snarled. "It's a free country, and I don't need to tell you shit."

Trent looked at Rebecca and asked her if she wouldn't mind retrieving his notebook from the car.

Rebecca stared at him with a look of confusion on her face and dutifully went outside to find the notebook.

As soon as the front door closed behind her, Trent's hand shot out and savagely grabbed Dutch Ferris's Adam's apple with a steel-like grip.

"Now, listen, you low-life son of a bitch," Trent snarled back. "You and I need to have a little understanding. You either cooperate with me right here and now, or I send my associate on another errand, and you end up being beaten to within an inch of your miserable, fucking life. And if you think you'll end up pressing charges against me, guess again, because like they used to say in the old western movies, 'dead men tell no tales!' Understand?!"

"Are you threatening me? I have rights." Dutch whined.

"I am absolutely threatening you, and the only rights you have right now are to decide whether you live or die. Those bastards in that truck shot me, and I don't care who I have to hurt, or kill, to catch them."

"You're that cop who got shot?" Dutch asked with a look of recognition on his face.

"Yeah, lucky me, huh?" Trent replied. "Now, let's see how smart and lucky you are before my associate returns."

Dutch saw the look of sheer determination on the police officer's face and blanched.

"Well, I ain't rightly sure, officer. I was just spouting off that night."

Trent squeezed Dutch's Adam's apple a little harder, and Dutch finally got with the program.

"I like going to gun shows to see who's buying and selling stuff, and I recall seeing that truck at a show near Louisville. There's a pair of twin sons who look exactly alike. One just seems to be a little swifter mentally than his brother. I think their names are Newt and Twit, but I don't know their last name."

"Anyway, I sold one of my .357 magnums to them in the parking lot. That's why I remember them. That, and I remember them having a big Confederate flag in the bed of their pickup and one for a front license plate. They told me they lived in Southern Indiana a few miles north of the Ohio River. That's all I know, I swear," Dutch pleaded.

Rebecca entered the house a few moments later and saw Dutch standing there massaging his throat.

"Well, thank you very much, Mr. Ferris," she heard Trent say. "You've been very cooperative, and the State of Indiana appreciates your spirit of civic duty. Anything else you care to add?"

"Uh, no," came Dutch's brief reply. "I take my civic duty seriously, sir."

"Well, Ms. Willett," Trent said to Rebecca, "I believe we're done here."

"Here's my business card, Mr. Ferris, if you think of anything else, I'm sure you won't hesitate to contact me."

"Uh, no, sir. I mean, yes sir, officer," Dutch managed. "Always happy to help the law."

Rebecca had an expression of bewilderment on her face as she and Trent exited the front door.

"You knew you hadn't left your notebook in the car, didn't you?" she said to Trent as they got in their car. "You sent me after it just to get me out of the way, didn't you?"

"Let's just say that Mr. Ferris has a remarkable memory once he feels properly motivated," Trent offered.

"Do you want to share the details of your interrogation technique with me?" Rebecca asked, still bewildered.

"Not really," Trent said. "But we now have a lot more information than we did before. Let's head back to the office, Rebecca, I've got some important searches for you to do with our databases."

Rebecca shook her head in a display of mock amazement and smiled.

"You are a mystery sometimes, Detective Reynolds—just a blessed mystery."

"Yeah, sometimes my wonderfulness is just a terrible curse," Trent rejoined, and he returned her smile.

Chapter 33

Clay's alarm woke him out of a deep sleep, and it took a few moments for him to remember that he was at the Monastery Lodge in Santa Fe. He walked to his window and marveled at the scene that spread out before him. The sun had barely set, and the western sky remained ablaze with the last embers of daylight.

Clay had always enjoyed the challenges and visual rewards of black-and-white photography, but the glorious sunset left little doubt in his mind that color trumped all.

He looked at his watch and saw that he had only fifteen minutes before he was to meet Maggie for dinner, so he rapidly cleaned up and put on fresh clothes. He selected black slacks and a dark gray sport jacket featuring a pale-blue windowpane weave. He wore a black knit shirt and placed a light-blue handkerchief in his blazer's breast pocket.

Clay looked at himself in the mirror and thought about how much his life had changed in the last six months. He wondered

what lay ahead. He breathed in and out slowly to calm himself, then went to meet a very intriguing woman for dinner.

Clay arrived at the main lodge first. He saw that the receptionist, Carmelita, was still on duty, and they exchanged greetings as he strode across the lobby toward the dining room.

The decor of the dining room was a display of southwestern elegance. The floor was laid with fourteen-inch-square ceramic tiles, and the walls were adorned with rich fabric coverings and large panoramic paintings. The tables and chairs were stunning with their rich cherry hues, and the rough-hewn beams in the ceiling gave the room its lodge effect.

What caught Clay's eye more than anything else, though, were the myriad of lit candles arranged throughout the room that created a warm and exotic ambience.

Clay selected a table by the fireplace, and he stared at the flames with his back turned toward the entrance to the dining room. His mind drifted back home. He pictured everyone's face and felt sad when he struggled to remember all of the details of Jennifer's voice and touch.

A few moments later, Clay was brought back to his present location by a gentle touch on his shoulder. Maggie Bodine had arrived. He immediately stood to say hello, but no words left his lips. The two of them stood two feet apart and silently eyed each other with a warm curiosity.

Maggie drank in every facet of Clay's face and stepped back to take in his full frame. Finally she managed to say, "It's very good to see you again, Clay Arnold. You haven't aged a day."

"You too, Maggie Bodine," was about all he was able to awkwardly utter at first. "You look lovely, as always. It's great to see you."

The two of them sat down and were saved from any more awkwardness by a waitress who materialized to take their drink orders.

The back of Maggie's chair was turned toward the fireplace, and when Clay looked across the table at her, she appeared to be celestially framed by the purifying light of the fire and the glowing candlesticks around the room. It was a scene Clay thought he would remember for a very long time.

It had been nearly five years since the two of them had last seen each other, and seeing her now literally took Clay's breath away. She was even more beautiful than he had remembered. Her long, auburn hair cascaded down her shoulders, and her green eyes sparkled with a brilliant intelligence.

Clay also enjoyed noticing that her figure still appeared to be delightfully trim, and her choice of ensemble accentuated her curves very nicely. Clay was duly impressed.

"Well," Clay began, "I'd really enjoy catching up with you on a personal level, so maybe we should get the business portion of our evening out of the way first?"

"That's sounds perfect," Maggie replied. "This is a very important account for me, Clay, not just for the fee I make, but because I want to create a promotional campaign that attracts thousands of people here. The artists' work deserves the attention. That's why I wanted you to shoot the images. You know: quintessential Clay Arnold artistry."

"Well, thank you. I'm really very flattered. I promise I will do my very best for you. I'm curious why didn't you just call me yourself?" Clay asked.

"I know it's weird, but we hadn't talked in a long time, especially after we had spent some really close times together, and I guess over time I felt awkward about contacting you."

"I'm really sorry you felt that way, Maggie. I understand what you're talking about and have to admit feeling much the same way. A lot of miles between our homes, and you'd have to think about the difficulty of making serious commitments. Anyway, it's really great to see you now. I'm excited about working with you and spending some time together."

Maggie and Clay spent the next thirty minutes talking about the overall theme that Maggie was looking for in promoting the galleries—festive, sophisticated, yet affordable for many pocketbooks. Maggie gave Clay a list of specific locations that she wanted included. She affirmed that Clay had full creative license, especially because she had confidence that he understood the importance of the business side of things as well.

Their waitress returned and took their orders, and Clay and Maggie settled into getting to know each other again.

"So, I take it you haven't gotten married since I last saw you," Clay led.

"No. I've dated a lot and have gotten to know some very interesting men, but nobody I wanted to make the big plunge toward matrimony with," Maggie admitted. "And, that's been okay, too.

"I understand," Maggie continued, "that you had someone very special in your life."

Clay looked past Maggie into the fireplace beyond and nodded yes.

"Jennifer and I were going to get married, but . . ." his words got caught in his throat.

"I'm very sorry, Clay," Maggie said softly. "I had heard about the bombing at the Planned Parenthood Center in Indiana. I'm sure she must've been very special."

Clay nodded affirmatively again.

The waitress brought their dinners a few minutes later and a fine bottle of red wine from Napa.

They settled in to enjoy their dinners and even found that their occasional silence was reasonably comfortable.

During the course of their dinner they talked about a broad range of topics, some humorous and some not so humorous before the subject turned to politics. Fortunately they held very similar beliefs, but Clay made certain that the alcohol he consumed didn't loosen his lips too much about his alter ego as a righter of wrongs.

After dinner they stepped out to the lodge's veranda and enjoyed a final drink under the night sky. It had gotten a little chillier since they'd arrived for dinner, and Clay offered Maggie his jacket. The stars overhead provided a dazzling show, and Clay pointed out several constellations in the southern sky.

"There's Orion the hunter, of course," Clay pointed out. "Lepus, the hare, is just below him, and Canis Major, the big dog, is to Orion's left."

A guitarist played for the guests on the veranda. Clay had always loved the sound of a classical guitar, and its rich melodies seemed perfectly matched with the starry display above.

"May I have this dance?" Maggie asked Clay with a warm smile on her face.

It was the first time that Clay had held another woman in his arms since Jennifer, and he privately admonished himself for enjoying the closeness. Clay closed his eyes as they slowly danced, and he inhaled the scent of Maggie's hair and skin. It had turned into a very lovely evening.

After an hour of getting reacquainted, Maggie said, "This has been a very special night, Clay. Alas, I need to get up really early tomorrow morning for work, and so do you," she said playfully. "Any chance you'd consider giving a girl a raincheck for some more time together when we don't have to think about work?"

"Yeah!" Clay said enthusiastically, "I'm sure that can be arranged."

Clay walked Maggie to her car, and for the first time in many months, he kissed another woman fully and passionately. She returned the intimacy.

"I've missed you, Clay Arnold," she whispered in his ear before kissing him goodnight a final time.

Clay kissed her back and said he'd see her in the morning. He held her car door open for her and waved as her car slipped into the darkness heading back to her place in old Santa Fe.

Clay stood there briefly and shivered a bit—not so much from the chilly night air, but more from the exhilaration of being with Maggie. He put his sport jacket back on and began walking back toward his room with a bit of extra spring in his step. He found himself humming a melody left in his mind by the seductive music of the classical guitar.

The foot path back to his room was dimly lit, and he enjoyed the solitude of the circuitous walk along the perimeter of the lot.

Before long he heard a muffled cry. At first he thought it was a fussy child who was having difficulty falling asleep, but then he noticed that the cry had more of a frantic sound to it, and he stopped to listen more closely.

There it was again! The sound was a combination of muffled cries and thrashing in the underbrush. He sensed there was a serious problem, and he immediately ran over to see what was going on.

"Shut up, *puta*!" he heard a rough male voice demand. "Shut the fuck up or I'll cave your pretty face in, bitch!"

Clay ran behind a housekeeping shack and immediately saw a man violently pinning a young woman to the ground. The attacker was tearing at the woman's blouse, exposing her breasts and trying to drop his pants at the same time.

Clay grabbed the man by the hair and wrenched him off the girl. The attacker immediately began swinging his arms trying to free himself from Clay's grip and managed to connect a glancing blow to Clay's chin. Clay leaped back on the man, and the two of them rolled around on the ground until the attacker managed to push away and fled before any more help arrived.

Clay regained his breath and staggered over to help the girl, who was curled in a protective position on the ground, whimpering softly.

Clay reached out and gently touched the girl's shoulder. In the low light Clay recognized the pretty girl, Carmelita, from the receptionist desk and sat beside her to comfort her.

"Carmelita, it's me, Clay Arnold. The attacker is gone now. You're safe." He covered her exposed breasts with his jacket and spoke soothingly to the terrified girl.

"Gone, safe?" she managed to say. "He hurt me and was going to rape me."

"C'mon," Clay said after a few moments of their both trying to collect themselves. "Let's get you up to the lodge and have you checked out and notify security."

Clay helped Carmelita to her feet, and they slowly walked back toward the main lodge. Clay had his arm tenderly around Carmelita's waist, and she laid her bruised head against his shoulder.

Once they entered the lodge, the new receptionist on duty saw that Carmelita had been hurt and began placing phone calls for assistance. Carmelita was led into a private staff office, and in the light Clay saw that she had a black eye and a split lip from where she had been brutally punched.

A security guard arrived shortly thereafter with a medical kit, and the night housekeeping supervisor moved him out of the way so she could gently wash and tend to Carmelita's wounds.

Several minutes later a male and female team of Santa Fe police officers arrived to take statements from Carmelita and Clay.

"I saw this man earlier today," Carmelita stated. "He came into the lodge saying he was looking for work as a groundskeeper, and like we do with all walk-ins looking for employment, I gave him our standard application and asked him to return it when it was completed. I didn't see him after that."

"Do you think you would recognize him again?" the female officer asked.

Carmelita shuddered at the thought, and replied, "I think so, maybe."

On the other hand, despite the low light conditions during the attack, Clay had gotten a very good look at the man, but he gave only a cursory description to the police officers. His blood temperature had calmed from boiling anger to a low-bubbling simmer, and he privately hoped he would have an opportunity to meet the bastard again.

The lodge staff and the police had things well in hand, and Clay was preparing to leave, but Carmelita held onto his arm and emotionally thanked him again for saving her. Fortunately, the episode hadn't turned out more tragically than it did.

For the second time in less than an hour, Clay walked along the foot path leading to his room. This time the only sound he heard was an owl calling from the distant trees. When he returned to his room, he had an e-mail from home waiting for him.

All's well here, Weed wrote, *I trust you're enjoying a peaceful time out West.*

"Yeah, real peaceful," Clay murmured to himself. "Bloody peaceful."

Clay e-mailed Weed back and told him about the drama at the lodge. He prepared his gear for the next day's photo shoot on Canyon Road and then stretched out on the bed.

He thought about the evening's contrasting events. He pictured Maggie's beautiful face and the excitement of holding and kissing her. Then he pictured Carmelita's tear-stained, battered face and thought about the tragedy they had narrowly averted.

The attacker had gotten away, but the feeling nagged at the back of Clay's mind that he might not be gone for good. Clay privately hoped that they would meet again. He would be better prepared next time.

"Timing," Clay thought. "Timing is everything . . . and maybe a little good luck, too."

Chapter 34

CLAY AWOKE EARLY THE NEXT morning and washed the cobwebs away with a close shave and a hot shower. He collected his camera gear and packed it into his car, and then went to the main lodge for breakfast. He also slipped the KGB Ring camera that Weed had modified into his jacket pocket. It contained a highly toxic dose of cyanide that Clay had ordered from his photochemistry supplier.

The bright light of day belied the dark human behavior that had occurred just a few hours earlier with Carmelita. As he walked through the lobby, Clay noticed that Carmelita was not on duty, which didn't surprise him given the trauma she'd endured. Clay left a message for Carmelita to call him when she could. He wanted reassurance that she was okay.

After breakfast Clay stopped briefly into the lodge's security office to ask if they'd been able to find out anything about the attacker. The officer on duty was a short, somewhat skinny chap

with the unlikely moniker of Holmes, as in Sherlock, but he didn't impress Clay as having the same penchant for deductive reasoning as the famed detective.

Clay offered his description of the attacker again, and officer Holmes told him that they were able to pull up a video of the man from the lobby's security camera. They reviewed it together, but the details were unclear.

Clay suggested that Officer Holmes might also want to ask the head of the lodge's groundskeeping crew if he recognized the attacker, since the man had applied for a position on his team. Holmes thought it was a good idea, and Clay hoped the officer would follow through. He gave Holmes his cell phone number in case he came up with anything solid.

Then Clay left the lodge and got in his car for the five-mile drive to Canyon Road, where he'd meet with Maggie to begin the day's shoot. On the drive over, he decided not to share any information with Maggie about the attack on Carmelita. He saw no sense in starting the day off recounting such an unpleasant episode. He frankly wanted to stay focused on his work, and to enjoy his time with Maggie.

Clay arrived a few minutes earlier than he and Maggie had discussed because he wanted some solo time to view the overall scene of trendy shops that lined both sides of Canyon Road. He knew that Maggie wanted him focused on specific galleries, but he also wanted to feel the mood on the street.

"Good morning, Clay," Maggie said brightly. "I thought that was you standing there looking all handsome."

"And top of the morning to you, too," Clay returned. "We have a beautiful light for taking pictures. I thought I'd get started early."

"It is a beautiful light," Maggie agreed. "Almost as nice as the candles and starlight last evening."

The two of them chatted for a few more minutes and agreed they would meet for dinner later that evening at a restaurant that

Maggie enjoyed. It was going to be a busy day for both of them, and their reward for working hard would be their time together later.

The hours passed quickly as Clay worked his photographic magic on scenes that most other photographers would've deemed commonplace. He captured facial expressions of delighted gallery patrons as they examined exciting pieces of art glass, stone and wood sculptures, weavings and tapestries, paintings, photographs, and jewelry . . . the displays of talent went on and on.

Around four in the afternoon, Clay found Maggie and told her he thought he'd achieved the look and feel that Maggie was looking for with her promotional materials.

It had been a very productive day, and the two of them reviewed a few of the images saved on Clay's camera.

"Very nice work, Mr. Arnold!" Maggie said enthusiastically. "I think a little celebration is in order later on. How's that sound?!"

"Sounds good to me," Clay said happily. "I'll meet you at the restaurant, say around eight o'clock again."

They chatted for a few more minutes, and then Maggie said she needed to check on several things yet before she could call it a day. Clay packed his camera gear and left Canyon Road in his rearview mirror as he drove away.

The late afternoon light was glorious in its intensity, and despite the fact that Clay had already shot over two hundred images for Maggie, he knew he didn't want to pass up an opportunity to photograph a landscape that was so different from the more subtle scenes he saw in the midwest.

Clay looked at his road map and found a remote road close to the lodge that connected Santa Fe to a smaller town named Tesuque a few miles away. As Robert Frost might've said, it looked like "the road not taken," which appealed to Clay's artistic sensibilities and his penchant for adventure. He saw that his gas gauge was indicating he was low on fuel, so he figured he'd fill up somewhere in Tesuque.

Clay's side trip proved to be fruitful. He saw large cacti and a small herd of mule deer. He loved the russet color of the surrounding rocks and the cries he heard overhead from a pair of soaring eagles. Once he reached the town of Tesuque, the scenery changed dramatically, and he saw the detritus that mankind's presence had left in its wake: old tires, skeletons of rusted vehicles, emaciated dogs, and dilapidated structures.

He pulled his vehicle up to what appeared once to have been a thriving general store and filled his gas tank from the old pump outside. Clay was thirsty from his drive and went inside the store to see what beverages they sold.

It took a few seconds for Clay's vision to get acclimated to the dimness inside, but he noticed two men sitting at a table nursing beers and talking idly. Clay nodded to them as he entered. They paid him little mind and went back to their beers and spirited conversation about the political dramas of the day. An ancient RCA television set showed a political rally that was going on.

"Now there's a sumbitch I could support," the grizzled-looking store owner slobbered between sips of beer. "Guy's gonna build a wall between us and Mexico and make the fucking wetbacks pay for it."

His buddy hummed his agreement.

"He's also gonna open up the federal lands so folks can graze their cattle. Hell, it's our land, not the freakin' politicians two thousand miles away."

Clay walked up to the chiller in the corner of the room and pulled a bottle of spring water out and held it up to cool his forehead.

"Hey mister, you're not from around these parts, are ya?" the loud-mouthed store owner asked.

"Nope," came Clay's reply. "Just passing through."

Clay noticed that the quieter of the men looked oddly familiar, and he tried to see him more clearly using the large mirror behind a counter that served as the bar.

"Hey, Earl?" the crude man asked. "Did you get that landscape job you were gonna apply for over at that Monastery Lodge?"

"Naw, I got the application, but I haven't done nothing with it yet. I got something else, though, or maybe I should say I came close to getting something else."

"What the fuck are you talking about?" the grizzled-looking owner asked quizzically.

"Damn near got me some pretty pussy last night," the man said, and Clay's ears immediately perked up.

Now Clay knew why the man looked vaguely familiar. It was the bastard that had attacked Carmelita. Fortunately, he didn't remember Clay.

"Wattaya mean *damn near*? You either scored or you didn't," the loudmouth said.

"Well, I got real close," Earl boasted. "I saw this pretty bitch working there, and I waited until she got off work and hid in the bushes. She came out and I cold-cocked her and dragged her sweet ass behind a shed. Woulda had her, too, if some asshole tourist hadn't jumped in. Mother fucker!"

Clay quietly sipped his water, slipped on his KGB ring, and looked at it appraisingly.

"Hey, mister!" the store owner shouted. "It's customary around these parts for strangers to buy the locals a drink," he lied.

"That so," Clay said matter of factly.

"Yeah. Tell him, Earl. A couple cans of those cold Coors would be good," he said as he pointed to the refrigerator.

Clay dutifully walked over to the chiller, retrieved two cans, and pulled the tabs off. Even with the door to the chiller open, his blood had begun to boil. While the two locals continued watching the RCA, Clay clandestinely opened the cap on his KGB Ring camera, poured equal amounts of the poison in each can, and gently shook the contents.

"Well, I sure wouldn't want to be rude to you fellas by not observing local traditions," Clay said as he placed the cans on their table. "I've got to head on now, but I hope you guys enjoy the rest of your day."

Clay watched each man take a big gulp of their free beers, and then he waited a moment by the doorway. Simultaneously, both men had looks of shock and terror on their faces as the poison coursed through their bloodstreams.

A frightening gurgling sound rose from the store owner's diaphragm, and a bloody froth oozed out of his lips. Soon both men were struggling against their destinies. It wasn't a pleasant scene, but Clay continued to watch.

Clay saw Earl's head lurch forward and smack the tabletop with an audible thud. The store owner stood up, took two steps, and fell over backward with all the grace of a drunken sot.

Both men were dead. Clay wiped his fingerprints off the cans and the handle to the chiller. He turned off the lights and flipped the door sign around to read *closed*.

Clay then shut the door behind him and calmly ambled back to his car. He looked around for any witnesses, and seeing none, he slowly pulled away and headed back toward the lodge. *Evening comes*, he thought to himself.

Chapter 35

WHEN CLAY ARRIVED BACK at his room, he looked at his watch and saw that he had a couple of hours before he needed to meet Maggie for dinner. He telephoned Weed to see how things were going back home.

"It's been busy," Weed said. "Tori is feeling her old self again, and she and Rennie have been working in the garden, harvesting some final veggies for Thanksgiving and getting the raised beds ready for winter."

"How about you and Mace?" Clay asked.

"Mace and I have been rummaging around your box of antique camera parts," Weed said, "and we may have a few more surprises for you when you return home. I have a couple of blues gigs coming up in Chicago soon, so I'll be gone for a few days. Mace says he'll be happy to keep an eye on things around here."

"We can always count on Mace," Clay said gratefully. "How're Rennie and Lex doing?"

"There's something special about a boy and a dog, isn't there?" Weed asked rhetorically. "Lex is beginning to play more, and he just runs around on three legs like nothing ever happened to him. Rennie's looking after him very well, and I think their playing together is helping both of them heal."

"How about you?" Weed asked. "How's your work going out in Santa Fe?"

"Well, I can answer that question on several levels," Clay replied. "I shot a couple of hundred images today on Canyon Road, and you'll never guess who's coordinating the promotional project."

"Florenz Zeigfeld?" Weed asked snarkily.

"Uh, no," Clay laughed. "Not even close. Would you believe Maggie Bodine?"

"Seriously!" Weed exclaimed. "The Maggie Bodine that you told me about a few years ago? I remember your saying she was a pretty special lady."

"Still is," Clay said. "Maybe even better. We had dinner at the lodge last night, and we're having dinner again this evening."

Before Weed could tease him about Maggie, Clay shifted the conversation to a more sobering subject.

"You remember me telling you about the attack on the pretty, young receptionist last night?" Clay asked. "By pure happenstance I ran into the attacker about an hour ago, and he was bragging to a buddy about it."

Weed was temporarily speechless. "You mean," Weed stammered, "you found the guy?"

"Suffice it to say," Clay replied evenly, "the KGB Ring camera works perfectly."

"Whoa!" was all that Weed was able to articulate.

"I'll tell you and Mace more about it when I get home instead of over the phone," Clay cautioned. "Go ahead and tell Mace though, okay?"

Weed and Clay chatted for a few more minutes, and then Clay said he needed to end their call so he could call Trent before he left to meet Maggie.

Trent Reynolds sat in his office chair wondering what else he and Rebecca could do to find the men responsible for several deaths, not to mention those bastards who blasted a huge hole in his Shoulder.

While Rebecca was poring over office files for any information about men named Newt and Twit living in southern Indiana, Trent reviewed the lab reports about the ANFO chemicals used in the Planned Parenthood bombing.

"Hey, Rebecca, c'mere and take a look at this," Trent said, pointing to a lab report on his desk. "It looks to me that the chemical composition is rather unique. It appears to include traces of motor oil in addition to the fuel oil. "

Rebecca looked over Trent's good shoulder at the report and said, "I see your point. Why don't I start researching some of the feed-and-grain stores in Southern Indiana and see if I can come up with a promising list of suppliers to investigate? Somebody has to know something about these guys."

A few moments later Trent's phone rang, and he answered it to the friendly voice of Clay Arnold.

"What do you mean you're not in the hospital?" Clay asked Trent with concern. "Where are you?"

"I'm where I need to be," Trent replied strongly. "Rebecca and I are in the office looking for any details in this case that'll help us catch these guys before they hurt anyone else. And by the way, thanks to Dutch Ferris, we now have the first names of two of the guys who likely shot me at Stella's and were probably the assholes who blew up the Planned Parenthood Center in Broad Ripple."

Clay sat stone still and listened for his detective friend to go on.

"We have some leads, Clay, and we have a plan that we hope will begin to finally produce results," Trent said.

"Anything I can do to help?" Clay asked hopefully.

"Not at this point, Clay, and believe me, I understand how important it is to you that we get these guys. It's very personal for me, too, but right now this is a job that law enforcement needs to handle. Don't worry, though, I'll keep you informed and even call on you if we need some extra help. Okay?"

"Yeah, okay," Clay said with a mixture of encouragement and some disappointment in his voice. "Yeah, I hear you, Trent. Just get these pricks for all of our sakes, okay?!"

"I promise you that I will do my very best, my friend," Trent said, and then the two men hung up.

Clay laid back on his bed and stared at the ceiling. His mind swirled tumultuously from one subject to another . . . the attack on Carmelita and his evening the score in Tesuque, his conversation with Trent about the possible leads, and his upcoming dinner with Maggie. It was all an emotional rollercoaster, and Clay was determined to maintain his equilibrium for whatever came next.

Before Clay left to meet Maggie, he e-mailed his agent, Lily Deupree, to confirm his upcoming travel schedule. He knew his next assignment would be a photo shoot at Balboa Park in San Diego, but he still wanted clarification of the dates for the projects coming after that.

Clay then cleaned up and put on fresh clothes. He refilled the KGB Ring camera with a new supply of poison and placed it in his jacket pocket. He also checked the firing status of his Ben Akiba Cane camera, the Stirn's Vest camera, and his Steineck ABC Wristwatch camera. He was loaded and ready to go.

The drive back to downtown Santa Fe was picturesque. The sun was very close to setting, and stars were beginning to appear high in the darkening sky. An orange ribbon of waning sunlight at the horizon was all that separated day from night. Clay was more than glad to have the violent aspects of the day over with, and he focused his attention on enjoying a pleasant evening with Maggie.

In his creative mind's eye, he imagined the darkness of night as a symbol of the murders, and the bright orange band of sunlight as a harbinger of hope for new beginnings. He chided himself for using the imagery in a bit of a trite way, but the dark-versus-light symbolism worked for him now.

Ten minutes later Clay found the Celestial restaurant that Maggie had chosen, and he parked his car just as he saw Maggie walking toward the entrance. He watched her as she spoke with the hostess and smiled at her loveliness. He also thought about how long it now seemed since Jennifer's death, and he grew sad thinking about what might've been. He took a deep breath and exited the car. His spirits improved with each footstep he took toward the Celestial and Maggie.

"Ah, yes, Mr. Arnold," the hostess said as Clay entered the restaurant's foyer. "Ms. Bodine is already here, so if you'll please walk this way."

Maggie Bodine was a picture of loveliness. Her long auburn hair lay gracefully on her smooth shoulders and framed her face like a Botticelli painting. She wore a stylish skirt with a brightly colored pattern and a cool tangerine-colored top that blended nicely with her hair. A splash of lip color, a little eyeliner, some silver jewelry, and the results were fun and stunning.

She looked up as Clay approached the table, and he was immediately drawn in by the depth of her brilliant green eyes and the warmth of her smile.

"Good evening, Maggie," Clay said warmly, and he took her hand and lightly kissed it.

"Why, Mr. Arnold, you certainly do know how to charm a lady!" she offered, and they both laughed.

"You look lovely tonight, Maggie. I'd never guess that you had worked hard all day long."

"Thank you, Clay, it was fun picking out something to wear for our dinner tonight."

Their server approached the table and asked for their beverage preferences, and after some deliberation they agreed on a pitcher of Sangria.

Clay began, "Why don't we talk about business first, and then we can settle in to a more relaxed mode. How's that sound?"

"Perfect," Maggie said, "because I'm buying your dinner tonight and writing you off as a business expense."

They both laughed again, and Clay joked that it wouldn't be the first time he was written off by a beautiful woman.

Their business discussion gradually left the topic of Clay's earlier photo shoot and morphed into a more personal conversation about each of their goals at this point in their already highly successful careers.

"I love my work," Maggie said. "And I'm way too young to think about retirement. I guess I'll just keep doing my design and promotional work until it's no longer filling my cup, so to speak."

Clay pondered how he would answer the same question about his goals. One thing was for certain: he wasn't about to share details about his mission to even the score with right-wing assholes and criminals.

"Photography is in my blood. It has been ever since my folks bought my first camera when I was a teenager. In some ways I've already accomplished much of what any photographer might hope to achieve. So I suppose I'll just keep doing what I'm doing, but perhaps I'll be even more selective about the projects I take on. Thankfully, money isn't a problem for me."

Clay's comments about money were a relief to Maggie. She had been a savvy business woman and had worked hard for many years, saving her money. The last thing she wanted was a relationship with a man who would freeload off of her success. With Clay she knew that wouldn't be a problem.

With their dinner nearly over, Clay asked if she wanted more Sangria or an after-dinner drink under the stars in the Celestial's courtyard.

"The hotel where I'm staying is just a few blocks away," Maggie said. "Why don't you walk me home and come in for a nightcap?"

Maggie paid the bill, and then she took Clay's arm as they exited the restaurant and were greeted by the chill of Santa Fe's mid-November air.

"It's nippy," she said as she snuggled closer to Clay's warm arm and shoulder.

As they walked along, Clay held her arm close and gently kissed her cheek. They entered the trendy hotel where Maggie was staying and took the elevator to the third floor. As they walked into her suite, Maggie adjusted the dimmer switch so that the room light provided an intimate glow.

"Why don't you select some music for us, Clay, and see what kind of beverages we have in the mini-bar? I'll be back in a few moments."

Maggie hummed a sweet melody as she walked back to the darkened recesses of her bedroom. Clay rummaged through the stereo cabinet and smiled as he found an older CD by his friend Weed Rawlins, but opted instead to go with the haunting sounds of Enya and Sarah McLaughlin.

He saw a bottle of Graham's port in the bar and filled two snifters. He took one and walked over to the window to admire the view of Santa Fe after dark.

A few minutes later Maggie quietly re-entered the suite's living room and placed her arms around Clay's torso from behind. She held him close and then turned him around so he was now facing her. Her lovely dinner attire had been replaced by a short, lavender-colored, satin robe, and her eyes sparkled like emerald gemstones in the dimmed room light.

"My, my, Maggie," Clay whispered softly, "I didn't know it was possible for you to be any more beautiful."

They walked over to the sofa, and Clay offered Maggie her snifter of tawny port. After a few sips, the glasses were placed on the cocktail table, and Clay pulled Maggie into his arms.

The combination of the music, the low room light, and the alcohol created an intoxicating mood, and they kissed and held each other passionately. It had been a long time since Clay had held a woman, and he found himself slipping further away from his past and moving into an alluring present.

They lay on the sofa and continued to kiss, and Clay untied the sash of Maggie's satin robe. It fell open to reveal her wearing a pretty lace bra and panties that matched the color of her robe. Clay nuzzled her neck and then her cleavage, and he lost himself in her skin and her perfumed scent.

"Come on," Maggie said and she stood and took his hand. They walked into the bedroom, and Clay saw that there was a candle flickering on her nightstand that would provide all the light that they needed.

Maggie unbuttoned Clay's shirt and slipped it off his shoulders. She reached down and undid his belt buckle, and he stepped out of his slacks and took off his socks. They stood holding and kissing each other for a few moments more, and Clay reached behind Maggie's back and undid her bra. Her firm breasts accepted his warm hand, and her nipples grew hard at his eager touch.

Maggie pulled the comforter off the bed, and Clay gently picked her up and laid her on her back. Clay lay down beside her, and their arms and legs became an intertwined tangle of flesh.

"It's been a long time for me," Clay confided. "I just hope . . ." he started, but Maggie felt his manhood growing and placed her finger up to his lips and gently said, "Sshh, you're going to be perfect."

They removed each other's underpants and enjoyed their foreplay for several more minutes. Clay moved his head down to Maggie's soft belly and continued nuzzling her until he was kissing the insides of her open thighs.

"Mmm," Maggie moaned, and she pulled Clay on top of her. "I've thought about this moment for a long time, Clay, ever since we made love a few years ago."

Clay responded by gently entering her, and they moved together slowly at first and then with a primal passion that swept them away to a climactic realm.

For Clay, there was only Maggie now. No killers that needed to be dealt with. No work projects that needed attention. No thought of folks back home in Indiana. No guilty thoughts about Jennifer. Just the warmth and wetness and scent of Maggie Bodine and a world populated by only two people on the planet. Spent, they finally fell asleep in each other's arms.

The next morning Clay was awakened by Maggie's soft cooing in his ear.

"Hey, sleepy-head, it's seven-thirty. Are you gonna sleep the whole morning away? I'll make us some coffee and see what I can conjure up for us from the fridge."

Maggie began to get out of bed, but Clay lightly put his arm around her waist and gave her a tender tug so that she fell back into his arms.

"Coffee and food can wait," Clay said sweetly. "Why don't we see if we can recapture some of last night's magic? Besides, I have to leave for San Diego in a little while, and I don't want to say goodbye to you yet."

Maggie wasn't ready for their time to end, either, and she slid back under the covers into Clay's embrace.

"So, Mr. Arnold," Maggie said, "any chance I'll get to see you again anytime soon, or do I have to wait another few years to contact your agent to get back on your calendar?"

"Ouch!" Clay replied. "I suppose I deserve that, but perhaps both of us can make a little more effort to be together going forward, without Lily's involvement."

"Well, sir, that sounds like a great plan," Maggie replied. "And since it appears that you've seen the light, maybe a nice reward is in order."

And with that, Maggie reached down and fondled Clay. Once she was certain he was fully aroused, Maggie climbed back on top of him and the two of them took their time rekindling the erotic sensations of the prior evening's lovemaking.

An hour later, Maggie and Clay emerged from bed, showered together and then prepared a petite breakfast of coffee, fruit, and croissants.

"I'm really sorry I have to leave for San Diego today," Clay said, "but being with you again has been terrific, Maggie. My travel schedule is going to be a little nutty for the next couple of weeks, and the holidays are always hectic, but I want you to know that you're very important to me, and I don't want us to lose touch, okay?"

Maggie buried her face in Clay's neck and nodded affirmatively.

"I'd like that very much, Clay."

Chapter 36

Accoʀᴅɪɴɢ ᴛᴏ Cʟᴀʏ's GPS, the drive time from Santa Fe to San Diego would be approximately thirteen hours. It meant spending a lot of time in a car, but Clay opted to drive instead of flying. He preferred not to risk going through airport security again with Weed's modified weapons. Just because he had successfully done it on his flight to Santa Fe didn't necessarily mean he could do it again. Besides, he had a lot to think about, and the alone time in the car gave him ample opportunity to do that.

His time with Maggie was still very fresh in his mind, and he fantasized about running away with her to a warm, secluded beach somewhere and leaving the world behind. Even as he thought about that, though, a pang of guilt about Jennifer rose up to meet him. He would never forget her.

But there were other thoughts that kept him company as the highway miles came and went. He thought about how much he loved living in the brewery mill complex with Weed, Tori, and

Mace. They were his family, and now Rennie was a new member who had certainly paid his dues by saving Tori and Lex. And, of course, there was his buddy, Satchmo. The big cat and Lex brought a wonderful dimension to his family, and he smiled at the strength of their personalities.

And he thought a lot about his last conversation with Trent. Was it really possible that Trent's interrogation of Dutch Ferris had given them the solid leads about the attackers that they'd been looking for?

"Newt and Twit," Clay said out loud. "What kind of dumb-ass, redneck names are those?"

Clay also reflected on his time in Charleston, which now seemed like a million years ago. Grace had been very lovely to him, and he wondered if he would ever see her again. Natalie Barrows's flirtation had brought a certain amount of amusement to his photography assignment, which helped soften the gravitas when he thought about his execution of Jefferson Talbot. Clay would never be able to think about Charleston in the same way again.

Clay continued his trek south through Albuquerque and then west on his way toward Phoenix and San Diego. He turned on the car's radio for some music to help lighten his mood again but made a mistake when he switched to a national news channel and caught the stories of the day.

A domestic terrorist takeover of federal lands in Oregon; a devastating series of bomb attacks in Brussels; another senseless school shooting; right-wing politicians calling for boots on the ground in the Middle East, and building a wall between the U.S. and Mexico. Then there were reports about the paranoid, vitriolic leadership of the NRA and religious educators' calls for students to arm themselves. The stories went on and on, and Clay's blood began to boil.

"Goddamnit to hell! Are we ever going to learn?!" he said out loud.

Clay drove along I-40 past exits for numerous small towns and decided to stop for gas and lunch in Gallup, New Mexico. He found an attractive cantina on the outskirts of town and e-mailed Lily while waiting for his lunch to be served.

Lily had scheduled another photography assignment for Clay on Chicago's Navy Pier prior to his returning home for Thanksgiving. He enjoyed being on the road, but his time with Maggie had made him a little wistful for a normal home life, whatever that meant.

With lunch over, Clay continued driving west and thought about his upcoming assignment in San Diego. Balboa Park had always been a favorite destination for Clay. Its museums and gardens were beautiful, and he was looking forward to photographing the magnificent Bonsai trees at the Japanese Friendship Garden.

Clay arrived in San Diego around dusk and checked into the hotel room that Lily had booked for him on Mission Bay. He thought it would probably be too late to call Maggie after dinner, so he sent her a brief but intimate message and told her he'd call her in the morning.

He was weary from his long drive from Santa Fe, but he needed to exercise his legs, and he chose to do so by walking to a nearby restaurant that the hotel's concierge had suggested. On a whim he grabbed his Ben Akiba cane handle camera to use as a walking stick.

He found the Harbor Inn about a half mile away and immediately noticed its rustic charm. As a guy who'd grown up in the midwest, he often marveled at the novelty of maritime motifs. The Harbor Inn did not disappoint.

It was constructed of fine, solid timbers and stained a medium gray. Its windows were divided with mutton bars, and flashes of color cascaded from the flower boxes. It had a cedar shake roof and copper gutters and flashing. The nautical theme was enriched by the glow of original glass mooring lights and colorful pennants.

It was clear that whoever owned the Harbor Inn took great pride in the building.

"Good evening, sir," came the warm greeting from a middle-aged Hispanic hostess as Clay entered the Inn. "Will you be dining with us tonight?"

"Yes, just one, please," Clay replied. "I prefer a booth if you have one available."

"Of course, sir. Please walk this way."

Clay settled into a booth by a window and placed his Ben Akiba Cane camera on the seat next to him. He looked west into the setting sun and thought about the immensity of the Pacific Ocean and the diverse cultures that existed beyond.

He ordered a vodka martini and a seafood salad. His long hours of driving were finally starting to really catch up with him, and he enjoyed the soft cushions and friendly ambience of the Harbor Inn. He took a sip of his martini, and it helped him settle in even more comfortably. The salad was delicious, and he would be sure to thank the concierge at his hotel for the recommendation.

As Clay was preparing to leave, he heard a disturbance back by the kitchen and assumed it was just normal kitchen clatter. He noticed a look of concern on the hostess's face as she hurriedly moved toward the kitchen.

"Dios mio!" she cried out, and through the open kitchen doorway Clay could see that a tough-looking man dressed in a cheap suit was holding a large knife up to a brown-skinned man's throat.

"Please, do not hurt my husband," she sobbed. "We will have your money tomorrow. I swear it!"

"You better," the tough man snarled. "Be a shame to see your nice little restaurant burned to the ground just because you didn't want to pay a little protection money. Comprende, greaseball?!"

The tough man threw the knife on the floor and gave the owner of the Harbor Inn a rough slap across the face. He then exited the rear kitchen door and went out into the night.

Clay had heard and seen enough. He dropped a hundred-dollar bill on the table, which included a generous tip, and left the Harbor Inn without saying another word. The only sound that was heard was the *tap, tap, tap* of his cane as he strode into the evening.

Once outside, Clay scanned his surroundings for the tough man. He wasn't sure which direction the guy had gone, so he took his time looking at all possibilities. He was about to give up and head back to his hotel when he looked along the wharf. There! A lighter flashed, and he noticed his target lighting a cigarette about forty yards away.

Tap, tap, tap came the steady staccato of Clay's cane as he walked along the wharf. The tough man leaned against the wharf's piling and idly watched the boats in Mission Bay as he smoked his cigarette. Despite the late hour, the harbor's maritime traffic was fairly loud.

When Clay was within ten feet of the man, he also leaned against a piling and looked out into the harbor. Being the thug that he was, the man looked over at Clay and assumed he was an easy mark for a shakedown.

"Hey you!" he said, turning to face Clay. "I'm a little short of dough. Let me see what you've got in your pockets, asshole."

Clay turned to face the man but said nothing in reply.

"Hey, I'm talking to you, asshole. Are you deaf or something?" he said menacingly.

The tough man closed to within six feet of Clay and pulled out a knife.

"Maybe you didn't hear me, jerk weed. I said give me your money."

Clay turned to face the man and made direct eye contact with him.

"If you think I'm some easy mark like that Hispanic couple you're putting the squeeze on, you might want to rethink that," Clay said sternly.

"Or what?!" the thug said to Clay. "Are you going to beat me with your little cane?"

"No," replied Clay as he flipped open the flap on his cane handle, revealing the gun barrel. "Now, why don't you just hand over your money, and we can peaceably go our separate ways."

The man took another step toward Clay and brandished his knife.

"That's far enough," Clay said, and he aimed the cane handle toward the man's upper torso.

The man took another step, and Clay pulled the firing mechanism.

Bang! came the report from the cane, and the man went down to his knees with a searing wound just under his right collar bone.

"Mother fucker!" he screamed in pain.

"Your money," Clay repeated, "or the next shot blows off your nuts. And, no one's around to save your sorry ass."

The thug reached into his pocket and pulled out a large, banded wad of cash. He threw the wad at Clay.

"You realize, you're a dead man," he snarled at Clay. "This ain't over!"

Clay bent down to pick up the cash and stuffed it in his jacket pocket.

"Oh, I'm afraid it is over," Clay said evenly, and he walked to within three feet of the thug.

The tough man took a swipe at Clay with his knife but missed badly, and Clay trained his cane handle on the man's hate-filled face. Bang! came another shot, and the man slumped and fell backward onto the dock. Clay walked over to make sure he was dead. Then he casually looked around for any witnesses, and, seeing none, he shoved the man's lifeless body into the dark water below. The doleful sounds of the harbor ships bid him farewell.

Clay closed the barrel cover on the cane handle and calmly retraced his steps to the Harbor Inn. It was nearly closing time at the restaurant, and Clay waited outside until it looked like no one was at the hostess station. He quickly wrote a note from a little notebook he carried and stuffed it inside the band that held the wad of cash together.

He stepped inside the Inn and placed the wad and note where the hostess would find it. No one saw him enter or leave. By the time the hostess returned and saw the large wad of cash, Clay was already halfway back to his hotel.

She looked around and read the note: "Compliments of a friend. You won't be bothered again."

Chapter 37

REBECCA WILLET WAS AN excellent investigator, and before long she had compiled a list of feed-and-grain stores located in Southern Indiana.

"There's a bunch of them," she reported to Trent. "I'm not sure that merely making phone calls to these folks is likely to produce the kind of information we're looking for."

"C'mon," Trent said. "It's time for us to make a road trip south. We're only a couple of hours away. Bring the list."

"You know, for a fella who just broke out of the hospital, you sure are pushing yourself awfully hard, Trent," Rebecca said with concern.

"Got to!" Trent replied. "These criminals have been very successful up to this point, and I can't think of any reason why they'd quit hurting people unless we stop them."

"Okay, but I'm driving," Rebecca insisted. "You still need to rest, or you're not going to be any good for anyone."

Trent knew better than to argue with Rebecca about this, and five minutes later he was comfortably strapped into the passenger seat. Rebecca gave the store list to Trent and steered their car toward the I-65 entrance ramp for southern Indiana.

Yesterday Trent Reynolds was a gunshot victim recuperating in a hospital bed. Today he was an officer of the law hell-bent on capturing or killing criminals named Newt and Twit.

Trent looked closely at the GPS and adjusted the size of the map to show an area encompassing all the feed-and-grain stores that Rebecca had identified. There were seven. A lot of territory to cover before dark.

"Which way, Trent?" Rebecca asked when they finally came to a point where they had to make a decision. There were seven red lights on the display, with two that were a little farther away from the others.

Trent examined the spread of red lights and said, "My guess is that these are men who like living deep in the country. No, I think these are more off-the-grid sort of people, and people who are very angry. And because I'm guessing these are back-country types, I think they probably prefer to shop at stores that are off the beaten track, too."

"So," he continued, "I say we go to these two red dots that are on the fringe of the cluster. That's where I say we start."

There was no way that Rebecca could argue with Trent's selections. He was going on pure gut instinct, and they had to start somewhere, anyway.

Trent selected the store marked by the red dot farthest away from the others. It was the Big River Feed Store, owned by a fella named Augustus Yoder. It was approximately ten miles from their current location, and Rebecca followed the GPS in that direction. They arrived some twenty minutes later, and Rebecca parked their car in a relatively empty parking lot.

"Good day," a pimply-faced kid said to Trent and Rebecca as they entered the store. "How can I help you?"

Rebecca and Trent flashed their badges and credentials at the teenager, and Trent said, "We're here to speak with Mr. Yoder. Is he available?"

"Uh, yessir," the young man responded quickly. "He's back in his office."

Trent saw the office located at the rear of the store, and he and Rebecca went off in that direction before the clerk could alert his boss about the official visitors.

Trent rapped on the office's door frame and entered without waiting for Mr. Yoder's invitation.

"Uh, yes," the startled store owner said. "Who are you?"

Again, Trent and Rebecca flashed their creds, and Trent said, "Indiana State Police, Mr. Yoder. We're here on official business. Mind if we have a seat?"

"What's this about?" Augustus Yoder stammered. "If it's about my noisy rooster, I'll see what I can do."

"No, sir," Rebecca said evenly, "it's not about your rooster. We have a few questions we need to ask you, though."

Trent continued, "You may recall hearing about a bombing at a Planned Parenthood Center in Northern Indy a few months ago. Our lab report indicated that the bombers used a device made of ammonium nitrate and fuel oil."

"ANFO. Huh. But what's that got to do with me and my store?" Mr. Yoder asked.

"Maybe nothing," Trent replied. "But that's what we're here to find out. We have reason to believe that the perpetrators live somewhere in Southern Indiana. Our source has suggested that two men named Newt and Twit might be involved."

"I'll be damned," Augustus Yoder said. "I know exactly who you're talking about, but I don't have a last name for them or an address because they never paid except in cash. About six months ago we had to stop extending credit to them because they weren't paying their bills. I finally kicked them off the premises because they kept coming up with lame excuses about not paying for stuff."

"Any idea where we can find these men or talk with someone who might know their whereabouts? It's very important," Trent said sternly.

"Detectives, I'd like to help you, but I just don't know for sure. A few months back I told them not to return unless they were prepared to pay their outstanding bills. I haven't seen them since."

"What were they buying from you, mostly?" Rebecca asked.

"Oh, the usual barnyard stuff. You know, hardware cloth for their chicken coop and bedding material. But some ammonium nitrate, too, as I recall, and a lot of it."

Trent and Rebecca shot each other a quick glance.

"And you don't know where they live, is that right?" Trent asked again.

"I don't rightly know for sure. Probably somewhere within twenty miles of here, but there's a lot of places for people to live without drawing attention to themselves."

"So if they're not doing any business with you now, where do you suppose they might go to buy supplies?" Trent asked.

"Oh, could be any number of places, but you might try Bobby Sweet's grain store over on County Road 225, about eight miles from here. Bobby might know something," Mr. Yoder suggested. "If you want I can give him a call."

"That's all right," Rebecca said. "We prefer to show up unannounced, but we appreciate your help."

"We'd also like you to keep this conversation between us, sir," Trent advised.

They handed the store owner their business cards and asked him to call them immediately if he saw or heard anything about the suspects.

Augustus Yoder walked the two detectives to the front of the store and said he'd keep his eyes open. The bewildered young clerk just stared into space.

Once back in their car, Rebecca entered the name of Bobby Sweet's grain store into their GPS and saw that it was the other red dot fairly close to Mr. Yoder's establishment.

"Hmm," Rebecca intoned. "I'd say that's damn near spot-on, Detective Reynolds. It appears that your reasoning may prove true."

"Maybe," Trent replied, "but before we head over there, Rebecca, I want to make something very clear. From this point forward it could get very rough, and I need you to trust my instincts on things. We've worked closely at the office, but we haven't out in the field, and things can go sideways quickly sometimes. We need to stay alert, and I want you to follow my lead, okay?"

"Of course. I understand, Trent. I seriously get it," Rebecca stated.

"Okay then," Trent said. "I've got two nine-millimeter Smith and Wessons in my pack. I'm loading one for each of us, and we each have two extra clips."

"Are you really expecting that kind of trouble?" Rebecca asked with concern.

"Not necessarily from this guy, Bobby Sweet, but you never know. You gotta remember the kind of men that we're dealing with. They won't hesitate to kill us, Rebecca. So from this point forward I trust no one but you."

Rebecca looked Trent straight in the eyes and nodded affirmatively. "Let's go have a conversation with Bobby Sweet."

As he often did, Clement Hacker muttered to himself as he worked alone in his pole barn.

"Probably shouldn't let those boys go to town. No telling what kind of mischief they'll get into. But we need the ammonium nitrate and fuel oil for the bombs. Oh, Ella Marie, I want this over. Totally over."

Newt and Twit were delighted with their newly found freedom. They had been holed up at their farm for several days, and they were thrilled that their pa had allowed them to venture out. At this point even being able to go to the feed store was a big damn deal.

"Now remember what Pa said, Twit," his twin admonished. "We keep our mouths shut and just take care of getting our supplies. No bragging, no storytelling, no picking any fights. We just get in and get out. Easy, right?"

"Sure," Twit replied, but Newt knew that his brother's acknowledgement was no guarantee going forward.

Several minutes later they pulled their dark pickup truck into the parking lot at Bobby Sweet's feed-and-grain store.

"Now, let me do the talking," Newt said firmly.

They entered the feed store, which at that hour was fairly quiet. Bobby Sweet manned the checkout counter, and Newt approached him to place their order.

"Wow, you fellers sure are using a lot of that ammonium nitrate," Bobby said. "I'm not sure what you're going to do with it this time of year, but hold on a few minutes, and we'll get you squared away."

Newt and Twit idly looked at merchandise while Bobby filled their order and told them to drive their truck around to the loading dock to pick it up.

"Now, be cool and keep your mouth shut," Newt reminded his brother. "We'll be out of here in a couple of minutes, okay?!"

They pulled their pickup around back, and a strapping young man helped fill the bed of their truck.

"You boys gonna blow up some stumps or something with all of this?" the employee said.

"Hell, no," Twit responded, laughing. "We got much bigger plans than that."

Newt shot his twin a cautionary look, but it was lost on him. Twit kept running his mouth, and there was nothing short of throttling him that Newt could do about it.

"We got us two buildings in Indy that our pa wants us to demolish. You know, just a couple of little projects," Twit chortled.

"What do you mean?" the young feed store employee said with concern. "Seriously, you're gonna blow up buildings with this stuff?"

Newt tried to save the situation and said, "What my brother means is that our pa has been contracted by a company in Indy to do some demolition work, and we're here to get supplies."

"Just be careful with this ANFO," the employee said. "I understand it is extremely powerful, and the amount that you got could probably take down a whole city block."

"Oh, we'll be real careful," Twit offered. "And, we've used it before."

"C'mon, Twit, we gotta go," was all that Newt could say to defuse his brother's braggadocio.

Once back in the truck, Newt looked at his brother and in no uncertain words called him the stupidest numbskull on the planet.

"What is your fucking problem, Twit? Can't you just shut the hell up for even a second?!"

"Now, Newt, who's that little prick gonna tell? And besides, we paid cash, and they don't know where we live. So, ease up, will ya? And there's no sense telling Pa, neither!"

Newt just shook his head in disbelief. "You're gonna get us both killed with that big mouth of yours. Now, let's get this stuff back home to Pa."

Newt steered their truck out of Bobby Sweet's parking lot and headed for home. About two miles down the road the brothers passed a nondescript sedan going the other way. It was occupied by a man and a woman, and they were heading toward Bobby's feed-and-grain store.

Chapter 38

C LAY AWOKE AT SIX-THIRTY in his hotel room on Mission Bay and lay in bed reflecting on the events of the last two days. He felt no pride in killing the man on the wharf, but he felt no remorse about it, either. The man had deserved a violent death, and Clay was willing and able to accommodate him.

Clay knew that he needed to get out of bed soon to do his photography assignment at Balboa Park, but he chose to stay warm beneath the covers for a few more minutes thinking about Maggie.

At the risk of calling too early in the morning, Clay really wanted to hear Maggie's voice. He felt that she somehow helped ground him in reality, and he needed a dose of that now. He speed-dialed Maggie's cell phone and was happily surprised when she answered on the second ring.

"Am I calling you too early?" Clay asked Maggie.

"Not at all," Maggie replied. "I've been lying here thinking about you."

They talked for several more minutes about the day ahead. As much as anything, they both enjoyed just hearing each other's voice.

"So, Thanksgiving is next Thursday," Clay said. "I don't think we ever got around to talking about your plans for the holiday. I'm heading to Chicago for an assignment after I'm done at Balboa Park and then back home for the holiday. If you're going to be alone for Thanksgiving, please feel free to come to my place. Tori, Weed, Mace, Rennie, and I will be together, and I know you'd be very welcome by everyone."

"That's very sweet, Clay, and I really appreciate the invitation, but my sister and her family are expecting me. In recent years we've made a family tradition out of it, so I don't want to disappoint them. I think my sister feels sorry for me because I'm not married, and it's her way of making me feel loved. Can we check our calendars and see about meeting somewhere in early December?"

"That would be great, Maggie. Lily is still finishing up some travel details for me, but I'm sure we can make it work," Clay said.

They talked for a few more minutes, and then both said they needed to get ready for their day ahead and would touch base in the next day or so.

Clay then decided to give a quick call to the farmhouse, and Tori answered the phone.

"Good morning, stranger," Tori said to Clay. "How're things in California?"

"Going well," Clay replied. "I wanted to know how you're getting along, and to see if Rennie and Mace are helping you out with Weed being in Chicago for his music gigs."

"Oh, yeah, I think both Mace and Rennie have signed a not-so-secret pact to keep a close eye on me," Tori laughed. "Rennie has been a huge help getting the house and courtyard decorated for our Thanksgiving dinner, and Mace has already made a run to the market for us, and the holiday is still a week away."

"I swear, Clay," Tori continued, "you'd think our family Thanksgiving dinner is the event of the century for Rennie. He's never known a Thanksgiving dinner before. It's very sweet and a little sad at the same time."

"Well, we'll make sure he's not disappointed. Despite all of the recent heartache for each of us, we still have much to be thankful for. I should be home the day before Thanksgiving, maybe sooner depending on how my work goes."

They chatted for a couple of more minutes, and Tori promised that she would send Clay's greetings to Weed, Mace, and Rennie. Clay finished washing up and dressed comfortably for a somewhat physical photo shoot. He collected his gear, and before he left his hotel room, he strapped on the ABC Steineck wristwatch camera that Weed had modified for him. He was ready to go.

Thirty minutes later Clay drove his rental car across the Cabrillo Bridge and entered Balboa Park. For some reason unknown even to Clay himself, he felt a special kinship with the park. The gardens and museums spread over twelve-hundred acres created a certain cultural atmosphere that made Clay feel at home.

As he scanned the scene before him, he marveled at the gardens and the architecture of the buildings constructed for the 1915 Panama-California Exposition. For Clay, the entire park setting was visually appealing.

As pre-arranged by Lily, Clay met with Max Watanabe to discuss the photo shoot at the Japanese Friendship Garden. The Garden was created in 1991 as an expression of friendship between San Diego and its sister city, Yokohama. Mr. Watanabe wished to create a large photo file of the Garden's trees and plant life, from which images could be selected for any number of promotional and archival purposes.

Mr. Watanabe's board of directors had specifically recommended that he retain the services of Clay Arnold.

"Ah, Mr. Arnold, it is a pleasure to meet you," the curator stated warmly. "We are honored to have you photograph our gardens."

"The pleasure is mine, Mr. Watanabe," Clay replied with a respectful bow. "Ever since my first visit here several years ago, I have developed a special fondness for bonsai trees. I hope to do them and your other exhibits justice."

Clay spent the morning hours arranging his equipment and shooting the Garden's magnificent collection of maple, juniper, fig, cedar, and cypress trees. It was a labor of love for Clay, and he became immersed in his connection with these diminutive trees grown in their shallow containers.

Characteristically, Clay required very little photography equipment. He preferred to keep it simple. He used his digital Hasselblad camera and a workhorse of an old Bogen tripod. Of course he had a couple of different lenses and camera backs, and a strobe, but Clay knew what equipment he needed to do the job and what he didn't need to haul around.

Clay worked intensely on every scene. He also worked fairly quickly in a fluid manner that at times almost appeared as a dance. When he was composing an image through his Hasselblad's viewfinder, though, he withdrew within himself and snapped the shutter only when the essence of the image convinced him of its worthiness. It was nirvana for Clay.

The shoot went very well, and Clay felt fortunate to have a bright Southern California light to work with. As he finished up some details in the Garden, he looked around at the other buildings, gardens, and promenades and thought he would like to visit here with Maggie sometime.

Mr. Watanabe invited Clay to be his guest at the park's Prado restaurant for a late lunch, and they sat outside enjoying the warmth of San Diego's mid-November weather.

"You live in a wonderful part of the world, Max," Clay said to Mr. Watanabe. "Back home in Indiana the deciduous trees have already lost their leaves, and the farmers have harvested their fields."

"Yes, we do live in a delightful place," Max agreed. "Sometimes the xenophobic political fervor bubbles over into something very unpleasant, often targeting Asians and other people of color. I usually remind myself that I have enough to keep my mind occupied with work, so I try not to listen to the ugliness. It is wise to remain vigilant, though."

Max changed the topic of conversation back to the photo shoot of the Japanese Friendship Garden and reviewed several of the images saved in Clay's camera as they enjoyed their lunches. Max was very excited by those he saw and couldn't wait to see how Clay would enhance them digitally.

After lunch Clay said that he would do a lot of photo-editing and send a large file of images for Mr. Watanabe to review. They agreed they would talk more some time after Thanksgiving to put the finishing touches on the garden project.

"So, where do you go from here today?" Max asked Clay.

"I have always enjoyed the drive through the countryside to the little town of Julian. I thought I'd take my time photographing around Palomar Mountain and have dinner in Julian. Then I'll head over to Palm Springs and spend the night somewhere.

"I'll fly to my next assignment the day after tomorrow in Chicago," Clay continued. That photo shoot along Navy Pier will take a couple of days, and when I'm finished there, I'll be only about a four-hour drive from home, just in time for Thanksgiving."

With this part of the photo shoot over, Max helped Clay load his gear into his rental car, and they said their goodbyes. Clay checked his GPS for directions and drove northeast toward the charming town of Julian.

The drive was very relaxing for Clay. He knew that the weather in the midwest was becoming chillier with each passing day, and he reveled in the warmth of the Southern California sun. As much as Clay enjoyed visiting this part of the world, he knew that his soul was firmly rooted in the midwest.

Clay drove through the curvy countryside that changed periodically from forests to deserts. He marveled at the range of flora nature produced from pine trees to enormous cacti and scatterings of blooming desert flowers. He found a great music station out of San Diego, and he smiled when one of the selections played was a classic Weed and Tori Rawlins blues medley.

The drive up Palomar mountain was foggy and provided Clay with opportunities to shoot cloud-shrouded scenes of the towering trees. Clay thought about his photo project at the Japanese Friendship Garden and mentally compared the size of the grand trees he was seeing on Mount Palomar with their much smaller counterparts at the Garden.

A little before 6:00 PM Clay arrived at the quiet town of Julian and parked by the Crazy Coyote pub for dinner. Before entering the restaurant Clay sat in his car and listened to the radio as he rearranged his gear. At the top of the hour, the radio switched from music to the news, and Clay listened to a string of news reports featuring the latest portrayals of ugly human behavior.

"Why do I persist in annoying myself with this shit?" Clay asked himself, as the news migrated from a story about a screwy psychiatrist who shot his fellow servicemen at a military base to the president of an evangelical college near Palm Desert who exhorted his students to carry concealed weapons on campus.

Clay had never been a religiously observant individual, but he knew enough about the sacred teachings in the Bible to shake his head in astonishment that a so-called educator and man of God would encourage hatred and violence.

Clay entered the restaurant and immediately drew some curious stares from the local folks who were there. He absently looked at his watch to confirm the time and immediately remembered that the watch he was wearing was his ABC Steineck Watch camera that Weed had weaponized.

"Evening, sir," came the greeting from the bartender. "I'm sorry we don't have any tables available, but you're welcome to sit at the bar."

It wasn't Clay's ideal choice of seating, but he was hungry and went ahead and sat down at the crowded bar next to a young couple who seemed to be drinking, rather than eating, their dinners.

Clay ordered a locally brewed beer and a corned beef sandwich and quietly read his e-mails on his phone. Lily had sent him his upcoming work schedule and hotel accommodations in downtown Chicago, and Clay wrote back to acknowledge his receipt.

Clay smiled when he saw an e-mail from Rennie that Mace had helped him compose with an attached photo of Rennie, Tori, Lex, and Satchmo. The subject line on the e-mail read, "When are you coming home? We miss you!"

Clay wrote him back and said, "Very soon, Rennie! Thanksgiving for sure."

The next e-mail Clay read was from Maggie, and he smiled inwardly at the intimate sentiments she expressed.

"Hey, mister," the young woman sitting next to him at the bar said, "that's a pretty fancy watch you're wearing."

"Yeah, I like it," Clay said politely but without really looking at her.

"Looks kinda old," she said. "Like an antique or something. What kind is it?"

Clay would've preferred to just quietly eat his dinner without any interruptions, but he fibbed and told her it was an old watch that had been given to him as a gift.

"It's called a Steineck," Clay finally said.

"I ain't never heard of that before, have you, Dickie?" the young woman said to her male companion seated next to her at the bar.

"Can't say that I have, Tanya," Dickie said. "Looks pretty expensive, though."

"Not really," Clay lied. "Just an old watch given to me by an old friend."

Clay finished his meal, paid his bill, and left the Crazy Coyote pub. He wanted to hit the road for Palm Springs before it got too dark, and he stood next to his car entering the location he wanted into his GPS.

"Hey, mister," a now familiar female voice called out to him as he prepared to get in his car. "Hold on there, mister. I want to talk with you some more about your watch."

"It's just an old watch," Clay said, with just a tinge of annoyance coloring his words.

Just then Clay noticed her male companion, Dickie, appear on the other side of a large, old metal trough filled with water. Together, they closed to within six feet of Clay.

"Like my girlfriend said, pal, we want to talk with you some more about that fancy watch you're wearing."

"Now look, folks," Clay said evenly, "it's been a long day. I'm tired, and I still have a long drive ahead of me, so why don't we just quit while we're all ahead and call it a day? How's that sound?"

"I want the watch, Dickie," Tanya said. "You told me you'd get it for me."

"Like the little lady said, mister, hand over the watch, and we all walk away ahead of the game."

Clay reached down to the Steineck watch and pushed the power button like Weed had shown him to do. Clay bent his left elbow and pointed the back of his wrist toward Dickie as if to show the watch to him.

"Well, since you've promised your little friend here that you'll get her the watch, why don't you come and get it?" Clay taunted.

Dickie, surprised by Clay's directness, hesitated at first.

"Go on, you big pussy," Tanya slurred at him. "Go get me my watch!"

Dickie took two steps forward, and Clay pressed the release button. A vivid blue light of electrical energy shot out from the face of the watch and attached itself to Dickie's twitching body. Tanya flung herself at Clay like a crazed banshee. She wrapped her legs around Clay's waist and tried clawing at his head and face.

Clay reached up and grabbed his snarling adversary by the hair and began peeling her off his body. Tanya, however, was one tough little fighter, and she managed to sink her teeth into a small part of Clay's earlobe and bite off a fleshy piece.

"Holy shit!" he bellowed, as he threw Tanya onto the ground and pushed the watch's power button. Again, a blue bolt of electricity arced from the watch and set Tanya into a writhing spasm.

Clay grabbed an old handkerchief that he carried and held it firmly up to his bleeding ear. He looked around to see who had witnessed the mutual assaults and was happily surprised that no one was around. When Tanya and Dickie finally stopped twitching, Clay bent down and lofted each one of them into the water trough.

The chill of the water immediately brought Dickie around, and he sputtered as the water splashed off the sides of the trough onto his face.

"You fucking son of a bitch," Dickie managed to snarl at Clay. "I'm gonna kill you, asshole."

Now Tanya was beginning to regain her faculties, but she was physically spent.

"Go get him, Dickie. I'm done," Tanya said.

"I really wouldn't do that, Dickie." Clay pointed the Steineck ABC Watch at the trough containing the wet couple.

Dickie leaned his soaking wet body forward and grabbed at Clay. Those were the last words that Tanya and Dickie ever heard as a brilliant blue light shot out of the watch and confirmed what an effective conductor of electricity water can be.

Clay again casually scanned his surroundings, and he saw that no one was around. He got into his car, backed it onto the street, and pulled away into the waning evening light.

Chapter 39

Trent and Rebecca entered Bobby Sweet's feed-and-grain store and were greeted by the proprietor.

"Help you folks?" came Bobby's friendly greeting.

"My name's Detective Reynolds, and this is Detective Willett. We're with the Indiana State Police, and we're here on official business. We want to speak with Mr. Sweet if he's available."

They showed the man their badges and credentials.

"I'm Bobby Sweet," the owner said. "Is there a problem?"

"We're looking for two men named Newt and Twit, last name unknown, and we have reason to believe they may be customers of yours."

"Yeah, I know them," Bobby said. "In fact, you just missed them by about five minutes. They were here picking up supplies. You probably passed them on the road."

Trent and Rebecca looked at each other, and Rebecca asked Bobby if he knew what they were driving and where they might live.

"I don't know where they live," the owner replied, "but they were driving a dark, unmarked pickup truck with a rebel flag as a front license plate."

Just then the young man who had helped Newt and Twit with their supplies on the loading dock came to the front of the store.

"Uh, excuse me, Bobby. Is it okay if I take my break now?"

"Hold on, Cody. These folks are detectives with the Indiana State Police, and they're interested in those two twin brothers you were just working with. Maybe you can help them out."

"They're weird," was the first thing that Cody said. "Especially that one who giggles a lot. I think his name is Twit, which sorta fits."

"Can you tell us the reason they came to the store today?" Rebecca asked.

"Well, yeah, they were here to pick up another supply of ammonium nitrate and a few gallons of fuel oil," Cody said.

"What do you mean *another supply*?" Trent asked. "Are they regular customers?"

"No, I wouldn't call them regular customers," Bobby answered, "but they've come in a few times, mostly to pick up the same supplies they got today."

"Got any idea what they do with that much ANFO?" Rebecca inquired.

"I really don't," Bobby said. "How about you, Cody?"

"I asked them if they were blowing up a bunch of stumps and stuff, and the brother that giggled a lot was kinda bragging about how they were going to blow up two buildings in Indy. It seemed like his brother was trying to get him to quit saying much, but he did say that their pa had been hired to do a demolition job there. That's about all I know."

"Did they say where in Indy or which buildings?" Trent asked.

"No, that's about it," Cody continued. "Oh, and when I warned them about how volatile the ANFO is, the goofy brother bragged that they had used it before. Like I said, they're a little weird."

"Any leads on who might know them around here, or which direction they headed when they left?" Trent asked.

Both Bobby and Cody shook their heads no. "They turned left out of the parking lot, but I think that's about all we know for sure. I wish we could help you further, detectives." Cody nodded in agreement.

Rebecca gave Bobby their business cards and asked him to call immediately if Newt and Twit returned. He said he would definitely do so.

Trent and Rebecca left Bobby Sweet's store, and they sat in their car in the parking lot trying to figure out their next steps.

"Where to, Trent?" Rebecca asked. "I hate the thought of this being a dead end for us."

"Me, too," Trent said. "I think it's time we stopped by our ISP Seymour office to see about putting more officers into the search. The thought of these guys buying that much ANFO with the intent of blowing up buildings in Indianapolis doesn't sound good at all. It's time to call in reinforcements."

Trent entered the location of the Seymour office into the GPS, and Rebecca sprayed a little gravel in the parking lot as they took off down the road.

Clement Hacker heard Newt and Twit's old pickup pull into the barnyard and stood in the doorway of his pole barn wiping his oily hands on an ancient cloth rag.

"You boys get everything we need at the feed-and-grain store?" Clement asked brusquely.

"Sure did, Pa," Twit replied. "Didn't we, Newt?"

"Yes, we got what you asked us to get, both the ammonium nitrate and fuel oil, Pa," Newt confirmed.

"Good boys," Clement said as if he was talking to a couple of hounds.

"Any problems at the store?" Clement asked. "Any issues, anything I need to be concerned about?"

"Naw, Pa, we did just like you asked, didn't we, Newt? No talking, no cussing, no fighting, no bragging. Just get the supplies and come back home. Right, Newt?"

"Well, Newt, is that right?" Clement asked his son sternly.

"Uh, sorta," Newt said weakly.

"Wattaya mean, sorta!" his father bellowed.

"Well, my shit-for-brains brother here," Newt said pointing to Twit, "couldn't keep his big mouth shut at the loading dock and told the guy helping us we were fixing to blow up two buildings in Indy."

A darkness grew over Clement's face like a solar eclipse, and he stepped up to Twit and backhanded him hard across his face. Twit yelped in pain.

"You stupid, stupid boy!" Clement yelled. "What am I going to do with you? You have jeopardized everything we've been working for to make those sons of bitches that killed your mother pay. I swear on your mother's grave that if you fucked this up, I will kill you myself. Do you understand me? Do you?!"

"Yes, Pa," Twit slobbered. "I swear I don't know what comes over me sometimes. I just sorta lose control, Pa. I'm real sorry. Tell him, Newt."

Newt stood stone still and didn't offer a word of support for his embarrassed and scared brother.

"Something else, too, Pa," Newt offered. "On the drive home I'm pretty sure I spotted two Indiana State cops in an unmarked car heading toward the grain store. I just caught a quick glimpse of the man in the passenger seat, but he looked kinda like that cop that Twit shot over at Stella's Diner."

"Oh no, no, no!" Clement seethed, and he tried to smack Twit again, but the agile cretin ducked just in time.

"Okay," Clement said once he finally regained his composure. "You boys get those supplies off the truck and safely set aside.

When you're finished, meet me up at the house. Because of your big mouth, Twit, we're now moving the timetable for the bombings up. I had originally wanted to blow up the insurance company and Conner Prairie Hospital on Christmas morning. Now, I'm aiming for Thanksgiving Day.

"And we sure as hell can't hang around here and wait for the law to close in on us," Clement continued. "So, tonight we'll mix up the rest of the ANFO and then leave early tomorrow morning and hide out at a place I know in Indy. This will be a Thanksgiving that people aren't likely ever going to forget."

The twins nodded their heads automatically.

Franklin Carter stretched his six-foot-four frame as he sat idly at his desk in downtown Seymour, Indiana. He had been a detective with the Indiana State Police for nine years and was resigned to being in charge of a remote post in the ISP's network of regional offices. It wasn't exactly the career move that he'd been hoping for.

Trent and Rebecca had no trouble finding the Seymour office. They pulled their car into the stall marked for official business only. They walked up to the entrance of an unremarkable building and entered a rather modest-looking reception area. There was no receptionist on duty.

Trent ambled over to Franklin Carter's office door, which was partially closed, and rapped his knuckles on the wooden frame.

"Yeah?!" came a beefy voice from within. "If you're here about the rooster that's waking up everyone on Locust Street, I've got my assistant handling it."

Trent pushed the office door totally open and said, "Crap, Carter, don't tell me that dealing with a noisy rooster is the high-light of your work day."

"Jesus, is that you, Reynolds? I didn't know that they let you out of the hospital yet."

Trent and Rebecca entered Carter's office, and the big man stood up to greet them.

"Yeah, I sneaked away and thought I'd come down here just to say hello," Trent fibbed.

Trent explained to Rebecca that Franklin Carter and he had gone through the Indiana State Police academy together, but they had pretty much lost track of each other as their careers progressed.

"I forgot you're stationed in the Seymour office," Trent said.

"Yeah, well, that's seems to be a common occurrence down here in the middle of nowhere," Carter said somberly. "It's not as cold as Siberia, but it's probably just as remote," he said sarcastically.

The three of them talked about the ISP and got caught up on office politics, and then Carter asked Trent how he was recuperating from the gunshot wound.

Rebecca interjected, "He'd be healing a lot faster if he'd stayed in the hospital for a few more days, but clearly that didn't happen."

"I'm all right," Trent said defensively. "Just a little tired and sore. Fortunately, Rebecca here has been a very good sport about driving and keeping me alert."

"So, what brings you down here, Trent? I thought you were mostly running investigations in the Indianapolis metro area," Carter said.

"We need your help, Carter. You remember hearing about the bombing at the Planned Parenthood Center in Broad Ripple and the attack at Stella's Diner?"

"Yeah, I do," Carter replied. "I remember you got shot at Stella's. Seems like I also recall hearing about a woman named Tori Rawlins getting attacked, too."

"You've got a good memory, Carter. Tori is actually a very old friend of mine. She and her brother Weed and the photographer Clay Arnold and I all grew up together. Anyway, you're correct. Tori was attacked, too."

"Thing is," Trent continued, "we know that the men responsible for all of these attacks live around here somewhere. According to information that we just got from Bobby Sweet over at the feed store, two men named Newt and Twit are planning on blowing up a couple of buildings in the Indy area. They're bad dudes, Carter, and Rebecca and I are trying to apprehend them before they do any more damage."

Just then, Franklin Carter's assistant, Blanche Curry, returned to the office in a huff.

Before she saw that Carter had visitors, she griped about that big-ass Rhode Island Red rooster that she had to quiet down.

"Biggest damn chicken I ever saw," she crowed, "and not very sociable, either. Mean bastard had some sizable spurs on his feet."

She wiped some chicken shit and feathers off her polished shoes and headed toward Carter's office to give him a full report.

"I threatened to shoot his ass in self-defense if he didn't shut up . . ." she began, and then stopped in midsentence when she saw Trent and Rebecca standing in Carter's office.

"Oh, sorry, folks. I didn't know you were here," she apologized.

"This here's Rebecca Willett, and this beat-up old cop is Trent Reynolds. They're from the Indianapolis ISP office," Carter said. "Trent and I went through the academy together. They're down here looking for two brothers who are suspects in some major crimes up Indy way."

"Pleased to meet you both," Blanche said. "Pardon my going on about the stupid rooster. I know it sounds pretty petty given the kinds of cases you're used to dealing with."

"Believe me," Trent replied, "some days Rebecca and I would prefer dealing with roosters than humans."

They all took seats in Carter's office, and Rebecca and Trent filled Blanche and Carter in on everything they knew about the two suspects with the first names Newt and Twit.

"Any information you have about these guys and their whereabouts would be very helpful. Plus, we would sincerely appreciate whatever manpower you can provide us," Trent said.

"As for manpower," Carter said, "you're looking at it unless we bring in the local sheriff, provided he's sober, of course. Blanche and I usually cover anything serious that goes on down here."

"Seems to me," Blanche began, "there were some guys with names like that that used to work over at the Wallace Concrete Company a while back. I recall Mr. Wallace calling our office once saying he was going to fire a pair of twins and their father for being obnoxious malcontents at work. He called us because he feared that he might need some help in escorting them off the premises."

"Why don't you give Mr. Wallace a phone call, Blanche, and see if he's got an address for these people," Carter suggested. "We should also crosscheck our records to see what we've got on file on these neanderthals."

Blanche departed Carter's office, and Rebecca joined her to offer assistance.

"We sure appreciate your help, Carter," Trent said. "This is personal for me since these are the jerks that shot me, and tried to rape our friend Tori, and killed Clay Arnold's fiancee in that Planned Parenthood bombing."

Just then Blanche hollered in from the outer office. "Mr. Wallace is gone for the day. You want me to try him at home?"

"That's all right," Carter said. "While you and Rebecca are checking our files, Trent and I are going to take a little drive over to Mr. Wallace's home. Call us if you find anything. C'mon Trent. We're burning daylight."

Chapter 40

CLAY LOOKED IN HIS rearview mirror as he pulled away from the Crazy Coyote pub. He saw an intoxicated man stumble out of the pub and walk in the opposite direction of the water trough. Clay breathed a sigh of relief. No one had seen what had occurred. Once again he had secretly executed his brand of personal justice.

It was nearly dark at this point, and Clay slid into a comfortable posture for the drive to Palm Springs. The traffic was not heavy, and the road conditions were very good. He tried not to dwell on what he had just done to Tanya and Dickie. He didn't feel good about it, but he certainly didn't feel bad, either. Emotionally, he was prepared to move on.

Clay reached for his phone and dialed Maggie's number. One thing was for sure: Clay really wanted to hear her warm and friendly voice.

"Good evening, Clay," came Maggie's welcoming voice. "And what have you been up to?"

"Hey there," Maggie. "Oh, you know, just a little of this and that," he said cryptically. "Just had dinner in Julian, and I'm on my way to Palm Springs now. I'll spend the night there and do some personal photography tomorrow in the desert, then fly to Chicago the day after."

The two of them talked for a few minutes longer, and with each minute that passed Clay felt more and more at peace. Maggie had a definite way of calming the savage beast inside him, and he was happy to have her in his life.

Maggie gave Clay some dates in early December for them to get together, and Clay said he would confirm what worked best for him when he wasn't driving and could check his calendar. Clay also suggested to Maggie that she consider flying to Indianapolis. She liked the idea of seeing where he lived and meeting his friends at the brewery mill complex.

They hung up shortly thereafter, and Clay eagerly welcomed the road ahead.

It was about nine-thirty by the time Clay arrived in Palm Springs. He drove along the main road through town, looking for a motel with vacancies, and finally pulled into the parking lot of the Mourning Dove motel.

He entered the motel lobby and was greeted by a rather rotund woman in her flora housecoat with curlers in her hair. She was accompanied by what was probably the ugliest pug dog Clay had ever seen.

"Good evening, sir. Snookums and I were just preparing to close up for the night. Good thing you came in when you did," she said.

Clay handed her his driver's license and credit card and said that he needed a room for only one night. Snookums sniffed at his shoes and broke wind as he waddled back toward his overflowing food bowl.

Once in his room, Clay placed his duffel bag and camera gear on the spare bed and turned on the television set. He stretched out on his bed and wearily stared at the ceiling fan as it made lazy, mesmerizing circles.

He thought about home and everyone he cared about there. He and Weed and Tori had been friends forever. Mace was like a wise uncle. Rennie was obviously new to the fold, but a very welcome addition. He smiled when he thought about Satchmo and Lex. He wondered how Trent was getting along.

"What a colorful lot," he mused to himself.

Now the ten o'clock news came on and led with a breaking story about a man and a woman in the town of Julian who had been found dead in an old water trough. A preliminary report from the medical examiner cited electrocution as the probable cause of death. Police say that they are stymied by how this could have happened because there wasn't a nearby source of electricity. They said they would release further details as they became available.

Clay listened intently to the report. He knew he was lucky to have escaped the scene undetected. Next time he might not be so lucky.

"Be cautious," he reminded himself. "Be very cautious. When in doubt, just walk away."

After a commercial break, the news turned to a story of the president of a local evangelical college exhorting his student body to carry concealed firearms on campus. Clay bolted straight upward into a sitting position to watch the report.

Rev. Clive Procter was the president and spiritual leader of the Living Desert College located twenty miles outside of Palm Springs. The college offered degrees in philosophy and evangelical living. It also offered religious services on Wednesdays and Sundays and Bible study classes every day. Its focus was very fundamental, and the faculty and student body, which numbered approximately two hundred, were expected to observe God's laws and those of Rev. Procter as well.

Procter pointed an arthritic index finger at the camera and said, "We are God's warriors in the fight being waged against Christianity. And it's not just the Muslim scum out there. It's also our own elected government officials, many of whom scoff at our way of life, that contribute to our vulnerability. We must be prepared to defend ourselves and our spiritual culture from all adversaries, foreign and domestic. That is why I encourage each of my students to carry firearms in the event that we are attacked by the evil lurking out there."

Clay's blood began to boil as he listened to this so-called man of God fuel the flames of hatred. This wasn't a real college, and this reverend was a false prophet. The Living Desert College was basically a fundamentalist cult that was indoctrinating impressionable young people for an American jihad. He thought about how often over the centuries God's name had been invoked for the righteous to vanquish their infidels.

Rev. Procter was a clever man. Whereas many fundamentalist leaders wouldn't welcome the prying eyes of the media, Procter relished it. He knew his views were so extreme that he had an opportunity to shine a global light on his Living Desert College and himself.

"And all of you in the media: If you got any questions, just come on out to our Living Desert College. We got nothing to hide, and a lot to share."

The local news program broke to another commercial, and Clay turned the television off. It had been a long day, and he was exhausted physically. Mentally, however, the last news story about the college president had him wide awake with righteous anger coursing though his veins. As Clay lay back down in bed, he slowly developed the germ of a idea, and the idea grew into a simple plan. Tomorrow he would meet Rev. Clive Procter.

The next morning broke with a celestial light that streamed through Clay's bedroom window like a clarion call. He knew it was going to be a very good day for taking pictures, and his feet hit the floor in eager anticipation of what was to come.

After enjoying a hearty breakfast at the Mourning Dove motel, Clay returned to his room to finish getting cleaned up. Surprisingly, he noticed a fake mustache and beard and sunglasses that Weed had apparently stowed with his gear.

"I swear," Clay said. "That man thinks of everything."

He placed a fresh battery in his camera and checked his settings for white balance and ISO speed.

He looked at the rest of his gear and made the decision to wear his antique Stirn's Vest Camera under a vest that he brought just for that purpose. The barrel of the lens, which Weed had modified into a .22 caliber gun barrel, protruded through a button hole. Clay made sure he packed everything else he had brought and departed the motel for his drive in the desert.

The countryside outside of Palm Springs was remarkable in its stark beauty. Even the desert holds life, Clay thought, as he entered Joshua Tree National Park. The rugged rock formations rose around him as he drove, and he imagined that he was being inspected by ancient tribal elders—strong, silent, watchful. Clay wondered if they found him worthy of admission to their sacred lands. The earth did not shake and no lightning appeared in the sky, so Clay proceeded forward respectfully.

At one point Clay came upon a secluded sunlit waterfall that beckoned to be photographed. He got out and positioned his camera on his tripod and removed the lens cap. He framed the scene he wanted in the viewfinder and manually set his aperture to f/11 for greater depth of field. He then set the exposure time for a full second to see if that long shutter speed would give the soft, white-feathered look to water that he enjoyed so much.

Clay drew in his breath evenly and slowly and then snapped the shutter at what the legendary French photographer, Henri Cartier Bresson, referred to as *the decisive moment.*

Clay snapped the shutter several more times and from slightly different vantage points. After each shot, he reviewed the image on the camera's display and then slightly modified his shutter speed and aperture for the precise look he wanted.

He continued taking a few more images of the waterfall and then moved on down the road, stopping every once in a while to shoot an abstract-looking rock formation, or the rough, weathered look of an old Joshua tree. He loved being a photographer.

Several minutes later Clay's GPS announced that he was approaching his destination. He rounded a corner and looked down into a broad valley below. Sure enough, there lie ahead the campus of the Living Desert College.

Clay pulled his car to the side of the road so he could inspect the campus. He replaced the lens on his camera with a 400 millimeter telephoto and mounted it on his tripod for stability.

The College was in the middle of nowhere, and it had no neighbors closer than five miles. Despite its isolation, there was a high security fence surrounding some ten acres constituting the main campus. Clay wondered if they were trying to keep the evil-doers of the world out or the students in.

The main administration building looked contemporary and professional. The rest of the dormitory and classroom buildings were more military-like in appearance. Simple, straightforward designs. No bright, flashy colors. Everything looked very well maintained, and the grounds were well kept. From this distance nothing appeared out of the ordinary to Clay.

Clay returned to his car and stowed his camera gear. Before continuing to the College, Clay bent down, and with a broad, short stick he scooped up a clump of wet mud and smeared it over his license plate, obscuring the numbers. He also put on the fake beard and mustache and dark glasses. Better safe than sorry, he thought, especially with a paranoid bunch of Bible thumpers in the middle of nowhere.

He slowly drove the road through the rough terrain that led to the entrance to the Living Desert College. When he was about one hundred yards from the campus entrance, he spotted a guard shack that he hadn't been able to see from his previous vantage point. He slowed to a stop by the shack and was greeted by a rather beefy-looking young man who was on duty.

"Good morning, sir," came the young man's greeting to Clay. "Welcome to the Living Desert College. How may I help you?"

"Good morning to you, as well. My name is Vance Berg," Clay lied. "I am a reporter for the Queen City Press, and I'm here to interview Rev. Procter."

"Is Rev. Procter expecting you?" the student guard asked.

"No," came Mr. Berg's reply. "I saw the good Reverend interviewed on television last night, and when he encouraged the media to come out to the college for a visit, I decided to take him up on his offer."

The young guard hesitated for a few moments. He knew about Rev. Procter's interview and his exhortation to the media to visit, but he didn't exactly expect reporters to drive out to the college.

"Er, uh . . . right," the guard stammered. He considered phoning the administration building to see if it was okay to admit the reporter.

"If you need to phone ahead to Rev. Procter, I certainly understand, since I'm showing up unannounced."

The young guard pondered this for a few moments, and he decided he didn't want to risk Procter's annoyance with an unnecessary interruption, so he chose the path of least resistance and directed "Mr. Berg" toward the parking lot for the administration building.

"Thank you, young man," came the reporter's reply when the gate was lifted, allowing his car to pass. "May the blessings of the Lord be upon you this fine day."

Clay drove the final hundred yards to the parking area for the administration building and parked in a space marked for visitors. He sat in his car to scan his surroundings and was surprised by how few students he saw walking across the campus quadrangle. Making sure no one saw him, Clay inspected his disguise in the visor mirror, and his new look surprised even him.

Clay reached for his camera gear and his notepad. He then carefully examined his Stirn's Vest camera that Weed had modified into a .22 caliber killing device.

The Stirn's camera was loaded with four .22 cartridges, with one in the chamber. The safety switch was turned off. Clay exited the rental car and strode casually for the building's entrance.

Once inside the administration building, Clay—a.k.a. Vance Berg—walked to a lovely water fountain that was the main focal point of the building's glass atrium. He was greeted there by an attractive coed who introduced herself as Miriam and offered to escort him to Rev. Procter's office. Clay noticed that she was wearing a holstered handgun on her curvaceous hip.

"Oh, I see you've taken up the good reverend's call for students to arm themselves," Clay said evenly.

"Certainly," Miriam said cheerfully. "Rev. Procter says we can't be too careful when it comes to defending our faith from the evil-doers out there."

When they reached Procter's office door, Miriam asked Mr. Berg to wait a moment while she informed the college president that he had a guest from the media.

A minute later a tall, thin man returned with Miriam. He instructed her to go ahead and take an early lunch while he was being interviewed. She bowed obediently and withdrew down an adjacent corridor.

With Miriam gone, the two men eyed each other curiously. Rev. Procter extended his hand to the reporter and welcomed him, but there was no warmth in his voice.

"Hello, Mr. Berg, is it? I am Rev. Clive Procter, president and spiritual leader of the Living Desert College. I presume you are here because of my interview on television last evening."

"I am," came Clay's reply. "It's not every day that a spiritual leader encourages his student body to arm themselves. I know our readers will be fascinated by your unique points of view."

"Well," Rev. Procter said, "I am always happy to speak with our friends in the media. Perhaps we can sit by the fountain and chat for a few minutes. My schedule is very busy, as usual, but I want the world to know about our mission to preserve our evangelical way of life. So, please ask whatever questions you wish, Mr. Berg."

Clay pulled out his notepad and pen and began asking a few prepared questions for the Reverend.

Clay asked about the College's origins and its sources of funding, which Rev. Procter easily deflected by saying how fortunate the College was that the Lord, in his infinite wisdom, had provided financial aid from true believers.

Clay asked about the College's academic programs and the credentials of its faculty. Rev. Procter claimed that their faculty was composed mostly of former students who wished to follow and advance Rev. Procter's vision of an armed evangelical world.

Clay asked Procter about his own credentials, and the Reverend went into a rehearsed litany about his wandering in the wilderness one day near the present site of the College and receiving an epiphany about training righteous crusaders on a pilgrimage in the Lord's name.

Clay dutifully listened and took notes, but after listening to Rev. Procter wax on philosophically about his own wonderfulness, Clay confronted him directly, "So, you basically walked out into the desert, put your hand on a rock, looked up in the sky, and said, *I am your prophet, oh ye who sits on high."*

Rev. Procter was not amused by Vance Berg's irreverence, and said so.

"Sir," he said very sternly to the reporter, "may I remind you that you are a guest here at our College, and as such, I expect you to exercise more professional decorum."

"Oh, excuse me for offending your sensibilities, Rev. Procter," Clay replied automatically. But then he charged ahead with his next question.

"Seriously, Reverend. Don't you find it just a bit incongruous that you are advocating violence in the name of God?"

"Not at all," Rev. Procter said, with annoyance creeping into his voice. "I do not advocate violence. I merely wish for our followers to protect themselves as they go about their missions to advance the cause of true biblical fundamentalism."

"How nice for you," the reporter replied dryly.

Rev. Procter picked up on Vance Berg's cynical sarcasm and dramatically looked at his watch.

"Well, Mr. Berg, if you have no further questions, I need to excuse myself to handle my spiritual responsibilities."

He stood up but made no attempt to shake the reporter's hand.

"We have a small campus. I'm sure you can find your way out."

"Thank you, Reverend, but I have one final question," Clay said. "How is it that you wish to spend eternity?"

Rev. Procter stopped walking midstride and turned to look at Vance Berg. His stare was icy with contempt.

"Ah, I expect to spend eternity with our Savior, Mr. Berg, bathed in love. However, I doubt that a nonbeliever like you will be joining me there."

"I suppose not, Reverend, but good luck with that," the reporter said.

Despite his best efforts not to lash out at this petulant guest, Rev. Clive Procter couldn't contain himself any further. His best human filters were beginning to fail him, and he lashed out verbally at Clay with a salvo of venom.

"YOU!" Rev. Procter hissed, as he pointed his arthritic index finger at Vance Berg. "YOU are anathema to these holy grounds. Leave now, or I will have you forcibly removed."

White spittle formed at the corner of the Reverend's sneering lips. Vance Berg met his cold stare with equal resolve.

"Hey, Rev. Procter, whatever happened to your welcoming the media to hear what you have to share?"

"Leave now, you accursed being!" He began to stalk toward Vance/Clay.

When he got to within arm's reach, Clay pushed the firing mechanism on the Stirn's Vest camera, and a .22 caliber bullet slammed into the Reverend's sternum. Thankfully, the loud sound of the water fountain helped drown out the shot's report.

Clay walked over to assess the situation and found the Reverend quite dead. Clay knew a lucky shot when he saw one, and he ironically looked heavenward and mouthed, "thank you!"

Clay swiftly lofted the Reverend's body into the fountain and watched it get swept under by the churning action. Without walking too quickly, Clay exited the administration building and went straight to his car. Thirty seconds later he was through the main gate and was gone. In total, he figured it had taken him two minutes to shoot the Reverend, dump his body in the fountain, get to his car, and exit the Living Desert College campus. So far, so good.

When Clay got to the high point of the road where he had previously spied the college campus, he pulled over to see what he could see. There was a lot of activity. Someone had found the Reverend's body. The place looked like a beehive that had been molested.

Clay took off his disguise and threw it down the hill into the brush below. He knew he had to get as far away as possible. Getting rid of his rental car was now his first priority. He drove on and saw a car wash. He pulled into a self-wash stall and proceeded to get the mud and other crud off his license plate and car body. He wanted to remove anything someone might recall.

He put the location for the car rental drop-off into his GPS and saw that he was only about twenty minutes away. Clay kept his speed very conservative and did not change lanes too frequently. Right now he wanted to be anonymous—just another car lawfully cruising down the road.

All of a sudden he saw flashing lights in his rearview mirror, and his blood chilled. Clay continued to maintain his speed and his cloak of anonymity. The lights drew closer, and the siren's blare was like a final wail before death.

The lights belonged to two police cars, and they bore down on Clay's position with a vengeance. Clay began to pull his car over to the side of the road in deference to his fate. One hundred yards, seventy-five, fifty yards, and then the police cars were in front of him, streaming away on a mission that apparently didn't require Clay Arnold's apprehension and incarceration.

Clay damn near lost control of his car. He was so surprised that the cops hadn't arrested him.

"Unfuckingbelievable!" was the only thing that came out of Clay's mouth.

As much as Clay wanted to pull his car over and stop until he could get his wits about him again, he just wanted to drop off the car and walk away. The car was the only thing that could link him to the campus. Two long minutes later Clay pulled the car into the rental agency's lot and exited the vehicle. An employee examined it and said everything looked fine. He even thanked Clay for washing it.

"You wouldn't have a shuttle going to the airport anytime soon, would you?" Clay asked.

"I just got back from a run to the airport," the employee said, "but c'mon; it's slow today. I'll run you over there."

He called over to his co-worker to say he was making a quick run to the airport and would be back in twenty minutes. Clay and his driver got in another car, and a minute later Clay Arnold, a.k.a. Vance Berg, had achieved his goal: anonymity. Next stop, Chicago.

Chapter 41

Franklin Carter and Trent Reynolds climbed into Carter's unmarked cruiser and took off for the address that Blanche Curry had given them for the Wallace residence. It was dark by the time they got to his home, and Mr. and Mrs. Wallace had just sat down for dinner when the doorbell rang.

"What now?!" Mr. Wallace grumbled as he rose from the table to answer the door. "It better not be those darn kids selling candy bars for school again. I swear, I feel like we're on every charitable organization's hit list for money."

But when he opened the door and saw Franklin Carter and another man standing on his porch, he lost his bluster.

"Evening, Mr. Wallace," came Carter's level voice. "I hope we're not taking you and the missus away from your dinner."

"You are, Detective Carter, but you're here, which means it's probably something pretty important. So you might as well come in and have a cup of coffee."

"This here's Trent Reynolds," Carter said. "He's an Indiana State Police detective assigned to the Indianapolis office. He's down here on a very important case, and we think you might be able to shed some light on a couple of domestic terrorists."

"Me?!" Mr. Wallace said with surprise. "You certainly know how to get a fella's attention, Detective. I don't know what I can do to help, but have a seat and let's hear what you have to say."

Mrs. Wallace brought the three men cups of coffee and then retreated to the kitchen to finish her dinner and let the three men talk among themselves.

Franklin Carter deferred to Trent. "Why don't you fill Mr. Wallace in on what's been going on around Indy and why we're here, Trent?"

"Thanks, Carter. Mr. Wallace, I'll come right to the point. Over the last several months, at least two men have been bombing buildings and terrorizing innocent people in the Indianapolis area. Through our investigation we have learned that two men with the first names Newt and Twit are highly likely suspects. We understand that they may live down around Seymour."

Carter interjected, "My colleague Detective Willett recalled that some time ago two men with names like that caused problems for you at the concrete plant."

"She's got a good memory," Mr. Wallace said. "Must be almost three years ago now that I called your office about some very aggressive and disrespectful employees that were causing headaches for me. The last name's Hacker, and their father's name is Clement Hacker. His nasty sons are rotten fruit that didn't fall far from the tree. Their old man is as bad as either of them, and he got even worse when his wife died of cancer."

"Where do we find them, Mr. Wallace?" Trent asked directly. "We have reason to believe that they're planning to blow up two more buildings in Indy fairly soon. Any help you can provide us, like a home address or a photograph could help save a bunch of lives."

Mr. Wallace hollered to his wife in the kitchen. "Honey, I'll be back in about an hour. I'm taking these detectives to the office to look over some employee files. And don't fret none. Everything's fine; just helping out, is all."

Fifteen minutes later the three men arrived at the offices of the Wallace Concrete Company, and Mr. Wallace immediately began pulling employee files looking for a home mailing address.

"All three of those men were a royal pain in the neck," Mr. Wallace declared as he deftly worked his way through personnel and payroll files. "Hell, I remember the last time I had a problem with them. They dumped wet concrete on another employee and tried to hold him still while it set up. A couple of the other guys intervened, but the poor guy had some fairly caustic burns from the chemicals in the cement. The guy was okay, but he missed nearly a week of work. I fired the Hackers on the spot. Good riddance!"

"All right, here's what we're looking for," Mr. Wallace said as he pointed to the file. "Apparently, they all live together on Crow's Bridge Road, but it doesn't give a house number. Seems I recall the one named Twit bragging about living in the sticks like a bunch of survivalists. Yeah, like that's something special to aspire to!"

"Do you know where their place is?" Trent asked.

"I think I have an idea," Mr. Wallace said, "but I seriously doubt that I could find it in the dark. It's pretty remote, and it sounds like these Hacker men have good reason to stay out of sight. My recommendation is for us to go looking for them at first light. Like I said, we'll never find them in the dark."

Carter and Trent thanked Mr. Wallace when they arrived back at his house. They agreed they would meet again at 6:00 AM at the concrete plant and head out from there.

The two detectives drove back toward Carter's office. Each wondered what the morning might bring.

"I really appreciate your involvement, Carter. You and Blanche have been very helpful. I feel like we're finally closing in on these people."

"I really want us to get these guys, too, Trent. They're obviously dangerous criminals, and on top of that I don't enjoy the thought of these assholes living in my jurisdiction."

Trent and Carter went back inside Carter's office and talked with Blanche and Rebecca about their conversation with Mr. Wallace.

"That was great work on your part, Blanche," Carter said. "Mr. Wallace knew exactly who Newt and Twit are, and he also identified their father, Clement Hacker, as another aggressive malcontent."

Trent added, "We're all meeting at the concrete plant at 6:00 AM tomorrow and then trying to locate where the Hackers live. Hopefully we can end this chapter in human depravity before they hightail it to Indy and cause more heartache for innocent people."

———

Clement, Newt, and Twit worked side by side for several hours mixing the fuel oil to the ammonium nitrate and packing the beds of the twins' pickup trucks to the maximum with ANFO. They then attached two truck caps to the tops of the beds and had their fertilizer bombs hidden from view.

"Good work, boys," Clement said to his sons as they completed the truck bombs around 4:00. "Now let's take some time for me to go over my plans with you—and I swear, Twit, if you fuck this up . . . ." He let his unfinished sentence hang like a death shroud.

"We're taking our three trucks with us," Clement continued. "You boys will be driving the ANFO trucks, and I'll have mine to pick you boys up after we blow the insurance company and the hospital. We all have our cell phones with us, which we'll use for communicating with each other, but also because they'll serve as the detonators for the ANFO once you have the trucks in position.

We have two other cell phones attached to the bombs. A simple phone call to those devices will set the bombs off. Understand?!"

"Yes, Pa," came their automatic reply, but Clement wondered if they were really paying close attention to his plans. "C'mon then," Clement said. "If those state cops are down here looking for us, we need to leave before sunrise and get up to my hiding place in Indy."

Ten minutes later the Hacker men were all packed up, and they formed a three-truck caravan heading north to Indianapolis.

Clay Arnold sat at the departure gate waiting for the boarding call for his flight to Chicago. He surreptitiously read his cell phone news apps, all the while keeping his eyes peeled for any sudden appearance by the police.

He knew he had been very lucky executing Reverend Procter and making a successful getaway, but he knew that his luck could run out at any minute. His flight was scheduled to board very soon, and he wouldn't feel entirely relaxed until his plane's wheels left the tarmac.

Clay's cell phone rang, and he was pleasantly surprised to see that it was Maggie calling him.

"Well, good evening, Maggie, this is a wonderful surprise. I wasn't expecting to talk with you until I got to Chicago. I'm sitting here in the Palm Springs airport getting ready to board my flight."

"Well, I'm glad I caught you, then," Maggie said brightly. "I've had a change of plans with my work, and I was wondering if you'd like me to join you in Chicago while you're there."

"You're kidding!" Clay replied with excitement. "That would be wonderful! I can't think of anything I would enjoy more."

"I know you have to work while we're there, but Chicago is one of my very favorite cities on the planet, and I'm sure I'll have no difficulty keeping myself occupied. Then, of course, we'll have our nights together," Maggie said with sexual innuendo. "I've missed you, Clay!"

They talked for a few more minutes, and Clay gave Maggie the name of the hotel where they'd be staying downtown along the Chicago River.

"I better scoot now, Maggie. Let's touch base when we arrive in Chicago."

They hung up, and Clay was preparing to get in line to board his flight when his phone rang again. This time it was Trent Reynolds calling.

"Hey Trent," Clay said as he answered his phone. "What's the good word?"

"The good word, my friend, is that my colleagues at the Seymour ISP post have helped us identify the attackers we're looking for, and we have a pretty good idea where they live. We're planning to regroup at 6:00 AM and raid their property. I just wanted you to know."

"Wow—great work, Trent!" Clay replied. "I can't talk very freely right now since I'm standing in line to board a flight to Chicago, but I'm really glad you gave me a call. Will you please keep me informed? And, by the way, I should be back home this Wednesday, just in time for Thanksgiving."

Trent and Clay talked for another minute, and Trent told Clay he would definitely keep him in the loop. Shortly after they hung up, the gate attendant scanned Clay's boarding pass, and twenty minutes later the jet's wheels left the runway, and he was on his way back to the Midwest.

Chapter 42

MORNING CAME VERY EARLY for the detectives from Indianapolis. Trent had set his alarm for five o'clock and gave a quick call to Rebecca's motel room to make sure she was awake and getting ready to go. He then sent a text message to Carter confirming that they'd meet at six at the Wallace Concrete Company. Carter replied affirmatively and said that Blanche would remain behind to cover the office.

It was still dark outside when Rebecca and Trent climbed into their car. Trent was physically improving each day from his gunshot wound, but Rebecca took over driving duties again to allow him more riding comfort. Fifteen minutes later they arrived at the Wallace Concrete Company. Mr. Wallace was outside waiting for them with a county map in his hands. As they were exiting the car, Franklin Carter pulled his car into the space beside them.

Dawn was breaking in the east as they all piled into Carter's cruiser. Mr. Wallace got into the front passenger seat to serve as navigator, and Rebecca and Trent got in back.

"Where to?" Carter asked Mr. Wallace.

"You remember the old Miller property on county road 250 N?" Mr. Wallace asked.

"Vaguely," came Carter's reply. "Remember, Mr. Wallace, I've only lived in Seymour a few years."

"Right," Wallace acknowledged. "Turn left out of the parking lot and go about four miles. When we get up to the old zinc mill, turn left again, and then I'll want to check the map more. Seems to me I recall that the old Miller place and the zinc mill bordered each other. I remember that there was a service road that led from the mill to the Miller farm. Now, I'm not totally sure, but I think that's where they live."

Trent checked his service revolver and clips to make sure they were loaded.

With each mile they drove, the sunlight was beginning to brighten the world again, and Trent became very encouraged that they would finally be able to apprehend the Hacker men.

"There's the zinc mill up ahead," Mr. Wallace advised. "Pull into their lot and go around back toward those conveyers. I think the service road is back there."

Detective Carter did as he was told and came to a stop once they were positioned by the big conveyers.

"I don't see any roads back here," Carter said with annoyance.

The four of them got out of the cruiser and looked around for the entrance to the road. Rebecca walked behind an old tool shed and noticed recent tire tracks in the moist November soil. The tracks came to an end by a couple of bales of hay from the Miller farm.

"Looks like there's been some recent truck activity over here," Rebecca, shouted out.

The three men trotted over to see what she meant. Sure enough, it was the entrance to the service road, and someone had used the bales of hay to block access to it.

"Give me a hand, will ya, Carter?" Trent said, and the two men began moving the bales out of the way. There were ruts in the soil imprinted by heavily laden vehicles.

"Looks like trucks came through here very recently. Hard to tell how many there were, but it looks like at least two," Carter ascertained.

"How far does this road go before it gets to the Miller homestead?" Carter asked Mr. Wallace.

"Oh, no more than maybe a quarter-mile," Wallace surmised. "Not far."

"All right," Trent said. "Mr Wallace, this is as far as you go. Wait for us over by the zinc mill office. We'll come back for you after we've completed our search."

Mr. Wallace wasn't happy about being left behind, but he understood the gravity of the situation.

Trent joined Carter in the front seat, and Rebecca pulled out her service revolver and chambered a round. She kept the safety on.

Carter pulled his cruiser into the entrance of the service road, where his car bogged down briefly in the wet truck tracks. He expertly used his low gear to slowly regain traction, and the cruiser reached firm ground. Cautiously, they pulled ahead into the tree-lined service road.

The sun had not fully risen over the horizon, but there was enough light now that the three police officers could see where they were going. The trees engulfed them as they proceeded forward, and Rebecca noticed that it was not an attractive grove. She felt as if they were entering a foreboding landscape.

With the autumn leaves off the trees, Carter noticed a metal barn roof about fifty yards ahead. He pulled his cruiser to a halt and checked his service revolver as well. He also pulled a riot shotgun from the gun rack and chambered a twelve gauge shell.

"We should go on foot from here," Carter advised. "Trent, you and Rebecca head down the service road, but give me a couple of minutes to swing around through the woods behind the barn."

Trent and Rebecca waited the amount of time they thought it would take Carter to get in position, and then they began stealthily walking down the road toward the old Miller place. Just before they got to the barnyard, Trent and Rebecca kneeled down out of sight, and Trent sent Carter a silent text to let him know they were in position.

The three detectives kneeled stone-still in their positions looking for any sign of activity. Five minutes passed without incident, and Rebecca grew impatient.

"Stay here, Trent, and cover me," Rebecca said. "I don't think they'd be expecting a woman, so I'm going to walk up to the door of the farmhouse and see if anyone's at home."

Trent was surprised by Rebecca's bravado, but he couldn't argue with her logic. He nodded his agreement and texted Carter to let him know what Rebecca was doing. Carter acknowledged the plan.

"Keep your eyes open, Rebecca," Trent warned. "They may have booby trapped the premises."

"Swell," came Rebecca's one-word response.

Rebecca placed her service revolver in the holster located at the small of her back and began a casual walk across the barnyard. Nothing stirred. Even the birds were silent as she approached the tired-looking property.

Trent saw Carter move to a corner of the pole barn that gave him a line of sight to the front porch of the farmhouse. Rebecca stepped onto the old wooden porch to the house and rapped on the doorframe.

"Anyone home?" she called out. She was greeted by silence. She knocked again on the door and waited for a response from within. Nothing came.

She pulled her revolver from its holster and tried the doorknob. It opened easily. "Anyone home?" she called out again. Only silence greeted her.

Trent and Carter quickly texted each other, and Carter swiftly moved to the rear door of the farmhouse while Trent joined Rebecca on the front porch. All three had their firearms ready, with the safeties off.

Trent moved past Rebecca into the house and motioned for her to check the upstairs. Carter came in through the back door and met Trent in the kitchen. Twenty seconds later Rebecca came down the steps and reported that the upstairs was clear.

Trent's adrenalin was keeping the wounded warrior keenly alert and relatively pain-free, but he began to feel deflated at the prospect of not apprehending the Hacker men.

"Let's check the pole barn," Carter advised. "I peeked in through a window when I was next to it, but it was too dark to see inside. We can come back here to complete our search after we have cleared the barn."

Trent nodded agreement, and the three officers went off in the direction of the barn. Once there, Trent inspected the large sliding door for wires that might be connected to an explosive device. He found none and very cautiously slid the door open. He was immediately hit by the offensive odor of ammonium and fuel oil, but the Hackers were gone, and so were their vehicles.

"Maybe they'll be back," Rebecca offered.

"Maybe," Carter replied. "But it sure looks like they've cleared out for a while."

Trent was very disappointed. "Damnit, we should've come here last night. My guess is that they've finished making their bombs, and they're heading back north to Indianapolis. I'll make sure our Indy command post alerts the bomb squad and the police departments for surrounding municipalities."

Carter was very disappointed, also. "It was too dark last night, Trent. We never would've found this place, even with Wallace's help. Let's do a thorough search of the house and the barn to see if they left us any clues about where they're heading."

The three officers began their search in the barn, and Rebecca motioned the men to where she was standing.

"Look here!" she said, as she pointed to Clement Hacker's old workbench.

There were detailed schematics for making fertilizer bombs and converting cell phones into detonation devices.

Franklin Carter let out a low whistle when he saw the schematics and the remainder of ANFO supplies behind the workbench.

"Not good. Not good at all," Carter said. "And right under our noses here in Seymour."

Trent suggested that Rebecca go up to the house to do a thorough search.

"Specifically, look for any information that might indicate where they're going and what they plan to blow up. Time is running short, and we need to speed things up."

While Rebecca began her search of the farmhouse, Trent and Carter looked for any clues at all. The schematics told them the kind of explosive devices and their detonators the Hackers had made, but they still didn't know what their intended targets were.

Trent took a load off his sore body and sat at Clement Hacker's workbench. When Rebecca found the bomb and detonator schematics a few minutes earlier, they all got so engrossed with them that they missed the two drawings that Trent was now staring at.

Hand-drawn on lined notebook paper were crude sketches of two buildings with various entrances, access points, and adjacent roads. The first sketch showed what appeared to be a single, large office building with an underground garage. The individual roads were not marked by name, but from the drawings, Trent's intuition was that it was in downtown Indianapolis south of interstate 70.

The second drawing was far more complex because it had a main building hub with several large wings radiating from the center. Several entrances were marked, with one in particular circled. It was the main hub.

Trent continued to look at the crude drawings to see if he could divine any further information. The first sketch could represent any one of scores of office buildings in downtown Indianapolis. They needed more information.

Trent stared at the second sketch, which looked like a building complex that was more institutional in nature, rather than an office building. He was about to get up and continue searching the barn when he noticed the letter "H" marked to the side of the second building.

"Hey Carter, come look at this," Trent said. "We missed these two drawings earlier. One looks like an office building, maybe somewhere in downtown Indy, and I think the letter 'H' refers to a hospital, but which one?"

Carter looked at the drawings but couldn't think of anything else to add.

"You know Indianapolis far better than I do, Trent. They look to me like places that could be anywhere."

"Wait a minute," Trent started. "Didn't Wallace say that Clement Hacker's wife died of cancer?"

"Yeah, I remember that," Carter replied.

"Listen, why don't you continue searching the pole barn, Carter. I want to go up to the house to see if Rebecca's come up with anything. I'm just wondering if his wife's death can point us in the right direction. Medical bills, invoices, things like that. Clement Hacker is one angry man, and losing his wife may have pushed him right over the edge."

"Rebecca!" Trent called out as he entered the Hacker's farm house.

"Up here!" she yelled back. "C'mon up."

Rebecca sat in a chair in what looked like a spare bedroom that had been turned into a sitting room. In her lap she held a loose stack of papers containing envelopes and bills and official-looking correspondence.

"I've just started going through this stack that I found in their family Bible," Rebecca said. "And at first glance it's pretty clear that Mrs. Hacker's cancer treatment racked up some very sizable bills, which isn't unusual."

"No," Trent said. "But how Mr. Hacker and his boys have been reacting to stuff is highly unusual."

Trent proceeded to tell Rebecca about finding the drawings of the buildings on the workbench. He told her about seeing the letter "H", which they agreed referred to a hospital.

"Look, I think we should get back to our car and then head straight home to Indy. Bring the papers along and look at them while we're driving. Something's going to happen soon, and I have a sinking feeling that not everyone's going to enjoy the Thanksgiving holiday."

Chapter 43

Clay's flight arrived at O'Hare International Airport around five in the afternoon, and he collected his luggage and camera gear and walked over to Ground Transportation to see about a shuttle to his hotel. There was one leaving in about ten minutes, which gave Clay time to try and reach Weed.

Weed saw that it was Clay calling, and he teased him by saying, "Is this the Robin Hood of Justice?"

Even though they had both promised never to make any references to Clay's other life as a righteous avenger, Clay couldn't help laughing at Weed's playful reference.

"Yeah, it's me, and I'm here in the forest surrounded by a bunch of guys in green tights!" came Clay's irreverent reply. "Hey, I just arrived in Chicago, and I thought you and Maggie and I might connect for dinner some time in the next two days."

"No can do, my friend. I finished my gigs in Chicago, and I'm already back home at the brewery complex," Weed said. "Although I would've enjoyed meeting your lady-friend, Maggie, and maybe

sharing some stories with her about what a weird kid you were, especially during puberty."

"Gee, thanks," Clay laughed. "Remind me never to introduce you to anyone special to me."

The two friends talked a bit more, and even though each was very tempted to talk about Clay's "adventures" with the antique camera parts that Weed had repurposed as weapons, they were smart enough to steer clear of the topic on the phone.

"There's a lot to share with you, but I'll be home on Wednesday, and I'll tell you and Mace at the same time."

Clay was informed that the shuttle was preparing to leave for the hotel, so he and Weed hung up, and Clay helped the shuttle driver safely stow his gear.

The Chrysalis Hotel was a new hotel along the Chicago River that boasted many luxury amenities that Clay normally didn't need. His agent Lily had found a great deal for him online, however, and decided to treat him to someplace special. Now that Maggie was joining him, he was very pleased that Lily had booked such a luxurious place.

"Very impressive," Clay thought to himself as he entered the Chrysalis's atrium and looked up at the towering glass ceiling. "I'll have to remember to get something very special for Lily for Christmas." He always did, anyway.

Clay checked in at the reservation desk and informed them that he would be joined by a woman named Maggie Bodine. He then rode the elevator to the twenty-first floor and entered his suite.

It was a stunning room with an equally stunning view of Lake Michigan and the Magnificent Mile. Clay prepared his camera gear for the next day's photography assignment on Navy Pier and shot an e-mail off to Rollie Evans, who was coordinating the assignment. They agreed to meet at nine-thirty, the following morning at the Pier.

Clay was exhausted from his work and his "extra-curricular activities" in southern California, and he lay down on the bed to take a quick nap before Maggie arrived. The next thing he knew, he was feeling a tickling sensation on his ear, and when he tried to move the annoyance away, he awoke to see a smiling, gorgeous Maggie Bodine seated on the bed with him.

"Is it really you, Maggie, or am I still dreaming?" Clay pulled her into his arms and gently shifted her body so she was now lying next to him.

"It's really me, you handsome hunk. You didn't think you could get rid of me so easily," she teased. "Why don't you give me five minutes to put some things away and freshen up, and I'll join you for a little reunion before you take me somewhere fun for dinner."

"Okay: five minutes, but not one second more," Clay replied. "Ooh, I've missed you."

They kissed passionately for another minute, and then Maggie pulled free to finish putting clothes away before she glided off to the bathroom.

"Four minutes now," Clay called out to her as she receded to the bathroom.

"Good things come to those who wait," she taunted him. "Don't go anywhere!"

Clay had no intention of going anywhere, and when Maggie reappeared at the foot of the bed a few minutes later, she literally took his breath away.

As a professional photographer, Clay Arnold had seen and photographed images of people and places that bordered on the magnificent. With his camera he had recorded many of those scenes and had been well-compensated for his talent. And he had shot portraits and fashion shots of some of the world's most gorgeous women. Clay knew beauty.

Maggie Bodine stood by the side of the bed wearing a short, lavender, satin robe. The candlelight from the nightstand highlighted her auburn hair like a fiery halo. Her complexion was radiant and a little flush. She felt warm. Clay gently put his arm around her waist and pulled her into bed. The bedding enveloped them like a chrysalis, just like the hotel's namesake.

Maggie and Clay took their time getting reacquainted and explored each other's virtues with respectful pleasure. Clay nuzzled Maggie's neck and fondled and kissed her lovely breasts. He gently caressed the inside of her smooth thighs and used his fingers to arouse her. Maggie fondled Clay beneath the sheets and was delighted by his responsiveness. They made love with primal passion, and afterward Maggie lay in Clay's arms and breathed in the smell of his skin.

Perhaps more than any other physical feature, it was Maggie's eyes that captivated Clay. As they lay in bed he peered deeply into them and saw an earnest sincerity that made him feel at peace. He flashed briefly on his lost love, Jennifer, and believed she would want him to move forward in his life.

Clay followed Maggie into the bathroom, and they made love again in the steamy shower. Afterward they held each other and let the warm water wash away their cares.

"My, my, Mr. Arnold, but you certainly know how to get a girl's attention," she teased. "I could get very used to having you as my sex slave."

"Bring on the whips and chains," Clay quipped. "You are an amazing lover."

"Now then, sir slave, there's only one other thing that I require from you to complete this romance."

"Oh?" Clay asked appraisingly as he wrapped his arms around her robed body.

"Dinner!" Maggie laughed. "A lovely candlelight dinner with wine, music, and a sinful dessert."

They both laughed, and Clay replied, "Coming right up, milady."

And while Maggie finished getting dressed, Clay phoned the hotel's concierge and made reservations at the hotel's four-star restaurant. It was a perfect way to end the evening, and any lingering thoughts about his executions in Charleston, Tesuque, San Diego, and Palm Springs simply wafted away like smoke on the wind.

Chapter 44

THE THREE HACKER MEN cruised along I-65 north toward Indianapolis in separate vehicles. Clement led the caravan and maintained a steady speed just below the 70 mph limit. Newt and Twit obediently followed their father in their pickup trucks and managed to stay out of trouble. So far, their two-hour drive through south-central Indiana was uneventful.

Clement scanned the horizon before him. The deciduous trees had already lost most of their leaves and were preparing for a five-month slumber. Winter was near.

"Ah, the great sleep!" Clement said out loud as he gazed at the tree shadows stretching across the road. "One last act of revenge against those who let you die, Ella Marie. One last rage against the hospital and insurance company. Then, come what may, and with the good Lord willing, I will be with you again."

The Hacker caravan drove past rolling farmland that now lay fallow. They crossed over the East Fork of the White River, past

Columbus, Indiana, and Camp Atterbury. Soon they came to the towns of Edinburgh, Franklin, and Greenwood, and by 8:00 AM they were on the southern outskirts of Indianapolis.

Clement texted the twins and told them to stick close to his truck and to mind all traffic laws. They hadn't come this far only to be apprehended because of a moving violation.

As they approached the neighborhood of Broad Ripple, Clement pulled his truck down a small service road he had found when the three of them were fixing to blow up the Planned Parenthood Center nearly six months ago now. At the end of the service road, Clement pulled up to an abandoned warehouse and motioned for his sons to pull their trucks behind the building.

There was a chain that locked the entrance to the warehouse's truck bay, but Clement made fast work of removing it with a bolt cutter he carried in his truck. The three of them pulled their vehicles inside and slid the large garage door shut. They had arrived undetected.

"Golly, Pa!" Twit exclaimed as he looked around. "You don't really expect us to stay here until Thanksgiving, do you?"

"I sure do," came Clement's viper-like hiss. "And if you think you're going anywhere, Twit, you better think twice. Now sit down and shut the hell up!"

Clement gave Newt fifty dollars in cash and told him to go get enough food and water to last them for two days.

"There's a grocery store three blocks away. Walk down there and get us some grub, and do not say one word that could lead anyone to us."

Newt nodded his understanding and sneaked out the door and into the shadows.

After Trent and Rebecca split up from Carter and Wallace, they sped up I-65 with Trent behind the wheel. They promised Carter that they would keep him informed about the Hacker men, and Carter said he and Blanche would return to search the Hacker homestead again and let them know if they found anything further.

Trent felt a real sense of urgency to get back to Indianapolis. His body ached from his gunshot wound, and it was only through sheer willpower and adrenalin that he was able to forge ahead. Rebecca worried that her partner was overdoing it, but she knew there was no way she would be able to get him to rest more.

Trent's heavy foot on the accelerator chewed up the road miles, and Rebecca used their time on the road to closely examine the stack of medical and insurance papers she had found in the Hacker's Bible.

"You know, Trent, it surprises me that cold-blooded killers like the Hackers would even have a Bible," Rebecca said. "As I think about it, though, human history is littered with stories of killing in the name of religion. If I were God, I think I'd be pretty pissed off."

"Amen!" came Trent's succinct reply.

The two detectives spent the next several minutes traveling quietly with the only sound coming from the tires humming on the pavement. Trent was doing a mental exercise trying to identify the large office buildings in downtown Indy and the area's plethora of hospital facilities. It was a daunting task.

Rebecca sat in the passenger's seat reading the documents she had found in the Hacker's family Bible. The documents did not paint a pretty picture of the last fifteen months of Ella Marie Hacker's life on earth. The glioblastoma multiforme was an insidious form of brain cancer that virtually no one ever survived. Mrs. Hacker's death was a painful testament to that fact.

"Whew," Rebecca exhaled audibly. "Not a pretty way to die," she lamented. "I can understand the fear and anger the family members must have felt. They obviously still do."

"Yeah, well, the fear seems to be gone, and only the anger remains," Trent said solemnly. "Do the papers give any indication about probable locations for the bombs?"

"A couple of insurance companies are documented here, but the main one is Hoosier Homestead Insurance. Apparently, that company refused to make good on the Hacker family's insurance claims because they say Ella Marie Hacker's cancer was a pre-existing condition. *Deny, deny, deny.*

"The insurance company refused payment, which left Conner Prairie Hospital on the hook for compensation from the family. I haven't been able to add up all of the claims, but we're looking at hundreds of thousands of dollars. No way the Hackers could pay that, so in addition to losing their wife and mother, they had to fight with huge corporations over money the family didn't have."

"So," Trent said, "it looks like we have two plausible leads as to where the Hackers might strike. Get on the horn to our Indianapolis post and let the superintendent know what we've learned. I figure we're still another hour from Indy. Let them know we're on our way back."

Rebecca did as Trent advised, and the two of them fell back into the silence of their thoughts and the humming of the tires on the road.

Newt Hacker considered his options as he walked back from the grocery store with his arms laden with two heavy bags of food and water. He could go back to the hidden warehouse and proceed with whatever plans his father had, or he could run like hell and leave all of this turmoil behind him. In the end, he decided that blood was thicker than water, and he walked back to rejoin his Pa and Twit. In truth, he believed he had no where else to go.

"Did you get everything we need?" Clement asked his son when he returned.

"Yes, Pa," came Newt's sullen reply.

"How about Twinkies?" Twit asked. "Did you get us any Twinkies or M&Ms?"

Newt threw him a package of Twinkies and said, "Here's your breakfast, dickhead!"

The three men sat in the dim light of the old warehouse and stared at one another while they munched on sandwiches and chips.

"Thanksgiving's tomorrow," Clement reminded his sons. "Now, listen up because this is important."

Clement then proceeded to recite his plans for blowing up the two buildings.

"We're going to leave here right before daybreak while most folks are still in bed dreaming about stuffing themselves with Thanksgiving dinner. Newt, I want you going to the Hoosier Homestead headquarters, and Twit, I want you going to Conner Prairie Hospital. Once both of you are in position near those locations, I want us to all call each other and confirm that you're ready to go. Nobody makes a final move to blow up the buildings until I say so, understand?!"

"Yes, Pa," came the twins' practiced response.

The three men spent the next couple of hours going over their plans for the umpteenth time. They cleaned and loaded their firearms and inspected the fertilizer bombs packed inside of the twins' pickup trucks.

Clement made sure the twins had all of their cell phone numbers saved, and especially the cell phone numbers that would detonate the bombs. Everything was ready, and now all they had to do was lie low in the warehouse and then move out before sunrise.

Chapter 45

Clay and Maggie lay in bed wrapped in each other's arms and legs. They had enjoyed a sumptuous dinner at the Chrysalis Hotel's restaurant, and afterward they'd snuggled beneath blankets and enjoyed a horse-drawn carriage ride beneath Chicago's sparkling skyline. It had been a great night.

It was early morning now, and the sunrise over Lake Michigan came pouring through their large picture windows. The scene of the sun on the lake was stunning, and Clay was tempted to run for his camera. The woman in his arms, however, was equally stunning, so he buried his face into her soft breasts and breathed in the scent of her skin.

Five minutes later Clay groaned as he peeked at the clock. It showed seven-fifteen.

"I've got to get ready and meet Rollie Evans at Navy Pier at nine-thirty. Would you call in sick for me, please?" he beseeched Maggie.

"Not a chance, sir!" she stated firmly. "Besides, you need to keep making money so we can go out to dinner again like we did last night," she teased.

"But!" Clay tried to begin.

"No buts, darling," Maggie cooed softly at him. "Perhaps this might help get your workday started with a smile," she said as she reached beneath the sheet and gently stroked him.

Once he was fully aroused, which may have taken as long as five seconds, Maggie climbed on top of her lover and the two of them moved in ways they were beginning to know gave the other the most pleasure.

"Oh, my!" Maggie said breathlessly. "Maybe I should call Rollie Evans for you."

They both collapsed in spent pleasure, and their bodies melted into each other. Their heartbeats were like a musical fugue with one of Maggie's heartbeats being echoed by one of Clay's.

"There is no place else on earth that I would rather be than with you," Clay spoke softly. "Thanks for wanting to come to Chicago."

They snuggled a few moments more.

"I know you have to get up and go to work. I'll be thinking about you, though—a lot I suspect," Maggie said. "And you can always call me if you get lonely." She kissed him gently again.

"And what do you have planned for today?" Clay asked.

"I thought I might do two things: go to the Field Museum, which I have always loved ever since I was a child when we'd take family trips to Chicago; then I thought I would cap off the afternoon with a shopping trip along the Magnificent Mile."

"Wow, that's quite a day. Do you think you'll have enough energy left for a nice dinner somewhere?" Clay kidded. "If so, why don't you think about where you'd like to go and make a reservation for around eight?"

"Oh, I can always eat," Maggie confessed. "Any idea what time you'll get back to the room?"

"Not totally sure, but probably by seven. The more work I get done today, the sooner I can finish tomorrow, and then we can play. I've told Weed and Tori and Mace that I would be back the day before Thanksgiving to help prepare for the festivities."

"And, Maggie," Clay continued, "I have a lot to be thankful for this Thanksgiving. You're breathing fresh life into me, and I just want you to know that I take our relationship seriously and that I am very grateful to have you in my life."

"I hope you know the feeling is mutual, Clay. I haven't felt this way about someone for a long, long time."

During the next thirty minutes Clay shaved, showered, and got dressed, while Maggie had the hotel's room service deliver coffee and breakfast. They enjoyed their breakfast on the balcony overlooking Lake Michigan. Twenty minutes later Clay grabbed his camera gear, called for an Uber driver, and was off to meet Rollie Evans at Navy Pier.

Rollie Evans was director of the Navy Pier Visitors Association and was responsible for a new marketing campaign that the Association had decided to roll out for the coming year. He was a very capable administrator who was meticulous in his attention to detail. For that reason he wanted no one other than the renowned Clay Arnold to provide the visual images for their new promotional campaign.

Clay arrived a few minutes before nine-thirty, and Rollie was waiting for him when his Uber car arrived.

"Ah, Clay Arnold! It is a pleasure to meet you in person. I'm Rollie Evans."

The two men walked over to a coffee emporium and began discussing the objectives that Rollie had for the photo shoot of Navy Pier. He had a well-conceived plan, and Clay thought he would be able to satisfy Rollie's goals.

Navy Pier is a 3,300-foot-long pier that was built in 1916 as part of architect and city planner Daniel Burnham's Plan of Chicago. Originally it was built as a mixed-purpose piece of public infrastructure whose main function was as a cargo facility for lake freighters and a docking space for passenger excursion steamers.

Today Navy Pier is the number-one tourist attraction in Chicago featuring sightseeing tours, the Chicago Children's Museum, the Chicago Flower and Garden Show, an IMAX theater, and the 150-foot-tall Navy Pier ferris wheel.

Clay marveled at the ferris wheel and knew he would ride to the top of it to shoot pictures before the day was over. He and Rollie talked for a few more minutes as they finished their coffee. They agreed they would meet again for lunch to review Clay's morning work.

Clay spent the first hour shooting random images of Navy Pier from various vantage points, making the best use of the cool, crisp November light. From the end of the pier Clay shot images of Chicago's skyline as the dramatic background for the pier's attractions. Sunlight poured onto the city's skyscrapers, and their glass windows reflected the light like a solar array.

Visitors began streaming onto the pier when it opened to the public at 10:00 AM. Most of them were families and couples who were visiting Chicago as tourists and couldn't wait to spend their precious vacation hours and dollars wandering the pier's many wonders.

As is often the case when large throngs of people gather, there were a few individuals who used the pier's popularity as a soapbox to voice their social and political views.

"Faggots and foreigners go home," proclaimed one sign in particular that was being held aloft by a seedy-looking young couple wearing armbands with Nazi swastikas.

"This here's America. We don't want their kind," the young woman taunted at anyone who would look their way.

Clay tried not to make eye contact with them because his blood was already beginning to boil from their xenophobic rants, and he wanted to stay on task with his photo shoot.

"Hey, Mr. Cameraman, why don't you take some pictures of us for the evening news," the male malcontent shouted at Clay.

Clay ignored him and continued to take pictures on the shot list he and Rollie had agreed on earlier.

"Yeah, asshole, I'm talking to you," the neo-Nazi male directed at Clay. "It's about time we sent them fucking faggots, Arabs, Chinamen, and Mexicans back to where they came from. C'mon take our pictures, you limp-dick prick."

Clay continued to try to ignore the mean-spirited couple and felt badly for the tourists who had to endure the verbal assaults during their vacation time. At one point a gay couple strode hand in hand along the pier enjoying the attractions when they unfortunately walked into the area that the Nazi couple occupied. It got ugly.

"Hey, you fuckin' fudge-packers," the female Nazi hollered. "You are an abomination in the eyes of the Lord."

The couple tried just to ignore the vitriol and walk away, but the strident couple followed after them.

"Yeah, you sissy boys!" came the young Nazi's taunt. "I'll give you something to suck on!" He began rubbing his own genitals. "Come and get it!"

Clay saw a security officer who was leaning on a dock piling looking at the boats on the lake. He decided it was time that this rent-a-cop earned his keep.

"G'morning, officer," Clay began. "I think we have a couple of people who are disturbing the peace." He pointed at the neo-Nazi couple. "You might want to have a conversation with them before things get out of hand."

The security officer looked at Clay with very little interest.

"Well, according to the Constitution of the United States, those folks have as much right to express themselves as anyone else. They ain't hurting nothing. Besides I agree with what they're saying."

"They may have their constitutional rights, and you may agree with them," Clay replied with annoyance rising in his voice, "but they're making a lot of people very uncomfortable."

"Yeah, well," the security officer said, "they'll get over it."

Clay recognized that he was getting nowhere with the rent-a-cop and walked away in disgust. He thought it was a sad commentary when even the authorities sided with ignorant people.

Clay sat on a bench changing camera lenses and spotted his antique KGB ring camera that he had used on the man who had attacked Carmelita at the Monastery Lodge. From a hidden pouch in his camera bag, Clay pulled out his final supply of poison and poured it into the ring's secret reservoir. He placed the ring on his finger and got up to take more pictures of the Navy Pier.

Rollie Evans met Clay at one in the afternoon for a late lunch, and the two men sat side by side reviewing images on the camera's screen.

"These are great!" Rollie exclaimed. "How about getting some shots from the top of the ferris wheel?"

"I'm glad you like," Clay replied. "I thought I'd ride the ferris wheel to the top once we finish lunch. Maybe you can get the operator to halt the wheel for me when I get to the top. I'll probably need only a couple of minutes, so it shouldn't disrupt the tourists' ride too much."

With lunch over, Rollie returned to his duties, and Clay stepped into a gondola for the ferris wheel and began the 150-foot ride to the wheel's apex. Clay was someone who never totally overcame his fear of heights, and he used his camera as a way to block out the rest of the world while he shot images of Navy Pier and Chicago's skyline. It was a disquieting experience for him, but he chose to face his fear of heights straight on and was rewarded with some stunning images.

From his vantage point high above, Clay observed the neo-Nazi couple exercising their constitutionally protected rights to insult and offend visitors. His blood continued to boil. Then he thought about Maggie and the pure pleasure he felt when he was with her, and his anger abated. He breathed in and out slowly and recalled words that he had said to himself a few days ago:

"Sometime, it's best to just walk away."

He completed his photo shoot from the top of the ferris wheel and then descended to terra firma with a sense of relief.

Back on solid ground, Clay was greeted by a cacophony of turmoil as the neo-Nazi couple, who had cornered an Indian man wearing a Sikh turban, mistakenly began calling him a fucking Arab.

"Hey, raghead! We don't want you fucking Muslims in our country!"

"I am a professor of mathematics at the University of Chicago, and I am a Sikh, not a Muslim."

His rational protests went unheeded by the Nazi couple, mainly because they didn't know, or care, about the differences of the cultures.

"Well, fuck you anyway, raghead! This here's America. Land of the free, and only our kind is welcome here."

The Sikh professor shook his head in clear disgust and receded into the crowd as quickly as he could. Clay's blood began to boil again.

"Just walk away," he reminded himself. "They're not worth it."

He tried to shift his thinking to happy thoughts about Maggie, but the neo-Nazi couple persisted in slinging their abuse.

Clay walked over to a juice bar adjacent to the ferris wheel and ordered a cool beverage to try to calm his rising anger. He was nearly calm again when he saw the mean-spirited couple enter a gondola to ride the ferris wheel.

"Hey, Mr. Cameraman, get a picture of us, will ya?!" the young woman shouted rudely.

"Sure," Clay replied, and he asked them if they'd like something to drink, too."

"Why, sure," the man said, and Clay purchased two more beverages while the couple settled in for their ride to the top.

The ferris wheel attendant told them they couldn't take their propaganda sign on the wheel, so they flung it to the security guard who had now walked over to see what all the commotion was about.

"Just walk away," Clay tried to remind himself again, and he was nearly at the point of doing just that when the couple began spewing their hatred toward anyone who didn't appear to come from white European stock.

Clay turned his back to the crowd and flipped the lid on his KGB ring camera. When he was certain no one was watching, he emptied the poison from the ring into the beverages. He walked back to the ferris wheel's unsuspecting occupants.

"Well, that's might neighborly of you, stranger," the young woman said as Clay handed them their drinks. "Your voice can sure get parched when you're trying to get people to see the light of day about foreigners."

"Well, these drinks should take care of that for you. Enjoy the ride!" Clay stated, and then he also receded into the crowd.

The ferris wheel began to move upward, and Clay watched the couple greedily drink their beverages. Clay walked back to an area that Rollie had set up as a temporary office on the pier and watched the wheel climb higher and higher into the autumn sky.

Several minutes later the ferris wheel returned to its starting point, and riders began to exit their seats. Only two occupants remained seated. Both had bloody froth on their lips and looks of agony etched onto the features of their white-supremacist faces. Dead!

The security guard heard a visitor scream and waddled over to investigate. When he saw the neo-Nazi couple sitting in their seats, stained by their own sputum, he barfed up his lunch and called the Chicago PD for back-up.

Rollie Evans was informed of the situation that had arisen at the ferris wheel, and he met Clay while hurrying over to offer assistance to the officer.

"I think the police are going to have me pretty busy now," Rollie said to Clay. "I know you can handle the rest of your assignment without me. Let's plan on meeting again tomorrow morning. I'll call you later to confirm things once the police have everything under control."

Clay said he totally understood the gravity of the situation and agreed they would talk later in the day.

As they parted company, Clay cast a final glance over at the dead neo-Nazi couple and said to himself, "Sometimes, you just can't walk away."

With Navy Pier cordoned off by the police as a result of the deaths, Clay called Maggie to see if she wanted him to join her on her jaunt down the Magnificent Mile.

"Are you all right?" she asked when he called. "I just saw a news report on my iPhone about two people dying mysteriously on the ferris wheel and prayed you weren't one of them."

"No, not me," Clay replied. "But the police have everything shut down on Navy Pier, so aside from some photo-editing, my work is pretty much done for the day."

"Well, I'm just leaving the Field Museum. Why don't we meet at the Chrysalis Hotel for a little afternoon delight and then do some shopping and enjoy dinner on the Magnificent Mile?"

"By 'afternoon delight,' are you referring to what I hope you're referring to?" Clay asked expectantly.

"Well, perhaps you might get a little lucky if you play your cards right, sir."

And that's what they did . . . but they didn't play cards.

Maggie looked like she was made for the Magnificent Mile. Her casual but trendy outfit sweetly complemented her trim figure, and with auburn hair cascading down her shoulders, she rivaled Botticelli's Venus. But it was her eyes and her smile that trumped all of her other features.

Maggie was someone who truly enjoyed life, and going out with Clay in a world-class city was a night she would remember. The walk down Michigan Avenue offered the quintessence of Chicago at Thanksgiving time: bluster and chill, but vivid with the sights and sounds of revelers on the street and merchants trying to attract holiday shoppers. Maggie held Clay's arm closely to stay connected to his radiant heat. He really enjoyed feeling her close.

They came upon an upscale seafood restaurant and decided to give it a try. It turned out to be a great choice, and the table arrangements made it easy to have an intimate dinner. Clay ordered sea bass and Maggie had scallops, and they shared a bottle of wine. They were not disappointed by the chef's skill.

They talked mainly about the holidays coming up and plans for Maggie to join Clay and his brewery crew for Christmas, and hopefully New Year's, too. Then they just chatted about things that were going on in their lives. It was fun for them to learn even the smallest of details.

During dinner, Clay briefly flashed back on his earlier encounter with the neo-Nazis. He did not like being deceptive with Maggie, but there was no way that he felt he could explain his actions without scaring the hell out of her. He didn't want to risk that, but he knew that at some point, his way of evening the score with deserving malcontents was a subject they would have to address.

With dinner over, they walked back to the Chrysalis Hotel. They knew that their time together in Chicago would soon be coming to an end, and they wanted to enjoy each remaining moment together. And so they did.

The next day came sooner than either Maggie or Clay wanted because it meant that they would leave each other for the Thanksgiving holiday. Clay had a little more work to do at Navy Pier, but the project was pretty well over.

Besides, Rollie Evans had enough on his hands with the police still trying to identify a suspect. They'd agreed to finish everything after the holidays.

Maggie and Clay said a tender goodbye to each other as Maggie left to catch her flight to her sister's home. Clay rented a car for the four-hour drive to Indy. The time alone in the car gave him ample time to think. He thought about the challenge of balancing his life as a photographer with his love for Maggie and his mission as a righteous avenger. He wasn't sure how this could possibly all work out, but he knew he wanted to find a way.

Chapter 46

I T WAS AROUND NOON WHEN Clay took the exit off I-65 for Merrillville. He gassed up his car and stopped at a Panera for lunch. While sitting alone at a table outside, Clay called Trent Reynolds's cell phone, which was answered on the second ring.

"Where are you?" Trent asked, as he and Rebecca sped north on I-65 toward Indy.

"I'm in Merrillville and should be home in a little over two hours. Do you have any further information you can share about the attackers?"

"A ton," came Trent's reply. "We're looking for three men named Hacker, a father and his twin sons. With help from our detectives at the Seymour post, we've found where they live and enough incriminating evidence to put these guys away for a very long time. Provided we catch them."

"That's great news!" Clay returned.

"Not so great, I'm afraid," came Trent's cautious response. "It appears they've made large fertilizer bombs, and they're preparing to do some major damage again. We believe they're planning to blow up an insurance headquarters building in downtown Indy and maybe Conner Prairie Hospital. I've alerted our ISP superintendent, and he said he'd get officers deployed to those sites, but he's concerned because we have several officers away on holiday leave."

"I know this is all official police business, but will you please let me know if you need additional manpower? Mace, Weed, and I would be more than happy to help you in any way we can."

"Thanks, Clay. I think we'll probably be okay, but keep your cell phones handy. Depending on staffing, I may need to call on you, after all."

The two old friends talked a few minutes more while each accelerated along I-65, one from the north and one from the south. They figured they'd both get back to Indy within an hour of each other.

"Trent, if your schedule permits, maybe we can meet at Stella's Diner for dinner. Stella obviously has a vested interest in our catching these Hacker pricks, too. Maybe you can fill us all in at the same time," Clay suggested.

"Sounds like a good idea to me," Trent replied. "Rebecca and I need to return to our office first and meet with the superintendent. Why don't we hook up at Stella's afterward—say around six, provided the world doesn't go to hell in a hand basket before then?"

"That'll be perfect," Clay said. "That'll give you time to do what you and Rebecca need to do in the office, and I can get home after being on the road for several days. See you around six o'clock, then."

About two hours later Clay pulled into the courtyard of the brewery complex and was greeted by Rennie, Satchmo, and Lex. Tori, Weed, and Mace came outside a few seconds later.

Clay smiled broadly at his welcoming committee and was engulfed by hugs and furry rubs as he stepped from the car.

"Man, it's great to be home!" Clay said as he held everyone close. "I've sure missed you all. I had an excellent trip, but it's always a relief to be home, especially after being on assignment in several cities."

"And just in time for Thanksgiving," Mace added. "Tori and Rennie have a great dinner planned for tomorrow, and I knew you wouldn't want to pass that up!"

"No way I'd miss that," Clay said, and he patted Rennie on his shoulder and gave Tori a peck on the cheek.

Rennie offered to help Clay carry his bags into his brewhouse living quarters, asking to hear all about his trips to Santa Fe, San Diego, and Chicago. Satchmo waltzed in with them and supervised their putting Clay's gear away.

"Someday I'd like to go to some of those places," Rennie sighed.

"I'm sure you will," Clay assured him. "Besides, I may need to have a great assistant to help me with my assignments from time to time. So maybe we can go on the road together someday, provided you also agree to study your schoolwork hard with Tori. How's that sound?!"

"Really?!" Rennie chirped with delight.

"Unless, of course, you'd rather go back to Hill Street to live," Clay kidded.

"No way!" Rennie retorted quickly. "I'll study hard with Tori, I promise!"

A few moments later, Weed and Mace came sauntering into Clay's living room. Lex stayed at the farmhouse with Tori as she continued preparations for the Thanksgiving holiday.

Weed spoke. "Hey, Rennie? Tori said she could use your assistance in the kitchen when you're finished helping Clay."

"Okay. Do you still need me, Clay?" Rennie asked.

"No, I think we're good here, Rennie. I appreciate your help, though. Why don't you head back to the farmhouse and see what kind of gastronomic delights you and Tori can conjure up?" Clay encouraged.

Rennie looked at Mace and asked, "Gastro-what?"

Mace shrugged and replied, "I think it means good-tasting food."

"Oh," Rennie replied. "So I guess I'll go help Tori make our gastros happy!"

They all enjoyed a good-natured laugh, and Rennie pivoted and went running out the door with Satchmo bounding after him.

"He's fitting in very well, isn't he?" Clay asked Mace and Weed.

"Yeah," Mace said. "He's come a long way in a very short time. He belongs here, and he knows it. For the first time in his life he feels safe and appreciated. I remember the feeling from when Mr. Jeffries allowed me to live here at the woodworking mill so many years ago. It's a feeling you never forget or take for granted."

Weed agreed. "I can't begin to tell you how happy Tori is to have Rennie around. Me, too—but for Tori especially his presence is reassuring after the attack on the path along the river. It's not something that she says in so many words, but I can tell. Rennie helped save her life, and that's something none of us would ever forget. With her being blind and vulnerable, having Rennie and Lex by her side gives her an added sense of strength."

"Then, of course," Weed continued, "Tori has made it her mission now to help educate Rennie. She's begun homeschooling him, and I can already tell that the experience is having a very positive effect on both of them."

"That's great," Clay said. "You guys have all been very patient and warm with him. I know we can't change the world, but if we can help this young man grow, we will have made a worthwhile difference."

"Amen to that," Mace offered. "And speaking about changing the world, do you have any 'adventures' from your travels that you would like to share with Weed and me?"

"Perhaps we should talk down in the sub-basement," Clay said softly, and he began walking toward the elevator that would take them down. Mace and Weed looked at each other and followed.

The sub-basement came alive with fluorescence as the three men entered this specialized workshop located thirty feet below Clay's residence and the antique camera museum. Weed and Mace had cleaned up the shop after Weed had worked his technical magic on the parts of Clay's antique cameras. Now it looked like any other workshop.

"Do we have any other parts left over that you might be able to use in the future?" Clay asked Weed.

"Some," answered Weed. "How did your weapons hold up? I assume you used at least one of them," Weed said with curiosity.

"I used all of them," Clay declared.

Mace and Weed looked at each other, speechless.

"And . . .?" Mace finally prodded.

"And, they worked perfectly," Clay reported.

Then Mace uncharacteristically stammered, "You mean that you actually used them to terminate some people?" Clay nodded affirmatively.

"Look," he said, "I don't know how much you guys really want to know. If we ever get caught, you'd both be charged as accessories. Plausible deniability might be your best defense."

"I think I speak for Weed, too," Mace said, "but we're not very concerned about getting caught at this point. Besides, you know that we've already bought into whatever it is you're doing out there in the name of justice. So, just do us all a huge favor and don't get caught."

"I promise you both I'll do my best. Right now, though, I actually need to leave. I'm meeting Trent Reynolds over at Stella's

Diner. He's got a really good lead on the pricks in the old pickup that have been causing so much misery. He wants to bring me and Stella up to date. If you really want details about the weapons, we can talk more when I don't have to rush off. Suffice it to say that the weapons were put to righteous use, and there are probably seven people who won't be enjoying a nice turkey dinner this year."

Weed let out a low whistle, and Mace quietly said, "Lordy, Lordy."

"I better scoot now," Clay said. "We can talk more when I get back. Besides, I'm sure you're going to want to hear what Trent had to tell me. I'll see you in a little while."

Chapter 47

"GODDAMNIT, I SWEAR I CAN'T take being cooped up in this nasty old warehouse one more minute," came Twit's petulant whine. "Can't we at least go out for a little drive? Besides, it'll make the time go faster, and then we can get a good night's sleep before blowing up the insurance company and hospital tomorrow."

Clement thought about what his nitwit son had just suggested. He knew the smartest thing they could do was lie low in the warehouse until the morning, but he was growing very antsy, too. Part of it was his feeling anxious about what they'd be doing in the morning. Another part agreed with Twit. He didn't enjoy sitting in some stinking old warehouse for hours at a time. Maybe a change of scenery would help ease the tension, he thought.

"C'mon Pa, wattya say?!" Twit tried again. "Newt, help me out here, will ya?"

Newt did not want to risk being on the receiving end of his father's ire, so he looked down at his feet and mumbled something incoherent.

"Maybe we could go out for a little while," Clement relented, "but I'll drive, and you boys do everything—and I mean everything—I say."

Twit whooped and hollered at his Pa's decision, and Newt looked at his Pa skeptically.

"Are you sure about this, Pa?" Newt asked.

"Just for an hour, no more," Clement replied. "Besides, I'd kinda like to see this Stella's Diner you boys keep talking about."

Clay left the brewery complex and drove his Tacoma truck over to Stella's Diner and arrived a few minutes before six. Stella and Abby greeted him as he arrived and escorted him to a table off to the side for privacy.

"Trent Reynolds will be joining me in a little bit," Clay said. "I think both of you might want to hear what he has to say. He finally has some solid leads about the men who bombed the Planned Parenthood Center, attacked your diner, and tried to rape and kill Tori."

"These men have been on the loose far too long," Stella sighed. "I don't think any of us will rest easy until they're caught, or better yet, dead."

The three of them chatted for a bit, and Stella asked Clay about his recent photography assignments. At ten minutes past six, Trent appeared in the doorway of the diner. With the late-afternoon sunlight streaming in behind him, he looked like a classic sheriff from an old western standing in the doorway of a saloon.

Abby went to greet Trent and pointed to the table where Clay and Stella were seated.

"Evening, Trent," Abby said. "It's good to see you up and around. I stopped by Conner Prairie Hospital to visit you again two days ago, but they said you had discharged yourself against medical advice."

"Well, it seemed like I'd laid around in bed long enough, and I saw no point in arguing with the nurses, so I had Rebecca pick me up," Trent replied.

"How're you feeling now?" Abby asked with sincere concern.

"All right," he replied stoically. "My shoulder is stiff and sore, but it's getting a little better."

"You know, Abby," Trent continued, "I don't believe I adequately thanked you for coming to see me in the hospital. I really appreciated your visits a lot, and maybe when this turmoil is over, you'll let me take you to dinner to thank you more properly."

Abby made eye contact with him and said, "I'd enjoy that very much, Trent. Just don't go getting yourself shot up again before we can do that."

"Yes, ma'am," he replied. "I'll do my best to make sure that doesn't happen."

Abby escorted Trent to Clay's table and told Stella that she would cover the hostess station while the three of them talked.

After Abby left, Stella said, "That woman has been a godsend for me. I've told her that if she decides to forget about her journalism career, she's got a job here as long as she wants. I've really come to rely on her."

Trent had a seat, but he told Clay and Stella that he couldn't stay long.

"So, Trent, what are you at liberty to share with us?" Clay asked.

"We now believe that three men named Hacker who reside in rural Southern Indiana are the men responsible for killing Jennifer Skyler, and for the attacks against the diner and Tori Rawlins. We also believe that they have left Southern Indiana and are presumably somewhere around Indianapolis planning on bombing at least two major buildings. Our department has officers covering the Hoosier Homestead Insurance Co. headquarters downtown and also Conner Prairie Hospital."

Trent explained that Ella Marie Hacker's insurance and hospital bills had tipped them off to their next probable strikes.

"We're not absolutely positive that these are their targets," Trent said. "But it seems pretty likely that they'll attempt to hit those buildings some time in the next couple of days."

Stella and Clay stared at each other and shook their heads in amazement. Just then Abby returned to their table with an intense look on her face.

"Excuse me for interrupting," Abby said. "But I thought you might like to know that our old friend Dutch Ferris just entered the diner. He's in the bar."

Trent and Clay shot each other a quick glance, and Trent said to Clay, "Why don't we go have ourselves a little conversation with Mr. Ferris?"

The two men walked over to the bar and saw Dutch sitting on a stool by himself with a cold beer that the bartender had just placed in front of him. Trent stood behind where Dutch was sitting and plopped his hands on the unsuspecting man's shoulders.

"Oh, shit!" came Dutch's reply when he saw who was joining him at the bar.

"How're you doing, Mr. Ferris?" Trent asked rhetorically. "What a lovely surprise running into you here."

Dutch stammered as he attempted to regain his composure. "Now, Detective Reynolds, I've told you everything I know already."

"Oh, now, why don't I believe that for a second?" Trent asked again quizzically.

"But, but . . ." Dutch attempted to reply unsuccessfully.

"This here's Clay Arnold, a very good friend of mine," Trent said pointing to his buddy. "You may know him by name as the famous photographer who owns that antique camera museum, but he also lost his fiancée when the Hackers blew up the Planned Parenthood Center a few months ago."

Dutch looked in Clay's direction and nodded his recognition.

"I'm really sorry about your loss, Mr. Arnold, but like I just said to the detective, I swear I don't know anything more than I've already told him."

Clay shot Dutch a steely look that removed any doubt he may have had about the resolve the two men shared for getting the Hacker men.

"Well, Dutch, this is your lucky day," Trent said mirthlessly. "You get to decide whether I haul your scrawny ass down to the station for several hours of unpleasant confinement, or you can leave here right now and head straight home and not return to the diner for a few days. How's that sound, Dutch?!"

Dutch didn't take long to respond. He immediately stood up, dropped a ten dollar bill on the bar, and turned to leave.

"Oh, gee," Dutch said as he glanced at his watch. "Look at the time! I think I'll head on home and watch me some television."

"You're a wise man, Mr. Ferris," Trent said. "And may I suggest that you keep our little conversation between the three of us. Sure would hate to have to come looking for you again."

Both Clay and Trent gave Dutch their business cards and told him to call either of them if he thought of anything else that would help lead them to the Hackers.

Dutch gulped, took their cards, and made a hasty retreat for the front door.

The three Hacker men piled into Clement's truck at the old warehouse and clandestinely drove away. Clement drove with Newt and Twit next to him on the front seat. The late November sun was beginning to set, which provided the men additional cover for their visit to Stella's Diner.

"Head north on Keystone Avenue," Newt directed. "The diner's located near the White River in Broad Ripple. I'll tell you where to turn when we get closer."

Clement followed his son's directions, and before long he began to see road signs for Stella's Diner. The diner was located in an attractive valley that was formed by the White River. Newt told his father to pull over at the crest of a hill above the diner's main parking lot. From here, they had a full view of Stella's property.

"So, this is the place where you boys shot that cop, huh?" Clement asked.

"Yeah, I shot him good," Twit guffawed. "The fucker dropped from the truck's running board like a ruptured duck, and we hightailed it out of there."

The three men sat in the truck watching people coming and going into the diner. It was getting darker with each minute that passed, and the towering lights in the parking lot began replacing the fading sunlight.

They were about to leave when Twit chirped, "Well, looky there, Newt. Isn't that our old friend Dutch Ferris heading this way in the parking lot? Pull on over there, Pa. I want to talk with him."

"I don't think that's a good idea, Pa," Newt offered. "We should head back to the warehouse before we attract any attention to ourselves."

"You're probably right, Newt," Clement said, but before they could exit the lot, Twit hollered out, "Hey, Dutch, you old limp-dick motherfucker, how're you doing?"

Clement pulled his truck over to where Dutch was standing and blocked his path.

Dutch Ferris took one look at the man hollering to him, and for the second time in less than ten minutes muttered, "Oh shit!"

"Now look, I don't want any trouble with you boys," Dutch said with fear rising in his voice. "And I sure don't recommend you going into the diner."

"And why's that?" Twit asked.

"Because that state detective you boys shot here a while back is in there, and he and this photographer named Clay Arnold just corralled me to see if I knew anything about you guys. The cop said he thinks you're fixing to bomb some buildings around here. Here's their business cards," Dutch said nervously.

Newt shot his father a quick look and said, "See, Pa? I told you it wasn't a good idea coming out for a drive."

"Hush up, boy!" came his father's censoring reply. He looked at the business cards and stuffed them in his shirt pocket. "Now, how do these assholes know what we're fixing to do?" he wondered out loud.

"I dunno," came Dutch's reply. "But Clay Arnold owns that antique camera museum not far from here, and he was also going to marry that lady doctor who got killed in that bombing of the Planned Parenthood Center a while back. They just told me to scram, and that's exactly what I intend to do."

And with that, Dutch Ferris pivoted around the rear of the truck and continued his hasty retreat for his car and home. The three Hacker men sat in their pickup and pondered their next move.

"I say we get the hell away from here, Pa, and head back to the warehouse until daybreak," Newt stated firmly. "I told you coming out here wasn't a good idea."

"Yeah, well, you're probably right, Newt. But now we know that the cops are on to us, so we'll need to be smarter than they are. We'll just have to move real fast tomorrow and hit the targets before they know what's happening."

With that said, Clement put his truck in gear and pulled away from the diner's parking lot under the cover of a growing darkness.

Meanwhile, back inside Stella's Diner, Abby and Stella coaxed the two men into staying for dinner.

"Trent, I know you need to get back to the office soon, but you need to keep your strength up, too," Stella declared maternally. "Abby will take good care of you gents, and your dinners are on the house."

Trent began to argue, but Stella looked him straight in the eye and said, "Sit!"

He sat.

"I feel like this is all coming to a climax soon, Clay," Trent said. "One way or the other we're going to shut these bastards down. I only pray we can do it without too much loss of life or property. These Hackers don't have much to lose at this point."

"I know," Clay stated. "Just tell me what you need, Trent. Mace, Weed, and I will do anything you want to bring these criminals to justice. Anything!"

Chapter 48

TRENT AND CLAY DIDN'T dawdle over dinner. Clay tried to pay the tab, but Stella insisted, and Trent knew better than to argue with her generosity.

"I'd better head on, Trent," Clay said. "I'll keep my cell phone handy, okay?"

Abby saw that Trent was preparing to leave, too, and she walked over to meet him at the door.

"You watch your back now, Detective Reynolds," Abby said rather formally, though her heart and concern were becoming much more personal.

"I will," Trent replied softly. "I've been shot once and didn't much care for it. Besides we're still going to have dinner together when this insanity is over. And, maybe you can tell me more about the article you're thinking of writing."

"It's a deal!" Abby said, and she leaned up and kissed Trent on the cheek.

It had already been an incredibly long day for Trent, but he knew that his place right now was at the office. He had no doubt that Rebecca would already be there, because in all likelihood she hadn't left since their return from Seymour.

Trent called her during his drive back to the office.

"What do we have?" Trent inquired "Any other information from the officers at the insurance building or the hospital?"

"It's been really quiet. I mean, not a peep," Rebecca reported back.

"All right," Trent said. "I'll be back in the office in about ten minutes, but there's no way I can just sit there waiting for something to happen. I won't stay long."

"You need to get some sleep, Trent," Rebecca insisted. "You can't keep pushing yourself like this."

"All right, maybe forty winks," he relented. "But you have to wake me the instant you hear anything."

"Yessir!" she replied with a smile on her face.

Clay returned to the brewery complex around the same time Trent arrived at his office. It had been a very long, emotional day for Clay, too, but he wasn't ready to turn in yet. He saw that the lights in the farmhouse were on and the lights in Mace's power plant were off, which meant that Mace was probably hanging out with Tori, Weed, and Rennie.

Clay sat in his Tacoma in the courtyard and listened to the sporadic tick of his truck's engine as it began to cool down. He pulled his cell phone out and called Maggie. She answered on the third ring.

"Hey there, Clay. I was hoping you'd call tonight. How are you, darling?"

"I'm doing okay, Maggie. I just needed to hear your voice," Clay admitted.

"Are you sure you're okay, Clay?" Maggie asked with concern.

Clay heard a door close on Maggie's end of the call and intuited that she had gone into another room for privacy.

"Actually, there's a lot going on, and some of it's pretty serious," Clay said. "Look, I don't want to scare you, and I'm sure things will be just fine. The police think they have a lead on the people who killed Jennifer in the Planned Parenthood bombing, and they've told me that they're expecting a violent confrontation with them very soon.

"Maggie, I'm sorry to have laid all of this unpleasantness on you. I guess I'm tired—and more than anything, I just wanted to hear your voice," he sighed.

"Clay, it's okay," Maggie reassured him. "You can tell me anything. I just feel very badly that you have to go through this pain alone. Will you call me again when you know something? Although I hope you know you can call me anytime."

"Thanks, Maggie. I really appreciate your being there for me. When we get off the phone, I'm going to go visit with Weed and Tori and everyone before I turn in. That should help a lot, too."

They talked for just a couple of minutes longer and then said goodnight.

Clay exited his truck and stepped onto the porch of the farmhouse. From that vantage point he turned and looked around the buildings in the brewery complex. He treasured these old buildings, and he thought about the decades of history that went with each. He had an uneasy feeling that after tomorrow things might be very different for all of them living there.

"Everything and everyone comes and goes," he whispered to himself. He sighed and then opened the door to the farmhouse to be with his family.

"There you are," Weed said to Clay as he entered the kitchen. "We were hoping you'd stop by before turning in for the night. Have you had dinner yet?"

"Yeah, thanks," Clay said. "Trent and I had a quick dinner at Stella's Diner, but that pumpkin pie sure looks good."

"Now, that pie is for tomorrow's Thanksgiving dinner," Tori chided. "But knowing how much you like my pies, I made two. So you're welcome to have a slice now if you want."

"Can I have some too, Tori?" Rennie, pleaded.

"Of course you can. Heck, anyone else want pie?" she asked in mock surrender.

Weed placed one of the CDs that he and Tori had produced into the player, and soon the kitchen was filled with mellifluous sounds and the aromas of a feast that Tori and Rennie were preparing for tomorrow.

Clay looked at everyone around the kitchen table and at Lex and Satchmo, who had curled up with each other on the carpet by the back door. It was a heartwarming scene to Clay. His parents were long gone now, and so was Jennifer Skyler. In their places were his friends in this room and Maggie Bodine. He wondered what other changes in his life would be forthcoming.

"Everything and everyone comes and goes," he murmured to himself again.

"So, how was your dinner with Trent?" Mace asked, knowing full well that Clay wouldn't go into too much detail with Rennie and Tori there.

"It was good," Clay responded without further details. "I'll fill you and Weed in later."

"That sounds rather ominous," Tori said from across the room.

"That's because it is," Clay answered honestly. "Trent's investigation has uncovered the names of the men who blew up the Planned Parenthood Center and likely attacked you and Rennie and Lex by the river. Trent thinks they're planning to strike again, and very soon."

That bit of news caught Tori off guard, and she replied, "I'm not sure I want to hear any more, but I sure hope Trent catches those jerks."

"Me and Lex do, too!" Rennie chimed in.

When they finished eating their pie, Clay helped Rennie wash the dishes, and then the length of the day finally caught up with him.

"Well, guys, it's time for this old photographer to hit the sack. Mace and Weed, can we get together early tomorrow morning to go over some details for the property? I feel like I've been gone forever, and I want you to fill me in on things that you need me to do around here."

Clay's words were actually a ruse. He wanted to let Mace and Weed know all of the details that Trent had shared about the Hackers and their destructive plans, but he didn't feel comfortable speaking freely in front of Tori and Rennie.

"Sure," came Mace's reply, and Weed nodded knowingly too. "Tomorrow."

Clay took his leave of the farmhouse and walked across the courtyard to his brew-house residence. Satchmo saw him leave and came bounding after him.

"Well, it looks like it's just us old cats together again, Satchmo," Clay said as the huge cat rubbed against this leg.

Back in his living room Clay poured himself a short glass of Glenmorangie scotch and placed an Enya CD into his stereo. He slid the glass door open, and he and Satchmo walked out onto his roof garden to finish off the day with sights and sounds that were both soothing and hauntingly beautiful.

Clay sat at his patio table, and Satchmo launched his corpulence onto his lap. Clay absently stroked the cat as he reflected on recent episodes from his travels and the people in his life. Despite the anger he continued to feel toward right-wing assholes, he also knew he had many reasons to be thankful.

"Let's try to keep it positive, shall we, Satchmo? After all, Thanksgiving's tomorrow, and surely nothing could go wrong on such a special day."

Chapter 49

CLEMENT HACKER LAY stretched out in the bed of his pickup truck. The gloom of the old warehouse where he and his boys had holed up enveloped him like a funeral shroud. He had not been able to sleep well. The truck's bed was not comfortable, but Clement had other distractions keeping him awake.

"Well, Ella Marie, I guess this is Armageddon day. Me and the boys are going to rock this town from its witless slumber, and we're going to exact our revenge on the people who let you die. This I swear to you!"

Clement looked at his watch and saw that it was half past four. He finally mustered the energy to get up, and he walked over to where the twins were sleeping on the ground and nudged each one.

"Time to go, boys," he said. "Up and at 'em. Today's the day the Lord made, and we're here to do his bidding."

"Aw, Pa, just five more minutes," came Twit's childlike plea.

"Now!" his Pa fired back at him.

The twins staggered to their feet and went off into a corner of the warehouse to relieve themselves.

"Hey, Newt?" Twit asked. "Do we have any more Twinkies? They say that breakfast is the most important meal of the day."

Newt just stared at his twin brother and shook his head in bewilderment.

"No, brother. You ate the last of the Twinkies yesterday. Remember?"

Clement had his sons join him as he inspected the two trucks filled with the ANFO fertilizer bombs. Everything appeared to be ready. They then pulled out the cell phones that they would use for communicating with each other and the cell phones that would be used to detonate the bombs.

"Now, remember," Clement said, "make sure you keep these cell phone numbers straight and don't go calling the wrong number before it's time. Understand?!"

"Yes, Pa," came their synchronized replies, but as usual Clement wasn't sure that Twit was paying attention to his admonitions.

"Now, listen up!" Clement said. "Here's what we're going to do."

And for the umpteenth time, Clement laid out his plan to blow up the two buildings.

"Newt, I want you to drive over to within a block of the Hoosier Homestead Insurance Company building on Massachusetts Avenue and scope things out. Twit, I want you to do the same thing over at Conner Prairie Hospital. Find a place in their parking lot and just hunker down until we're ready to go."

"From what your pal Dutch Ferris told us," Clement continued, "the cops are probably on to us. So we're going to leave here in a couple of minutes and get you boys situated by the targets while it's still dark out. When I tell you to move, I want both of you to rush the buildings in your trucks in a coordinated attack that'll have this city reeling for years to come. We have to do it fast, though, so the cops don't have time to respond. After that, you go run and hide and call me. I'll come pick you up. Understand?!"

"Yes, Pa." But neither of them really did understand. They were following their father's orders, and that was all they needed to know.

"Okay, I guess that's it then," Clement said to his sons. "I just want you boys to know that I'm counting on you to avenge your mother's death. I know I haven't always been easy on you fellers, but I did what I thought was the right way to teach you to respect and fear the Lord . . . and me. It was the only way I knew. Now, let's saddle up and make our move before daybreak comes!"

The three Hacker men got into their pickup trucks and exited the old warehouse near downtown Indianapolis for the last time. Newt had only a ten-minute drive to the location of the Hoosier Homestead Insurance Company headquarters, and Twit needed an additional twenty minutes to drive north to the sprawling complex of Conner Prairie Hospital. Clement decided on a location midway between their targets where he would await the bombings. He called the twins.

"Let me know when you're in position," Clement instructed. "And tell me what kind of police presence you spot."

Rebecca Willett walked across the hall to the break room at their Indiana State Police office in central Indianapolis and lightly touched Trent's shoulder to awaken him.

Trent immediately bolted upright into a sitting position, and his sore shoulder reminded him that he was still recovering from a serious gunshot wound, compliments of Twit Hacker.

"Whoa. It's almost 5:00 AM," Trent lamented as he rose from the break-room cot. "I thought you were only going to let me get forty winks, Rebecca."

"It's been totally quiet at both locations, and you needed the sleep," Rebecca replied.

Trent knew he couldn't be cross with Rebecca for letting him sleep. She had not closed her eyes for nearly two days now and had maintained regular communication with the ISP officers on duty. She was pulling double-duty to let her partner get the rest he needed.

Trent got up and poured himself a cup of the strong coffee that Rebecca had made. He looked at himself in the mirror and raked his fingers through his ruffled hair. He needed a shave and a shower, but those luxuries would have to wait.

"I'm going to drive up to Conner Prairie Hospital," Trent said. "That's a much bigger complex than the insurance headquarters, and our officers could probably use another pair of eyes. Let's keep in close touch, Rebecca."

Trent grabbed another cup of coffee and piled into his cruiser for the drive to the hospital. He radioed ahead to let the officers there know he was coming. He was told that it had been very quiet aside from the ambulance that had arrived around 2:00 AM with an elderly heart attack victim.

Meanwhile, back at the brewery complex, Clay woke up around five and checked his watch. Satchmo's enormous body lay spread-eagle across the bed, and he barely moved when Clay got up to use the bathroom.

With everything going on, Clay knew it was pointless to try to go back to sleep, so he washed up, dressed, and took the elevator down to the sub-basement workshop. Mace was already there working on a project for the power plant.

"Good morning, Clay," Mace said as his friend entered the subterranean workshop. "And happy Thanksgiving to you!"

"Same to you, big fella," Clay replied. "You haven't been here all night, have you?"

"No, just doing a little tidying up around here," Mace said, but Clay knew that Mace didn't require much sleep.

A few minutes later the whirring sound from the elevator announced Weed's arrival.

"Morning, gents," Weed said sleepily as he entered the sub-basement. "I had a feeling you'd both beat me down here. Have you heard anything from Trent?"

"No, it's been quiet," Clay stated. "I'm hesitant to give him a call because I know he's very focused on catching the Hackers. I'm sure he'll be in touch with us if he needs assistance or has anything significant to report."

"All the same," Weed said, "I feel powerless just sitting here by the phone waiting for a call. I vote that Clay and I drive up to the hospital while Mace keeps an eye on things around here. You comfortable with that, Mace?" Weed asked.

"Yeah, I've got things covered here. I thought I'd go over to the farmhouse around seven to see if Tori and Rennie are stirring yet. Let's all keep our cell phones handy though, just in case."

It was still dark by the time Twit arrived just outside the grounds of Conner Prairie Hospital. Given the early hour, the main parking lot was sparsely filled, but he knew that hospitals were like self-contained towns that never slept. There'd be a lot of people inside.

He saw an unmarked ISP cruiser driven by Trent Reynolds enter the main entrance to the lot and drive over to join another unmarked police cruiser. Twit chose a hiding spot on the other side of the lot and awaited word from his father that Newt was in position at the insurance headquarters.

The three-way call from Clement came a few minutes later.

"Tell me what you boys see," Clement instructed.

Newt answered first. "I see two uniformed officers standing by the main entrance to the insurance building and two more officers working the grounds on foot. Plus, we have another cop patrolling the perimeter in his squad car. There's no one watching the entrance to the underground garage, though."

This was good news to Clement. He had expected a far larger complement of cops, but apparently the Thanksgiving holiday had left them short-staffed.

"And what about you, Twit? What's happening up at the hospital?" Clement asked.

"Well, sir, I just saw that Indiana State cop that I shot at Stella's Diner show up by himself. He's over talking with two other cops in another unmarked state car. The hospital security staff has been patrolling on foot, but they don't seem to pose much of a problem. I'm not sure if there are other security guards inside the hospital. I've got myself a good hiding place, and I'm ready to go when you say the word, Pa."

"All right then," Clement said somberly. "I want to change our plans now just a little, so listen up. Instead of both of you moving on your targets at the same time, I want Newt to blow the insurance building first. Then, once he's done that, Twit, I'll call you to make your move. Understand? First Newt—then you, Twit."

"Yes, Pa. We understand," Twit said. "First Newt and then me."

"Now then," Clement said. "If for some reason this whole thing goes south, I just want you boys to know that I'm proud of you. Just do as I say, and we should be able to put a serious hurt on the bastards that failed your sweet, departed mother."

The twins mumbled unintelligibly.

"Okay, Newt. It's time to go, son. Go make us proud! Once you blow the building and get away, give me a call, and I'll come pick you up."

Newt acknowledged his father's order, and the three men hung up.

"Gee," Twit said to himself after they hung up. "I would've liked to wish my brother good luck, but Pa hung up too fast. Dang!"

It was nearly 6:00 AM now, and the sky to the East was just beginning to show signs of dawn's arrival. It was Thanksgiving Day.

Newt Hacker brought his dark, unmarked pickup truck to life but kept his headlights off. He slowly rolled down the side street that would bring him to Massachusettes Avenue and came to a stop for a final survey of the lay of the land. It was still quiet, and the police officers he'd spotted before were pretty much in their same position.

As a show of bravado, Newt texted Twit a final message: "Kingdom Come!" Then he rolled another forty yards forward before he stomped on the accelerator. The pickup shot forward like a beast released from Hell.

Before the officers could understand what was happening, Newt's truck had covered nearly half the distance to the entrance of the parking garage. The truck's all-terrain tires cut a nasty, jagged scar across the insurance company's manicured lawn and mowed down several ornamental shrubs bearing holiday lights. The sound of the truck was fearsome in its intensity.

The two officers on foot immediately saw the commotion and came running. The officer in the squad car did likewise, but they arrived only in time to see the building's large garage entrance engulf Newt's pickup truck like a giant, dark maw.

Once inside, Newt spotted the main elevator shaft located in the middle of the garage. As he and his Pa had planned, Newt accelerated again and crashed his truck through the glass walls with such destructive force that he was able to penetrate the elevator shaft itself.

It took him a few moments to collect his wits again after such a violent crash, but he managed to exit the truck and get the bomb detonator primed and ready to receive its phone-call signal. He looked outside the garage entrance and saw that the cops had established a perimeter blocking his exit. He had anticipated this and was already running for the stairwell so he could exit the building through a ground-level door.

As he opened the door to the stairwell, he received a text on his phone. It was Twit, wanting to know how things were going.

"I'll call you," Twit texted.

"Oh, shit, brother—not now!" was Newt's impassioned reply. He prayed Twit remembered the correct phone number to call.

The next thing Newt knew, there was a blinding flash, accompanied by an enormous cacophony, followed by a brief but all-encompassing sensation of searing heat. Twit had called the wrong cell phone number and blown the twelve-story building and his twin brother to kingdom come.

Even from his vantage point several miles away, Clement heard the sound of the ANFO bomb as it totally leveled the Hoosier Homestead Insurance Company headquarters. True to their word, the Hacker men had destroyed the company that had denied Ella Marie the insurance coverage they'd paid for.

"One down and one to go," Clement said out loud. "Now I need to wait for Newt's phone call and go pick him up."

But the call didn't come. Instead Clement was greeted by the insistent wail of emergency vehicles apparently heading toward the tragedy on Massachusetts Avenue. Clement waited several more minutes for Newt's call, but when it still didn't come, he thought he'd better drive up to Conner Prairie Hospital to be close by Twit when he gave the order to attack.

"Dang it, Newt, where the hell are you?" Clement muttered to himself as he pulled his truck into traffic and headed northeast on Allisonville Road.

Chapter 50

Clay and Weed pulled into the visitors' lot at Conner Prairie Hospital a few minutes after Trent had arrived and saw him talking very dramatically to whoever was on the other end of the phone.

Trent put his finger up as Clay and Weed approached him to let them know he was in the middle of an important conversation. He hung up moments later and turned to face his friends.

"Well, the sons of bitches actually did it. Those fucking Hackers just blew up the Hoosier Homestead Insurance headquarters on Mass Ave. Fortunately, because it was so early on Thanksgiving Day, very few people were hurt, but the building is nothing more than a huge pile of rubble now. The Indy police and firefighters have several blocks cordoned off because of concerns over gasline leaks and downed power lines. The area's a mess! I can't believe they actually pulled it off."

"Any idea if the bomber got away?" Clay asked.

"Not really," Trent answered. "But from the size of the explosion, the officers on site have questioned whether anyone could've gotten away in time. Their guess is that the bomber died in the explosion. It'll take days to sift through all of that rubble, but I would be surprised if we ever find anything resembling human remains."

Trent picked up his radio and called all of the officers on patrol at the hospital. He shared the news of the Hoosier Homestead bombing and made certain everyone knew that there could still be a second attack.

"All right, people. This is not a drill. I want everyone to close ranks and protect the entrances to the hospital. We have a lot of property to cover, and I need each of you to stay in radio contact. We're not going to let happen here what just occurred on Mass Ave."

Trent turned to Clay and Weed and told them to stay by the main entrance and keep alert in case the Hackers outflanked any of his men.

Clement Hacker arrived several minutes later and parked his car on a street adjacent to the hospital that gave him a full view of the medical complex. He called Twit to ask where he was, and Twit whispered his location to him.

"Have you heard from Newt?" Clement asked his son. "He was supposed to call me after he got away, but I never heard from him."

"Uh, no, I haven't heard from him, either," Twit replied. "Uh, Pa? I need to tell you something."

"Don't tell me you're getting cold feet about blowing up the hospital, are you?" Clement challenged.

"Uh, no, it's just that I . . . well, I think I may have fucked up and called the wrong number when I tried to reach Newt and see how things were going."

There was dead silence on the phone until Clement finally said, "You mean to tell me that you called your brother, but you called the wrong number. Is that what you're telling me?"

"I," Twit stammered, "I thought I had the right cell phone number, but I think I really fucked up this time. I'm sorry, Pa."

"You mean to tell me that you blew the insurance building by mistake with your twin brother still in it?"

Twit gulped and said, "I'm real sorry, Pa. I feel awful about Newt. I'll try to make up for it. I swear."

Clement Hacker was filled with rage and heartache at the same time. He always knew that Twit was a bit of a challenge, both intellectually and emotionally, but he never dreamed that things could go this badly.

Clement was beside himself with contempt. "You're damn right you're going to make up for it, although I don't know how anyone could make up for killing their own brother, you worthless moron!"

The sun was just beginning to cast its first light on Conner Prairie Hospital, and Clement knew that Twit needed to act fast before even more cops showed up to protect and defend the medical complex.

"All right, Twit, it's time you showed me what you're made of. Go blow up the hospital. Aim for the front entrance and don't stop until you get the truck deep inside the main lobby, then get outside and detonate the fertilizer bomb. Understand?!"

Twit didn't respond verbally. Instead the rumbling resonance of a heavy pickup truck was heard at the rear of the visitors lot. Twit was on the move and coming fast.

Trent was conversing with a police officer when the sound of the death-delivering truck stopped him in midsentence. Instinctively, he just felt like something wasn't quite right about the thunderous sound, and he immediately put out another alert to secure the perimeter around the hospital and protect the entrances.

Clay and Weed took up positions on one side of the main entrance, and Trent took up a position opposite them. Everyone was armed except Weed and Clay.

The scene that Clay witnessed that morning was grand in cinematic proportions. It looked like something out of an epic novel. Twit's dark, stripped-down pickup truck sporting a Confederate flag for a front license plate came charging out of the early morning mist. It was a spectral scene, reminiscent of the Gray Ghost of Civil War fame, charging out of the fog.

Twit's truck accelerated and was now within one hundred yards of the main hospital entrance. Trent had no choice but to order his men to draw their weapons and take cover behind their vehicles.

"Steady!" Trent shouted. "Hold your fire. Await my order. Steady, now!"

Twit's truck was one stout, powerful machine. He and his late brother had done a lot to reinforce the steel in both the body and frame, plus strengthening the suspension system for off-road use. Now Twit pulled up a steel shield that he and Newt had fabricated to fit inside the windshield.

Twit drew a direct sightline on the hospital's front doors and stomped on the accelerator.

Trent screamed, "Open fire!"

The sounds that came next were horrific. Twit's truck shrieked like an ancient banshee, and gunfire from half a dozen officers launched an angry response. Trent saw that the truck was gaining purchase and would soon break through the hospital entrance. Bullets flew in furious numbers, but the assault had little effect on the armored pickup.

As Twit's truck got to Weed and Clay's position by the entrance, Weed leaped on to the truck's running board on the driver's side, and Trent gasped as he saw his friend repeat what he had attempted to do at Stella's Diner.

Unfortunately, history repeated itself.

Twit saw that he had an unwanted passenger and pulled his handgun out and pointed it back toward Weed. Weed grabbed the muzzle of the gun and attempted to wrench it away, but Twit fired, and a searing pain shot through Weed's left hand. The bullet went straight through his hand, and he fell off the truck as the pickup went tearing through the steel and glass entrance of Conner Prairie Hospital's finely decorated main lobby.

Twit's truck ravaged chairs and tables as it devoured the furnishings like a starved beast. It came to rest on the opposite side of the lobby near the front desk. The only good news was that there was virtually no one in the lobby at this early hour, but security officer Troy Snodgrass had the misfortune of being in the wrong place at the wrong time as the truck pinned him against the desk just below a polite sign that read, "How may we help you?"

Clay immediately ran to assist Weed, whose hand was bleeding badly. A uniformed security guard came to offer assistance and carefully helped Weed to his feet and led him in the direction of the emergency room.

"Go help Trent!" Weed hollered to Clay. "I'll be all right!"

After Twit's pickup came to a crashing halt, there was a brief, eerie silence made even more alien by the dust and debris that clouded the air. Then Twit recovered from wrecking his truck, exited the ruined pickup, and began firing his gun in the direction of the trashed entrance. Trent and another officer dove into the lobby and began returning fire at Twit, who was attempting to find another exit before detonating the fertilizer bomb.

Clay sneaked into the opposite side of the lobby from Trent and crawled over shattered glass in the direction of the truck. The gunfight in the lobby continued, and Clay heard the wail of multiple sirens as help was on the way.

Clement Hacker maintained his position just outside the hospital's grounds, but knew he would have to leave soon or risk being captured when the police cordoned off the area surrounding the hospital complex.

"Damn it, Twit, blow the fucking hospital already!" Clement screamed in frustration, but Twit had his hands full attempting to fight off Trent and the other officers.

Clay crawled another thirty feet and eventually came up alongside the menacing pickup. He wasn't sure what he should do next, but he reckoned that there had to be a detonating mechanism for the fertilizer bomb. While Trent kept Twit occupied returning fire, Clay tore the canvas cover off the bed of the pickup and saw the enormous load of ANFO.

"Oh, no!" he moaned.

Clay figured that a blast could come at any second, and he searched feverishly for anything that looked like a mechanical device. Trent and the officer had Twit pinned down behind a large planter, but there was no telling how long that distraction would keep Twit from blowing up the hospital. Clay continued digging his way through the truck's wreckage and spotted several wires that looked different from the others.

"There!" Clay said out loud to himself, and he quickly but carefully cleared away the detritus partially concealing the wires and the detonator. He knew time was of the essence, and he could only speculate on how the Hackers had connected the wires. Time was running out fast. Clay knew that as soon as the officers and Twit ran out of ammo, Twit would blow the building.

"Give it up, Hacker," Trent yelled at Twit. "We've got you totally surrounded. There's no point in trying to escape."

"I don't need to escape, asshole," Twit hollered back. "I've got my own little insurance policy right here in my hand. Now, back away. I'm walking out of here, and there's nothing you can do about it."

Trent fired another shot in Twit's direction, but it harmlessly ricocheted off the planter. Twit hunkered down and entered the detonating signal into the cell phone. One punch of a button would be all that it took to ruin a major medical facility whose mission was to preserve life.

Clay thought about Maggie and his family at the brewery complex and grabbed the wires. He figured this could be the last thing he ever did, and he yanked the wires free from the ANFO bomb's cell phone receiver. Nothing happened, and Clay breathed a major sigh of relief.

At that point Trent and the officer and Twit were all out of ammunition, and Twit called out, "Okay, copper, I guess you win. Hold your fire. I'm coming out!"

And then Twit stood up with a leer on his face and the detonator in his hand.

"I guess you lose, lawman," Twit taunted at Trent. "This is for my ma and my pa and Newt," he snarled and then he pushed the cell phone button to blow the building. Nothing happened. He pushed the button again, and again nothing happened. Then Clay stood and held up the wiring he had just yanked free from the truck bomb. He held it high so both Trent and Twit could see it. Further disaster had been averted.

When Trent saw that Clay had saved the day by defusing the bomb, he rushed at Twit with the swift moves of a pro linebacker and tackled Twit as he tried to escape. Unfortunately, Trent's wounded shoulder compromised his ability to hold the crazed twin, who broke free and ran for the front entrance.

From his vantage point outside, Clement saw his son's failed attempt to escape as Twit was nearly cut in half by a fearsome fusillade of bullets that came from multiple law enforcement officers who had arrived to render assistance.

Twit Hacker lay dead, and Conner Prairie Hospital, though seriously damaged, had survived an attempted Thanksgiving Day massacre.

Clement Hacker hung his head and wept as he saw his last chance to exact his revenge for Ella Marie fizzle to nothingness.

The wail of police sirens ruined the quiet of the early holiday morning as Trent began coordinating the security operations for the hospital.

Twit's body was carted off to the hospital's morgue, and Clay sat on the floor of the lobby still clutching the disabled detonator wires. He was dirty and bleeding from a myriad of superficial cuts.

Trent came over to Clay and had to unwrap Clay's clinging fingers from the device.

"You did it, Clay," Trent said to his friend. "You saved the hospital and countless lives."

Clay looked his friend in the eye and simply nodded his understanding. He was stunned by his own actions and could barely move. Trent helped him to his feet and took the detonator from Clay.

"Why don't you go check on Weed in the ER while I get things under better control here?" Trent suggested.

Clay nodded his understanding again but was still dealing with the shock of what had just occurred. Medical personnel from the hospital came up to Trent, and he asked an intern to please take Clay to the ER to get checked out and to see Weed.

From his vantage point above the parking lot, Clement Hacker saw that there was nothing more that could be done for Twit. He started his truck and slowly pulled away as the morning sunlight brought clarity to the destructive scene that his son had left behind.

When Clay got to the emergency room, he saw Weed sitting up on a hospital gurney with his hand wrapped in a large, gauzy bandage. For having just been shot through his hand, he looked halfway human, and he smiled as Clay entered his cubicle.

"I guess we lived, huh?" Weed said to his lifelong friend.

"Yeah, I guess we did," came Clay's soft reply. Then he put his arms around Weed's neck and sobbed uncontrollably, releasing a torrent of raw emotions that came from deep within his very being.

Chapter 51

THE NEXT HOURS WERE A BLUR for everyone involved. Clay called Tori to let her know about the attack on the hospital, explaining that Weed had been wounded but that his injury was not life-threatening. He told her that Weed was being taken to surgery soon to stabilize his injured left hand, and he promised to keep her and Mace and Rennie informed of Weed's status.

"Mace and I have been watching the news," Tori said. "We can't believe this happened in our community, and especially on Thanksgiving morning. I'm so relieved that Weed is going to be okay. When can I be with him?"

"Tori, I'm not sure how long he'll be in surgery, but if I had to guess, he's going to be pretty heavily sedated for the next twenty-four hours. My suggestion is that you wait until tomorrow morning, when he'll be more lucid."

Tori thought that Clay's comment made a lot of sense, but she made him promise to keep her informed of any changes.

"I just pray that this is all over," Clay added somberly. "There's still one more Hacker out there, and none of us will be able to rest easy until he's apprehended. It's another good reason for you to stay safe where you are."

Clay then briefly handed the phone to Weed, who reassured his sister that he was going to recover and that Clay would keep in touch with them.

"I gotta go, Tori," Weed said. "Looks like they're pretty serious about dragging my sorry butt into surgery."

They all knew that Weed's hand would probably never be quite the same again, but he was alive, and for that they were all very thankful.

Clay returned to the main lobby and found Trent working with the bomb squad personnel to get the truck bomb extricated from the hospital lobby as safely and quickly as possible. To no one's surprise, media vans were lining up outside the hospital to satisfy the public's insatiable right to know everything about anything.

A reporter from station WSAF was already attempting to get an exclusive interview with ISP Detective Trent Reynolds. Trent never enjoyed media attention, and so he deflected the reporter's request by saying, "Here's the man you should be interviewing," as he pointed to Clay. "Clay Arnold not only saved the hospital, he also saved countless lives by defusing the truck bomb that surely would've killed scores of people. He's a true hero!"

The reporter immediately wheeled around to interview Clay, who shot Trent a look that conveyed, "Oh, gee, buddy—thanks for throwing me to the wolves."

Thirty minutes later the entire world knew that world-famous photographer Clay Arnold had thwarted an urban terror attack and saved hundreds of patients and medical personnel at Conner Prairie Hospital near Indianapolis.

It came as no surprise to Clay that he received a very concerned call from Maggie, who wanted to make sure he was all right.

"Good lord, Clay, what were you thinking? Are you all right?" Maggie asked tearfully. "I just saw the news reports on CNN, and your name is all over social media."

"Yeah, I'm okay, Maggie. I guess with a truck bomb in the hospital lobby and a lot of shooting going on, none of us really had much time to think."

"Thank God you're okay," Maggie cried. "Next time will you please let someone else be the hero?!"

"Amen to that!" Clay replied. "I'm no hero, Maggie; I just knew something had to be done with the bomb, or we were all going to die."

Clay and Maggie talked for a few more minutes, and then Trent came over and asked him to come for an initial debriefing.

"I'll call you back later today, Maggie, when things calm down here. I'm really glad you already had Thanksgiving plans with your sister. This is sure no way to celebrate my favorite holiday."

Clement Hacker drove aimlessly trying to comprehend what had occurred that morning. The total destruction of the Hoosier Homestead Insurance Company headquarters gave him little consolation in the wake of losing his twin sons and their failure to cause more than partial damage to the hospital where Ella Marie had died.

He felt very alone. Numb. "Oh, Ella Marie . . . what is to become of me? I have nothing left."

Clement Hacker's truck meandered along River Road near the White River. He was close to the place where, a few weeks earlier, his twin sons had attacked the golfers and that blind woman.

There was very little traffic, and he kept his speed under the posted limit. With no particular place to go, Clement just drove and let his mind begin to calm and regain focus. He looked at his watch and saw that it was the top of the hour, so he turned on the truck's radio to listen to the local news.

The news was devoted entirely to the "Thanksgiving Day Attacks," as the media began calling them. The reporter gave a sketchy narration of events surrounding the bombing of the Hoosier Homestead Insurance Company headquarters. The superintendent of the Indiana State Police was interviewed, but he offered little of substance, since the forensics team was still collecting and processing information.

The news report then switched to an interview with ISP detective Trent Reynolds on location at Conner Prairie Hospital.

Trent didn't mince words. "We got very lucky at the hospital today. Thanks to the bravery of one man in particular, a disaster of major proportions was averted. Clay Arnold, who many of your listeners know as a famous photographer and the owner of the antique camera museum that bears his name, single-handedly found and defused the fertilizer bomb that was set to blow up the hospital. Had it not been for Mr. Arnold's clear thinking, under heavy gunfire and unarmed, hundreds of people would've been killed."

Clement Hacker listened intently to the news accounts and grew angrier by the moment. He and his boys had waited a long time to avenge his wife, and this pissant photographer had scuttled their plans. Clement fumed. He tried to remember where he had heard that name before, and then it struck him. That seedy-looking man, Dutch Ferris. The guy Twit knew at Stella's Diner.

Clement reached into his pocket and pulled out the two business cards that Dutch had given him. Clement saw that one was for the ISP detective Trent Reynolds and the other was for a photographer named Clay Arnold.

Clement leered at himself in the rearview mirror.

"Gotcha!" he said out loud.

Mace and Rennie listened intently as Tori told them about her conversation with Clay and Weed.

"Is Weed gonna be okay?" Rennie asked.

"We'll just have to wait and see, but Clay told me his injuries aren't life-threatening. We'll know more later in the day after he comes out of surgery," Tori said.

Mace shook his head with dismay. "I'm sure he'll be all right. Weed's a pretty tough cookie."

"Well, I suppose we'll just have to play it by ear regarding tonight's Thanksgiving dinner," Tori said. "Weed obviously won't be here, and I'm not sure about Clay, either. This is one Thanksgiving that none of us will ever forget."

Rennie and Mace nodded their agreement.

The three of them chatted for a few more minutes about the bombing of the insurance headquarters and the attack on the hospital.

"Why do people do stuff like that?" Rennie asked. "It's just plain hateful."

"That is the question that must be on a lot of people's minds right now," Mace replied. "I am afraid that we live in a time when tragedies like these will occur. I guess the fact is it's always been this way, all throughout human history. There's always been people who feel justified to act above the law and harm other people. Actually, sometimes for good, but more often for evil. Anyway, there's no easy answer to your question, Rennie, but these Hacker men were certainly extremely angry and on some level very desperate."

Rennie nodded affirmatively, but he still didn't really understand.

Mace said he needed to finish some work in the brew house's sub-basement, but he planned to be around all day if Tori and Rennie needed him.

"Tori, please give me a buzz on the intercom if you hear anything further from Clay, okay? I'm tempted to run up to the hospital, but I seriously doubt that they'll let any unauthorized people onto hospital grounds."

Rennie and Tori said goodbye to Mace and went back to working on their projects around the farmhouse. Mace walked alone across the courtyard and entered the elevator for the special workroom thirty feet below Clay's old brew house. He typed in the password Clay had given him: "Evening."

Clement Hacker pulled into a gas station to fill his truck and to buy a map of the Indianapolis area. He had a cell phone, but he used it mainly for phone calls and wasn't adept at using GPS or the Internet. His boys usually handled those applications. He sat in his truck studying the map. He saw Clay Arnold's address printed on his business card, and after just a few moments of staring at the map, Clement knew precisely how to get to the location.

"One last stop on Armageddon Day, Ella Marie. Just one final act of revenge, and I'll consider this retribution all done."

Clement pulled his truck into light holiday traffic and steered toward the White River north of Broad Ripple.

"Okay, Mr. Clay Arnold, let's see how you feel about someone fucking with your family."

Chapter 52

Tori and Rennie worked side by side at the shed behind the farmhouse. It was nearly noon, and they would be stopping before too long to get a bite to eat. The beauty of the azure November sky belied the ugliness that had already occurred in Indianapolis on this day of giving thanks.

"I still don't get it," Rennie said. "I don't understand why some people are so mean. When I was living alone on Hill Street, I made it a point to steer clear of certain people, but the mean ones always had a way of dragging you into their shit. I mean stuff."

"Maybe that's why the Thanksgiving holiday is so special to folks," Tori offered. "It reminds us that despite all of the harshness in the world, there are still many things, and lots of people, we should be thankful to have in our lives."

"I suppose," Rennie allowed. "I'm sure grateful to all of you for taking me in, and I get to have Lex and Satchmo as friends, too."

Tori smiled. "C'mon. I'll go make some lunch, and you can play with Satchmo and Lex outside until it's ready. Oh, and why don't you buzz Mace on the intercom and see if he wants anything?"

Rennie walked over to the intercom unit on the wall and pushed the button to speak.

"Hey there, Mace, it's Rennie. Pick up if you're there. We're fixing lunch and wanted to know if you want to join us."

A few seconds later Mace replied, "I just had my lunch, but thank you very much. I've still got some work to do down here that will take me a while. I may not see you until dinner tonight, but holler if you need me, okay?"

Rennie took Satchmo and Lex outside to play in the courtyard, and Tori continued to fix lunch.

Mace returned to a project that had captured his imagination. He had marveled at Weed's ability to fabricate lethal weapons out of parts of Clay's antique cameras. The Stirn's Vest camera, the Ben Akiba Cane camera, the KGB Ring camera, the Steineck ABC Watch camera: these were devices that fit into Clay's psyche as a photographer, a collector, and a righteous avenger.

But Mace had become fascinated with one old detective-style camera in particular, and he dutifully toiled on it now. He hoped to have it finished by tonight's dinner and to surprise Weed and Clay afterward with what he'd made. And as much as Mace enjoyed the overall quirky appearance of this small metal camera, its very name brought a smile to his face: The Demon Detective camera.

The Demon was originally introduced in England in 1889 and had a funnel-shaped front and a flat back. It measured just a little more than two inches by two inches. The name *Demon* was attractively stamped into the metal on the back, making it visually more appealing than the front of the camera.

But make no mistake: this device that Mace was fabricating promised to be demonic in its killing ability once completed. The tricky part now was charging and storing enough power in a small battery to produce lethality on demand. With electrical and digital diagrams he borrowed from Weed and a healthy stash of spare parts, Mace was getting very close to completion.

As he drove on a road along the White River, Clement Hacker listened to the continuing news reports about the blast that leveled the Hoosier Homestead Insurance Company and the attack on Conner Prairie Hospital. It was hard for him to believe that both Newt and Twit were gone. He was all alone now with only frustration, grief, and anger to keep him company as he approached the address listed on Clay Arnold's business card.

It was nearing noon as Clement spied the brewery complex, and he pulled over to the side of the road to scope out the property. He saw the sign and entrance for the antique camera museum and what appeared to be a spacious living quarters with a roof garden above it. He saw another old building that had a tall, brick chimney that he presumed was the original power plant for the complex. And across the courtyard from those large structures, he saw what looked like an old wooden-frame farmhouse.

Clement sat in his truck for several minutes looking for any activity. The only thing he saw was some black kid playing in the courtyard with a big cat and a three-legged dog. He saw no cars and no adults. It was quiet.

Clement was eager to get on with his revenge. He pulled out his loaded .357 magnum pistol and threw some extra shells in his jacket pocket. His sawed-off, twelve-gauge, semiautomatic shotgun hung in the truck's gun rack. He started the truck, put it in gear, looked around for cops, and then started moving cautiously toward the entrance to Clay Arnold's complex.

Lex was the first one to notice the unusually harsh sound of a rough pickup truck coming their way. He barked a couple of times to alert the others, and Rennie looked in the direction Lex was barking. Satchmo stood still, too, and the three of them stopped playing as the pickup entered the courtyard and came to a stop about twenty feet away from the farmhouse.

Lex let out a low growl. Rennie noticed that there was something about this vehicle and the stranger that Lex did not like one bit.

"Does that dog bite?" came the gruff question from the truck's driver.

"Sometimes," Rennie said. "And sometimes it's hard to get him to let go."

"Yeah, had me a dog like that once," came the man's reply. "I'm looking for a fellow named Clay Arnold. I understand he lives around here."

Lex continued to emit his low, menacing growl, and Rennie was streetwise enough to trust his canine friend's judgement.

"He's not here right now, and I don't know when he'll be back," Rennie answered truthfully.

"Well, don't that beat all. And here I drove all this way to see him, special," Clement lamented.

"Like I said, he's not here, and no telling when he's coming back. He travels a lot."

"Okay. Hold your dog, will ya? I want to get out and stretch my legs," Clement said.

Clement got out of the truck, and Lex's growl immediately went from a low rumble to a full-blown menacing bark.

"Easy, Lex," Rennie said to the large Labrador, but Lex was on full alert.

Tori heard Lex's uncharacteristically angry barking and stepped outside onto the front porch.

"Oh, I didn't know that we had company," Tori said.

"Howdy, ma'am. Sorry to bother you on Thanksgiving, but I was just hearing on the radio what a hero this Clay Arnold feller was at the hospital this morning, and I thought I'd stop by to meet him."

Tori Rawlins was about the kindest and most generous person on the planet, but she wasn't stupid, and she heard bullshit when she heard it. That, coupled with Lex's protective behavior, told her that this was a potentially threatening situation.

"Rennie, why don't you take Lex inside and check the stove, and Satchmo, you go with them, too."

Rennie turned to go into the farmhouse, but Lex stood his ground by Tori on the porch.

"Now, mister, I don't mean to be rude, but I heard Rennie tell you that Mr. Arnold isn't here, and we're not sure when he's returning. Perhaps if you'd like to leave a phone number, he could get back to you."

Clement stared at Tori. "You're blind, aren't you?" he started. He waved his hand in front of her face to see if she reacted. "Yeah, you are."

Tori didn't respond, and Lex maintained his protective posture.

"Are you his girlfriend or something?" he pushed.

"Sir, really, I don't mean to be rude, but Mr. Arnold's not here, and I've got things I need to tend to on the stove, so I need to go now. Give me your name, though, and I'll be sure to tell Clay he might expect a phone call from you."

"Hacker," Clement said matter of factly. "Clement Hacker."

The last name, Hacker, was the name that Tori had been hearing on the news reports all morning long. It took a split-nanosecond for her to recognize that this man standing in front of her was a member of the horrible family that had brought the Thanksgiving Day Assaults to her hometown.

Clement immediately saw recognition in Tori's sightless eyes. He took a step toward Tori, and Lex let loose a ferocious snarl. Rennie heard the commotion and came running from the kitchen.

"Hey, get out of here!" Rennie screamed at the man, but Clement tried to kick the dog while drawing his handgun from his coat pocket.

"Whoa!" Rennie yelled as he saw the nasty-looking man pull out the gun. "He's got a gun, Tori!"

"That's right, nigger boy. Now let's all go inside and wait for Clay Arnold to return, and put this damn dog up or I swear I'll blow another one of his legs off."

Tori pulled Lex inside the house and into Rennie's bedroom. She closed the door. Lex yelped and barked his displeasure.

Once inside the house, Clement pushed Tori and Rennie into the kitchen. He took a chair at the table that gave him a view of anyone driving into the courtyard. Satchmo took one look at the stranger in their midst and took off running into another part of the house.

"Smells good, whatever it is you're cooking. Why don't you serve up something for me, bitch?" he directed at Tori. "And don't you go getting any funny ideas about pouring shit on me. I'll shoot you and this little coon if you get any funny ideas."

Tori poured the last surviving Hacker a bowl of soup and sat down next to Rennie as far away from the killer as possible.

"Now, let's just settle in and wait for your pal to return," Hacker said as he slurped the soup greedily. "According to the news reports, he was responsible for defusing the truck bomb at the hospital and for getting my boy killed. We'll see how much of a hero the sonovabitch is when he gets back."

"Don't you think you and your boys have already caused enough pain and suffering for people?" Tori hurled at him.

"Don't you go telling me about pain and suffering," Clement spit back in return. "I've lost everything and everyone dear to me, and I'm not going to listen to your pitiful lecture. I ain't even close to ending the pain and suffering. Just you wait and see."

Rennie shot Tori a glance and saw the fear and concern etched on her face. Neither of them said a word back to the intruder. Rennie moved even closer to Tori and stood in front of the intercom located on the kitchen wall.

Clement looked at Tori and said, "My boys told me that they tried to take a blind woman on a path by the river not far from here. You wouldn't be that woman, by any chance, would you?"

Cold fear shot through both Tori and Rennie. They already knew they had a serious problem with this intruder's pursuit of Clay, but learning that this criminal was the father of the men who'd attacked them and shot Lex brought back a flood of memories that they thought they'd put behind them.

Rennie had to think of something to do. He and Tori just couldn't wait for Clay to show up, or for Mace to walk into a trap. Rennie looked around the room for anything that they could use as a weapon, and although there were lots of sharp cooking utensils, the size of Clement Hacker's gun kept them from trying to launch a counter attack.

"You and your boys are pure evil," Tori said with anger. "You're real brave men, aren't you, Mr. Hacker? I'm sure Mrs. Hacker would be very proud of everything you've been doing in her name. You're just a bunch of cowardly criminals, and I'm glad your sons are dead."

With that Clement stood up and slapped Tori hard across her face. She yelped briefly in pain and her sightless eyes shot daggers at her assailant.

Rennie started to go after Clement for hitting Tori, but she grabbed him roughly by the sleeve and yanked him back against the kitchen wall.

"Now, you just stay there and shut the fuck up," Clement bellowed. "We're staying put until your pal Arnold shows up. Then we'll see who the coward is when he begs me to spare your lives."

Rennie and Tori desperately needed a plan. Rennie looked around the kitchen for anything that could help them, and then he remembered the intercom on the wall. He sidled in front of the intercom and clandestinely reached his hand behind his body and pushed and held the intercom button on the wall. He prayed that Mace would be within earshot and would recognize that he and Tori were in imminent danger.

Rennie whispered to Tori, "Keep him busy talking; I'm trying to alert Mace with the intercom."

Tori immediately recognized Rennie's clever plan and began engaging Clement Hacker in conversation in case Mace was listening.

"So, Mr. Hacker, you and your boys were the ones that blew up the Planned Parenthood Center, right? And your boys are the ones that attacked me and Rennie and Lex near the river, right? And, of course, you and your spawn were the ones who blew up the insurance building and tried to kill a lot of innocent people at the hospital, right?"

From deep within the sub-basement Mace stood listening to Tori's voice on the intercom. At first, he thought it was just a ruse that Rennie and Tori were playing on him, and he was very close to replying when he heard Clement Hacker's voice.

"That's right," Clement said with venom in his voice. "And there's nothing you can do about it, so sit there and shut up. Like I said, we're gonna just hang out and wait for your buddy to show up."

Rennie didn't know whether Mace heard the danger that was happening in the kitchen, but he couldn't continue to hold the intercom button much longer. He let go of the button and moved closer to Tori again.

But Mace had indeed heard Tori's confrontation with Clement Hacker and anxiously tried to think of a plan of action. He reached for his cell phone on the workbench and punched in Clay's number.

"Hey, Mace," came Clay's weary reply. "How're things at home?"

"We have a serious problem, Clay," Mace said, and then he proceeded to inform him of what he heard on the intercom in the sub-basement.

"Oh, no!" Clay lamented. "I'm on my way home," he said and hung up.

Chapter 53

CLAY RAN LIKE THE WIND. Trent saw him running frantically and caught up with him just as he was exiting the hospital's devastated entrance.

"What's up?" Trent asked Clay, who was obviously distressed.

"I just got a call from Mace. Clement Hacker's at the farmhouse, and he's holding Tori and Rennie hostage. He's waiting for me to return. Please make sure Weed gets excellent medical care. I've gotta go!"

Then Clay took off running again and leaped into his Tacoma. He sprayed a rooster-tail of gravel as his truck roared to life and launched itself out of the hospital's parking lot. He was only ten minutes from home.

No sooner had Clay exited the lot than Trent reached him on his cell phone again.

"Hold up, Clay! You can't do this all by yourself. Wait until I get some officers over there!"

But given the number of police trying to control the carnage at the insurance company and the hospital, Trent wasn't sure how much help would be immediately available. He got on the radio to alert the Indiana State Police superintendent.

Clay called Mace in the sub-basement and told him he was on his way. Clay wasn't sure what he was going to do when he got home, but he advised Mace to stay put until he got to the courtyard and called him back.

True to his word, Clay pulled up to the entrance of his brewery complex ten minutes later and came to a stop. He surveyed the buildings and courtyard that were his home and saw a menacing-looking pickup truck parked in front of the farmhouse. He felt like he was looking at an unwanted alien from another world.

Clay called Mace to let him know that he had arrived. Mace told him he hadn't heard anything further from Rennie on the intercom, and they weren't quite sure what to make of that.

"I think Hacker is waiting for you to arrive; then he'll show himself," Mace speculated. "Did you bring any weapons with you?"

"No. All of my antique camera weapons are either with you in the sub-basement or still with my gear upstairs," Clay reported.

"That's not good," Mace said. "And I think he'll definitely see you if you try to sneak past him to get to where I am."

"Yeah, not good," Clay acknowledged. "But since we don't have much choice in the matter, let's give it a try anyway. I'm gonna give it just five more minutes to see if the police come, and then I'm going in."

Clay hung up and checked his watch. Five long minutes came and went. No cops. He texted Mace to let him know he was going in. He put the Tacoma in gear and moved steadily forward onto his property. When he was within twenty yards of the farmhouse, he saw an older, grizzled-looking man step out onto the porch. He had Tori roughly grabbed by the arm with a gun pointed at her head. Clay came to a halt.

Down in the sub-basement Mace became very concerned very quickly about what was happening in the courtyard thirty feet above his head. Clay had just hung up, and Mace didn't have a clue what his unarmed friend was going to do. Clay said he was going to wait for five minutes for the police and then do something. One thing was for sure: It wasn't in Mace's makeup to wait around idly for a nasty outcome to occur.

He pondered a plan of action for a long ten seconds and then leaped into action. He went to the workbench and picked up his newly-improved Demon camera. It had performed remarkably well during its test firing, and it was fully charged and ready to go.

Next he went to the wall-mounted coatrack with the five bronze hooks and pulled the hook on the far left side. He heard the audible click he was expecting, and the wall panel opened an inch. It was wide enough for him to get his fingers behind the panel. He reached in and found the hidden latch. A second later the doorway to the secret tunnel slid open. The passageway had been built over one hundred and fifty years ago by the Block brothers, and it connected the sub-basement with the shed behind the farmhouse.

Mace found the light switch that illuminated a string of lights running the length of the tunnel. He entered the tunnel and found the air to be dry with an earthy sweetness. The tunnel was tall enough for him to stand in, and he moved quickly.

He had about sixty yards to cover, and he moved with a grace that belied his seventy years of age. He came to the end of the tunnel and climbed thirty feet up a strong ladder that ended at an old wooden landing. He was now immediately below the floor where the workbench sat. He saw the latch and hinges he was looking for. He undid the latch.

Mace breathed in and out evenly to get his heart rate to slow. He listened for any sounds that would give him guidance. He couldn't wait any longer. He used his shoulder to heave at the floor, knowing full well he was also trying to lift the bench itself and whatever rested on it. It was incredibly heavy, so much so that Mace wondered for a moment whether it had been secured to the floor.

Another heave, and then another. Sweat began to form on Mace's forehead, and he wasn't sure his plan would work in time. Another heave, and yet another, and then he felt the workbench slide off to the side. It came to rest at a precarious angle against the shed's wall.

Mace tried to be as quiet as possible, but he had to move the workbench even more in order to get out. An empty flower pot slid off the workbench onto a bag of peat moss and made a muffled crunch. Mace waited a second to see if the crunch brought any attention. It didn't.

In five seconds Mace was on his feet inside the shed. He was now only fifteen feet from the farmhouse's back door. He heard voices coming from the front of the house, and he quickly but quietly crossed the space between the shed and the back door.

Mace stepped inside and again focused on his breathing to calm his heart rate. He felt the Demon camera in his right hand. It was charged and ready to release an electronic pulse that could take down a Cape buffalo.

Mace saw Clement Hacker and Tori standing on the front porch with their backs to him. Hacker had Tori's arm in a strong grip with his gun pointed at her head. Clay was some twenty feet farther away.

"What's the matter, Mr. Arnold? Are you still feeling like a famous hero now?" Clement challenged. His words spewed like flowing magma.

Clay ignored him. "Are you all right, Tori?" were Clay's first words. "Where's Rennie?"

"I'm okay, Clay," Tori said evenly. "This rough stuff is getting a little tedious though," she deadpanned. "He locked Rennie in the guest bedroom with Lex. He's okay, for now."

"Shut up, bitch!" Clement snarled at her.

"You didn't answer my question, Arnold. Are you still feeling like a famous hero?"

Clay gave serious thought to the question. Hero. It wasn't a concept he was comfortable with. He was just a guy trying to get by with his professional talent and a fairly well-defined set of ethics. He was no hero. In fact, he preferred not to be.

"Mr. Hacker, let her go. She can't hurt you, and I'm the one you want anyway," Clay said.

"Shut up!" Hacker fired back at Clay. "I don't need you telling me what to do."

"Let her go," Clay said again.

And this time Clement Hacker pushed Tori away from him and pointed the gun at Clay.

"Hell, you're right," Clement admitted. "The poor bitch is blind. My boys would've done her a favor to rape and kill her instead of her having to fumble around in the dark all the time."

Tori looked in Clement Hacker's direction with more rage than she had ever felt in her life. She knew what her limitations were, and she also knew what her strengths were. As a person without sight, Tori had cultivated an almost preternatural sense of hearing. She was able to identify sounds' locations and felt almost bat-like with her echo-locational capabilities. She focused her entire being on the sound of Clement Hacker's voice.

"And now, Mr. Clay Arnold—famous photographer and hometown hero—it's time you pay the price for your interference."

He pointed his gun at Clay, and just before he pulled the trigger, *Whomp!* came the sound of a vicious strike as Tori's right leg shot up and her work shoe connected solidly with Clement's jaw. Her sense of hearing was true. Clement stumbled with a pitiful yelp of pain and went down. His gun skittered away from him, and Clay charged. Clement regained control of the gun, but Tori delivered another brutal kick to the sound of his voice. Hacker went down hard again but held on to the gun.

There was so much commotion that Mace didn't have a clear shot with the Demon. He stepped out on the front porch and stood ready.

Clement's mouth was bloody from Tori's last kick, and he spit blood as he hollered, "Damn you all! Damn you all to hell."

Clay had reached Tori and placed his body between her and Hacker.

"Nice," Clement said. "This way I get to shoot both of you with just one shot. Have any last words, Mr. Hero?"

Clay saw Mace emerge onto the porch with something familiar in his hand.

"Yes, Mr. Hacker, I do," Clay said with finality. "Evening Comes!"

"What the fuck does that mean?" Clement asked with contempt as he kept his pistol trained on Clay.

"It means this, asshole," Mace said from behind him. And with that he pressed the shutter button on the Demon camera, and an angry, blue bolt of electricity shot out of the modified antique and engulfed Clement Hacker.

Hacker had a look of astonishment on his face as he sizzled, shook, and quivered for an interminably long five seconds before he finally dropped to the floor in a heap. He was dead.

Mace immediately ran to see whether Clement Hacker needed another jolt but quickly saw that the patriarch of Indiana's worst domestic terror family was finally history.

Clay led Tori into the farmhouse, and together they liberated Rennie and Lex from Rennie's bedroom. Lex came bounding out to Mace on the front porch and smelled the singed carcass lying there. Rennie came to the front door and looked at the sprawled figure.

"Is he dead?" Rennie asked. "He smells funny."

Mace nodded affirmatively. "Why don't you go see if Tori has a sheet or something we can place over him until the police get here?"

Rennie took another look at Clement Hacker's fried body and ran to find Tori.

Fifteen minutes later two Indiana State Police cars showed up, one carrying the ISP superintendent.

Within two hours the crime scene had been processed and the medical examiner had released Clement Hacker's body to the morgue. Mace felt an unusual sense of pride when the medical examiner took a look at his Demon camera and pronounced it the most intriguing killing device he had seen in a very long time.

By mid-afternoon the authorities were gone, and Clay, Tori, Mace, and Rennie were left to try to enjoy what was left of the Thanksgiving holiday.

They all sat at the kitchen table, relieved that they had survived the final saga of the Thanksgiving Day Assaults. Lex and Satchmo lay curled up with each other on the rug by the back door.

"How'd you know about that secret tunnel?" Tori asked Mace. "No one was more shocked than me when you showed up like you did."

"Well, I think maybe Clement Hacker was," Mace said. "This old brewery has many secrets," he said cryptically. "This tunnel is just one of them."

"I don't know about you guys," Tori said sadly, "but I'm not feeling quite in the mood for the Thanksgiving dinner Rennie and I had planned for tonight."

Mace and Clay knew how hard they'd worked to make Rennie's first real Thanksgiving special. They both felt badly that no one was in a festive mood right now.

"How about if we do this," Clay suggested. "If it's okay with you, Tori, why don't we just put our dinner off until tomorrow? That way Weed will most likely be with us, and we can have our whole family together. Besides, I could use some time to process everything that's gone on today. I'm pretty wiped out."

They all thought that was a very good idea, and they spent the remainder of the day together hunkered down in the farmhouse, reconnecting with one another, and trying to regain their emotional equilibrium.

Around 5:00 PM Trent Reynolds called Clay to check in.

"My superintendent tells me you guys did a helluva job taking down Clement Hacker," Trent stated proudly.

"Yeah, well—I think we just got lucky," Clay replied. "No more hero stuff going on here. Just trying to stay alive."

Mace nodded affirmatively to Clay. "We got real lucky."

"How's Weed doing?" Clay asked.

"He's out of surgery and sleeping now," Trent replied. "The surgeon said Weed's hand won't have full range of motion, but with physical therapy and exercise, it shouldn't be a major handicap for him. I think he got lucky, too."

At about eight o'clock Clay and Mace said goodnight to Tori and Rennie and walked across the courtyard to their respective residences. Lex hobbled alongside Mace to the power plant, and Satchmo bounded after Clay and ran up the stairs to Clay's living quarters.

"Well, big fella," Clay said to Satchmo. "It looks like it's just you and me again."

They stepped out onto Clay's roof garden like they had done many times before, and the two of them stood staring at the crisp autumn sky.

Clay shivered in the cool night air and scratched the big Maine coon cat behind his tufted ears.

"It's all a big mystery to me, Satchmo. Who gets to live and who has to die. In the end everything and everyone comes and goes, and we're all destined to become stardust. It's how we live our lives that defines our legacies."

Clay took a full sip of his Glenmorangie scotch and thought about the recent months that had passed: Jennifer's death; his avenging executions in Charleston, Santa Fe, San Diego, Palm Springs, and Chicago; and the awful calamities of the Thanksgiving Day Assaults.

The thoughts brought an even greater chill to the night air, but the best news was that he still had his family, and he and Maggie were falling in love. Despite the tragedies, he knew he had a lot to be thankful for.

Right now, though, Clay was a weary guy and very content being alone in his home with an enormous cat, a glowing November moon, and the rhythmic beating of his calming heart. He welcomed a peaceful night's sleep.

Chapter 54

THE NEXT DAY DAWNED with a special radiance that belied the ugly violence that had occurred at the brewery complex and all across Indianapolis. Thanksgiving Day had thankfully come and gone, but very few area residents would ever forget the tragedies that transpired on a day dedicated to expressing gratitude for our blessings.

Clay awoke early as he usually did and enjoyed a simple breakfast on his rooftop garden. He knew that Tori's holiday dinner would be a sumptuous meal, and he didn't want to spoil his appetite. Satchmo spent a few hours asleep at the foot of Clay's bed but had taken his leave in the middle of the night to make his appointed rounds.

Clay called Maggie to hear her voice. He felt hesitant to tell her about Clement Hacker's assault and subsequent death at his place, but he knew it would all come out at some point so he chose the direct approach. He told her everything, and she listened intently.

"How are Tori, Rennie, and Mace doing?" were the first words out of her mouth.

Clay was relieved that Maggie didn't run away kicking and screaming when he recounted the dangerous events. He loved that she was concerned about his friends.

"They're all okay," Clay said. "We just got word from the hospital that the doctor is releasing Weed today. Mace and I are going to Conner Prairie Hospital to get him around eleven, and then we're going to have our family Thanksgiving dinner around noon."

"And how are you doing, my handsome hero?" Maggie asked. "You always seem to be there for other people, but how are you holding up?"

"I'm okay, too," Clay allowed. "I'd sure be a helluva lot better if you were here."

"I know. Me, too," Maggie said. "I can't wait to see you in early December and then again for Christmas, and who knows where that will lead?"

Maggie shared her Thanksgiving experience at her sister's, and again Clay was relieved that she hadn't been exposed to Clement Hacker's ugly revenge. They talked for a few more minutes and agreed they'd talk later in the day.

Clay got cleaned up and dressed and went downstairs into his antique camera museum. He wandered from one display case to another until he had paid homage to every special camera he had collected along the way. He felt like he was among old friends.

From there he took the elevator down to his darkroom and turned on the orange-glowing safelight. It had been several months since he had worked down here, and he felt a rush of desire to shut himself away and lose himself in the photochemistry of his fine art. He would do it soon.

Clay opened a drawer beneath his enlarger and saw the contact sheet with Jennifer Skyler's portraits, and this time he felt a pang of guilt for not continuing to grieve for her like he once had.

"I'm not a perfect man," Clay whispered aloud. "I will never forget you, Jennifer."

Clay heard the whir of the elevator and figured that Mace was in the building looking for him. He placed the contact sheet back in the drawer and left the darkroom. Clay found Mace one floor below the darkroom in the sub-basement workshop.

"I don't know that I have adequately thanked you for saving our lives, Mace. You were amazing, and we are all forever in your debt, my friend."

"You're welcome, Clay. Truth is I was scared to death. We just got very lucky. Besides, Clay, you made it very clear from the beginning that this brewery complex belongs to all of us. We're family, and we stick together. No way I was going to let some deranged wacko ruin that."

The two friends rummaged around the sub-basement for a while, and Mace showed Clay the diagrams he had borrowed from Weed to construct the Demon camera.

"You never cease to amaze me, Mace Davis, and I can't wait to hear what Weed says when you tell him about how you fried Clement Hacker."

They finished their rummaging around in the sub-basement and went up to the courtyard to go see Tori and Rennie. They knew she would already be up and putting the finishing touches on their noon meal and getting things ready for Weed's return.

"G'morning!" they called out to Tori as they entered the farmhouse's front door.

Lex came hobbling up to them and buried his face between Mace's knees.

Tori came out of the bathroom wearing her robe and a smile that could whisk away any lingering thoughts of yesterday's deadly intrusion.

"Now, if you guys came here looking for breakfast, you can forget about it," she kidded. "I'm only preparing one meal today, so you'll have to go to Stella's if you can't wait until noon."

"Why, Tori!" Mace feigned innocence. "We just stopped by to offer any help before we run up to the hospital to fetch Weed."

Tori enjoyed the sentiment and repaid them each with a pecan roll.

"Now, scoot on out of here," she said. "Rennie and I have everything under control, so why don't you two just bring my wounded brother back home?"

And that's what they did. Mace and Clay found Weed sitting in a wheelchair by the outpatient entrance when they arrived at the hospital. Trent was with him, and despite all of the violence that they'd been through, both men seemed in reasonably decent shape.

"Goddamnit, Weed, you scared the crap out of me!" Clay said as he gave his life-long friend a strong hug. "Let me look at you. Okay, except for that ginormous bandage around your hand, you look almost human."

"Yeah, well—just a flesh wound, as they say," Weed replied. "Let's get out of here. I've seen enough of hospitals for a while."

"I'd say a lot more than just a flesh wound," Trent added. "He had a large caliber bullet go right through the middle of his hand at point-blank range. The hospital has a great hand specialist on staff, and he thinks the prospects for full usage are good but not great."

Weed sighed. "I'd do it again, guys," he said. "It was worth it. No hero thing going on here. There were just too many lives at stake. I got lucky."

"It was awfully brave, my friend," Trent said to Weed. "Of course, you realize that we're oh-for-two when it comes to jumping on moving trucks driven by terrorists."

Clay turned to Trent and said, "We're going home to have our Thanksgiving dinner that we didn't get to have yesterday. If you're free, why don't you join us? We'd love to have you."

Weed and Mace said "amen" to that.

"You know, I'd really enjoy that, but I have a couple hours of work back at the office that I just can't let slide. Then I've asked Abby West to join me for dinner. She wants to talk about that article about gun violence she wants to write. And I . . . well, I just enjoy her company. However, if you old guys are capable of staying awake past eight-thirty, we would be delighted to join you around then."

"That's great! We'll see you around then," Clay said. "Old guys, huh?!"

"Oh, and one last thing," Trent began again. "The heroic actions all of you took to protect the public have not been forgotten. Law enforcement agencies from here to Seymour, Indiana, to Washington, D.C., are still in the midst of thoroughly investigating the case. When they're far enough along in that process, don't be surprised if they don't go lofting you up on their shoulders as true American heroes."

"Oh, no," Clay said. "Trent, please don't let that happen. The three of us have great lives. Getting tagged as heroes will ruin it for us. Do you guys agree?"

"Trent, you know we appreciate the kind words," Mace said. "And we know they're heartfelt, but what Clay said is true. Take it from a real 'old guy.' Keep us below the radar if you can, please."

Trent heard their words, and as their friend and a realist he agreed to do what he could to keep the politicians and the press away.

"But perhaps a very small, very private little ceremony in the governor's office might be arranged instead," Trent suggested.

"Maybe," Clay allowed. Then they took their leave.

Clay, Weed, and Mace pulled away from the hospital in Clay's Tacoma. Clay took a final look at the demolished entrance and shivered at the thought of what might've been. He would never forget how close to death he and so many others came at this place for healing.

None of the men spoke for a minute. Each one was settling into the companionship of the others. They'd been through a lot together. Clay thought about how he had evened the score with several right-wing bastards and criminals over the past weeks. He had a feeling he wasn't finished expressing his avenging mantra, "evening comes."

Weed called Tori to let her know they were on their way and that they were all starved.

"And tell that Rennie kid that if he's nice, I'll let him see where I got shot," Weed exclaimed.

The men pulled onto the road that ran along the White River. Seeing the flowing river water had a healing effect on them. They remained contemplative.

"So, tell me the truth, Mace," Clay said. "If you'd known how much turmoil we'd put you through when I originally bought the brewery complex, would you have stayed or gone somewhere else?"

Mace thought for a moment, and Clay and Weed glanced at him.

"Some things are just a roll of the dice, I guess," Mace said. "Fact is, I have no regrets. Look at us! What a hodgepodge of humanity. We've got us a ghetto kid, a blind woman, an old black man, a guy who goes by the name 'Weed,' and a serial killer. On top of that we have a three-legged dog and a huge cat that thinks he's human. And you know what? I wouldn't have it any other way."

About the Author

OVER THE LAST FOUR DECADES, Stuart Fabe's creativy has focused on three genre: photography, weaving, and writing. He has published several books showcasing his fine-art photographs and his intricate weavings. He has exhibited his artwork at numerous art shows and gallaries, and his work is widely collected.

Evening Comes is Stuart's second novel. He enjoys the role of storyteller and in examining the conflicts inherent to vigilantism and good versus evil. His writing is intended solely as entertainment.

Stuart lives in the countryside near Greencastle, Indiana, with his partner, Marla, two dogs, two cats, and nine chickens.